The
DEVIL
YOU KNOW

The DEVIL YOU KNOW

MIKE CAREY

WARNER BOOKS

NEW YORK   BOSTON

Warner Books
Hachette Book Group USA
237 Park Avenue
New York, NY 10169

Visit our Web site at www.HachetteBookGroupUSA.com.

Printed in the United States of America
Originally Published in Great Britain in April 2006 by Orbit

First Warner Books Edition: July 2007
10 9 8 7 6 5 4 3 2 1

Warner Books and the "W" logo are trademarks of Time Warner Inc. or an affiliated company. Used under license by Hachette Book Group USA, which is not affiliated with Time Warner Inc.

Library of Congress Control Number: 2006935148
ISBN: 978-0-446-58030-4

Book design by Charles Sutherland

To Lin; as if there's any other direction that matters

Acknowledgments

With thanks to all the staff at the London Metropolitan Archive who were so hospitable and so generous with their time—especially Jan Pimblett and Dorota Pomorska-Dawid. Also to my ever-inspiring agent, Meg Davis, who helped out with my stumbling Russian, and my editor, Darren Nash, who provided both a sounding board for ideas and a large quantity of Belgian beer to help with the acoustics for said board. To desk editor Gabriella Nemeth, whose London A–Z, unlike mine, is the right way up. And finally to my wife, Lin, the superpowered offspring of a lawyer and a Litvak, who spotted no fewer than six massive errors in the original typescript. Great work, team: now into your starting positions for book two.

The
DEVIL
YOU KNOW

One

NORMALLY I WEAR A CZARIST ARMY GREATCOAT—
the kind that sometimes gets called a paletot—with pockets sewn in
for my tin whistle, my notebook, a dagger, and a chalice. Today I'd
gone for a green tuxedo with a fake wilting flower in the buttonhole,
pink patent-leather shoes, and a painted-on mustache in the style of
Groucho Marx. From Bunhill Fields in the east, I rode out across
London—the place of my strength. I have to admit, though, that
"strong" wasn't exactly how I was feeling; when you look like a pistachio-
ice-cream sundae, it's no easy thing to hang tough.

The economic geography of London has changed a lot in the last
few years, but Hampstead is always Hampstead. And on this cold
November afternoon, atoning for sins I couldn't even count and probably looking about as cheerful as a *tricoteuse* being told that the day's
executions have been canceled due to bad weather, Hampstead was
where I was headed.

Number 17, Grosvenor Terrace, to be more precise: an unassuming
little early Victorian masterpiece knocked off by Sir Charles Barry
in his lunch hours while he was doing the Reform Club. It's in the
books, like it or not; the great man would moonlight for a grand in
hand and borrow his materials from whatever else he was doing at the
time. You can find his illegitimate architectural progeny everywhere

from Ladbroke Grove to Highgate, and they always give you that same uneasy feeling of déjà vu, like seeing the milkman's nose on your own firstborn.

I parked the car far enough away from the door to avoid any potential embarrassment to the household I was here to visit and managed the last hundred yards or so burdened with four suitcases full of highly specialized equipment. The doorbell made a severe, functional buzzing sound like a dentist's drill sliding off recalcitrant enamel. While I waited for a response, I checked out the rowan twig nailed up to the right of the porch. Black and white and red strings had been tied to it in the prescribed order, but still . . . a rowan twig in November wouldn't have much juice left in it. I concluded that this must be a quiet neighborhood.

The man who opened the door to me was presumably James Dodson, the birthday boy's father. I took a strong dislike to him right then to save time and effort later. He was a solid-looking man, not big but hard-packed, gray eyes like two ball bearings, salt-and-pepper hair adding its own echoes to the gray. In his forties, but probably as fit and trim now as he had been two decades ago. Clearly, this was a man who recognized the importance of good diet, regular exercise, and unremitting moral superiority. Pen had said he was a cop—chief constable in waiting, working out of Agar Street as one of the midwives to the government's new Serious Organized Crime Agency. I think I would have guessed either a cop or a priest, and most priests gratefully let themselves go long before they hit forty; that's one of the perks of having a higher calling.

"You're the entertainer," Dodson said, as you might say, "You're a motherless piece of scum and you raped my dog." He didn't make a move to help me with the cases, which I was carrying two in each hand.

"Felix Castor," I agreed, my face set in an unentertaining deadpan. "I roll the blues away."

He nodded noncommittally and opened the door wider to let me in. "The living room," he said, pointing. "There'll be rather more children than we originally said. I hope that's okay."

"The more the merrier," I answered over my shoulder, walking on through. I sized the living room up with what I hoped looked like a professional eye, but it was just a room to me. "This is fine. Everything I need. Great."

"We were going to send Sebastian over to his father's, but the bloody man had some sort of work crisis on," Dodson explained from behind me. "Which makes one more. And a few extra friends . . ."

"Sebastian?" I inquired. Throwing out questions like that is a reflex with me, whether I want answers or not; it comes from the work I do. I mean, the work I used to do. Sometimes do. Can live *without* doing.

"Peter's stepbrother. He's from Barbara's previous marriage, just as Peter is from mine. They get along very well."

"Of course." I nodded solemnly, as if checking out the soundness of the familial support network was something I always did before I started in on the magic tricks and the wacky slapstick. Peter was the birthday boy—just turned fourteen. Too old, probably, for clowns and conjurors and parties of the cake-and-ice-cream variety. But then, that wasn't my call to make. They also serve those who only pull endless strings of colored ribbon out of a baked-bean tin.

"I'll leave you to set up, then," Dodson said, sounding dubious. "Please don't move any of the furniture without checking with me or Barbara first. And if you're setting up anything on the parquet that might scratch, ask us for pads."

"Thanks," I said. "And mine's a beer whenever you're having one yourself. The term 'beer' should not be taken to include the subset 'lager.'"

He was already heading for the door when I threw this out, and he kept right on going. I was about as likely to get a drink out of him as I was to get a French kiss.

So I got down to unpacking, a task that was made harder by the fact that these cases hadn't moved out of Pen's garage in the last ten years. There were all sorts of things in among the stage-magic gear that gave me a moment's—or more than a moment's—pause. A Swiss Army penknife (it had belonged to my old friend Rafi) with the main blade broken off short an inch from the tip; a homemade fetish rigged up out of the mummified body of a frog and three rusty nails; a feathered snood, looking a bit threadbare now, but still carrying a faint whiff of perfume; and the camera.

Shit. The camera.

I turned it over in my hands, instantly submerged in a brief but powerful reverie. It was a Brownie Autographic No. 3, and all folded up as it was, it looked more like a kid's lunch box than anything else. But once I flipped the catches, I could see that the red-leather bellows was still in place, the frosted viewfinder was intact, and (wonder of wonders) the hand-wheeled stops that extended the lens into its operating position still seemed to work. I'd found the thing in a flea market in Munich when I was backpacking through Europe. It was nearly a hundred years old, and I'd paid about a quid for it, which was the whole of the asking price, because the lens was cracked right the way across. That didn't matter to me—not for what I principally had in mind at the time—so it counted as a bargain.

I had to put it to one side, though, because at that moment the first of the party guests were shepherded in by a very busty, very blonde, very beautiful woman who was obviously much too good for the likes of James Dodson. Or the likes of me, to be fair. She was wearing a white bloused top and a khaki skirt with an asymmetric hang, which probably had a designer name attached to it somewhere and cost more than I earned in six months. For all that, though, she looked a touch worn and tired. Living with James Supercop would do that to you, I speculated; or, possibly, living with Peter, assuming that Peter was the sullen streak of curdled sunlight hovering at her elbow. He had his father's air of blocky, aggressive solidity, with an adolescent's wary stubbornness grafted onto it. It made for a very unattractive combination, somehow.

The lady introduced herself as Barbara in a voice that had enough natural warmth in it to make electric blankets irrelevant. She introduced Peter, too, and I offered him a smile and a nod. I tried to shake hands with him out of some atavistic impulse probably brought on by being in Hampstead, but he'd already stomped away in the direction of a new arrival with a loud bellow of greeting. Barbara watched him go with an unreadable, Zen-like smile that suggested prescription medication, but her gaze as she turned back to me was sharp and clear enough.

"So," she said. "Are you ready?"

For anything, I almost said—but I opted for a simple yes. All the same, I probably held the glance a half moment too long. At any rate, Barbara suddenly remembered a bottle of mineral water that she was holding in her hand and handed it to me with a slight blush and an apologetic grimace. "You can have a beer in the kitchen with us afterward," she promised. "If I give you one now, the kids will demand equal rights."

I raised the bottle in a salute.

"So . . . ," she said again. "An hour's performance, then an hour off while we serve the food—and you come on again for half an hour at the end. Is that okay?"

"It's a valid strategy," I allowed. "Napoléon used it at Quatre Bras."

This got a laugh, feeble as it was. "We won't be able to stay for the show," Barbara said, with a good facsimile of regret. "There's quite a lot still to do behind the scenes—some of Peter's friends are staying over. But we might be able to sneak back in to catch the finale. If not, see you in the interval." With a conspiratorial grin, she beat her retreat and left me with my audience.

I let my gaze wander around the room, taking the measure of them. There was an in-group, clustered around Peter and engaged in a shouted conversation that colonized the entire room. There was an out-group, consisting of four or five temporary knots spread around the edges of the room, which periodically tried to attach themselves to the in-group in a sort of reversal of cellular fission. And then there was stepbrother Sebastian.

It wasn't hard to spot him; I'd made a firm identification while I was still unfolding my trestle table and laying out my opening trick. He had the matrilineal blond hair, but his paler skin and watery blue eyes made him look as if someone had sketched him in pastels and then tried to erase him. He looked to be a lot smaller and slighter than Peter, too. Because he was the younger of the two? It was hard to tell, because his infolded, self-effaced posture probably took an inch or so off his height. He was the one on the fringes of the boisterous rabble, barely tolerated by the birthday boy and contemptuously ignored by the birthday boy's friends. He was the one left out of all the in-jokes, looking like he didn't belong and would rather be almost anywhere else—even with his real dad, perhaps, on a day when there was a work crisis on.

When I clapped my hands and shouted a two-minute warning, Sebastian filed up with the last of the rear guard and took up a position immediately behind Peter—a dead zone that nobody else seemed to want to lay claim to.

Then the show was on, and I had troubles of my own to attend to.

I'm not a bad stage magician. It was how I paid my way through college, and when I'm in practice, I'd go so far as to say I'm pretty sharp. Right then I was as rusty as hell, but I was still able to pull off some reasonably classy stuff—my own scaled-down versions of the great illusions I'd studied during my ill-spent youth. I made some kid's wristwatch disappear from a bag that he was holding and turn up inside a box in someone else's pocket. I levitated the same kid's mobile phone around the room while Peter and the front-row elite stood up and waved their arms in the vain hope of tangling the wires they thought I was using. I even cut a deck of cards into pieces with garden shears and reconstituted them again, with a card that Peter had previously chosen and signed at the top of the deck.

But whatever the hell I did, I was dying on my feet. Peter sat stolidly at front and center, arms folded in his lap, and glared at me all the while with paint-blistering contempt. He'd clearly reached his verdict, which was that being impressed by kids'-party magic could lose you a lot of status with your peers. And if the risk was there even for him, it was clearly unacceptable for his chosen guests. They watched him and took their cue from him, forming a block vote that I couldn't shift.

Sebastian seemed to be the only one who was actually interested in the show for its own sake—or perhaps the only one who had so little to lose that he could afford just to let himself get drawn in, without watching his back. It got him into trouble, though. When I finished the card trick and showed Peter his pristine eight of diamonds, Sebastian broke into a thin patter of applause, carried away for a moment by the excitement of the final reveal.

He stopped as soon as he realized that nobody else was joining in, but he'd already broken cover—forgetting what seemed otherwise to be very well developed habits of camouflage and self-preservation. Annoyed, Peter stabbed backward with his elbow, and I heard a *whoof* of air from Sebastian as he leaned suddenly forward, clutching his midriff. His head stayed bowed for a few moments, and when he came up, he came up slowly. "Fuckwit," Peter snarled, sotto voce. "He just used two decks. That's not even clever."

I read a lot into this little exchange—a whole chronicle of casual cruelty and emotional oppression. You may think that's stretching an elbow in the ribs a touch too far, but I'm a younger brother myself, so the drill's not unfamiliar to me. And besides that, I knew one more thing about birthday boy than anybody else here knew.

I took a mental audit. Yes. I was letting myself get a little irritated, and that wasn't a good thing. I still had twenty minutes to run before the break and the cold beer in the kitchen. And I had one surefire winner, which I'd been meaning to save for the finale, but what the hell. You only live once, as people continue to say in the teeth of all the evidence.

I threw out my arms, squared my shoulders, tugged my cuffs—a pantomime display of preparation intended mainly to get Sebastian off the hook. It worked, as far as that went; all eyes turned to me. "Watch very carefully," I said, taking a new prop out of one of the cases and putting it on the table in front of me. "An ordinary cereal box. Any of you eat this stuff? No, me neither. I tried them once, but I was mauled by a cartoon tiger." Not a glimmer; not a sign of mercy in any of the forty or so eyes that were watching me.

"Nothing special about the box. No trapdoors. No false bottoms." I rotated it through three dimensions, flicked it with a thumbnail to get a hollow *thwack* out of it, and held the open end up to Peter's face for him to take a look inside. He rolled his eyes as if he couldn't believe he was being asked to go along with this stuff, then gave me a wave that said he was as satisfied of the box's emptiness as he was ever going to be.

"Yeah, whatever," he said with a derisive snort. His friends laughed, too; he was popular enough to get a choric echo whenever he spoke or snickered or made farting noises in his cheek. He had the touch, all right. Give him four, maybe five years, and he was going to grow up into a right bastard.

Unless he took a walk down the Damascus Road one morning and met something big and fast coming the other way.

"O-o-okay," I said, sweeping the box around in a wide arc so that everyone else could see it. "So it's an empty box. So who needs it, right? Boxes like this, they're just landfill waiting to happen." I stood it on the ground, open end downward, and trod it flat.

That got at least a widened eye and a shift of posture here and there around the room—kids leaning forward to watch, if only to check out how complete and convincing the damage was. I was thorough. You have to be. Like a dominatrix, you find that there's a direct relationship between the intensity of the stamping and trampling and the scale of the final effect.

When the box was comprehensively flattened, I picked it up and allowed it to dangle flaccidly from my left hand.

"But before you throw this stuff away," I said, sweeping the cluster of stolid faces with a stern, schoolteacherly gaze, "you've got to check for biohazards. Anyone up for that? Anyone want to be an environmental health inspector when they grow up?"

There was an awkward silence, but I let it lengthen. It was Peter's dime; I only had to entertain him, not pimp for him.

Finally, one of the front-row cronies shrugged and stood up. I stepped a little aside to welcome him into my performance space—broadly speaking, the area between the leather recliner and the running buffet.

"Give a big hand to the volunteer," I suggested. They razzed him cordially instead—you find out who your friends are.

I straightened the box with a few well-practiced tugs and tucks. This was the crucial part, so of course I kept my face as bland as school custard. The volunteer held his hand out for the box. Instead, I caught his hand in my own and turned it palm up. "And the other one," I said. "Make a cup. *Verstehen Sie* 'cup'? Like this. Right. Excellent. Good luck, because you never know . . ."

I upended the box over his hands, and a large brown rat smacked right down into the makeshift basket of his fingers. He gurgled like a punctured water bed and jumped back, his hands flying convulsively apart, but I was ready and caught the rat neatly before she could fall.

Then, because I knew her well, I added a small grace note to the trick by stroking her nipples with the ball of my thumb. This made her arch her back and gape her mouth wide open, so that when I brandished her in the faces of the other kids, I got a suitable set of jolts and starts. Of course, it wasn't a threat display—it was "More, big boy, give me more"—but they couldn't be expected to know that look at their tender age. Any more than they knew that I'd dropped Rhona into the box when I pretended to straighten it after the trampling.

And bow. And acknowledge the applause. Which would have been fine if there'd been any. But Peter still sat like Patience on a monument, as the volunteer trudged back to his seat with his machismo at half-mast.

Peter's face said I'd have to do a damn sight more than that to impress him.

So I thought about the Damascus Road again. And, like the bastard I am, I reached for the camera.

This isn't my idea of how a grown man should go about keeping the wolf from the door, I'd like you to know. It was Pen who put me up to it. Pamela Elisa Bruckner—why that shortens to Pen rather than Pam I've never been sure, but she's an old friend of mine, and incidentally the rightful owner of Rhona the rat. She's also my landlady, for the moment at least, and since I wouldn't wish that fate on a rabid dog, I count myself lucky that it's fallen to someone who's genuinely fond of me. It lets me get away with a hell of a lot.

I should also tell you that I do have a job—a real job that pays the bills, at least occasionally. But at the time currently under discussion, I was taking an extended holiday, not entirely voluntary, and not without its own attendant problems relating to cash flow, professional credibility, and personal self-esteem. In any case, it left Pen with a vested interest in putting alternative work my way. Since she was still a good Catholic girl (when she wasn't being a Wicca priestess), she went to Mass every Sunday, lit a candle to the Blessed Virgin, and prayed to this tune: "Please, Madonna, in your wisdom and mercy, intercede for my mother though she died with many carnal sins weighing on her soul; let the troubled nations of Earth find a road to peace and freedom; and make Castor solvent, amen."

But usually she left it at that, which was a situation we could both live with. So it was an unpleasant surprise to me when she stopped counting on divine intervention and told me about the kids' party agency she was setting up with her crazy friend Leona—and the slimy sod of a street magician who'd given her an eleventh-hour stab in the back.

"But you could do this so *easily*, Fix," she coaxed over coffee laced with cognac in her subterranean sitting room. The smell was making me dizzy—not the smell of the brandy, but the smell of rats and earth and leaf mulch and droppings and Mrs. Amelia Underwood roses—of things growing and things decaying. One of her two ravens—Arthur, I think—was clacking his beak against the top shelf of the bookcase, making it hard for me to stick to a train of thought. This was her den, her center of gravity—the inverted penthouse underneath the three-story monstrosity where her grandmother had lived and died in the days when mammoths still roamed the Earth. She had me at a disadvantage here, which was why she'd asked me in to start with.

"You can do real magic," Pen pointed out sweetly, "so fake magic ought to be a doddle."

I blinked a couple of times to clear my eyes, blinded by candles, fuddled by incense. In a lot of ways, the way Pen lives is sort of reminiscent of Miss Havisham in *Great Expectations*: she only uses the basement, which means that the rest of the house apart from my bed-sitter up in the roof space is frozen in the 1950s, never visited, never revised. Pen herself froze a fair bit later than that, but like Miss Havisham, she wears her heart on her mantelpiece. I try not to look at it.

On this particular occasion, I took refuge in righteous indignation. "I can't do real magic, Pen, because there's no such animal. Not the way you mean it, anyway. What do I look like, eh? Just because I can talk to the dead—and whistle up a tune for them—that doesn't make me Gandalf the bastard Grey. And it doesn't mean that there are fairies at the bottom of the sodding garden."

The crude language was a ploy intended to derail the conversation.

It didn't work, though. I got the impression that Pen had worked out her script in advance for this one.

"'What is now proved was once only imagined,'" she said primly—because she knows that Blake is my main man, and I can't argue with him. "Okay," she went on, topping up my cup with about a half-pint of Janneau XO (it was going to be dirty pool on both sides, then), "but you did all that stage-magic stuff when we were in college, didn't you? You were *wonderful* back then. I bet you could still do it. I bet you wouldn't even have to practice. And it's two hundred quid for a day's work, so you could pay me a bit off last month's chunk of what you owe me . . ."

It took a lot more persuasion and a fair bit more brandy—so much brandy, in fact, that I made a pass at her on my unsteady way out the door. She slapped off my right hand, steered my left onto the door handle, and kissed me good night on the cheek without breaking stride.

I was profoundly grateful for that when I woke up in the morning, with my tongue stuck to my soft palate and my head full of unusable fuzz. Sexy, sweet, uninhibited, nineteen-year-old Pen, with her autumn bonfire of hair, her pistachio eyes, and her probably illegal smile would have been one thing; thirty-something Earth Mother Pen in her sibyl's cave, tended by rats and ravens and Christ only knew what other familiar spirits, and still waiting for her prince to come even though she knew exactly where he was and what he'd turned into—there was too much blood under the bridge now. Leave it at that.

Then I remembered that I'd agreed to do the party just before I made the pass, and I cursed like a longshoreman. Game, set, and match to Pen and Monsieur Janneau. I hadn't even known we were playing doubles.

———

So there was a reason, anyway, even if it wasn't good or sufficient, why I now found myself facing down these arrogant little shits and prostituting my God-given talents for the paltry sum of two hundred quid. There was a reason why I'd put myself in the way of temptation. And there was a reason why I fell.

"Now," I said, with a smile as wide as a Halloween pumpkin, "for my last and most ambitious trick before you all go off and feed your faces, I need another volunteer from the audience." I pointed at Sebastian. "You, sir, in the second row. Would you be so good?" Sebastian looked hangdog, intensely reluctant. Stepping into the spotlight meant certain humiliation and possibly much worse. But the older boys were whistling and catcalling, and Peter was telling him to get the hell up there and do it. So he stood up and worked his way along the row, tripping a couple of times over the outstretched feet that were planted in his path.

This was going to be cruel, but not to stepbrother Sebastian. No, my un-birthday gift to him was a loaded gun that he could use in any way he wanted to. And for Peter . . . well, sometimes cruelty is kindness in disguise. Sometimes pain is the best teacher. Sometimes it does you no harm to realize that there's a limit to what you can get away with.

Sebastian had made his way around to my side of the trestle table now, and he was standing awkwardly next to me. I picked up the Autographic and slipped the hooks on either side, wheeling the bellows out fully into its working position. With its red leather and dark wood, it looked like a pretty impressive piece of kit; when I gave it to Sebastian to hold, he took it gingerly.

"Please examine the camera," I told him. "Make sure it's okay. Fully functional, fully intact." He glanced at it cursorily, without enthusiasm, nodded, and tried to hand it back to me.

I didn't take it. "Sorry," I said, "you're my cameraman now. You have to do the job properly, because I'm relying on you."

He looked again, and this time he noticed what was staring him in the face.

"Well—there's black tape," he said. "Over the lens."

I affected to be surprised and took a look for myself. "Gentlemen," I said to the room at large. "Ladies." A five-second pause for howls of mocking laughter, nudges, and pointing fingers. "My assistant has just brought something very alarming to my attention. This camera has black masking tape over the lens, and it can't therefore take photographs"—I let the pause lengthen—"in the normal way. We're going to have to try to take a *spirit* photo."

Peter and Peter's friends looked pained and scornful at this suggestion; it sounded to them like a pretty lame finale.

"Spirit photographs are among the most difficult feats for the magician to encompass," I told them gravely, paying no attention to the sounds of derision. "Think of an escapologist freeing himself from a mailbag suspended upside down from a hook in a cage that has been dumped out of a jet plane flying about two miles up. Well, this trick is a little like that. Less visually spectacular, but just as flamboyantly pointless."

I gestured to the birthday boy. "We're going to take your picture, Peter," I told him. "So why don't you go and stand over there, by the wall. A plain background works best for this."

Peter obeyed with a great show of heavy resignation.

"You have another brother?" I asked Sebastian, quietly.

He glanced up at me, startled. "No," he said.

"Or a cousin or something—someone your own age who used to live here with you?"

He shook his head.

"You know how to use a camera?"

Sebastian was on firmer ground here, and he looked relieved. "Yeah. I've got one upstairs. But it's just point and shoot, it doesn't have any . . . focus thing, or . . ."

I dismissed these objections with a shake of the head, giving him a reassuring half smile. "Doesn't matter," I said. "This one focuses manually, but we're not going to bother with that anyway. Because we're not using either the lens or ordinary light to form the image.

But the thing you're going to be clicking is this." I gave him the air bulb—sitting at the end of a coil of rubber tubing, it was the only part of the camera that I'd had to replace. "You squeeze it hard, and it opens the shutter. When I say, okay?"

I hadn't loaded the Autographic for more than a decade, but all the stuff I needed was right there in the box, and my hands knew what to do. I lined up a new plate, peeled away one corner of the waxed cover sheet, then slammed it into place and tore the cover free in one smooth movement. It wasn't what a professional would have done, partly because there was bound to be some seepage of light if you loaded the camera like that in an ordinarily lit room—but mostly because I was loading print paper rather than negative film. We were cutting out one stage of the normal photographic process. Again, it didn't matter, but I noticed as I was tightening the screws up again that James and Barbara Dodson had wandered in and were standing at the back of the room. That was going to mean a louder eruption, but by this stage I didn't really give a monkey's chuff; Peter had gotten quite seriously under my skin.

I got Sebastian into position, steering him with my hand on his shoulders. Peter was getting bored and restive, but we were almost done. I could have ratcheted up the tension a bit more, but since the outcome was still in doubt, I thought I might as well just suck it and see. Either it would work or it wouldn't. "Okay, on my mark. Peter—smile. Nice try, but no. Kids in the front row, show Peter what a smile is. Sebastian—three, two, one, now!"

Sebastian pressed the bulb, and the shutter made a slow, arthritic *whuck-chunk* sound. Good. I'd been half afraid that nothing would happen at all.

"Now, we don't have any fixative," I announced as my memory started to kick in again, piecemeal. "So the image won't last for long. But we can make it clearer with a stop bath. Lemon juice will do, or vinegar, if you . . . ?" I looked hopefully at the two grown-ups, and Barbara slipped out of the room again.

"What about developing fluid?" James asked, looking at me with vague but definite mistrust.

I shook my head. "We're not using light," I said again. "We're photographing the spirit world, not the visible one, so the film doesn't have to develop; it has to translate."

James's face showed very clearly what he thought of this explanation. There was an awkward silence, broken by Barbara as she came back in with a bottle of white-wine vinegar, a plastic bowl, and an apologetic smile. "This is going to stink," she warned me as she retreated again to the back of the room.

She was right. The sweet-sour tang of the vinegar hit and held as I poured out about two-thirds of the bottle, which covered the bowl to half an inch or so deep. Then, with Sebastian still standing next to me, I slipped the plate out of the camera, very deliberately blocking with my body the audience's line of sight. "Sebastian," I said, "you're still the cameraman here. That means you're the medium through which the spirits are working. Please, dip the print paper in the vinegar, and slosh it around so that it's completely soaked. An image should form on the paper as you do this. Do you see an image, Sebastian?"

Peter hadn't even bothered to move from his place over by the wall. In fact, he was leaning against it now, looking more sullen and bored than ever. Sebastian stared first in consternation and then in amazement at the paper as he sluiced it round and round in the bowl.

"Do you see an image?" I repeated, knowing damn well that he did.

"Yeah!" he blurted. Everyone in the room was picking up on his tension and astonishment now; I didn't need to go for any verbal buildup.

"And what *is* that image?"

"A boy. It's—I think it's—!"

"Of course you can see a boy," I interrupted. "We just took a photo of your brother, Peter. Is that who you can see, Sebastian?"

He shook his head, his wide eyes still staring down at the muddy photograph. "No. Well, I mean, yeah, but—there's somebody else, too. It's—"

I cut across him again. Everything in its place. "Somebody you recognize?"

Sebastian nodded emphatically. "Yeah."

I like to see what I was doing here as siding with the underdog, but if there had been no element of sadism in it, I wouldn't have been looking at Peter as I said the next few words. "And does he have a name, this other boy? What dark wonders from the spirit world have we captured and pinned to the wall, Sebastian? Tell us his name."

Sebastian swallowed hard. It was genuine nerves rather than showmanship, but the strained pause was better than anything I could have choreographed myself.

"Davey Simmons," Sebastian said, his voice a little too high.

The effect on Peter was electrifying. He yelled in what sounded like honest, naked terror, coming away from the wall with a jerk and then lurching across to the bowl in three staccato strides. But I was too quick for him. "Thank you, Sebastian," I said, whipping the print out of the bowl and waving it in the air as though to dry it—and as though keeping it out of Peter's reach was only accidental.

It had come out pretty well. In black and white, of course, and darkened around the edges where the light had got in at the paper, but nice and clear where it needed to be. It showed Peter as a sort of grainy blur, only recognizable by his posture and by the darker splodge of his hair. By contrast, the figure that stood at his elbow was very distinct indeed—sad, washed out, beaten down by time and loneliness and the fact of his own death, but not to be mistaken for marsh gas, cardboard cutout, or misapplied imagination.

"Davey Simmons," I mused. "Did you know him well, Peter?"

"I never fucking heard of him!" Peter yelled, throwing himself at me with desperate fury. "Give me that!" I'm not hefty by any means, but for all his solidity, Peter was just a kid; holding him off while I showed the print to his friends wasn't hard at all. They were all staring at it with expressions that ran the gamut from sick horror to bowel-loosening panic.

"And yet," I mused, "he stands beside you as you eat, and work, and sleep. In his death, he watches you living, night into day into night. Why do you suppose that is?"

"I don't know," Peter squealed, "I don't know! Give it to me!"

Most of the audience were on their feet now, some surging forward to look at the print, but most pulling back as if they wanted to get some distance from it. James Dodson waded through them like a battleship through shrimp boats, and it was he who took the print out of my hands. Peter immediately turned his attentions to his father and tried again to snatch the photo, but James pushed him back roughly. He stared down at the print in perplexity, shaking his head slowly from side to side. Then, with his face flushing deep red, he tore it up, very deliberately, into two pieces, then four, then eight. Peter gave a whimper, caught somewhere between misery and the illusion of relief, but from where I was standing, it looked like he'd be living with this for a while to come.

Dodson was working on thirty-two pieces when I turned to Sebastian and solemnly shook his hand.

"You've got a gift," I said. He met my gaze, and understanding passed between us. What he had was a lever. Peter wasn't going to be as free in the future with his elbows, or his fists, or his feet—not now that everyone had seen his guilt and his weakness. There wasn't any extra charge for this; I work on a fixed rate.

I'd noticed the miserable little ghost hovering around Peter as soon as he'd come into the room. They're harder to spot in daylight, but I've got a lot of experience on top of a lot of natural sensitivity, and I know what to expect in a house where they don't keep their rowan sprigs up to date. I didn't know what the connection was, but unless Davey Simmons had no family at all, there had to be a damn good reason why he was haunting this house rather than his own. He couldn't get away from Peter; his soul was tangled up in him like a bird in a briar patch. You could read that in any number of ways, but Peter's violent reaction had ruled out some of them, changed the odds on others.

Anyway, things got a bit confused after that. Dodson was yelling at me to pack up my things and get out, and spitting and spluttering about a lawsuit to follow. Peter had fled from the room, pursued by Barbara, and barricaded himself in somewhere upstairs, to judge by the bangs and yells that I could hear. The party guests milled around like a decapitated squid—lots of appendages, no brain, faintly suspect smell. And Sebastian stood watching me with big, solemn eyes and never said another word as long as I was there.

When I asked Dodson for the money he owed me for the performance, he punched me in the mouth. I took that in my stride—no teeth loosened, only a symbolic amount of bloodshed. I probably had that coming. He went for the camera next, though, and I went for it, too. Me and that Brownie went back a long way, and I didn't want to have to go looking for another machine with such sympathetic vibes. We tussled inconclusively for a few moments for control of it, then he seemed to remember where he was—in his own living room, watched by a gaggle of his son's best friends, whose fathers he also no doubt knew well in work or club circles.

"Get out," he told me, his eyes still wild. "Get out of my house, you irresponsible bastard, before I throw you out on your ear."

I gave up on the money. It wouldn't be easy for me to argue that traumatizing the birthday boy was within my remit. I packed everything up laboriously into the four cases under James's glaring eyes and stertorous breathing. He was suffering a kind of anaphylactic reaction to me now, and if I didn't get out soon, he might crash and burn as his immune system tore itself apart in its desire to remove the irritation.

Out into the hall, and I caught sight of Barbara on the upstairs landing. Her face was pale and tense, but I swear she threw me a nod. With four suitcases' worth of heavy freight, I was in no position to wave back—and it might have been tactless in any case.

———————

It was about half past six by this time, with the November dark already settled in. Pen would be waiting for me back in her basement, eager for hard news and harder currency. Under the circumstances, I couldn't really give her either.

The moon was three days from the dark. Like most people these days, I kept my eye on the almanac when I was planning to be out after nightfall. The dead don't follow the phases of the moon, of course, but there are lots of nastier things that do—and the dead I can deal with, in any case.

So I drove around to Craven Park Road. It was somewhere to go, and I have to stop by the office once every couple of months if only to throw out the mail. Otherwise, the slowly accumulating weight of unpaid bills would threaten the structural integrity of the building.

Harlesden isn't the best place in the world to put up your shingle. You have to park your car out on the main road if you want to have an even chance of it being there when you get back to it. The Yardie boys tout coke out on the street and stare you down hard if you accidentally make eye contact. And the beggars who sit exhausted in the doorways, their hollow-eyed stares spearing you like the Ancient Mariner's as you walk by, are mostly the risen-again. Not ghosts, I mean, but those who've come back in the body—zombies, for want of a less melodramatic word. They're a sad bunch, on the whole, but that doesn't stop your flesh from crawling slightly as you walk by.

But tonight, everything was pretty quiet. Even the sign over my door was holding up pretty well. Sometimes the kids from the Stonehouse Estate come by with their airbrushes and turn the sign into something whimsical and baroque, obliterating in the process the simple, dignified face I present to the world. But tonight the words F. CASTOR ERADICATIONS stood out in all their austere clarity.

Grambas, the proprietor of the kebab house next door, was leaning in his doorway, enjoying a roll-up cigarette whose heavy smoke hung around him like a shroud. He grinned at me as I unlocked the street door, and I shot him a wink. We've got an understanding: he's promised me that he won't lay ghosts or bind demons so long as I don't serve greasy fried food and overmatured salads.

My office is actually above the kebab house. Once inside the door, there's a narrow flight of awkwardly high stairs that leads up, with a sharp, right-angled bend, to my second-floor premises. Pen says the stairs are high because the conversion was a weird one, swapping between three stories and four, depending on which of the original residents sold out and which ones stayed. I reckon the builders were working on margin; twenty high steps are quicker to throw up than thirty normal-size ones.

I scooped up a thick handful of mail and headed on up. Even if you're fit, you get to the top of those steps a little breathless. I'm not fit. I kicked open the office door, breathing like a dirty phone call, and flicked on the light.

It's not much of an office, even by Harlesden standards. Being over a kebab shop—while it has its advantages in terms of daily sustenance—tends to lend a greasy miasma to the walls, the furniture, and the air you breathe. And Pen had never made good on her promise to get me some decent furniture (although her offer still stood if I ever got even on the rent), so all I had was a Formica-topped self-assembly desk and two tubular steel chairs from IKEA. The filing cabinet was a two-drawer midget that also served as a table to hold the kettle and tea things. By way of decoration, I had six framed illustrations from *Little Nemo in Slumberland*, which I'd got from IKEA on the same expedition that brought me the chairs. They made clients feel relaxed and receptive. Also, they weighed in at less than four quid each.

Yes, it was pathetic. But it was mine.

Or, at least, it had been.

I sat down in one of the chairs, put my feet up on the filing cabinet, and started to flick through the post. For each piece of real mail, there were two curry-house fliers and a great investment opportunity, which made progress fairly fast; not many envelopes actually needed to be opened before making the fall of shame into the already-overflowing wastepaper basket. An electricity bill, black, and a phone bill, red . . . these colors change with the seasons and are a gentle reminder of time's passing.

I stopped short. The next envelope in the stack was pale gray and bore a return address that I recognized: the Charles Stanger Care Facility, Muswell Hill. My name was written on the front of the envelope in a pained, cramped hand in which curved lines were approximated by collections of short, angular jags. It was fractal handwriting; looking at it, you imagined that under a microscope, every stroke of the pen would open up into a thousand angled flecks of tortured ink.

Rafi. Nobody else wrote like that. Nobody sane *could* write like that.

I opened the envelope carefully, peeling back the gummed flap rather than just tearing off one end and running my finger along. Rafi had caught me with a razor blade once, taped into the corner of the envelope. I'd almost lost the top joint of my thumb. This time, though, there was nothing except a single sheet of paper torn from a notepad. On it, in very different handwriting from that which had addressed the envelope (but still Rafi's hand—he had several), there was a message that, if nothing else, was admirable in its brevity.

YOURE GOING TO MAKE A MISTAKE YOU NEED TO TALK TO ME BEFORE YOU MAKE A MISTAKE YOU NEED TO TALK TO ME NOW

I was still staring at the letter, unsure whether to put it into my pocket or let it fall into the basket, when the phone rang. Picking it up was a reflex action; if I'd thought about it, I would have let it lie, because it was bound to get me into a conversation that I didn't want or need.

"Mr. Castor?"

It was a male voice, dry and harsh with an overtone of stern disapproval. It conjured up an image of a preacher with a Bible in his hand and his finger pointing at your heart.

"Yes?"

"The exorcist?"

I considered lying, but since I'd confessed to my name, there wasn't any point. Anyway, it was entirely my own fault. Nobody had made me pick up the frigging phone; I'd done it of my own free will, as a consenting adult.

And now I had a customer.

ᵔᵒ Two

THIS WAS TEN YEARS OR MORE AFTER THE DEAD first began to rise—I mean, to rise in sufficient numbers that it wasn't an option anymore just to ignore them.

They'd always been there, I guess. Certainly as a kid I was seeing them on and off whenever I was in any place that was quiet or where the light was dim. An old man standing in the street, staring at nothing as the mothers pushed their strollers right through him and kept on walking; a little girl hovering irresolute by the swings in the local playground, through all the watches of the night, and never clambering on for a ride; a shadow in the deeper shadows of a narrow alley that didn't move quite in sync when a car went by. It wasn't ever much of a problem, though, even for people like me, who could actually see them; most ghosts keep themselves to themselves, and it's not like you have to feed them or clean up after them. Ninety-nine out of a hundred will never give you any trouble at all. I learned not to mention them to anybody and not to look at them directly in case they cottoned on to me and started talking. It was only bad when they talked.

But something happened a few years before the page turned on the old millennium, as though some cosmic equivalent of a big, spiteful kid had come along and poked a stick into the graveyards of the world, just to see what would happen.

What happened was that the dead swarmed out like ants—the dead, and a few other things.

Nobody had any explanation for it, at least not unless you counted the many variations on "we are living in the last days, and these are the signs and wonders that were foretold." That was an argument that played fairly well, up to a point. The Christians and the Jews had put their money on a bodily resurrection, and that was what some people seemed to be getting. But the Bible is strangely coy on the subject of the were-kind, hedges its bets on demons, and draws a big fat blank on ghosts, so the Christians and the Jews didn't really seem to be any better placed than the rest of us to call the toss.

The theological arguments raged like brush fires, and under the smoke that they threw up, the world changed—not overnight, but with the slow, irrevocable progress of an eclipse, or ink soaking into blotting paper. The promised apocalypse didn't come, but new testaments were written anyway, and new religions kick-started. New and exciting careers opened up for people like me. Even the map of London got redrawn, which as far as I was concerned was the hardest thing to believe and accept.

I was born elsewhere, you have to understand—up North, two hundred miles from the Smoke—and my view of London is an outsider's view, assembled in easy pieces over the last twenty years. When I picture the city in my mind, I tend to see it in simplified, schematic terms—like the cageful of snakes, orange on green on blue, that you see on the inside cover of the A–Z. Where the biggest snake—the king python, the Thames—runs right through the middle, that's the null zone. Ghosts can't cross running water, and they don't even like the sound of it all that much. Lesser demons and were-things will usually balk at it, too, although that's not so widely known. So the river's a good place to be, unless for any reason communing with the dead is something that you actually *want* to do.

Walk a few streets in any direction, though, until you can't see the Thames at your back anymore, and you're in a city that's been a major population center ever since Gog and Magog sat down on their two hills some time around the middle of the Stone Age and put their feet up. Sacked by war, gutted by riot, razed by fire, and scoured by plague, it's got a ratio of about twenty dead to every one living inhabitant, and that ratio is weighted most heavily in the center, where the city is oldest.

It's not as bleak as it sounds, because not everyone you lay in the earth comes back; there are a whole lot who are content to sleep it out. And those who do come back will often stay in one place rather than wander around and inspire sphincter-loosening terror in the living. Most ghosts are tethered to the place where they died, with the place where they were buried coming in a close second (a fact that turned the blocks around inner-city cemeteries into instant slums). Zombies are just spirits even more tightly circumscribed than that, effectively haunting their own dead bodies, and as for the *loup-garous*, the were-kind . . . well, we'll get to them in their place. But sometimes ghosts go walkabout, impelled by curiosity, loneliness, solicitude, boredom, mischief, a grudge, a concern, an addiction—some unfinished business, anyway, that won't let them lie quiet until some still-distant Judgment Day.

I'm talking about the dead as if they had human emotions and human motivations. I apologize. It's a common mistake, but any professional will give you a different point of view on the subject, whether you ask for it or not. Ghosts are reflections in fun-house mirrors—distorted echoes of past emotions, lingering on way past their sell-by date. Sometimes there's a fragment of consciousness still there, directing them so that they can respond to you in crude and simple ways; more often not. The last thing you want to do is to make the mistake of thinking of them as people. That's the bottom line, as the Ghostbusters count it. Sentimental anthropomorphisms aren't exactly an asset in my line of business.

But sentient or not, a close encounter with a ghost can be an upsetting, not to say seat-wetting, experience. That's where the exorcists come in—both the official church-sponsored ones, who are usually either idiots or fanatics, and the freelancers like me, who know what they're doing.

My vocation had shown itself on the day after my sixth birthday, when I got tired of sharing my bed with my dead sister, Katie, who'd been run over by a truck the year before, and made her go away by screaming scatological playground rhymes at her. Yeah, I know. If ever there was a poisoned chalice that had a clearer Hazchem warning written down the side of it, it's one I never came across.

But how many people do you know who actually get to choose what they do for a living? My careers teacher said I should go into hotel management, so exorcism it was.

Until now. Now I was on sabbatical. I'd had my fingers burned pretty badly about a year and a half before, and I was in no hurry to start playing with matches again. I told myself I'd retired. I made myself believe it for a good part of every day.

So now, as I listened to the voice of this solidly respectable citizen who was reaching out to me for help across the London night, the first thought that came into my mind was how the hell I was going to get rid of him. The second was that it was lucky he hadn't called in person, because I was still dressed like a clown. On the other hand, the second would probably have helped with the first.

"Mr. Castor, we have a problem," the voice announced in a convincing tone of anxiety and complaint. Was that the royal *we*, or did he mean himself and me? That would be a bit pushy for a first date.

"I'm sorry to hear it," I offered. And since the best defense is a good offense, "My books are pretty much full at the moment. I don't think I'll be able to—"

He shot that one down well before it got to the bushes. "I find that hard to believe," he snapped. "Very hard to believe. You never answer your phone. I've been calling you for four days now, and you've never picked up once. You don't have an answerphone; you don't even use a voice-mail service. So how would you be booking appointments?"

At any other time, this litany would have sounded like good news to me. A client who's been calling for four days already has a lot invested in the deal, which makes him that much more likely to see it through.

At any other time.

Even now, as I considered my response, I felt the familiar quickening of my pulse; the familiar sensation of standing on the high diving board and looking down. Only this time I wasn't going to let myself jump.

"I'm not taking on any new clients right now," I repeated after slightly too long a pause. "If you tell me what your problem is, I can refer you to someone else who can help you, Mr. . . ."

"Peele. Jeffrey Peele. I'm the chief administrator at the Bonnington Archive. But I'm coming to you as the result of a personal referral. I'm not prepared to consider employing a third party who's a complete unknown to me."

Too bad, I thought. "It's the best I can do." I dumped the sheaf of letters I was still holding on top of the filing cabinet, the muffled boom testifying to how empty it was, and stood up. I wanted to wind this up and get moving; the evening was already looking problematic. "Why do you need an exorcist?" I prompted him.

This seemed to wind Mr. Peele up even tighter. "Because we have a *ghost*!" he said, his voice sounding slightly shrill now. "Why else would you imagine?"

I chose to let that question hang. He'd be amazed. But fireside tales didn't seem like a very attractive option just then.

"What sort of ghost?" Getting a little more information out of Peele would probably be the quickest way of seeing him off. Depending on what he told me, I could almost certainly steer him in the direction of someone who could do the job. If it was a sympathetic someone, I might even be able to claim a finder's fee. "I mean, how does it behave?"

"Until last week, it was entirely inoffensive," he said, sounding only slightly mollified. "At least—in the sense that it didn't do anything overtly hostile. It was just there. I know this sort of thing has become a fairly commonplace occurrence, but this"—he tripped on whatever he was trying to say, came back for a second pass—"I've never experienced anything like this before."

For what it was worth, I commiserated. We got them often enough, even now—people who because of luck or lifestyle or straightforward reasons of geography had never met one of the risen, either ghost or zombie. Pen called people like that vestals, to distinguish them from virgins in the more conventional sense. But Peele had just lost his spectral cherry, and it was obvious that he wanted to talk about it.

"The Bonnington Archive is in Euston," he began. "In Churchway, off the end of what used to be Drummond Street. We specialize in maps and charts and original documents—with a London provenance, of course, because a lot of our running costs are met through the Corporation of London and through the boroughs' JMT funding." He translated the acronym with an automatic air, like a man used to speaking in jargon and not being understood. "Joint Museums and Trusts, an initiative of the mayor's office. We also have a maritime artifacts collection, funded separately by the office of the Admiralty and the Seamen's Union, and a very sizable library of first editions, somewhat haphazardly acquired . . ."

"And the ghost is haunting the archive itself?" I prompted him, alarmed at the prospect of listening to an itemized list. "Since when, exactly?"

"Since the late summer. Perhaps the middle of September, or thereabouts. There was a lull in October, but now she's returned, and she seems to be worse than ever. Actually threatening. Violent."

"Are the sightings clustered? I mean, does the ghost haunt any particular room?"

"Not really, no. She—she wanders around, to a large extent. But within limits. I believe she's been seen in almost every room on the first floor and in the basement. Sometimes, less often, on the upper stories."

That peripatetic aspect was unusual, and it piqued my interest. "You say *she*, so I assume her form is recognizably human?"

This question seemed to alarm Peele a little. "Yes. Of course. Are there some who aren't? She appears to be a young woman, with dark hair. Dressed in a hood and a white gown or robe of some kind. It's only her face that"—again he seemed to have a brief struggle with some word or concept that was difficult for him to get a handle on— "her face is very difficult to see," he offered at last.

"And her behavior?" I glanced at my watch. I still had to confess to Pen that I'd screwed up badly at the party, and now there was Rafi's letter to deal with. The quicker I got through the sympathetic-ear routine and got on my way, the better. "You said she was inoffensive until recently."

There was a pause on the line, a long enough pause that I was opening my mouth to ask Peele if he was still there, when he finally spoke.

"Most of the time, when people saw her, she'd just be standing there—especially at the end of the day. You'd feel something, like the gust of air when a door opens, and you'd look around and see her. Watching you." There was a very meaningful pause before those last two words; Peele was reliving an experience in his mind as he spoke, and it wasn't a pleasant one. "Never from close by. From the other end of the room or the bottom of a staircase. We have a lot of stairs. The building has a very distinctive design, with a great many . . ." He pulled himself back to the point, with some effort. "We have thirty people on staff, including several part-timers, and I believe everyone has seen her at least once. It was very frightening at first. As I said, she tended to favor the end of the afternoon, and at this time of year, it's often dark by four. It was very disconcerting to be looking for a book in the stacks and then to look up and see her standing at the end of the aisle. Staring at you. With her feet a few inches above the floor or her ankles sinking into it."

"Staring at you."

"I'm sorry?"

"You said that twice," I pointed out. "That she looks at you. But I believe you also mentioned that her face is indistinct. How do you know what it is she's looking at?"

"Not indistinct," Peele objected. "I never said that. I said you can't see her face. Not the upper part, at any rate. It seems to have . . . a curtain over it. A veil. A red veil. I can't quite describe the effect, but it's probably the most disconcerting thing about her. The veil covers everything from her hairline to just below her nose, so that only her mouth is visible." He paused for a moment—consulting his memory, I assumed—and his voice became even more hesitant. I could hear him picking his words, turning them over in his mind to check for nuances. "But you feel her attention," he said. "You know you're being watched. Examined. There's no possibility of doubt on the matter."

"You get that in a lot of hauntings," I agreed. "Ectoplasmic eyeballing. You can even get it without the ghost itself ever showing up; and then, of course, it's a lot harder to deal with—a lot harder to spot for what it is. What you've got is the more usual variety: she looks at you, and you feel the pressure of her gaze. But"—and once again I forced him back to the real issue—"she's doing more now than just looking, right?"

"Last Friday," said Peele unhappily. "One of my assistants—a man named Richard Clitheroe—was mending a document in the staff workroom. A lot of the original manuscripts in our collection have been indifferently cared for—inevitably, I suppose—and so a large part of our work is maintenance and reconstruction. He picked up a pair of scissors, and then there was—there was a commotion. Everything on the table started to fly around wildly, and the scissors were snatched from his hand. They cut his face, not deeply but visibly, and—and mutilated the document, too."

He fell into silence. I was impressed that he'd put the damage to the document last. To judge from his hushed tone, it was obviously the thing that had frightened him the most. So Peele's archive had a harmless and passive ghost who had suddenly become enraged and active. It was unusual, and I felt curiosity stir in my stomach like a waking snake. I clenched my teeth, holding it sternly down.

"There's a woman I used to work with sometimes," I said to Peele. Work *under* was the truth, but I went with the face-saving lie. "Professor Jenna-Jane Mulbridge. You've probably heard of her. The author of *In Flesh and Spirit*?" Peele exhaled—a sound halfway toward an "Aah." JJ's magnum opus was one of the few textbooks of our trade that had genuine crossover appeal, so everyone had heard of her even if they hadn't read it. "The woman who raised Rosie?" Peele confirmed, audibly impressed.

Actually, it had taken a whole bunch of us to raise the ghost known half jokingly as Rosie Crucis—and it took a whole dedicated team of people to keep her raised once we'd got her—but I let that pass. "Professor Mulbridge still practices occasionally," I said. "And she also heads the Metamorphic Ontology Clinic in Paddington, so she's in daily contact with dozens of the best men and women in the business. I can drop her a line and ask her to get in touch with you. I'm sure she'll be able to help you."

Peele mulled this compromise over. On the one hand, JJ was a very sizable carrot; on the other hand, he'd obviously been hoping, as clients usually do, for instant gratification.

"I thought you might come yourself," he said pointedly. "Tonight. I really wanted to have this dealt with tonight."

I have a stock lecture for clients who take this tack, but I felt as though I'd already given Peele more than his fair share of tolerance and patience.

"Exorcism doesn't work like that," I said tersely. "Mr. Peele, I'm afraid I'm going to have to get back to you later—unless you choose to follow this up yourself elsewhere. I have another appointment, and it's one that I don't want to be late for."

"So Ms. Mulbridge will perform the exorcism for us?" Peele pursued.

"Professor Mulbridge. I can't promise that, but I'll ask her if she's free to take it on. If she is, I presume the archive's number is listed in the phone book?"

"We have a Web site. All the contact details are on the Web site, but my home number—"

I broke in to tell him that the Web site would be fine, but he insisted that I take his home number down anyway. I wrote it on the back of Rafi's envelope. "Thank you, Mr. Peele. Really good to talk to you."

"But if the professor *isn't* available—"

"Then I'll let you know. One way or another, you'll hear from me or from her. Good evening, Mr. Peele. Take care."

I hung up, crossed to the door, and headed down the stairs. I'd reached the bottom before the phone rang again.

I flicked the lights off, turned the key in the lock, and walked away, heading for the car. It was still where I'd left it, and it still had all four wheels. Even at its worst, there are tiny holes in the midnight canopy of my bad luck.

A glass of whisky was calling out to me, a sultry siren song floating above the hoarse and ragged voices of the night.

But I was like Ulysses, tied to the mast.

First I had to go and see Rafi.

———————

I changed my clothes in the car, experiencing a palpable prickle of relief as I dumped the green dinner jacket in the backseat. It wasn't the ridiculous color of the thing, it was the feeling of being without my tin whistle, as necessary to me as a piece is to an American private eye. As I shrugged my greatcoat back on over my shoulders—hard work in that confined space—I had to reassure myself that the whistle was still there, in the long, sewn-in pocket on the right-hand side at chest height, where I can hook it out with my left hand while it looks like I'm just checking my watch. The dagger and the silver cup are useful tools in their way, but the whistle is more like a part of me—an extra limb.

It's a Clarke Original, key of D, with hand-painted diamonds around the stops and the sweetest chiff I ever came across. It comes in a C, too, but like David St. Hubbins once said, "D is the saddest chord." I feel at home there.

Satisfied that the whistle was back where it was meant to be, I started the car and drove away from the office with the familiar mixed feelings of relief and cold-turkey disgruntlement.

The Charles Stanger Care Facility is a discreet little place about a third of the way down the long bow bend of Coppetts Road, just off the North Circular. The spine of it was made by knocking a whole row of workers' cottages together into one building, and although there are some odd, misshapen limbs growing off that spine now, with Coldfall Wood as its backdrop the place still manages to look idyllic if you approach it on a summer's day—and if you can ignore the colonnade of spavined bed frames and dead fridges left along the margins of the lane in the venerable English pastime of fly-tipping.

But a wet November evening shows the place off in a bleaker light, and once you get through the entrance door, which is actually two doors and can only be released by buzzer from the inside, you have to dump what's left of the idyll in the receptacle provided. Pain and madness seem to be stewed into the walls of the place like stale sweat, and there's always someone crying or someone cursing at the limit of hearing. For me, it's as though I'm walking out of sunlight into shadow, even though they keep the heating turned up a degree or two too warm. I don't know how far that's down to me being what I am and how far it's purely autosuggestion.

Charles Stanger was a paranoid schizophrenic who murdered three children in one of those workers' cottages just after the Second World War. The books say two, but it was three—I've met them. He spent the rest of his life in Broadmoor at Her Majesty's pleasure, and in his more lucid stretches—because Charlie was Cambridge-educated and could turn a sentence like a joiner turns a table leg—he wrote eloquent letters to the Home Secretary, the president of the Howard League for Penal Reform, and anyone else who showed an interest, bewailing the lack of adequate facilities for the long-term incarceration of those whose crimes were occasioned not by malice or deviant passion but purely and simply by their being as crazy as shithouse rats.

After he died, it was discovered that he owned not just the cottage he lived in but the one next door, too. His will stipulated that they should be given over to a trust in the hope that they might someday become the seed and template for a more humane and less alienating institution in which the dangerously disturbed could live out their days safely sequestered from ordinary punters.

It's quite a touching story, really. A bit sad for the three little ghosts, of course, because they're now spending the afterlife in the company of an endless stream of violently disturbed men who probably bring back to them the circumstances of their own demise. But the dead have no rights. The mentally ill do, at least on paper, and the Charles Stanger Care Facility walks the usual line between respecting those rights and trimming the edges of them. Mostly the inmates are treated pretty well, unless they cut up rough with the wrong attendant at the wrong time. The place had only had four deaths in care in the last twenty years, and only one that could fairly be called suspicious. I would have liked to have met *him*, too, but he hadn't stuck around.

The Stanger doesn't pin its faith to last April's rowan switch, and if you've ever seen the effect a haunting can have on the psychologically fractured or fragile, you'll know why. The wards here are maintained on a week-by-week basis, and they come in all three flavors: a cross and a mezuzah, representing the religious worldview, a sprig of pagan woodbine, and a necromantic circle meticulously drawn around the words HOC FUGERE—flee this place.

The staff nurse at the reception desk looked up as I walked in and gave me a warm smile. Carla. She's an old hand, and she knows why I have strolling-in-off-the-street privileges here.

"Evening, lover," she said. That's her usual form of address for me, but she knows I won't get the wrong idea; her husband, Jason, is a burly male nurse and could make a novel origami sculpture out of me in the space of about five seconds. "I thought he'd been pretty good lately."

"He's been fine, Carla," I said, scribbling my name in the daybook. "Tonight I'm just visiting. He wrote me a letter."

Her eyes widened, and interest quickened on her face. Carla is an inveterate gossip. It's her only vice, and she regrets bitterly the failure of real-life hospitals to live up to the same standards of intrigue and promiscuity as fictional ones.

"Yeah, I saw," she said, leaning in toward me a little. "He had a hard time with it, too. You know, the strong hand writing, the other one trying to snatch the paper away."

I raised and lowered my eyebrows in a virtual shrug. "Asmodeus won," I said tersely, and Carla made a sour face. Asmodeus always wins. It wasn't even worth commenting on anymore, and I'd only said it to avoid giving any other answer to her implied question.

"I'm going to go on in," I said. "If Dr. Webb wants to talk to me, I can stick around for a while afterward. But really this one is just private stuff."

"You run with it, Felix," she said, waving me on. "Paul's got the keys."

Paul was a lugubrious black man so tall and broad that in a 4-4-2 formation, he'd count as one of the 4s all by himself. He scarcely ever spoke, and when he did, he kept it short and to the point. When he saw me walking up the corridor toward him, he said the single word "Ditko," and I nodded. He turned around and led the way.

There's a left turn at the end of the main hallway with a subtle upward gradient underfoot as you pass from the converted cottages into a newer, purpose-built wing. It has a different feel to it, too—on a psychic level, I mean. Old stones put out a sort of constant, diffuse emotional field like the glow of a dead fire; newly poured concrete is blank and cold.

Which may be why I shuddered when we stopped in front of Rafi's door.

Paul bent down to check the inspection window, made a tutting sound with his tongue against his teeth. Then he put the key in the lock and turned it. The door swung open.

I always forget in between visits how small and bare Rafi's cell is. I suppose forgetting makes the whole thing easier to bear. The place is a cube, essentially, ten feet on a side. No furniture, because even when it's bolted down, Rafi can rip it up and use it, and there are people still working at the Stanger now who remember the last time that happened. "If in doubt, don't," is their fervent creed. The walls and ceiling are bare white plaster, but out of sight underneath them, instead of plasterboard, there's a layer of silver and steel amalgam, one part to ten. Don't ask me how much that cost. It's the main reason why I'm poor. On the floor, the metal isn't even covered over. It shines dully up from between old scuff marks.

Rafi was sitting in the corner in the lotus position. His long, lank hair hung down over his face, hiding it completely. But he looked up at the sound of my footsteps, parted the foliage, and grinned out at me from under it. Someone had released one of his arms from the straitjacket and given him a deck of cards; they were spread on the floor in front of him in the pattern of a game of clock patience. Hard-edged, plastic-coated—that looked like a really bad idea in my book. I made a mental note to tell Carla to slap Webb over the back of the head for me and ask him what he thought he was doing.

"Felix!" Rafi growled in one of his more unpleasant voices—all in the back of his throat, gutturals so harsh they sounded like slowed-down shotgun blasts. "I am honored. I am so fucking privileged. Come on in, now. Come right on in. Don't be shy."

"He gives you any trouble," Paul said, stolid and matter-of-fact, "you just call, all right?" He closed the door behind me, and I heard the key turn again.

Rafi was watching me in silence, expectant. I let my coat fall open and touched my fingers to the pocket where the tin whistle nestled, the top inch or so of its gleaming metal visible against the gray lining, like half-cooled cinders. He sighed when he saw it, a sigh with a jagged edge to it.

"You gonna play us a tune?" he whispered. And it was really Rafi for a moment, not Asmodeus stealing Rafi's voice.

"It's good to see you, Rafi," I said. "Yeah, I'll whistle something up for you in a minute or two. Give you some peace—or at least some headspace."

Rafi's face twisted abruptly—seemed to melt and re-form in an instant into a brutal sneer. "You fucking wish!" snarled the other voice.

Well, I knew this wasn't going to be easy. It never is. With the feeling of a man about to jump up over the top of the trench and go charging across no-man's-land, I sat down in front of him and got into a cross-legged posture that mirrored his own. I took the letter out of my coat pocket, unfolded it, and held it out for him to see.

"You wrote to me," I said, deliberately leaving the "you" hanging in the air. Despite what I'd said to Carla, I still wasn't 100 percent certain whether it was Rafi or his evil passenger who had really been sailing the ship when that letter got written—and I felt like I needed to find out.

Rafi took the letter out of my hand and stared at it for a second with a calm, half-amused look on his face. Flame blossomed between his fingers, shot in an instant to all four corners of the crumpled sheet of paper, and consumed it in a single *whoof* of heat that I felt from where I was sitting. Rafi's fingers opened, and black ash drifted down onto the floor between us.

"Yeah," was all he said. "I did that." He dabbled his finger in the ashes, staring at the ground.

"You said that I was about to make a mistake," I prompted him, feeling more pessimistic by the second. "What mistake was that, Rafi?"

He glanced up at me again, and our stares locked. Rafi's eyes were brown, normally; these were liquid black, as though tears of ink were welling up in them.

"You're going to take this case," Asmodeus rasped. "And it's going to kill you."

⌇ Three

WHEN I FIRST MET RAFAEL DITKO, I WAS NEARING THE bottom of a spiral. I was nineteen, and I'd been in Oxford for less than a year—as a student, mechanically following a degree in English because it was my best subject at school and because my dad hadn't sweated in shipyards and factories for forty years to see his children go on and do the same.

But despair and nihilism had been eating into me for years. The more I saw of the sad and futile dead, hovering at the edges of life like beggars at the door of a fancy restaurant, the grimmer and more hopeless the whole universe looked to me. If there was a God, my reasoning went, he was either a psychopath or a fuck-up—nobody you could respect would ever have created a universe where you got one chance to warm your hands at the fire, and then you spent the rest of eternity out in the cold. Even when I could manage to forget my sister Katie's scared little ghost and the way I'd slammed the door in its face, life didn't make enough sense for me to want to engage with it.

Ditko was twenty-two, an exchange student from Czechoslovakia, which was a rare thing back then ("then" being the hedonistic 1980s, the dawn of the new age of heroic capitalism). With his dark hair and dark eyes, he looked like the bastard son of an archangel and a temple dancer, and he poured scorn on the dreams of entrepreneurial apotheosis that afflicted most of his fellow students. A job in the Square Mile? Retirement at thirty? Fuck that. He was hurrying headlong into life and sex and death with a fervor that ruled out even that degree of calculation.

Rafi borrowed the self-worship of the Thatcher generation, tried it on, and turned it into something graceful and ironic. Yeah, he stole his mates' girlfriends, smoked their grass, colonized their floors, and ram-raided their fridges, but he paid us all back by giving us tickets to the show. Nobody ever managed to hate him for it, not even the women he scooped up and sifted through like trinkets on a market stall. Not even Pen, for whom he was the first and (ultimately) the only one.

I wonder sometimes what his life would have been like if he'd never met me. Certainly he was already fascinated by the occult, but it was an academic thing back then, because he was too flippant and too sharp really to believe in anything. But in our drunken conversations about the dead—the ones who never leave and the ones who come back—that interest started to quicken into something else. Even as he tempered my bitter atheism with his own agnostic, indulgent gospel (suck it and see, hold your fire, look at the pretty pictures), he listened to my descriptions of London's ghosts with an enthusiasm that was way too intense to be healthy. I was so stupid and self-absorbed back then I didn't see it, but I was giving him something new to get hooked on.

I gave up on university just after the start of my second year and set out on the aimless but intense round-the-world ramble that would consume the next four years of my life—my where-do-you-go-after-nowhere tour. Rafi had provided the emotional fuel for that journey—had pointed me and aimed me and lit the blue touchpaper—and that meant, on a practical level, that I probably owed him my life. But I didn't see him for another two years after I got back, and when I did, he'd changed. He'd turned into one of those guys who hang out in basement bookshops and pay ten times over the odds for Aleister Crowley's laundry lists.

We had a pint or seven at the Angel, on St. Giles's High Street, but for me, at least, it was a disturbing and dispiriting experience. What had drawn me to Rafi was that he had a handle on life that I was keen to get close to and if possible to imitate. Now all he wanted to talk about was death—as state, as destination, as source, as trout pond. He said he was learning how to be a necromancer. I told him that was bollocks; just because some of us could see and talk to the dead (I'd met five sensitives by then and heard about a handful more), that didn't make death itself any less irrevocable. There was a line. Each of us would only get to cross it once, and we'd all be heading in the same direction. I'd never heard of anyone popping back to turn the gas off. I was talking bollocks, of course. But the zombies weren't widely known about back then, and I'd never come across one.

In any case, Rafi didn't listen. He was onto something, he said, and this something would make the things that I could do irrelevant overnight. "Quicker, even," he repeated, snapping his fingers in my face with a wild grin. "As quick as that. Your round again, Fix."

It was my round all seven times, and I drew some comfort from that afterward. In some respects, at least, Rafi hadn't changed. He was still an elegant parasite who managed to make you feel you should be thanking him while he scrounged off you. Maybe the Ditko core was still intact under all this other bullshit. Maybe he'd ride it out and find yet another brand-new high.

The next time I saw him was in the spring of 2004. A phone call at midnight dragged me out to a studio flat in the Seven Sisters Road, where Rafi was sitting slumped and blank-eyed in a claw-foot bathtub with the taps running. His girlfriend, who was skinny and wasted, with the kind of wispy white hair that always reminds me of daffodil puffballs, had to top the bath off with a couple of packets of ice from the liquor store every ten minutes when the water started to boil.

"Rafi done a spell," she said. "Something fucking big." He'd summoned a ghost, but something had gone wrong, and instead of ending up in the circle, the loose spirit had gone into him. Then he'd started burning up.

I sat with him through that night, listening as he rambled and raged in what sounded like four different languages, trying to get a feel for the spirit that was sticking it to him. By about six a.m., we'd run out of ice, and I was scared that if I waited much longer, he'd just burn himself out. So I took out my whistle, cleared the girl out of the room, and started to play. That's how I do it. The music is a cantrip, and if it works, it has the same effect on bodiless spirits as flypaper does on flies. The ghosts get wrapped up in it, and they can't get free. Then, when the music stops, abracadabra, there's nothing for them to hang on to—so they stop, too. When the last note fades, they're just not there anymore.

If that sounds easy, put it down to the fact that I never did finish that English degree. In reality, it's hard and slow, and it only works at all if I can get a real fix on the ghost in question. The clearer my mental image of it, the better the tune and the more reliable the effects.

In this case, the ghost had such a strong presence, it was almost like smoke coming off Rafi's overheated skin. I thought I had it nailed. I put the whistle to my lips and blew a few notes on it, high and fast, to get things started.

It might just as well have been a gun—something big and heavy, like a .38 Trooper, say—pointed at Rafi's head.

———————

I sat on the silver-steel floor of the cell while the chill of the metal, never less than glacial, crawled slowly up my spine. A nurse shouted in the distance, something jovial and probably obscene, and a door slammed heavily.

Rafi's black-on-black eyes closed and then opened again, keeping me pinned in their lazy, mad crosshairs. A smell of stale meat wafted off him, which I knew was because I'd just come from my office over

Grambas's kebab shop. One of the hallmarks of Asmodeus's presence was that Rafi would start to smell of the last place you'd been, which was typical of the demon's peekaboo bullshit.

"You're going to die," he said again, almost absently, turning over a couple of cards in his sprawling game of patience.

"You're wrong," I said, feeling a premature sense of relief. "A job did come my way tonight, but I already said no."

"Of course you did," the smashed-glass voice grated again, in open mockery. "You're still in mourning for your old friend, aren't you? You made a promise to yourself that you wouldn't screw the pooch like that again. 'First, do no harm'—which in your case means 'Don't do a blind fucking thing.'"

Rafi's tongue snaked out and rasped around the edges of his mouth with a sound like newspapers being chased down the street by a strong wind. I suddenly realized that his lips were dry and cracked, flakes of desiccated skin hanging onto them in a light, irregular frosting. I should have noticed that before; it's another of the signs I usually keep a watch for, and it confirmed what I'd already noted from Rafi's smell. It meant I was definitely talking to Asmodeus now, and Rafi wasn't going to surface again unless the demon allowed him to.

Slowly, absently, he tore a huge gash in his own forearm with his thumbnail. Blood welled up and spattered on the floor of the cell. I ignored it. Asmodeus does that kind of stuff for show, but he always makes good the damage afterward. He's got a vested interest in keeping Rafi's body in good working order.

"Too late to do much, anyway," he murmured, more to himself than to me. "The big picture—that's set now, more or less. And it's not like you're even asking the right questions . . ."

There was a silence. When he spoke again, it was in a different voice—almost liquid, with a fluting modulation that was insidious and unpleasant.

"So you said no. But here's the thing, Castor. You're gonna change your mind. I'm nearly certain about that. You see, time is different for my kind, by which I mean it's slower. Feels to me like I've been stuck in here for a thousand years already. Got to do something to keep my edge, you understand? So I tune into things. Things that are on the edge of happening. Things that might might might just slop over the edge of the possible and soil the carpets of the real. I know what I'm talking about. After the final no there comes a yes, and you'll be getting to that before the night is out. I mean, you're so agonizingly predictable when it comes to your friends, well"—he ducked his head left, right, left—"I think it's pretty obvious whose tune you're gonna end up dancing to."

I took the whistle out of my pocket and laid it on the floor next to me. Rafi—or the thing that lived inside him—eyed it with cold amusement.

"I don't dance," I said. "Don't ask me."

He laughed—not a nice sound at all.

"You *all* dance, Castor. Every bastard one of you. I never met a man, woman, or child yet who made a real fight out of it." He stretched out his free arm, made his index and middle fingers into the barrel of a gun, aimed them at my feet. "Bang, bang, bang. If I wasn't serving my time inside this heap of pulp and gristle, I could make you dance. But since I am . . . indisposed, someone else is going to take a shot at it. And this someone else—well, they're too big for you."

"You prefer 'Oh Danny Boy' or 'Ye Banks and Braes'?" I asked him, my face set in a cold deadpan.

"Now that's just crude," he sniggered. "Give me 'O Fortuna.' I like music that sounds like the end of the fucking world. But anyway, coming back to the point—even though it's not gonna get me anywhere—you should say no to this case, because you don't have more than a cat in hell's chance of coming out of it in one piece."

"You know, I'm always flattered when you put it like that," I told him. "I shouldn't take the case? Lawyers and private detectives take cases. The people who use my services generally see me more in the light of a garbage disposal unit."

Asmodeus dismissed this red herring with a slow, contemptuous shrug.

"Well, if you've got the balls to say no and stick to it, then that's fine—you don't have a problem. But that's not where the smart money's sitting, Castor. And when it comes to the study of human behavior, I've got a few years' lead on you. I started watching when the entire human race only had two balls to share between them—and both of 'em were in my hand. Speaking of which, how's Pen?"

The sudden shift of subject false-footed me—and he switched to Rafi's own voice, too, to get as much impact out of it as he could.

"That's none of your damn business," I snapped back, which got me a supercilious grin.

"Everything that's damned is my business," he leered. "You ought to pick your words more carefully, Castor. Words are the birds that break cover and show your enemy where you're hiding. Here. Get into practice."

He picked up one of the cards and skimmed it across to me, so it fell facedown at my feet. I picked it up and turned it over, expecting the ace of spades or maybe the joker, but it was blank on the face side—the spare card they give you in some decks to stand in for the first one you lose.

"No, the smart money says you're gonna fall for it," Asmodeus said. "So I'm just telling you—you need to watch your back better than you're doing. You're too easy, Castor. You've got to kick up some dust once in a while so it's harder to see where you're going. Otherwise, you'll get there and you'll find a hanging party waiting for you." His eyes narrowed to coal black slits. "You're looking to play me back down into the basement right now. But one of these days, you're gonna come around and play me right the fuck out of here. Set me free. Set little angel Rafael free, too. I mean, those are the rules, right? You break it, you fix it. But you're no fucking use to me dead. So you got to do three things. Take the card when she gives it to you. Watch out for burning booze and wicked women. And don't put your finger on the trigger until you know what you're shooting at. Kiss, kiss."

He kissed his fingers—the same two fingers that had previously been the gun—and pointed them at me again. I put the whistle to my lips and started to play, and after that, I went at it solidly for half an hour.

———————

When I banged on the cell door for Paul to come and let me out, Rafi was sleeping. It *was* Rafi, now, and he'd probably tear up the zeds until morning, so there was no point in me hanging around. I took a glance at the wound on his arm just before I left. It was already healed, only a faint scar showing where it had been. Fucking demons. All mouth and trousers, most of the time.

But as I drove back to Pen's house, Asmodeus's words worked their way down into my brain like grit into a paper cut. So I was going to change my mind about Peele's job offer? I didn't think so. Right then I couldn't think of anything that would turn me around. The whole business with Rafi was what had made me say my farewell to arms the best part of a year ago, and tonight had just served as a vivid reminder of what happened when I made a mistake. Like I needed reminding anyway. I live with it every fucking day.

But I still carried the tin whistle around with me. I still felt cold and exposed without it. And my pulse still slid up a gear or two when I heard a ghost story.

Grit in a paper cut, ground all the way down, where you couldn't get it out again.

I backed the car into Pen's overgrown driveway, crushing a few tough strands of bramble that had had the guts to put their heads back up since I'd left that afternoon. I got out and retrieved Rhona the rat's cage from the backseat. She gave me a fairly unfriendly look; in her books, I was one of those guys who lead you on, take what they need, and then leave you hanging. All things considered, it was a fair cop.

The key fob played the first bar of "Für Elise" as I locked the car up. I hoped that Beethoven's ghost was out there somewhere, making the night hideous for the managing director of Ford.

There was no sign of a light. I live at the top of the great, three-story pile, and Pen lives at the bottom of it, but it's built into the side of a hill, so from this side, her rooms are underground. On the other side, they look out onto a garden that is ten feet below the level of the road. But I didn't need to see a light; I knew she was in there, waiting for me.

The Peter's Birthday Party Massacre seemed a long time ago now, and its sting had faded. But for Pen, it was still the big story of the day, and she'd be wanting to know how well I'd gone down. She'd also be wanting to count the pennies.

Well, I'd gone down like the *Titanic*, and the pennies were still in James Dodson's wallet. Now I had to face the music—which was likely to be a lot more like "O Fortuna" than "Ye Banks and Braes."

I let myself in and locked the door behind me. I bolted it, too, and I lifted up my hand to put a ward on it, which is still automatic with me even after living in Pen's house for three years. But I remembered in time and turned away with a vague sense of coitus interruptus. She's a priestess now; she does her own blessings.

But just as I put my foot on the top of the basement stairs, I saw that I was wrong about where Pen was. There was a light on in the kitchen, not visible from the street, and there were noises of purposeful, even slightly violent activity.

I walked on through. Pen was sitting at the kitchen table with her back to me, the bare bulb swinging gently over her head in the draft from the cracked window, and she didn't look up. She was too absorbed in her work. She had her toolbox open on the table in front of her and the remains of a sprawled, broken necklace. I came a step or two closer and saw what she was doing. She was filing the beads from the necklace, laboriously and carefully. A saucer on her left-hand side was full of beads that she'd presumably already finished to her own satisfaction. There was also a bottle of Glen Discount and a glass.

"You can share," she said, as if reading my mind. "I broke the other glass when I tried to scrub the turps smell off it."

I was right behind her now. I picked up the glass, took a long sip of the whisky, and set it down again. While I was doing this, I looked more carefully at the necklace and saw that it was her rosary.

"Pen," I said, because there was no way I couldn't ask, "what are you doing?"

"I'm filing the beads down," she answered, matter-of-factly.

"Because . . ."

"They were too big." She looked up at me now, twisting her head around and squinting against the light. "You changed," she said, sounding disappointed. "I hope you brought the suit back with you."

"It's in the car," I said, putting Rhona's cage down on the table. "Thanks for the loan."

She pursed her lips and made kissing noises at Rhona, who sat up and scratched at the bars.

"Would you put her back in the harem?" Pen asked.

I was glad to. The alternative was to come clean about the party then and there, and every minute I could put that conversation off was one more minute of happiness. But the beads were still weighing on my mind, probably because I'd only just seen Rafi, and this looked so much like something that one of the inmates at the Stanger would do to while away the hours between ECT sessions.

"Too big for what?" I asked.

Pen didn't answer. "Take Rhona downstairs," she said. "I'll be right behind you. I found something of yours, by the way—it's on the mantelpiece next to the clock."

As I walked down the stairs into Pen's basement citadel, I heard something that made a sudden wave of unease crest inside me. It was "Enola Gay" by OMD. Pen often left her old vinyl playing on the turntable when she went out of the room, and the turntable was of the kind that goes back to the start of the record when it finishes. But if she was playing eighties stuff, that wasn't a good sign.

The door to her sitting room was open. Edgar and Arthur watched me mournfully from their favorite perches—the top of the bookcase and a pallid bust of John Lennon, respectively—as I transferred Rhona from the carry cage to the big rat penthouse where she lived with her entourage of big, hunky guy rats who'd be happy to give her what I'd so signally failed to deliver.

I looked over at the mantelpiece. There was something leaning against Pen's ludicrous antique carriage clock: a curled-up piece of glossy card, off-white on the side that was facing me. A photo. I crossed the room, picked it up, and turned it over.

I knew roughly what it was going to be—the music and Pen's mood had filled in some of the blanks ahead of time. But it still hit me like a punch in the chest.

The back quad at St. Peter's, Oxford—the one with the fountain that tends to run with things other than water. Night: a scene caught in the baleful eye of someone's inadequate flashgun, so there was no background to speak of. Just Felix Castor, age nineteen, all chestnut curls and strained grin, trying hard to look like he wasn't eight months out of a state comprehensive school. I was already affecting a long coat, but back then it was a poncy black Burberry—I hadn't yet joined the pre-Revolution Russian army. And since the coat was made for someone a lot broader across the shoulders, I looked like five foot ten inches of sweet Fanny Adams.

To my left, Pen. Christ, she was beautiful. The photo didn't exist that could do justice to the colors of her, the quickness and the life of her. In a feathered snood, a red sequined boob tube, and a slit black skirt (marking this as the morning after a party), and with her gaze cast so demurely to the ground, she looked like a hooker who's just tossed it all in to become a nun but hasn't told anyone yet. Her hand was raised to the heavens, index finger extended.

To my right, Rafi. He was wearing the black Nehru jacket and pants that were his trademark, and he was smiling the smile of a man who's got a great secret in him. Herman Melville says that's an easy trick, but then, he also thought Moby Dick was a whale.

Both Rafi and I were crouching down, each of us with one leg extended behind us, the other flexed at the knee. I remembered that night with a vividness that had never faded, and I knew the reason for the strange pose. We were on our marks, and Pen was about to say go.

"I found it in the garage," Pen's voice said from behind me. "After you moved all your magic stuff. It was lying on the floor."

I turned to face her, feeling like I'd been caught out in something. An emotion, maybe—something unworthy and unspoken that made me ashamed. Pen had the saucer of beads in one hand, the maimed rosary in the other. She looked a little wistful.

"What's the score?" I asked her, groping for something to say that wouldn't relate to the photo. I indicated the saucer with a nod of the head.

"The score?" She chewed this over, setting the beads down on the arm of the sofa before sitting down heavily herself right next to them. She seemed to find the words a bit perplexing, unless that was just the whisky. The silence lengthened.

"The match was called," she said at last, not quite managing the flippant tone she was aiming for. "Rain stopped play. Bloody hell, I wish I was rich. I wish you played the guitar, like Stoker."

It was a standing joke that had started to lean over and fall down by this time. Mack Stoker—Mack the Axe, Mack Five—matriculated in the same year as us, and he dropped out of university, too, only he did it to become lead guitar with Stasis Leak, the thrash-metal band, and was so successful that he'd already been in rehab three times.

I managed a tired smile, which Pen didn't return. She stared at me solemnly, then looked down at the saucer of beads, then back at me. "I worry about you, Fix," she said. "I really do. I don't want you to get hurt. I went to see Rafi last week, and he told me you were going to get yourself into trouble. In over your head." After a moment's silence, she went on, her voice a lot lower. "I wonder sometimes . . . if things could have turned out differently. For him. For all of us."

"There's no room for a tin whistle in a hardcore band," I parried ineptly. But she was talking about the photo now, and her words took me back, unwillingly, to the memory I'd been avoiding.

It wasn't just a party, it was a May Ball. Overprivileged kids playing at being decadent adults, but with none of the poise and probably not enough of the cynicism. Pen had Rafi on one arm, me on the other, all three of us aroused way past our safety limits by alcohol and close dancing and teenage hormones. Rafi, with his characteristic chutzpah, suggested a three-way. Pen smacked him down. She was a good Catholic girl, and she didn't put it about. But she countersuggested. We could race across the quad and back to her. The first one to touch her . . .

"How did the party go?" Pen asked, bursting the bubble.

I stared down at her like a rabbit caught in headlights.

"Fine," I lied. "It went fine. But the guy—Mr. Serious Crimes Squad—paid me by check. I'll give you the money tomorrow."

"Brilliant!" said Pen. "And I'll show you what the beads are for. Also tomorrow. Fair exchange, Fix."

"The motto of all good landlords in this world and the next," I agreed.

"Thank God one of us is earning, anyway," Pen muttered, grimacing around another swig of whisky. "If I don't get some money in the bank, I'm going to lose this place."

She said it lightly, but for Pen that was like saying "I'm going to lose an arm." I knew damn well how much she loved the house. No, more than that—how much she needed it, because she was the third Bruckner woman to live there, and three was a magic number. The devotional stuff she did, the rituals and incantations—her bizarre post-Catholic version of wicca—they depended on 14 Lydgate Road. She couldn't do them anywhere else.

"I thought the mortgage was paid," I said, trying to match her off-the-cuff tone.

"The first one is," she admitted. "There've been other loans since. The house is the collateral for all of them."

Pen only likes to talk about her get-rich-quick schemes on the upswing. The fact that they always leave her poorer than she was when she started is a truth that she finds unpalatable.

"How bad is it?" I asked.

"I need a couple of grand before the end of the month," she sighed. "When the money starts to come in from the party bookings, I'll be fine. But right now, every little bit helps."

I know when I'm beaten. I kissed her goodnight, went upstairs to my own room, and threw myself down, exhausted, on the bed. Something in my trouser pocket dug into my thigh, so I arched my back, rummaged for it, drew it out into the light. It was a blank playing card.

After the final no, there comes a yes. And you'll be getting to that before the night is out.

"You bastard," I muttered.

I flicked the card away into the corner of the room. Turned out the light and went to sleep still dressed. The number of the Bonnington Archive was in the book, and I still had the envelope with Peele's home number on it; but there was no point in calling anyone before the morning.

Four

THERE'S A SPRAWL OF STREETS BETWEEN REGENT'S Park and King's Cross that used to be a town. Somers Town, it was called, and still is called on most maps of the area, although that's not a name that many of the residents tend to use very much.

It's one of those places that got badly fucked over by the Industrial Revolution, and it never really recovered. In the middle of the eighteenth century, it was still mostly fields and orchards, and rich men built their estates there. A hundred years later, it was a pestilential slum and a thieves' rookery—one of the places that got Charles Dickens salivating and sharpening his nib. St. Pancras Station sits in the middle of it like a great, overblown wedding cake, but it was Somers Town as a whole that got sliced up, by roads and railways and freight yards and warehouses and the cold, commercial logic of a new age. It's not a slum anymore, but that's mainly because it isn't a place anymore. It's more like the stump of an amputated limb—every street you walk down is sliced off clean by a railway cutting or an underpass, or a blank wall that usually turns out to be part of the gray, moldering hide of Euston Station.

The Bonnington Archive was on one of those truncated avenues, off the main north-south drag of Eversholt Street, which connects Camden Town with Bloomsbury. The rest of the street was mainly warehouses and office spaces and discount print shops, with dust-blinded windows and the occasional exoskeleton of scaffolding; but in the distance, on the far side of the railway lines, there was a block of flats of 1930s vintage, all brown brick and rust-burned wrought iron, its crumbling balconies set with lines of drying knickers like flags of surrender—and bizarrely enough, bearing a white stone virgin and child just above the portico of the main entrance, the name of the block being Saint Mary's.

The Bonnington Archive itself stood out from the low-rise concrete monstrosities around it like a spinster among sprawling drunks. It looked to be early nineteenth century, in dark brick, four stories high, with meticulous patterns set into the brickwork underneath each row of windows, like vertical parquet. I liked it. It had the look of a palace that had been built at the whim of some senior civil servant who wanted a fiefdom, but then had died, like Ferdinand the First before he could walk across the threshold of his Belvedere. Close up, though, it was clear that this palace had long ago been divided and conquered: one of the first-floor windows was covered by a nailed-up slab of hardboard, and a doorway close by was choked with rubbish and old, sodden boxes. The real entrance to the archive, although it looked to be part of the same building, was twenty yards farther on.

The four-paneled double doors were made of varnished mahogany, liberally scarred with dents and scuff marks at the bottom, but obviously real and solid all the same. There was a brass plate beside the door that proclaimed with serifed formality that this was the Bonnington Archive, maintained by the Corporation of London and affiliated to the Joint Museums and Trusts Commission. There were opening hours listed, too, but this didn't look like the sort of place that had the world beating a path to its door.

I stepped through into a very large and very impressive entrance hall.

Maybe I was a decade or so out in my estimation of how old this place was—the stark black and white tiling on the floor had the

moral seriousness of Her black-and-white Majesty, Victoria. There
was a countertop on my left-hand side made of gray marble, currently
unoccupied, but as long and as impregnable as the wall of wood at
Rorke's Drift and looking as if it came from the same school of defensive fortification. Behind it, though, there were half a dozen wardrobe rails where rows of coat hangers clustered thickly. They were all
empty, but at least this showed willing. The comfort and convenience
of any rampaging hordes that might come through here had already
been taken into account. There was an inner office farther back, on
the other side of the desk, with a sign that bore the single word SECU-
RITY. In conjunction with the deserted desk, that struck me as slightly
ironic.

On my right-hand side, there was a broad, gray-flagged staircase,
and above my head, a vaulted skylight with an impressive stained-
glass rose emblazoned on it, struggling to shine through dust and
pigeon shit. At the foot of the stairs, there were three modern office
chairs covered in bright red fabric, that looked badly out of place.

I stood very quiet and still in that tired, grimy light, waiting, listening, feeling. Yes. There was something there—a gradient in the air,
so subtle it took a few moments to register. My eyes defocused as I
let the indefinable sense that I've honed through a couple of hundred
exorcisms slowly open itself to the space that surrounded me.

But before I could begin to focus on the fugitive presence, a door
slammed loudly on my left, making it skitter out of reach. I turned
to look over my shoulder as a uniformed guard came through from
the security office. He looked the business, despite being somewhere
in his fifties: a hard man with mud brown hair that wasn't so much
receding as fleeing across his forehead and a nose that had been broken and reset at some point in his career. He straightened his tie like a
man walking away intact from a nasty bit of rough-and-tumble. For a
moment, I thought he was going to ask me to assume the position.

But as soon as he smiled, you could see that it was all show. It was
a puppy-dog smile, a smile that wanted to be friends.

"Yes, sir?" he said, briskly. "What'll it be?"

I fought the urge to say a pint of heavy and a packet of crisps. "Felix Castor. I'm here to see Mr. Peele."

The guard nodded earnestly and pointed a finger at me as if he was really glad I'd brought that up. Rummaging for a moment under the counter, he came up with a black Bic biro and nodded me toward a large daybook that was already out on the countertop. "If you'd like to sign in, sir," he said, "I'll let him know you're here."

As I signed, he picked up a phone and tapped the hash key, then three others. "Hello, Alice," he said, after a brief pause. "There's a Mr. Felix"—he glanced down at the daybook—"Castro down at the front desk. Yes. Fine. All right. I'll tell him." Alice? I'd remembered Peele's first name as Jeffrey.

The guard put the phone down and waved expansively in the direction of the chairs—the same gesture that actors use when they want you to applaud the orchestra. "If you'd like to take a seat, sir, someone will come along and see to you shortly."

"Cheers," I said. I went and sat down, and the guard invented things to do at the desk in a transparent effort to look busy and purposeful. I closed my eyes, shutting him out, and tried to find that teasing presence again—but there was nothing doing. The small noises of the guard's movements were enough to shake my fragile concentration.

A minute later, there were footsteps on the stairs. I opened my eyes again and looked up at the woman who was coming down to meet me.

She was something to look at. As I sized her up, I slid my professional detachment into place like a visor over my eyes. I'd have put her in her late twenties, but she could have been older and just wearing it well. She was on the tall side and very slim—wiry, workout slim, rather than just slim-built—with straight blonde hair drawn back into a tight bun, which in other company might have been called a Croydon face-lift. Not here, though. She was well dressed—even immaculately dressed—in a gray two-piece that consciously and stylishly mocked a man's business suit. Her shoes were gray leather with two-inch heels, plain except for a red buckle on the side of each, the red being picked up by a handkerchief in her breast pocket. At her waist, looped around a gray leather belt, was a very large bunch of keys. With that detail, and with the stern haircut, she looked like the warden in the kind of immaculate women's prison that only exists in Italian pornography.

Then she spoke and, just as it had with the security guard, her voice made all the other details break apart and come together in a new pattern. The timber was deep enough to be thrilling, but the cold tone checked that effect and put me firmly back in my place. "You're the exorcist?" she asked. I had a momentary flashback, without the benefit of acid, to James Dodson saying, "You're the entertainer?" There wasn't an inch or an ounce to choose between them.

I'm used to this. Cute and fetching though I am in my own right, the job casts its ineluctable pall over the way people perceive me and deal with me. I looked this high-gloss vision right in the eyes, and I saw exactly what she was seeing—a snake-oil salesman offering a dubious service at a premium rate.

"That's me," I agreed amiably. "Felix Castor. And you are?"

"Alice Gascoigne," she said. "I'm the senior archivist." Her hand came out automatically as she said it, like a cuckoo when the clock hits the hour. I took the hand and gave it a firm, lingering shake, which in theory gave me a chance to add a little more depth to those first impressions. I'm not psychic, at least not the kind with all the ribbons and bells, the kind who can read people's thoughts as easily as picking up a newspaper or get newsflashes from their possible futures. But I *am* sensitive. It goes with the job. I've got my antennae out on wavelengths that other people don't use all that much or don't consciously monitor, and sometimes skin contact gets me tuned in strongly enough to take an instant reading of mood, a flash of surface thought, an elusive flavor of personality. Sometimes.

Not from Alice, though. She was sealed up tight.

"Jeffrey is in his office," she said, taking her hand back at the earliest opportunity. "He's actually busy with some month-end reports, and he won't be able to see you. He says you should go ahead and do the job, and then you can send your bill in to him whenever it's convenient."

My smile took on a slightly pained tilt. We were really getting off on the wrong foot here.

"I think," I said, picking my words with care, "that Jeffrey—Mr. Peele—may have a mistaken impression of how exorcism works. I *am* going to need to talk to him."

Alice stood her ground, and her tone dropped a few degrees closer to zero.

"I've told you that won't be possible. He'll be tied up all day."

I shrugged. "Then would you like to suggest a day that will be more convenient?"

Alice stared at me, caught between perplexity and outright annoyance.

"Is there some reason why you can't just do the job right now?" she demanded.

"Actually," I said, "there are a lot of reasons. Most of them are fairly technical. I'd be happy to explain them to you and then wait while you relay them to Mr. Peele. But that seems like a very roundabout way of doing things. It would be better if I could talk you both through it together—along with anyone else who needs to know."

Alice considered this. I could see it didn't sit well with her. Also—although this was just a guess—that her initial urge to tell me to sod off was tempered by the reluctant conclusion that she lacked the full authority to back it up.

"All right," she said at last. "You're the expert." The emphasis on the last word fell a fraction of an inch this side of sarcasm.

She pointed toward the lockers opposite. "You'll have to leave your coat here," she said. "There's a rule about personal effects. Frank, could you please take Mr. Castor's coat and give him a ticket?"

"Okey-dokey." The guard unhooked a hanger from one of the racks and laid it on the counter. I considered making an issue of it, but I could see I was going to have a bumpy enough ride with Alice as it was without going out of my way to make things difficult. I transferred my tin whistle to my belt, where it fits snugly enough, and handed the greatcoat over the counter to the guard. He'd been watching my exchange with Alice without any visible reaction, but he gave me a smile and a nod as he took the coat from me. He hung it up on the otherwise empty rack and gave me a plastic tag into which the number 022 had been die-cut. "Two little ducks," he said. "Twenty-two." I nodded my thanks.

Alice stood aside to let me walk up the stairs in front of her, no doubt mindful of how short her skirt was and of the consequent need to maintain the dignity of her station. I went on up with her heels clattering on the stone steps behind me all the way.

On the second floor there was a set of glass-paneled swing doors. Alice stepped past me to open them and walk through. I followed her into a large room that looked something like a public lending library, but with more sparsely furnished shelves. In the center of the space, there were about a dozen wide tables with six or eight chairs arranged around each. Most of the tables were empty, but at one of them a man was turning over the pages of what looked like an old parish register, making notes in a narrow, spiral-bound notebook as he went; at another, two women had spread a map and were laboriously copying part of it onto an A3 sheet; at a third, another, older man was reading The Times. Maybe The Times gets to jump the queue and become history straight away. Elsewhere there were shelves full of what looked to be encyclopedias and reference books, a few spinner racks loaded with magazines, a couple of large map chests, a bank of about eight slightly battered-looking PCs ranged along one wall, and at the end farthest away from us a six-sided librarians' station, currently staffed by one bored-looking young man.

"Is this the collection?" I hazarded, prepared to be polite.

Alice gave a short, harsh laugh.

"This is the reading room," she said with what seemed like slightly exaggerated patience. "The area that we keep open to the public. The collection is stored in the strong rooms, which are mostly in the new annex."

She launched out across the room without bothering to look back and make sure I was still following. She was heading for an ugly steel-reinforced door that stood diagonally opposite us on the other side of the big open space. To either side of it there were two scanning brackets—the kind you get at the exits of large stores to discourage technologically challenged shoplifters.

Alice opened the door not with one of the keys that she wore on her belt but with a card that she ran through a scanner to the left of the door, making a small, inset red light wink to green. She held the door open for me, and I stepped through into a corridor that was narrow and low-ceilinged. She closed the door again behind us, pushing against the slam guard until the lock clicked audibly, and then slid past me again—it required a little maneuvering—to lead the way.

There were doors on both sides of the corridor, all of them closed. Narrow glass panels crisscrossed with wire mesh showed me rooms lined with filing cabinets or full of bookshelves from floor to ceiling. In some cases, the windows had black sugar paper pasted up over them, graying with age.

"What does a senior archivist do?" I asked by way of polite conversation.

"Everything," Alice said. "I'm in overall charge here."

"And Mr. Peele?"

"He's responsible for policy. And funding. And external liaison. I'm in charge when it comes to actual day-to-day running." She was testy, seeming to resent being questioned. But like I said, it's an automatic thing with me. You can only decide what's useful information and what's trivia when you see it in the rearview mirror.

So I pressed on. "Is the archive's collection very valuable?"

Alice shot me a slightly austere glance, but this was clearly something she was more disposed to talk about. "That's really not a question that has a meaningful answer," she responded slightly condescendingly, the keys jingling at her waist. "Value is a matter of what the market will bear. You understand? An item is only worth what you can sell it for. A lot of the things we've got are literally priceless, because there's no market anywhere where they could be sold. Others really have no value at all.

"We've got seventy-five miles of shelving here—and we're eighty percent full. The oldest documents we hold are nine centuries old, and those don't ever come out to the public except when we mount an exhibition. But the bulk of the collection consists of stuff that's much more mundane. Really, they're not the sort of thing that people pay a fortune for. We're talking about bills of lading from old ships. Property deeds and company incorporation deeds. Letters and journals—masses of those—but most of them not written by anyone very famous, and in a lot of cases not even all that well preserved. If you knew what you were looking for, theoretically, you could steal enough to keep yourself very comfortably. But then you'd have a lot of trouble selling them on. You'd never get an auction house to take them, because they're ours and they're known. Any auction house, any dealer who cared about his reputation, they'd check provenance as a matter of course. Only fences buy blind."

We turned a corner as she talked, and then another. The interior of the building had clearly gone through as baffling and messy a conversion as my office. It seemed we were detouring around rooms or weight-bearing walls that couldn't be shifted, and after the austere splendor of the entrance hall, the shoddiness and baldness of all this made a bleak impression on the eye. We came at last to another staircase, which was a very poor relation to the one Alice had descended before. It was of poured concrete, with chevroned antitrip tape crudely applied to the edges of each step. Again, Alice hung back to let me go up first.

"You've seen the ghost?" I asked as we climbed.

"No." Her tone was guarded, clipped. "I haven't."

"I thought everybody—"

She came abreast of me again at the top of the stairs, and she shook her head firmly. "Everybody apart from me. I always seem to be somewhere else. Funny, really."

"So you weren't there when she attacked your colleague?"

"I said I haven't seen her."

It seemed as though that was all I was getting. Well, okay. I'm pretty good, most of the time, at knowing when to push and when to fold. Another bend in the corridor, and now it joined a wider one that seemed to be more in the spirit of the original building. We followed this wider hallway for about twenty yards, until it passed the first open doorway I'd seen. It looked into a large room that was being used as an open-plan office: six desks, roughly evenly spaced, each with its own PC and its own set of shelves piled high with papers and files. One man and one woman glanced up as we went past—the man giving me a slightly grim fish-eye, the woman looking a lot more interested. A second man was on the phone, talking animatedly, and so he missed us.

The sound of his voice followed us as we walked on. "Yeah, well as soon as possible, to be honest. I'm not that great with the language, and I can't—yeah. Just to establish authenticity, if nothing else."

A few yards farther on, Alice abruptly stopped and turned to face me.

"Actually," she said, "you'd probably better wait in the workroom. I'll come and get you."

"Fine," I said. With a curt nod, she walked on. I swiveled on my heel and went into the room that we'd just passed, and this time all three of its occupants gave me the once-over as I walked in.

"Hello there," said the man who'd been on the phone before. "You must be Castor." He was about my age or slightly older—midthirties, free-falling toward the big four-oh. He had a fading tan, made more uneven by freckles, and light brown hair that was as wild as if he'd just woken up. He was dressed down, to put it politely: torn jeans, a Damageplan T-shirt, and flop-top trainers. But the bundle of keys he carried at his belt was as big as Alice's own. On his left cheek, there was a square surgical dressing.

He gave me an affable grin and held out his hand. I shook it and read a certain tension behind the smile—tension and perhaps expectation. He wasn't sure how to take me yet, but he had hopes that I could live up to my billing. Of course, this was the guy who had the most reason to want the ghost cleared out of here.

"Pleased to meet you, Mr. Clitheroe," I said. Behind me, the woman whistled appreciatively and then hummed the opening bars of the *X-Files* theme tune. Clitheroe laughed.

"It's just Rich," he said. "You knew because of the bandage, right? I mean, that wasn't some sort of—emanations from the ectoplasm—kind of thing?"

"Who you gonna call?" the woman drawled. "Gho-o-ostbusters!"

I turned to face her, and Rich made the introduction on cue. "This is Cheryl. Cheryl Telemaque—our IT specialist." Cheryl was very compact, very striking, and very dark-skinned—the shade of brown that can legitimately be called black. She looked to be in her early twenties, and her taste in clothes clearly ran to rhinestone-studded Von Dutch tops and a weight of chunky jewelry that skirted the glittery borders of bling.

"Which one are you?" she demanded with a cheerfully piss-taking grin. "The nerdy one, the cute one, or the anally retentive one?"

"I'm amazed you have to ask," I said. Again, I shook hands. Her grip was firm and strong, and I got an instantaneous flash of warmth and amusement and mischief—Cheryl was a real live wire, clearly. Exact voltage yet to be determined.

"Do you have to use pentagrams and candles and stuff?" she asked me eagerly.

"Not usually. A lot of that palaver is just for window dressing. I skip the candles and pass the benefits on to the customer."

"And this is Jon Tiler," said Rich. I turned again. Rich's arm was thrown out to indicate the other man—the one who'd followed me with a cold-eyed stare when I walked past earlier. The youngest of the three, I guessed, and the least prepossessing physically—he was five six in height, overweight by about forty pounds or so, and his flushed face was replete with burst blood vessels. He wore a short-sleeve shirt with some kind of floral design on it in shades of orange and pink and green—as if he was dressed for jungle operations in a fruit salad.

"Hi," I said, holding out my hand. He gave me a curt nod, but he didn't take the hand, and he didn't speak.

"Jon teaches all the little kiddies," said Cheryl, in a tone that—though jokey—seemed slightly loaded.

"I'm the interpretation officer," said Jon with a sullen emphasis.

The soft answer turneth away a whole heap of wrath and makes people take you for a pliable idiot into the bargain. "Interpreting what, exactly?" I asked.

"The collection," Jon said. "People come in. I do sessions for them. And it's not just kids, Cheryl. We lay on plenty of programming for adults, too."

"Sorry, Jon," said Cheryl, casting her gaze down like a chidden schoolgirl.

Rich jumped into the pause that followed before it could get awkward. "We've got a remit from the Education Department," he said. "They're one of our funding streams, and they set us targets. We're supposed to run one-day courses for kids in National Curriculum stages two, three, and four, and outreach sessions for adult learners. Alice oversees, Jon delivers. With help from a couple of the part-timers."

Jon went back to what he'd been doing, which was photocopying pages from a book on an oversized and slightly antiquated printer/copier. He turned his back on me fairly pointedly, and I wondered what it was about me he objected to so strongly. A possible answer suggested itself at once, and I made a mental note to check it out when I got the chance—assuming that I was still on the job after my interview with Peele.

There was still no sign of Alice, so I decided there was no harm in starting to collate a bit of information.

"Rich," I said, "if you don't mind talking about it, how did you come to get hurt?"

Cheryl jumped in before he could answer. "I've got the film rights," she said cheerfully. "He signed them over to me on a beer mat, so you're too late."

Rich grinned, a little sheepishly. "It was really weird. I was just wrapping up for the night, right? Three-quarters of an hour late, as per usual."

"Who else was around to see this?"

He thought about that for a moment. "Everyone," he said. "Cheryl. Jon. Alice. Farhat must have been around, too, because Friday's the day when she comes in. She's one of Jon's assistants."

"Alice?" I repeated. "Alice saw what happened?"

"Oh yeah." He gave a short laugh. "It was hard to miss. Everyone saw it—and heard it, too. Cheryl reckons I screamed like a—"

"Mr. Castor," said Alice. "Would you like to come through?"

Quite an impressive display of ninja stealth. She was standing in the doorway with her arms folded, and Rich tailed off when he saw her. For a moment I thought of asking her to clarify the mystery: she said she wasn't there; Rich said she was. But it might come across badly to bring it out in public—like a challenge or a taunt. It was probably better to let that one keep for now. "Well, I look forward to hearing the whole story," I said blandly. "Go over it in your mind; the more detail you can give me, the better. I'll see you in a few minutes."

"Sure, man," said Rich.

Nodding to the pair of them, I joined Alice and she led the way down the corridor, around another odd bend. The doors here were open, all but one, and some even had windows onto the corridor. At the same time there was a subtle change in the background feel of the place, like the silence when a fridge cuts out, making you aware for the first time that you were hearing a sound. I suspected that we'd just passed into the new annex.

Just beyond the bend in the corridor there were two doors. One was tersely labeled SENIOR ARCHIVIST, and the other had Peele's name on it, above the emblazoned words CHIEF ADMINISTRATOR.

"He's very busy," Alice said, making it sound almost like an accusation. "Please keep this as short as you can." She knocked on the door, then walked in.

The name plaque on Peele's door may have been impressive, but his office was barely wide enough to fit his desk into. You'd have thought a man with that big a title could have finagled himself a bit more elbow room.

Peele himself was sitting not exactly behind the desk—because this was a corner room with some odd angles to it, and the desk was against a wall—but in as commanding a position as logistics allowed. He looked up as I came in and closed a window on his computer's desktop. Probably Minesweeper, judging by how hastily and jerkily he did it.

The man who swiveled his chair toward me was in his late forties; tall and cadaverous in build, with a great ruddy hawk bill of a nose spoiling what would otherwise have been the handsome and ascetic face of a Methodist minister. He had red worry-marks on either side of his nose, but he wasn't wearing spectacles. His thinning hair was brown grizzled with gray, and his suit, which was dark blue, shimmered with a faint and incongruous two-tone effect.

I say he swiveled his chair toward me. Actually, he only made it through a few degrees of arc, and when he stopped, he was still only three-quarters on to me. His gaze made contact with mine for all of a second, then darted back down to the desk.

"Please sit down, Mr. Castor," he said. He waved toward the other chair, which had been positioned so far away from his own that it was only just inside the room. I took it. Alice stayed standing.

"Thank you, Alice," Peele said over my head.

Alice read that right, but she didn't take the hint. "I think I should probably stay," she said. "I'll need to know how we're going forward with this."

"I'll discuss the situation with Mr. Castor and then let you know," said Peele, sounding almost petulant.

I counted five seconds before the door closed behind my back, not with a bang but with a whimper, or rather a complaining *whoof* of displaced air. There was something a little off-kilter in that whole exchange, but I didn't know either of them well enough to tell what it was.

"I'm pleased you reconsidered," Peele went on, sounding if anything a bit irritated. "But I confess, after our conversation last night, I was expecting to hear from Professor Mulbridge."

My own fault. I'd talked up option B too much and made myself look like the stand-in instead of the main event.

"Well, that's still a possible way forward, Mr. Peele," I allowed. "But I found myself with some free time after all, and I thought time was a factor here. If you're prepared to wait a little while, I can certainly refer your problem to the professor. I should be seeing her next week. Or the week after, maybe."

He grimaced. As I'd hoped, he swallowed this suggestion with a definite lack of relish. "No," he said, shaking his head emphatically. "We couldn't possibly wait that long. After the attack on Richard, I think the staff are looking to me to act—to resolve this problem. If I can't, then . . . well, morale will suffer; it will certainly suffer. I really can't have it said that I didn't act. And the archive is hosting a public function on Sunday. No, it needs to be settled. The whole business needs to be settled."

I couldn't tell what was going on in Peele's mind, but he'd become quite animated now. He risked another glance at me, no longer than the first one. "This is a crucial time for us in many ways, Mr. Castor," he said. "I have a meeting in Bilbao tomorrow—at the Guggenheim Museum. A very important meeting for the archive and for me. I need to know that matters here are in train—that I'm not going to come back to chaos and recriminations. If you're free to start now, today, then I think that's what we should do."

The tone of his voice was merely fretful and peevish, but the fear underneath seemed genuine. He was out of his depth, he expected dire consequences if he screwed up, and he wanted an expert to take the whole thing off his hands and make it go away.

Well, here I was. I just wished to Christ he'd look at me or acknowledge me in some way. This relentless cold shoulder reminded me disturbingly of a passive-aggressive girlfriend I'd once had. Was he autistic?

Peele seemed to guess what was going through my mind.

"You're probably finding my body language a little disturbing," he said. "Perhaps you're even wondering if I have a psychological or neurological condition of some kind."

"No, I wasn't—"

"The answer is that I do. I'm hyperlexic. It's a condition similar in some ways to high-functioning autism."

"I see."

"Do you? Perhaps not. If you're mentally classifying me as somebody with a debilitating disease, then you don't see. Not at all. I could read at the age of two and write just after my third birthday. I can also memorize complex texts after a single reading, even if I'm not familiar with the language they're written in. Hyperlexia is a gift, Mr. Castor, not a curse. It does, though, make me react in unusual ways to other people's social signals. Eye contact in particular is very uncomfortable for me. I'm sorry if you're finding this interview disorienting or unpleasant as a result."

"It's fine," I said. Embarrassed and slightly thrown, I overcompensated and spoke just to fill the silence. "In fact, it fills a hole in the jigsaw. I can understand now why you laid so much emphasis on the way the ghost stares at you. That's probably more upsetting for you than for the rest of the staff here."

Peele nodded. "Very perceptive," he said without warmth. "Another aspect of my condition is that I find most metaphors . . . opaque. Confusing. Such as your reference to me as a jigsaw puzzle, for example. I hear it, but it doesn't mean anything to me. If you could avoid metaphors when you're speaking to me, I'd be very grateful."

"Right." I decided the best bet was to pull the discussion back onto a strictly business basis. "Let me just check the timetable with you again," I said. "The sightings started in September, is that right?"

"I believe so, yes. At least, that's the first time anything was said to me about it, and so that's the first entry in the incident book. I didn't see her myself for a few weeks after that."

"Do you have an exact date? For the first sighting, I mean?"

"Of course." Peele seemed slightly affronted at the question. He opened his desk drawer and took out a double-width ledger with a marbled hardboard cover, put it down on the blotter in front of him, and started to leaf through it. I'd assumed that "incident book" was a quaint, archaic title for a database file, but no, here was a real book with real writing in it. Maybe working in a place like this gave you an exaggerated respect for tradition.

"Tuesday, September the thirteenth," he said. He reversed the book and offered it to me. "You can read the entry, if you like."

I glanced down at the page. The entry for September 13 ran to most of a side, and Peele's handwriting was very small and very dense. "No, that's fine," I assured him. "It's unlikely I'll need to refer to it in detail. In any case, the attack on Mr. Clitheroe—Rich?—happened a lot more recently?"

"Yes." He turned the book back around to face himself and consulted it again. "Last Friday. The twenty-fifth."

I pondered this for a moment. Active versus passive is one of the ways I tend to classify ghosts—with passive making up more than 95 percent of the total. The dead keep themselves to themselves, most of the time; they scare us just by being there, rather than by actually going out of their way to harm us. But what was even rarer than a vicious ghost was one that had started out docile and then turned.

Well, let that lie for now. What I needed more than anything was a place to start from.

"Go back to September," I said. "Did you bring in any big acquisitions in the days or weeks before that first sighting? What else was happening in late August or early September? What else that was new?"

Peele frowned, visibly rummaging through the interior archives of his memory. "Nothing that I can think of," he said, slowly. But then he looked up—as far as my chin, anyway—as a mild inspiration struck him. "Except for the White Russian materials. I believe they came in August, although we were expecting them as far back as June."

My ears pricked up. White Russians? A female ghost who wore a monastic hood and a white gown? It sounded like a link worth clicking on.

"Go on," I prompted him.

Peele shrugged. "A collection of documents," he said. "Quite extensive, but it's hard to tell how much of it is going to be of any use. They're letters, mostly, from Russian émigrés living in London at the turn of the century and just after. We were very pleased to get them because the LMA—the London Metropolitan Archive, over in Islington—was showing an interest, too."

"Where are they kept?" I asked.

"They're still in one of the storerooms on the first floor. Until they're fully referenced and indexed, they won't be added to the rest of the collection."

"I'd like to go down there and see them later, if that's okay."

"Later?" Peele seemed perturbed by this concept. "Is there some reason why you can't do the exorcism straight away?"

And here we were again. But he didn't know, of course, how closely he was echoing his senior archivist. "Yes," I said. "Yes, there is. Mr. Peele, let me explain to you how this is going to work—what you'll get if you decide to hire me. I'd like to go through it in a bit of detail, because it's important to me that you understand what's likely to happen. Is that all right?"

He nodded curtly, his face saying louder than words that he really wasn't interested in the traveling hopefully—only in the arrival. I ploughed on anyway. It would save time and tears later, assuming this wasn't break point in itself.

"If you've ever thought about the act of exorcism at all," I said, "you've probably thought of it as something that goes down in sort of the same way that weddings do. The priest, or the vicar, or whoever, says, 'I now pronounce you husband and wife,' and there you go; it's done. By saying it, he makes it happen."

"I'm not naive, Mr. Castor," Peele interjected, in my opinion a little over-optimistically. "I'm sure that what you do is a very exacting discipline."

"Well, it can be. But that's really not the point I'm making. Sometimes I *can* just walk into a place, do the job, and walk out again. Mostly, though, it's not that straightforward—or at least, it's not that fast. I have to get a fix on the ghost—a sense of it. That comes first. Then, when I've got that sense really nailed down hard in my mind, I can call the ghost to me, and I can get rid of it. But there's no telling how long that process will take. Exorcism isn't a one-size-fits-all kind of thing. And if I'm going to do this job for you, I'm going to need to know right now that you won't be drumming your fingers and looking for things to happen within an hour or a day. It will take as long as it takes."

I waited for Peele to mull this over, but he changed the subject—I suppose as a delaying tactic while he weighed up what I'd just said. "And how much—"

"I charge a fixed price. Whether it takes me a day or a week or a month, you pay me a thousand pounds. Three hundred of that is up front."

That "fixed price" stuff was outrageous crap, of course. I take the same approach to the prices I charge as I do to most other things, which is to say that I make it up as I go along. This time around, the main thing on my mind was the down payment; I needed some cash in hand, and three hundred was more or less the amount I needed to clear myself with Pen—plus a little danger money, since this ghost had shown that she liked to play rough.

But the opposition was stiffening. Peele didn't like what he was hearing one bit.

"I'm sorry, Mr. Castor," he said, his gaze making it as far as my lapels as he darted a quick glance at me, "but I'm not prepared to pay anything in advance for what seems to be such a precarious and ill-defined service. If you're really saying that you could be here for—for as long as a *month*, disrupting our work, and that for all that time we'd still have to contend with the haunting, too . . . well, it's just not acceptable. Not acceptable at all. I think I'd prefer you to work on the basis of payment by results. I think that's the only kind of contract I'm prepared to enter into here."

I blew out a loud breath, shook my head.

"Then I think we're back to where we started," I said, standing up and pushing my chair away from the desk. "I'll let the professor know that you need a job done here, and she'll get in touch with you at her convenience. Sorry I wasted your time."

I headed for the door. It was only half bluff. What I'd told Peele about how I do the business was true enough, and it was also true that I needed the money now. If I'd set the bar too high, well, then that was too bad for me; but either way, he didn't get to buy me on credit.

I got the door open, but he called out to me before I could walk through it. I turned on the threshold and looked back at him—indecisive, sullen, glaring at his desktop with bitter distaste, but obviously thinking that starting again with someone else would mean all the time he'd wasted already would just be sunk costs.

"Could it really take as long as a month?" he demanded.

"If it did, it would be a new world record. Most likely, I'll run your ghost to ground inside of a couple of days and be out of your hair before you've had time to notice that I'm around. I'm not saying I'm slow, Mr. Peele—just that the work I do doesn't proceed according to a fixed timetable."

"Are there ways to make it proceed faster?"

That one set off a small carillon of alarm bells in my mind.

"Yes, there are," I admitted. "But they're not going to be my first options, because they're—unpredictable."

"Dangerous?"

"Potentially, yes. Dangerous."

He nodded reluctantly. "Well, then. I presume you know your business, Mr. Castor. I think—I may have spoken too hastily before. Three hundred isn't an unreasonable sum to ask for as a deposit. But if progress is slow, then perhaps we might consider using some of those other methods?"

"We can talk about that later," I said firmly, wondering what I was letting myself in for here.

"Later," Peele agreed. "Yes, very well. Perhaps you can come back at the end of the day and let me know how it's all gone. Or tell Alice," he amended, and he seemed to brighten at that second, better reflection. "And Alice can report back to me."

I let it go. It was obvious I was going to have him breathing down my neck whatever I said. "Fine, I'll do that. First, though, I'd like to talk to Rich Clitheroe about the incident where the ghost attacked him. And I'd also like to take a look at those Russian letters you were talking about—or rather, the room where you're keeping them."

"Certainly. Ah—I'll have to get the money signed out of the safe, which means waiting until after lunch, when I do the financial review with Alice. But I hope you won't wait until then to get under way?"

"Mr. Peele," I assured him gravely, "I was under way as soon as I walked in the door."

———————

Peele didn't go back into the workroom with me; he just picked up the phone and summoned Alice. I had to wonder if he was trying to distance himself from the decision to hire me—or was this just another aspect of his condition? Was he so uncomfortable around other people that he preferred to rule by proxy?

Peele broke the news that I'd be around for a while. Alice took it on the chin, but it was clear that she viewed this prospect with about as much enthusiasm as root-canal work. If I were sensitive about stuff like that, I could have got my feelings hurt. Before I let myself be led away, though, I decided to clear up one thing.

"The incident in which Rich Clitheroe was attacked," I said, as Alice held the door open for me to walk on through. "You told me you weren't present for that, right?"

"No." Alice's tone was exasperated. "That's *not* what I said. I said I didn't see the ghost. I saw what happened to Rich, but there wasn't any ghost there. As far as I'm concerned, there never has been."

"So you just saw the scissors—what? Levitate? Move themselves through the air?"

Alice shot a look at Peele before replying. He was staring at the desk, but seemed to be listening closely. I don't know what cue she was looking for or what she got. "His hand twisted around," she said. "The scissor blade scraped along his arm and then came up and grazed his face. You should be asking him about this, not me."

"Yeah, well, I will ask him, of course. But I wanted to establish—"

Alice cut across my words, speaking past me to Peele. "Jeffrey," she said. "If you give me a direct instruction to cooperate with this, then I'll do it. If I'm free to refuse to be questioned, I'm going to refuse."

There was a strained pause.

"Alice has strong feelings about this," Peele said very quietly. He stared at his computer monitor as he said it, so the only clue I had that he was talking to me was that he referred to her in the third person.

"I can see," I acknowledged.

"If you can work around her . . . it would probably be best. I'm sure everyone else will be happy to tell you what they know."

I looked at Alice, who was glowering at me now, making no attempt to hide her resentment.

"Fine," I said, after a moment. She nodded curtly, her point established, and her lines drawn. I followed her out to the workroom, and the door closed on Peele, no doubt to his immense relief.

It wasn't fine; it was thick, lumpy bullshit. But the cardinal fact hadn't changed—I still needed the money.

Back in the workroom, I gave the Exorcism 101 speech again, with minor modifications, for the benefit of Rich and Cheryl, who ate it up, and Jon, who pretended I wasn't happening.

"So I'll be asking all of you to tell me what you've seen and what you've experienced," I wound up. "You, and any other colleagues who've been involved in all this. And I'll start with what happened to you, Rich, because that's obviously the most extreme incident and probably the one that will give me the best launch point for what I need to do. First off, though, I was wondering if someone could show me the Russian stuff that came through in August. Letters from émigrés, that kind of thing?"

Rich gave me a double thumbs-up. "We can do both things at the same time," he said. "It's me that's cataloging all that stuff."

"What about me?" Cheryl demanded, pretending to be hurt at being left out. "When are you gonna interview me?"

"Straight afterward," I promised. "You're second on my list."

She brightened. "Go to hell, copper. I won't talk."

"I'll make you talk," I promised. I wondered if all conversations with Cheryl had this surreal edge.

Rich glanced at Alice as if for permission, and she made a gesture that was the hybrid offspring of a shrug and a nod. "Don't take all day about it," was all she said.

The building was even more of a maze than I'd thought. Our route to the storeroom where the Russian materials were being kept led us back down the rough-and-ready cement staircase, but then up another and through a fire door held shut by a spring hinge stiff enough to constitute a serious risk to outlying body parts. After a minute or so of similar twists and turns, I felt like a country mouse being given the runaround by a London cab driver.

"Is there a shortcut?" I asked, slightly out of breath.

"This *is* the shortcut," Rich called out from up ahead of me. "See, we're going to the new annex. The other way is back out through the entrance hall and around."

He stopped and pointed in through an open door. Inside, I saw when I joined him, there was another open-plan space, a fair bit smaller than the workroom I'd already seen, and made more cramped still by half a dozen library trolleys parked along one wall. A carrot-haired man who looked to be still in his teens wheeled one of these trolleys past us, getting up a good turn of speed so that we had to stand aside smartly or be run down. In among some shelf units at the back of the room, two other figures, indistinct in the half gloom, were transferring books and boxes from shelf to trolley or vice versa, exuding an air of focused haste. They didn't look up.

"SAs," said Rich. "Services Assistants. The keepers of the Location Index. They're the ones who collect all the stuff that's been requested and take it up to the reading room—then put it back again afterward. It's a bastard of a job. Will you want to talk to them, too?"

I shrugged. "Maybe later," I said. I didn't want to make this any more complicated than it already was. I was just looking for a clue as to where I should start fishing for the ghost—so that I didn't waste my time sitting in the wrong room, on the wrong floor, while Peele was watching the meter and waiting for results.

We moved on, and it was clear that we were now in a different sort of space. The doors here were all steel-faced, and the temperature had dropped by more than a few degrees. I pointed that out to Rich, and he nodded. "British Standard 5454," he said. "That's what we work to. When you're storing valuable documents, you want less than fifteen percent humidity and a temperature that's kept as stable as you can get it within a range of fourteen to nineteen Celsius."

"And the light?"

"Yeah, there are limits for that, too. Can't remember what those are."

Finally, Rich stopped in front of a door no different from any of the others, swiped with his ID card, and then unlocked it with one of the keys from his belt. He held the door open for me to enter. A sharp smell of must came out to greet us.

"Is this where it happened?" I asked him.

He shook his head vigorously. "The attack? Jesus, no. That was upstairs, in the workroom—where we just were. If it had happened while I was down here on my own, I would've shit myself."

I went into the room. It was warehouse size, slaughterhouse cold. My eyes flicked from the mostly bare shelves around the walls to the collection of FedEx boxes piled up on the two tables and the floor. One box was open, and it seemed to be filled with old birthday cards. A spiral-bound reporter's notebook sat open beside it, one page half filled with scribbled notes. On the other table there was what looked to be a laptop computer connected up to an external monitor and mouse.

I turned back to face Rich, who had followed me into the room.

"This is?" I asked.

"One of the new strong rooms. One we haven't expanded into yet—so we use it for sorting and short-term storage. This"—he indicated it with a wave of his hand—"is the Russian collection. I'm about a third of the way through it."

I took another look around, second thoughts often being best.

"Are both the laptop and the scribble pad yours?" I asked.

"Yeah. When you're cataloging new stuff, you start by just jotting down everything that comes into your head. Then you decide what goes into the item description and what the catalog headers should be. Some people enter it all directly into the database, but I find it's best to go through the two stages."

"Do you mind if I have five minutes alone in here?" I asked him. "Maybe you could go and make yourself a cup of coffee, and then come back down."

Rich seemed a little startled, but he rolled with it. "Sure," he said. "I don't drink coffee, though. Here." He squatted beside the nearest table and reached under it. I tilted my head and noticed what I'd missed—a portable fridge, about the size of one of the courier boxes. He took two bottles of Lucozade isotonic out of it, handed one to me, and put the other into his jeans pocket.

"In case of emergency," he said with a grin, "break glass. If you don't tell BS 5454, I won't."

He went out and closed the door. Nice guy, I thought. One of nature's gentlemen. But then again, the ghost had tried to part his hair about six inches too low. I was the Seventh Cavalry, as far as he was concerned.

Putting the bottle down on the edge of the table, I reached into the box and gingerly took a handful of whatever was in there. They were just what they'd looked like from the door—birthday cards in antiquated designs. The printed greetings were in English, but the writing inside was in a dense Cyrillic script that I knew from nothing.

I screwed my eyes tight shut and listened to the cards with my hands, but they weren't talking. After a minute or so, I opened my eyes again and took a closer look at the boxes. There were about three dozen of them, and each of them could probably hold anything up to a couple of hundred documents. They wouldn't all be cards, of course; letters and photographs could be a lot smaller, so the total might be that much higher.

Even if the ghost was anchored to something in this room, the chances of me finding that something on a quick pass like this were close enough to zero that it wasn't a viable option. But if the ghost itself was here now or anywhere close by, then I ought to be able to get a trace of it.

I sat down on the floor and slid the tin whistle out of my belt. Unhurried, emptying my mind as much as I could of other thoughts, I played "The Bonny Swans" right through from start to finish. This wasn't a cantrip; I wasn't trying to snare the ghost or even to drive it out of cover. This was just one of the tunes I used to help me focus. My own thoughts flowed out of me, riding on the music, and took a little stroll around the room, taking in textures and sounds and smells, poking their tiny, irresponsible fingers into every nook and cranny.

And there *was* something moving there, more or less out on the limits of what I could reach. Something very quiet; but whether that quietness was weakness or stealth or something different from either, I couldn't really tell. I could barely sense it at all. That was strange. A violent ghost would usually stain the very air around it with its psychic spoor. They might be rare, but they were hard to miss.

I reached the last verse, reciting the words in my mind as the plangent music wailed out of the old whistle into the still air.

> And yonder sits my false sister, Anne,
> Fol de rol, de rally-o,
> Who drowned me for the sake of a man . . .

The tenuous presence grew a little stronger, a little more vivid in my listening mind. But at the same time it grew stiller and more silent. I felt its attention slide over me like a ripple through cold water, breaking against my skin.

As if it was listening. As if the music had drawn it in, not because of any power I had but just because of something in the tune itself that it was responding to. But in any case, I knew it was close. I knew that

that silence was the mark of its attention, a greedy silence swallowing the old tune and opening wide for more. Was it really going to be this easy? I let the last notes linger, drew them out into a tapering thread of sound like a fishing line, pulled gently, ever so gently . . .

. . . And she was gone. So abruptly, it was like the bursting of a soap bubble. One moment, the teasing sense of her, hovering over me, wrapping herself in the sweetness of the music. The next, nothing. Dead, empty, intransitive silence.

Skittish, I thought bitterly. I shouldn't have reached out. Should have stayed passive and just let it happen. Fuck.

The door opened with a squeal of neglected hinges, and Rich looked in, cautious and solicitous.

"How are you doing?" he asked.

"So-so," I said flatly.

Five

IT WAS A FRIDAY, RICH SAID, AND IT WAS ALREADY a quarter to six. His hours were from eight-thirty to five, and he didn't get any overtime, but it was nothing special for him to be working late. Sometimes you just had a job to finish, and if you went home before it was done, then something you'd spent days or weeks putting together might fall through. In this case, he was finding and retrieving a whole stack of maps and plans on London's hidden waterways for a group of primary-school kids who were going to be coming in on the following Monday.

"That's part of business as usual, is it?" I asked. Just checking.

"Oh Jesus, yeah. We're a public facility, don't forget. Not many people wander in here off the street, but one of our official targets is throughput. We've got to make sure that the archive gets used by at least ten thousand people this year. And next year it's twelve thousand, and so on. We've got two classrooms and an open-access library up on the third floor."

"But taking the sessions is Jon Tiler's job, not yours? I mean, he's the teacher."

"Interpretation officer. Yeah, too right—I wouldn't take that job on for a big clock. But London rivers are one of my specialties, so I ended up doing some of the prep for this one. And there was a particular map that had it all—all the original tributaries superimposed on a surface map of the city. Only it was splitting right down the middle, on one of the folds, and I could see what was going to happen if Jon used it in that state. So I decided to fix it. I got sidetracked.

"Cheryl was up there, too, finishing off some bits and pieces of her own before the weekend. Alice was going over the next week's schedules with Jon, and Faz—Farhat, I mean; she's a part-timer—was doing some typing for Jon off in the corner. A worksheet or something.

"And I was more or less done. I mean, I'd found all the bits and pieces I'd set out to find, and all I had to do with the map was put a patch in it. It sounds dodgy, but that's how we deal with splits and tears, unless the original is too precious to mess with. We paste in new material—unbleached Japanese paper and pH-neutral paste—and stain it the right color so it doesn't look like a pig's breakfast. I was cutting my patch to size. We're meant to tear rather than cut, but I usually cut and then fray the edges with the edge of a scissor blade. Anyway, that's where I'd got to."

Rich took a long swig on the Lucozade bottle, wiped his mouth.

"And then the lights flickered. Just for a second. Alice said something about brownouts, and Jon turned that into a joke—I can't remember what, just something crude. But then it happened again, and suddenly it was like we were at a disco and they'd turned on the strobes. I stood up—I was going to walk over and turn the lights on and off a few times, see if that did the trick.

"But I never got there. Something pushed me back down into the chair. There was a bang—like something heavy landing on the table in front of me—and the floor shook. The map, the stain pots, all the stuff I was using, it just went flying into the air. The lights went out altogether, then a second later they came back on again. And the scissors"—he lifted a hand to touch the bandage on his cheek—"they sort of twisted around in my hand. I could see it happening, but I couldn't stop it. It hurt like a bastard, too. I managed to slip my finger out of the grip, but my thumb was still trapped, all twisted around.

"I was shit-scared, mate, I don't mind saying. I shouted out some-thing. 'Fuck,' or something like that. 'Look what's fucking happen-ing.' Cheryl came running over to help me, but the scissor blades were pulling me around by my own thumb—up and down and all over the place. I must have looked like Peter Sellers in that movie where he's trying not to do a Nazi salute.

"The scissors were hacking at my body and my face, and the only way I could protect myself was to turn with them and keep ducking out of the way. I barged into Cheryl, and she went over on the floor. Christ knows where Jon and Alice were. Farhat just kept screaming and screaming, which was a sod of a lot of use. Then I got the idea of banging my hand against the edge of the desk. It took about five or six goes, but in the end I got my thumb free, and the scissors just fell to the floor. Cheryl was thinking more clearly than I was—she trapped them with her foot in case they got up again.

"I looked across at Cheryl. I was going to say something like, 'Bloody hell, that was intense.' But then I saw she was looking at my face, so I put my hand up and touched my cheek. And it was wet. There was blood pouring down out of this cut. Spattering all over the worksheet and the desk, all over everything.

"I think I fainted for a few seconds. The next thing I remember, I was sitting down again and Peele—Jeffrey—was in the room. Bit of a rarity in itself, that—like a visit from royalty. Everyone was shouting, arguing about what to do. Alice said she was going to call for an am-bulance, but I said I was okay and I was going home. I'd deal with the cut myself. Jeffrey wasn't happy about that because he thought there might be some sort of insurance angle to all this shit, but I more or less said bollocks to that and got out of there. I was shaking like a leaf and I felt sick—like I might really throw up. I just had to get out.

"I almost didn't come back in on the Monday. The whole thing re-ally shook me up. But this is my job, for fuck's sake. What am I going to do, pull a sickie because I'm scared of ghosts?"

Rich took another belt of Lucozade, grimaced.

"Warm," he explained, without much conviction, putting the bottle down on the table and shoving it away from him.

I didn't say anything for a moment or two. What he'd said made some things easier to get a handle on, but it made others even murkier than they'd been before.

"You're right-handed?" I asked him at last. It wasn't a question, really. He'd been holding the phone in his right hand when I'd walked past the workroom earlier.

"Yeah. So?"

"But you were holding the scissors in your left hand, because it was your left cheek that got slashed."

He looked at me, obviously impressed.

"You're good at this, aren't you? Yeah, that was what pissed me off more than anything, to be honest. I was using my left hand because my right one already had a big thick dressing on it from where I'd trapped it in the desk drawer a few weeks earlier. It was just starting to get better, and then I got my face opened up. Someone's really got it in for me."

"The desk drawer. Was that the ghost, again, or—"

Rich laughed sardonically.

"No, that was just me. It's not like I need any help to mutilate myself. I've got a name for accidental self-immolation. It's a good job I'm the bloody first-aid man." He hesitated, nonplussed. "Mind you—it would have been around about the right time. Maybe it *was* her. I thought it was just me being cack-handed."

I turned my attention back to the boxes on the table.

"Have you been working on these ever since August?" I asked.

He followed my gaze and blew out his cheeks. "On and off, yeah," he answered, sounding a little defensive. "I've got other stuff going on as well, obviously. There's a huge amount of material there, and it's never been sorted. It was in a private collection somewhere over in Bishopsgate. Well, that's what Jeffrey likes to say, anyway. But I was in on the whole deal, so I can translate that into English for you—he means it was stuck under someone's bed next to the pisspot."

"You were in on the deal?"

"Yeah, I found the stuff, and I acted as broker. I wasn't allowed to claim a finder's fee because I'm on salary here—you can only pay a fee when someone from outside has brought something to you. But I acted as a go-between and a translator, anyway. It made a change from routine. And as a reward I get to catalog the whole damn collection myself because I'm the only one here who can speak Russian."

"Was that why the Bonnington hired you?" I asked him. "As a language expert?"

"I suppose it made a difference—but it was the classical education that was my unique selling point, not the Russian and Czech. The archive has got a load of old deeds and certificates written in medieval Latin." Rich picked up one of the birthday cards, opened it, and read the message inside. "To be honest, I don't mind doing this stuff, because I like to give myself a linguistic booster shot every now and then to make sure I don't get too rusty. Normally I do it with a foreign holiday, but this is cheaper."

"Is there a story attached to this collection?" I hazarded. "Or to how you got your hands on it?"

He looked blank and shrugged. "No, we just put in a bid for it and got it. But there's no scandal or murder or anything, if that's what you mean. Not that I heard about."

"And you haven't come across anything sensational or unusual in the documents themselves?"

By way of answer, Rich read aloud from the card he was still holding. "'To Auntie Khaicha, from Peter and Sonia. With all our love and thanks. We hope to see you again before the baby arrives, God willing, and to hear news from our dear cousin.'"

He let it fall back into the box.

"That's one of the racier ones," he said resignedly.

———

Time flies when you're enjoying yourself. It was after midday when Rich and I got back up to the workroom. The archivists had all clocked off for lunch, leaving a note for Rich that they'd be at the Costella Café on Euston Road. He invited me along, but I wasn't going to lose this opportunity to have the place to myself.

"Could you leave me your keys?" I asked him, thinking of the locked fire door.

He hesitated, and various thoughts passed visibly across his face. In the end, he shook his head. "I can't," he explained with a certain amount of embarrassment. "There's only the three of us who are key-holders—me, Alice, and Peele himself. It's a sacred trust sort of thing; they practically make you swear an oath. We're supposed to keep them on us all the time. We can lend them out to the other people who work here, but there's a form for it, and they've got to be timed out and timed back. If Alice sees you with my set, she'll go for me like a bloody pit bull."

"Is each set different, then?" I asked, looking down at the hefty collection of ironmongery. I wasn't trying to get around him, I was just curious, because the keys were of so many different sizes and varieties. I take a keen interest in keys and locks—they're somewhere between a hobby and an obsession with me.

Rich shook his head, following my gaze and still looking a little awkward—as though he'd disliked having to genuflect to the rules. "No, they're all the same. And to be honest, we only ever use about half of them. Less than half. I bet some of the locks that these things open don't even exist anymore—they just get added to, and nobody ever remembers to take anything off the ring." He shrugged. "But there's only three sets—or four, if you count the master set down in security. So it's not like there'd be any doubt about it if I lent you mine. I'm sorry, Felix—if there's anywhere you need to get into, Frank's probably your man."

"Yeah, no problem," I assured him.

It occurred to me that Peele might not have joined his troopers for lunch, so I wandered along and knocked on his door. There was no answer, so I tried the handle. The door was locked. Alice's door was open, though, and her office—neat, clean, monastically bare—was unoccupied.

Okay, so I wouldn't be able to get back to the room where the Russian stuff was sitting. But the ghost had manifested in the workroom, too, so it was probably worth whistling up a tune in there.

In the end I went through several old favorites, but without getting anything in response. If the ghost was still there, I couldn't feel it anymore.

Rich, Cheryl, and Jon got back from lunch dead on one, and Cheryl's eyes lit up when she saw me. "You gonna do me now?" she demanded.

"Absolutely," I said. "That's what I'm sitting here waiting for."

"You gonna use a drippy tap and a rubber truncheon?"

"I'm on a budget. You'll just have to smack yourself around the face while I ask the questions."

For the sake of privacy, Rich unlocked a room for us on the main corridor opposite the workroom. Cheryl sat on the edge of a table with her legs swinging, and I prepared to play one half of the nice-cop, nasty-cop double act. But she got her question in first.

"What if ghosts started to exorcise real people?" she demanded.

I was momentarily floored. "Sorry?" I asked.

"I was just thinking. If they started to fight back, they'd start with you, wouldn't they? They'd take out the blokes who could do them some harm. Then they'd have the rest of us at their mercy." She warmed to her theme. "You should probably train up an apprentice, like. And then when you die, the apprentice can track down the ghosts that did you in and get revenge for you."

"Are you volunteering?" I asked.

Cheryl laughed. "I could do it," she said. "I quite fancy it, to be honest. Can you do it as an evening class?"

"Correspondence course only. By Ouija board."

She made a face. "Har har har."

"How long have you been working here?" I asked her.

"Cheryl Telemaque. Catalog editor, first class. Mainframe log-in number thirty-three."

"How long?"

She rolled her eyes. "Forever!" she said, with a rising pitch. "Four years in February. I only came in to do some indexing work. Three months, it was meant to be."

"So being an archivist suits you?"

"I just got stuck, I suppose." She sounded comically morose now. Her voice was performance art, and I found it hard not to laugh. "I was good at history, at school, so I did it for my degree—at King's. That was pretty amazing in itself, you know? Not many kids from South Kilburn High going on to uni. Not from my year, anyway.

"But I didn't really think I was going to end up doing it for a career, you know?" She gave me the look that a center forward gives the ref when he's holding up the red card. "I mean, there aren't any history careers. But I couldn't get a job, and I was gonna do postgrad, only I already owed about twelve thousand quid on my BA, so they wouldn't give me a loan. Then this job came up—for a catalog editor, not an archivist—and my stepdad said I should go for it." Cheryl consulted her memory, frowning. "I think he was my stepdad by then. Anyway, it was Alex—my mum's boyfriend. Then her third husband. Currently her ex."

"Is that important?"

"I like to keep score. You know that thing Tracey Emin did—the bed with all her lovers' names sewn into it? Well, if my mum did it, it'd have to be a circus big top."

For someone who had a more methodical mind or a tighter time budget, I could see where talking to Cheryl could quickly lead to homicide or madness. For now, I was happy to roll with it, because I suspected that underneath all the clowning around, she'd asked me to question her because she had something to tell me.

"So you came here four years ago," I pursued, deadpan.

She grinned at the memory. "Eventually, yeah. I've got a motto, right? You've got no right saying you don't like something if you haven't tried it. But this time I just didn't fancy. We had a big row about it. I said I'd rather be on the game than work in a bloody library, then Alex said he was going to take his belt off to me."

"And?"

"I told him I didn't expect to get my first customer so quick." The grin faded abruptly, and she became brusquely matter-of-fact. "Anyway, after that I really needed a job, because my mum chucked me out. So I applied for this, and I'm still here four bloody years later."

"What does a catalog editor do?" I asked.

"Almost everything. Sorting new collections. Data input. User support. Most of the time, though, it's bloody retroconversion." Cheryl pronounced the word as if it was a kind of toxic waste. "Putting the old printed catalogs onto the database. See, lots of collections are still on these really nasty old printed lists that haven't even been looked at for a million years. I copy them across. Hundreds of thousands of them. It'd drive you frigging well mad. Sylvie's the only excitement we ever get around here."

"Sylvie? Is she another part-timer?"

Cheryl laughed, short and loud. "No, you pillock. Sylvie's the ghost."

"That's—"

"Just my name for her. Yeah. You've got to call her something, haven't you?"

"Why? Does she talk to you?"

She shook her head, a frown appearing and then disappearing again on her expressive face. "Not anymore. She used to be nattering on all the time when she first come round. Now you don't hear a peep out of her."

I pricked up my ears. "What sort of thing did she talk about?" I asked, trying to keep my tone casual.

"I don't know, do I?" Cheryl said, looking severe and slightly affronted. "I don't speak the language. She talked in Russian or Swedish or German or something, and I didn't understand a word of it. Except when she went on about roses. I got that."

Russian or Swedish or German. Or something. Quite a wide range. "So you see a lot of her?" I pursued, giving that one up for now.

Cheryl nodded. "Oh yeah. I see her every day, more or less. I think I'm on her wavelength."

"And you're not afraid of her? Even after what happened to Rich?"

"Nah. She wouldn't hurt me. You get a feeling if you're safe with someone, and I feel safe with her. She just stands there and watches me work—for ages, sometimes. I'm the only one who doesn't freak out about her, so I reckon she's more comfortable with me. Or maybe she just doesn't like men."

Cheryl paused and thought for a moment, staring at me with a forbidding seriousness.

"I ought to hate you," she said. "Because you're coming in to get rid of her. That's almost like murder, isn't it? Like she's already dead, and you're killing her again."

There was a long enough break that I thought she'd finished. "Well, obviously I don't see it like—"

"But the truth is, I think she's really, really sad."

She traced a line on the desk with her fingertip and frowned at it, her expressive face solemn, almost somber.

"I think you'd be doing her a favor."

———

Jon Tiler was almost as reluctant to talk to me as Alice was—but Alice had reappeared by this time, and she hypocritically told him that Peele had insisted on everyone's full cooperation. I was taking against Alice, which was something I'd have to watch. I didn't like the way she threw Peele's weight about.

In the interview room, Tiler was terse and monosyllabic. But then he'd been terse and monosyllabic in the workroom, too. Had he been at the Bonnington long? No. Did he like it there? Sort of. Had he seen the ghost? Yes. Often? Yes. Did it scare him? No.

I was only doing this for the sake of form. I felt like I already had the beginnings of a handle on the ghost—or at least an idea of how it had come to be here—so I probably didn't need any additional insights from Tiler. It just goes against the grain with me to leave stones unturned. I guess I *am* the anally retentive Ghostbuster, after all.

So I stirred up the pot a little.

"Do you have any idea," I asked him, "what ghosts really are?"

"No," Tiler answered with something like a sneer. "That's your thing, isn't it? Not mine."

"Most of the time they're not the spirits of the dead but emotional recordings of the dead. Imprints that just persist in the places where a strong emotion was felt for reasons that we don't understand."

I watched him for a moment or two, and he watched a spot on the ceiling somewhere behind my left shoulder. His expression was a glum deadpan.

"So you see," I said, "I'd normally expect to find evidence of some kind of strong emotion associated with this ghost's appearance at the archive. Something intense enough to leave a psychic echo." Pause for effect. Still nothing. "And the only strong emotions I've experienced here so far are yours."

Tiler's eyes widened and his stare jerked back to meet mine.

"What do you mean?" he yelped. "That's not true. I didn't show any emotion at all. I didn't do anything!"

"You radiate hostility," I said.

"I don't!" He was indignant. "I don't like all this stuff going on around me, that's all. I like to do my job and just"—he groped for words—"be left to get on with it. This is nothing to do with me. I just want it sorted."

"Well, that's what I'm here for," I said. "And the more I can find out about the ghost, the quicker I'll be done. So for starters, why don't you tell me about your encounters with it? When was the most recent?"

"On Monday. As soon as I came in." Tiler was still truculent, but something in him had loosened up. He went on without being prompted. "I was down in the stacks, and I felt her. I mean, you know, I felt she was there. And I was a bit rattled because of what had happened to Rich, so I got out of there fast. She was coming toward me, and it got—it felt cold, suddenly. Really cold. I could see my breath in front of me. I don't know if that was because of her, or if it was just . . ." his voice tailed off. "I got out fast," he repeated glumly, and his gaze flicked down to the floor.

"What does the ghost look like?" I asked him.

He looked at me again, surprised.

"She doesn't look like anything," he said. "Her face has gone. The top half of it, anyway. There's nothing there."

"When Mr. Peele described the ghost to me, he said that it wore a veil . . ."

Tiler snorted. "It's not a veil. It's just red. All her face except for her mouth is just red. She looks like one of those people who talk on TV programs and they want to stay anonymous so they get their heads blurred out. It's just a big red blob with her real face hidden behind it."

"And the rest of the body?"

He thought about this for a moment. "There's only the top half of her. She's all white. Shiny. You can see through her. And she sort of gets fainter the farther down you go, so from here"—he gestured vaguely at his own torso—"you can't see her anymore."

"Clothes?"

He shrugged. "She's got a hood on. And she's all in white. She keeps fading out. You can't see much."

After a few more questions, I let Tiler go. He didn't seem to be holding out on me, but all the same, it was still like drawing teeth.

And after that I went for a wander. Every cubic inch of the building had been turned into usable space, but it had obviously been done piecemeal, with no overall plan, and with a willingness to punch a new door through any wall that got in the way or to build a corridor around or a staircase over anything that couldn't be made to move. And it seemed that the work was ongoing; on the attic level, the rooms were mostly empty shells, and there was some builders' stuff piled up on the stairwell. The balcony railings had been removed to allow a block and tackle to be put in, and several palletloads of bricks had already been hauled up.

My tour of the building took about an hour and fetched me up back at the first-floor room where the Russian collection was stacked up. Rich met me there by prior arrangement and let me in again. "You can just slam the door behind you," he said. "When you're ready to go, I mean. It will lock automatically, and you won't be able to get back in. Happy trails, partner." He headed for the door. There was something I wanted to ask him about, but for a moment I couldn't remember what it was. Then it came to me just before he disappeared.

"Rich," I called. "Did the ghost ever talk to you?"

He shook his head emphatically. "No, mate. She never says a word to me."

"Cheryl said it used to talk a lot. Then it stopped."

Rich nodded. "That sounds right. A few people said they heard her talk in the first couple of weeks. Now she just goes at people with scissors. Better than bottling it up, isn't it?"

He let the door swing to behind him, and I was alone. That was annoying. If I was right about there being some kind of link between the ghost and this room, this collection, then she'd probably have been speaking Russian, and Clitheroe could have confirmed that. But if God had meant us to climb the mountain in a day, he would have put in a chairlift.

I tried a few more tunes to lure the ghost; it didn't bite. There was an obvious alternative, but I was reluctant to start on that just yet. Searching through all those thousands of cards and letters for an elusive emotional footprint wasn't a very attractive prospect. And it wouldn't even work unless I got a more vivid sense of the ghost itself first. As things stood, even if I found what I was looking for, I probably wouldn't recognize it.

Sometime after four o'clock, Alice came looking for me.

"Jeffrey wants to know how far you've got," she said, remaining in the doorway. She seemed to like doorways—or perhaps that was only when I was in the room.

"I'm still doing the groundwork," I said.

"Which means?"

"I'm trying to find out what exactly the ghost is haunting."

Alice cocked her head, innocently inquiring. "I thought she was haunting us," she said. "Did I get that wrong?"

I nodded, playing straight man. "It's not that simple," I said. "Not usually. I think it may have come in with these"—waving my hand over the cards and letters on the table—"but even if it did, it's not going to be easy to find out exactly where its fulcrum is. It's obviously wandering around the building a lot—but the first floor is its favorite stamping ground. That means we can probably assume that it's tied to something down here. I'm trying to find out—"

"So can I tell him you've made some actual progress?" Alice broke in. "Or just that you're still looking?"

"I've met the ghost," I answered, and I was gratified to see her narrowed eyes widen slightly. "That's a useful start, but it was a very brief contact, and I've only got the barest beginnings of a sense of her. Like I said, it's still early days."

She stepped into the room and put six fifty-pound notes down onto the table in front of me, along with a receipt for me to sign and a pen for me to sign it with.

"Enjoy," she said sourly. "No one can say you haven't earned it."

———

I called it a day a little after half past five. The ghost was still being coy, and the building was getting colder by the minute; the heating was evidently on a timer, even if the staff weren't.

Alice escorted me back through the maze to the lobby, where Frank liberated my coat from the rail where he'd stowed it that morning. He handed Alice a couple of FedEx packages, and she stopped long enough to sign her name in the mail book. As I was transferring my whistle back into its rightful place, the others came past in a huddle. Cheryl paused in passing.

"It was my birthday on Saturday," she said.

"Many happy returns."

"Cheers. So I'm standing drinks. D'you want to come?"

It seemed churlish to refuse, so I said yes. It was only after that that Cheryl seemed to notice Alice, still signing for her packages at the other end of the counter.

"Sorry, Alice," she said. "You're welcome, too, if you want to come."

Even I could hear the insincerity. "No, thanks," said Alice, her face setting into an inexpressive blank. "I'm going to be tied up here for an hour yet. Have a good time."

Six

RICH AND JON WERE ALREADY WAITING OUT ON the street, and they fell into step with us. Jon didn't react to my being there, but I didn't imagine he was thrilled at the prospect.

We went to a free house on Tonbridge Street that didn't seem to know quite what its freedom was for, at least if the choice of beers was anything to go by. I opted for a pint of Spitfire, which shone out from among the otherwise lackluster options.

Cheryl got the drinks in while Rich, Jon, and I found a table. It wasn't hard; the after-work crowd were just starting to trickle in, only sluggishly drawn to the plastic gilt and the sandwich menu, and completely indifferent to the two ranks of fruit machines giving their synchronized salutes off in the far corner.

"What do you think of the Bonnington?" Rich asked with a sardonic grin.

I think he was hoping for an extreme response—one that he could savor. I temporized. "Well, it's an office," I said. "The more you see of them, the more they come to look alike."

"Have you ever worked in one?" Tiler asked pointedly.

"I've always done what I do now," I said, glossing over the fact that for the past year and a half, I hadn't been working anywhere. "So apart from the odd vacation job back when I was a student, no. But I've been called into a fair few."

"Well, I've seen loads," said Rich. "But I've never seen anything like this place."

"It's a bit of a swamp of fear and loathing," I allowed. "What's with Alice? Is she always like that?"

He raised his eyebrows. "No. She's always been a bit of a bitch, but now she's fallen out with Jeffrey, hasn't she? She probably hasn't had breakfast in bed all week."

"So she and Peele are knocking boots?"

The quaint euphemism made Rich grin and Tiler purse his lips. "Yeah," Rich said. "Exactly. But only because Jeffrey is the CA. If they made a new post of Executive Big Bastard over the Chief Administrator, Alice would roll up her mattress and move on down the corridor. Whoever's in the boss's chair, there are some women who'll always be under the desk bobbing for apples in his crotch."

This was said with a certain amount of bitterness. Alice was younger than Rich, I realized. But he was her junior in the pecking order. No telling what sort of hatchets were buried there, or how shallowly.

"What did Peele and Alice fall out about?" I asked, trying to stay with the subject without responding directly to what he'd said. I thought he might be wrong about Alice. I didn't like her, but she didn't seem like the sort of person who'd give a pole dance in exchange for a pole position.

"I don't think this is something we should be talking about," Tiler said a little prissily. "It's just gossip, anyway. No one even knows if they—"

"About you," Rich interrupted, as if he was surprised that it needed saying. "You and the ghost. Jeffrey was all in favor of getting someone in to deal with it back when it first turned up. But Alice dug her heels in—said we were all just hallucinating, and there was nothing there. God, she was smug back in October, when the sightings stopped. But then they started up again, and I got this." He touched his bandaged face. "And Jeffrey said right, we'll have to deal with it now. But Alice still said no. And in the end, he went ahead and got you in without even asking her."

"That must have been upsetting for her," I allowed.

Rich nodded vigorously, looking as if he was enjoying the memory. "Yeah, you could say that. I mean, basically, she rules the roost while Peele hides in his office. And if he gets this Bilbao job he's going for, she's tipped for the big chair. So for him to disagree with her . . . well, it made her look stupid in front of the rest of us. Especially since he did it just by calling you up out of the blue, rather than by telling her to her face that she was wrong. He can only stand up to her behind her back, you see."

I remembered that Peele had mentioned Bilbao to me—something about a trip that he was about to take out there. I asked Rich what that was all about.

"He's been greasing up to the Guggenheim," said Rich with absolute scorn. "If he's an art historian, I'm the archbishop of Canterbury. But he loans himself out to them for lectures, and he's really cosy with the trustees there now. So they've called him over for a little chat tomorrow, which he's hoping is really a recruitment interview. And so is Alice, because then she walks into Peele's job."

"I don't think it's as simple as that," said Jon.

"I do," Rich replied, bleakly deadpan. "It's always looked like a racing certainty from where I'm—"

Cheryl came back with the drinks then, and Rich stopped fairly abruptly to help her unload the glasses from the tray she was carrying.

"So you reckon you've got her in your sights?" he asked me as he settled down with his bottle of Beck's.

"Alice?"

"The ghost."

Cheryl handed me my pint with practiced hands that didn't spill a drop.

"Not yet, no. I'm working on it. It shouldn't take too long."

"Can't be quick enough for Rich," said Cheryl. "He hates my Sylvie."

Rich shook his head emphatically. "No, fair's fair. I don't hate her. I just want her to sod off to her eternal reward. Preferably with her engines belching hellfire."

Cheryl laughed and prodded him with her elbow as she sat down next to him.

"Bastard," she said.

We toasted her in beer and vodka, and she responded with a mock-solemn bow. "Thank you, thank you," she said. "And next year in Jerusalem. Or at least somewhere that's not here."

Chink, chink, drink. Cheryl wiped her mouth with the back of her hand and belched unapologetically. For some reason, I found that endearing.

"So is this your first ghost?" I asked, shifting the topic from the loaded issue of how far I was along with the job—and, to be fair, the seemingly even more loaded issue of Alice's right of succession. Tiler and Rich nodded, but Cheryl, taking another swig of her drink, made a negative wave of the hand.

"No," she said when she'd downed her mouthful. "Not mine. I've had two already. And one was a bloke I went out with."

"You went out with a—" Tiler echoed, bewildered.

"When he was still alive, I mean. I was haunted by the ghost of my ex-boyfriend. Is that sick or what? Danny Payton, his name was. He was lovely. His hair was all goldy-blond, and he worked out, so he had muscles on him." She gestured vividly.

"But he was bisexual, which he didn't ever tell me, and he was two-timing me with a bloke. And this bloke had another bloke, who beat Danny up and threw him in the Thames. Except he didn't, because he missed. I mean, he threw Danny off Waterloo Bridge, but it was right up close to the edge, and Danny landed on the bank, in about two inches of water. Broke his neck." Cheryl was getting into her story, and she clearly enjoyed our silent attention.

"Anyway, I went to the funeral, and I had a good cry. But mostly I was thinking you dirty bugger, you should've kept it in your trousers when you weren't with me. What goes around, comes around."

"Cheryl, that's sick," Tiler protested, wincing. "You can't go to a funeral and be thinking stuff like that!"

"Why not?" Cheryl asked, appealing to the rest of us with her arms outspread. "You can't make your thoughts wear black, Jon. It's just the way I am, okay? I was missing him, yeah, and I was sorry he was dead. But he was dead because he'd been shagging another bloke, so I couldn't help feeling a bit pissed off about it. That's part of what funerals are for, in my opinion. You get it out of your system. You get closure, yeah?

"Except it turned out that Danny didn't." She paused dramatically, rolling her eyes at us. "I got back home, and he was only there in my bloody bedroom, wasn't he? Not a stitch on him! I screamed the place down, and my mum and my stepdad came running in, and then they hit the roof. Mum was wetting herself because it was a ghost, and Paulus, my stepdad—husband number two, Felix, yeah?—was all crazy-eyed because it was the ghost of a *white* boy. He was calling me all the sluts and whores, and Danny was reaching out to me like he wanted to give me a big hug, so Paulus tried to hit him and smashed his hand through the window instead."

Cheryl laughed at the memory, and I laughed along with her. It was a dark enough scene, but she made it funny because her voice orchestrated it like a Whitehall farce. Tiler was looking like a hanging judge, though, and even Rich was shaking his head in pained awe.

"You always do that," he said. "You tell these awful stories, and then you laugh. And there's never a punch line."

"There *is* a punch line. I exorcised him."

"You what?" Rich exclaimed, and Cheryl cast a sly look at me.

"There's not a closed shop or something, is there?" she asked. "You know, like for actors, or train drivers?"

"Yeah, sorry," I said. "There is. The union's going to have your arse."

"Well, it's my best feature." She smirked. "See, I didn't mind him being there, at first. You've got no right saying you don't like something—"

"—if you haven't tried it," Rich finished. "But Jesus wept, Cheryl. A ghost!"

"The ghost of someone I really liked. It was nice still having him around. I used to chat with him about stuff. He never said anything back, but I knew he was listening. He was like a mate you can share secrets with.

"But you know, time goes on, sort of thing. I couldn't really take another bloke up to my room if the ghost of the last one was still sitting there. And he was so sad—like Sylvie's sad. In the end, I thought it was probably best if we ended it.

"So what I did, right, was I gave him the standard dump speech. Like as if he was still alive. I sat down on the bed next to him, and I said I wanted us to still be friends and everything, but I didn't love him in that way, and I wasn't going out with him anymore. You know how it goes. At least I'm assuming you do. And all the while I was talking to him, he was getting fainter and fainter. Until . . . when I'd more or less finished . . . he just went out like a light." Cheryl pondered on that for a moment, her expression sliding down the register from sunny to somber. "And then I really cried."

The silence from the rest of us was a testament to Cheryl's skills as a storyteller. It was broken by Jon Tiler. "You really know how to throw a party, don't you?" he said gloomily.

"Yeah," said Cheryl, pointedly. "I do. And if you get snarky on me, Jon, you won't be coming on Sunday."

"Sunday?" I asked.

"My mum's getting married," said Cheryl. "Again. At the Brompton Oratory. Fourth time around the track, this is. They don't say 'Till death us do part' for my mum; they say 'Who's holding ticket number twenty-three?' Anyway, I had a brain wave. I asked Jeffrey if we could have the reception in the reading room at the archive, and he said yeah, we could. So everyone's invited."

"So you don't hold it against your mum that she threw you out on the street?" I asked, more surprised at that than at the ghost story—I already suspected it would take a lot to shake Cheryl.

She laughed. "We tear pieces off each other, and then we're all right again. We've always been like that. I've got no time for all her bloody boyfriends and fiancés and husbands, though. They're a right shower. This latest one's worse than Paulus and Alex put together, if you ask me. But he won't last. They never do."

"What about your dad?" I inquired.

"Nothing about my dad," Cheryl answered shortly. She made a face and shook her head.

"Here," said Rich, trying to pull the agenda back onto safe ground. "Joke about ghosts, right. This big expert on paranormal phenomena is doing a lecture tour of the UK, and he gets to Aberystwyth on a Friday night. And he goes into the hall, and it's packed. Shuffles his notes, clears his throat, and says, 'Let's just see where we stand. How many people here believe in ghosts?' Every hand in the room goes up. 'Excellent,' says the professor. 'That's what I value. Truly open minds. Okay, how many of you have actually seen a ghost?' Half the hands go down, half stay up. 'Good enough,' says the professor. 'And out of you lot, how many have spoken to a ghost?' Maybe twenty hands stay up, and the professor nods. 'Yes, that takes some courage, doesn't it? And how many of you have touched a ghost?' All but three hands go down. 'Finally,' the professor says, 'how many of you have made love with a ghost?' Two hands go down, but one right at the back of the room stays up. It's a little old guy in a grubby mac. 'Sir, you amaze me,' says the professor. 'I've asked that question a thousand times, and nobody has ever answered yes to it. I've never met anybody before you who's had sex with a ghost.'

"'Ghost?' says the old guy. 'Oh, sorry, I thought you said goat . . .'"

Cheryl guffawed, and Jon said he'd heard it. Jokes about goats followed, and for a while, we all tried to think of one that was clean. It turns out there aren't any.

Rich bought the next lot of drinks, and I took care of the one after that. Jon downed his third vodka breezer with indecent haste and claimed a prior engagement. Rich gave him a meaningful look, but he clearly wasn't going to be shamed into standing his round. He wished us all good night and left without a backward glance.

"Tight bugger," muttered Rich.

"Oh, leave him alone," said Cheryl. "He can't help it. You've seen what he buys himself for lunch. He just gets off on counting his pennies, that's all."

"What are his politics?" I asked, casually.

"His politics?" Cheryl repeated blankly. "I haven't got the foggiest. I don't think he's got any, unless supporting Fulham counts. Why?"

"He looked really unhappy to see me. I wondered if he was a Breather."

"Ohh." She saw what I was getting at then, and her eyes widened as she considered the possibility. "I don't know. Maybe. He's never seemed to give much of a toss for his fellow man, to be honest, but they're an odd bunch, aren't they? My flatmate where I lived before was one of them, and she used to go along to the cemetery at Waltham Abbey at weekends and read aloud from Gibbon's *Decline and Fall*—I suppose because she thought the ghosts might need the intellectual stimulation. It always seemed a bit cruel to me."

The Breath of Life movement—or the Breathers, as most people refer to them—are a grassroots pressure group campaigning for changes in the law governing the risen dead. Ghosts and zombies, they say, are still people; they have rights that need to be recognized and defined in law. Some of them feel the same way about the more colorful groups among the undead, but there's a certain amount of contro-versy there. What rights do the possessed have, for example, and who gets to enjoy them? Host body or invading spirit? And what about the were? It had all turned into a bit of a circus. The government—New Labour, but with a bit of the shine gone—had made some cautious statements about legally recognizing the dead, causing the Tories to point dramatically quivering fingers at the law of inheritance. How could it be expected to work if it turns out that you *can* take it with you after all? What about criminal trials? Could a dead man give evidence against his murderer or stand trial for murder himself? And if he were found guilty, how in hell are you supposed to punish him? And so on, and so on.

And my own profession, of course, had come in for a whole lot of attention. If the dead had rights, then presumably one of those rights was not to be blasted into the void by a cheerful tune from a tin whistle—or by a poem, a mechanical drawing, a series of complicated hand gestures, or whatever other form of cantrip the exorcist hap-pened to favor as he slashed and burned his way through the natural order of things.

I let all this wash over me as far as I could, but the Breathers were getting to be something of a worry for me—as the other, earlier right-to-lifers had been for the staff at abortion clinics.

However, neither Rich nor Cheryl remembered Jon Tiler ever say-ing anything on the subject one way or the other, which made it more or less certain that he wasn't part of the movement. You could never get them to shut up about it short of gagging them with moldering grave cloths.

The party passed its cusp and started to wind down. Cheryl went off to powder her nose, and Rich, who was a bit maudlin-drunk by this time, started in to tell me about some of his walking tours in Eastern Europe, but ran out of steam in the middle of a rambling anecdote about a club in Prague called Kaikobad, where they have transsexual strippers. His eyes seemed to defocus, which, when a guy is in his cups, either means he's thinking deeply or he's about to pass out. Either way, I figured it was about time to call it a night.

"Hey, mate," Rich said, rousing suddenly. "I think you've made a new friend."

"What, Cheryl?" I asked, a little thrown. He obviously couldn't mean Jon Tiler.

Rich waved that suggestion away impatiently. "No, not Cheryl. Cheryl talks a good fuck, but she's never been known to deliver. I meant the oversize geezer in the corner."

He didn't point, just rolled his eyes off to the right and then back. I followed his lead, not jerking my head around but picking up my drink and then letting my gaze traverse the bar slowly and casually.

It wasn't hard to guess who he meant—a big, heavyset guy sitting near the door, jammed into a tight booth that made his already impressive bulk loom even larger. His oddly shapeless body was packed into an antique-looking gray herringbone suit, and whatever it said on the label, there had to be a whole lot of Xs in front of the L. His bald head glistened, and his pale, almost colorless eyes shied away as they caught my stare.

As he looked away, I experienced the sudden cessation of a feeling so tenuous, it had slipped under my guard. It was the sensation that Peele had described to me over the phone: the sensation—like a light, even pressure over the whole of my skin—of knowing that I was being looked at.

Okay. File that one for later, I guess. I didn't know who he was, but I knew *what* he was well enough, and he probably knew what I was, too. That could even have been why he was watching me. Exorcists excite very real and very natural fears in certain quarters.

Cheryl came back from the loo right then, which was my cue to head on out. I made my excuses, gave the birthday girl a kiss on the cheek, and left.

I walked past Euston Station and back up Eversholt Street for reasons I can't even remember. Maybe I just fancied a walk, although it was still cold and blustery, or maybe I was deliberately choosing a route that would take me by the archive.

I was on the other side of the road, though, so when I saw the woman standing out on the pavement next to the doorway of the Bonnington, her arms hanging at her sides and her head bowed, my first thought was that it was Alice calling it a day after a stupendous stint of unpaid overtime.

Then I registered the hood, and a moment after that, the way her body became more and more washed out and hard to distinguish from its surroundings the closer you got to the ground. And finally she raised her head to stare at me, which stopped me dead in my tracks, because the stare was being conducted without the benefit of eyes. The upper half of the woman's face was a formless, rippling plane of undifferentiated red. Dark hair, decorously tousled, then cherry red lips and a neotenously rounded chin. Nothing, nothing but redness in between.

What she was wearing was harder to determine. She was dressed in white, the way everybody said, but white what? There was too little of her to form a judgment from. She raised an arm to point toward the building, and it was a bare arm, spectrally pale. It seemed as though she was fighting against the pull of gravity, her movements as strained and slow and full of terrible effort as the way your legs pump in dreams when you're running away from the bogeyman.

I pulled myself together and stepped out into the road—almost into the path of a Routemaster bus; the blare of its horn floated behind it like the bellow of a wounded animal as I jerked back at the last moment, out of its path.

I thought she'd be gone now, her dramatic exit hidden by the bus in line with all the best movie clichés. But she was still there, and as I broke into a run, I tried to assemble the sense that went with the vision—the fix. I began to drop the mesh of my weird perceptions over her, dredging up notes in sequence, turning her into music. It was hard. Even though she was there in front of me, the trace was so faint, it almost wasn't there at all. It was as though I was looking at her through the wrong end of a telescope. That wasn't something that had ever happened to me before, and I didn't understand it. But if she stayed where she was for just a few moments longer, it wouldn't matter.

Then a door opened about twenty feet behind her, and bright white light stabbed through her. She turned away, and as she turned, she disappeared. I found myself staring at Jon Tiler, who was looking at me with a startled-rabbit expression on his face. He had a satchel in his hand, which he lifted up by way of explanation—or protection, because he looked like he was expecting to be spanked.

"I went back for my bag," he said. "Was that . . . Shit, were you—"

I ran through a range of answers in my mind, most of them revolving around the word fuckwit. But none of them would achieve anything beyond the immediate emotional catharsis.

So "Lock the door behind you" was all I said over my shoulder as I walked away.

Seven

THE DINNER PARTY WAS FLAGGING.

In fact, that was a polite word for it. It had died. Even my father, who when he's in full flow can be silenced by nothing short of decapitation, had finally given up and was just staring at his plate. My headmistress from primary school, Mrs. Culshaw, was fiddling with her greens. The clown sitting next to my mother picked his nose forlornly, and she wagging a finger at him without any real conviction.

All around the table, faces turned to me.

"Give us a tune, Fix," Pen said with an insinuating lift of the eyebrows. "I bet you know some amazing ones."

I shook my head, but they were all nodding. Old school friends, old enemies, women I'd slept with, the man from the corner shop back in Arthur Street, everyone wanted some free entertainment, and I was on the spot.

Slowly, I stood up.

"Play the one your sister Katie liked," my father said. "The one you played to her before she died." A chuckle went around the table at his little joke. He exchanged a glance with my mother, who nodded appreciatively as if he'd scored a point in some unacknowledged game.

"Play her back to life again," my brother Matthew suggested. He blessed me ironically with the sign of the cross.

That did it. That always did it. I wanted to make them all shut up, and the quickest way to achieve that was to do what they said. I put my whistle to my lips and blew a single note—strident, shrieking, sustained. The faces around the table went in an instant from smug challenge to dismay. Then I modulated that one high note into a wailing, skirling tune, and they gasped.

I don't always remember what song I play in this dream, but this time it was "The Bonny Swans." By the time I got to the first refrain, everyone was clutching their heads or their stomachs, sliding down off their chairs, collapsing across the table with moans of agony.

It was clear that the music was killing them. That made me feel a little bad, in a way, a little sick with myself, but it didn't make me stop. They'd asked for a tune. I gave it to them, as the ones who were trying to crawl toward the door collapsed and curled in on themselves, and the ones who'd just slumped in their chairs withered and decayed in fast-motion.

I killed them all. No more embarrassment. No more demands. They asked for it, and they got it. Finally I lowered the whistle, which now felt hot to my touch, like a gun after it's been fired. I slotted it back into my pocket, grimly satisfied.

Then there was a liquescent gurgle from behind me. It was a terrible sound—a sound of indescribable distress and pain. The sort of sound that means either pull me back or finish me off, but don't leave me stuck here in between like a rabbit on a barbed-wire fence.

The whistle had let me down. This one I was going to have to kill with my bare hands.

I turned around slowly. I didn't want to see, but it was my responsibility. I knew if I didn't do this, the next time I blew into the whistle, no music would come. This was the price I had to pay for the gift that had been given to me. This was the place and time where the rent fell due.

The body slumped at my feet was twitching feebly, like a goldfish on the bathroom floor. It was too dark to perceive anything apart from that vague sense of movement. I gripped its shoulder, hauled it onto its back. It didn't resist as my hands found its throat.

The lights came up slowly as I squeezed.

———————

"Couldn't sleep?" Pen asked. She padded into the kitchen in bare feet and scarlet silk dressing gown, rubbing her eyes.

I took a sip of coffee. I'd made it on the stove top, using Pen's 1930s moka pot, and it was thick and black and lethally strong—not exactly calculated to cure insomnia, but just right to stop my hands from shaking.

"Have you ever noticed," I asked her, "how characters in movies always sit bolt upright when they get to the scariest part of the dream? It's like they've got some kind of psychic ejector-seat mechanism. They get to the money shot and *boing*, they're awake."

She poured herself a cup from what was left in the pot. It would be three sips and some sludge, but they'd be potent sips.

"You dreamed about your sister again."

I shook my head. "This time it was Rafi," I said glumly.

She sat down opposite me, in silence. I finished the cup, and she offered me hers.

"Nobody blames you," she said, at last. "Nobody thinks you screwed up."

"I *did* screw up."

"You tried to help him. It didn't work. Nobody else could have done anything."

I was sorry I'd mentioned it. Honesty isn't usually a vice I indulge, but with Pen, you get into the habit. She never lies—not even the white kind that spare feelings and avoid embarrassment. You tend to give her the same courtesy back.

"Maybe nothing would have been the best thing to do," I muttered.

Exorcism is both more and less than a job. You do it because it's something you find you *can* do, and because once you've started, there's something about it that doesn't let you stop. But, in the long run, it gets to you. Exorcists who live long enough to be old are very strange people indeed—like the legendary Peckham Steiner, who lived the last few years of his life on a houseboat on the Thames and wouldn't set foot on dry land because he thought the ghosts were about to launch a blitzkrieg on the living, and he was the first target.

I thought about Rafi as he was when I first met him: elegant, selfish, and beautiful, a dancer with a thousand delighted partners. Then I thought about him steaming in that bathtub full of ice water, his eyes shining in the dark, looking as though the fire that was inside him was about to break out through his skin at any moment and leave nothing but black ash.

It wasn't that I convinced myself I knew what I was doing. I didn't. I'd never seen anything like this, and it made me literally piss my pants. But it didn't seem possible to just sit there while Rafi burned; it seemed like I had to do something, and there was only one thing I knew how to do. So I took out my whistle and I closed my eyes for a moment, looking for the sense of him, the fix. Easy. The place was saturated with it. So I started to play—just like in the dream.

At the sound of the first note, the demon Asmodeus hissed and bubbled like a kettle with the lid left off and opened Rafi's eyes wider than they were meant to go. Weakened from his long climb up from Hell, he clawed at me without strength and cursed me in languages I'd never encountered, but he couldn't lever himself up out of the bath, and all I had to do was to step back out of his hands' reach. I played louder to drown out the harsh gutturals that were spitting and frothing on Rafi's lips.

And it seemed to be working. That's the only excuse I can give for not thinking it through—not realizing what it was I was actually doing. Rafi's body twitched and shuddered, and the steam that was boiling off him turned into roiling, curdled light. I was playing faster now, and louder, playing what I could see and feel and hear in my mind, letting the music spill out like scalpels to operate on the world. I was lost in it, mesmerized by it, part of a feedback loop that filled me up with sound as a cup is filled with sweet wine.

Then for a moment the curses stopped, and the writhing thing in the bathtub looked up at me with Rafi's terrified, pleading eyes. "Fix," he whispered, "please! Please don't"—his face twisted. Asmodeus's features surfaced through Rafi's like oil through water, and he roared at me like a wounded animal. Except that his horns protruded in clusters through the flesh of his cheeks, and his black-on-black eyes boiled like snake pits.

Idiot though I was, the truth hit me in the face then. Rafi hadn't been possessed by a ghost at all but by something much bigger and more terrifying. That meant that there was only one human spirit inside him, that the fix I had was on Rafi, not on his ruthless passenger. I was exorcising Rafi's own spirit from his body.

I almost faltered into silence, but that would have been the worst thing I could possibly do. It would probably have extinguished Rafi's soul right there and then. Instead I tried to turn the tune into something else—to break it free from the Rafi-sense that filled my head and latch it onto something else.

I played through the night, and the night was endless. The thing in the bathtub flailed and cursed, wept and moaned, laughed drunkenly and begged for mercy. Then the frosted glass of the bathroom window lit up with a dim, weary glow of yellow-pink dawn light. That seemed to be the signal for hostilities to cease. The thing closed its eyes and slept. About a half second later, the whistle fell from my mouth, and I slept, too. I didn't surface again for eighteen hours.

I woke to the sick realization of what I'd done. I'd managed not to snuff out Rafi's soul, but in some way I didn't understand and couldn't undo, I'd knotted that soul and the demon that was possessing him into one inextricable psychic tangle—turned Rafi and Asmodeus into some obscene ectoplasmic equivalent of Siamese twins.

And that was when I'd thrown my hand in—made my New Year's

resolution in midsummer and packed the tools of my trade up in a shoe box in Pen's garage. There had to be something else I could do with my life—some job where they didn't give you the keys to the poison cabinet until you'd learned how to mix the antidotes.

Only it turned out that keeping resolutions was another thing I couldn't do to save my life.

———————

"Nobody told me to let you into anything," said Frank, rubbing his earlobe between thumb and forefinger as an adjunct to thought.

"I'm assuming that nobody told you not to, either," I countered.

The burly security guard laughed good-naturedly, but he shook his head. "I'm sorry, Mr. Castro," he said. "You can use the reading room, same as anybody. And anything that's in the public-access collections, you can get it out on a pink slip. But if I let you into the strong rooms, and then it turns out you wasn't authorized or anything, that's my job right there, isn't it? No, I've got to have either Mr. Peele or Miss Gascoigne come down here and tell me it's okay. Then I'll happily take you through."

I gave up and headed for the stairs. "You—er—you've got to leave your coat down here, too. Sorry." Frank sounded genuinely embarrassed. It wasn't in his nature to be hard-arsed, despite his scary face, but he had to walk the walk as best he could. I came back, transferring a whole lot of paraphernalia to my trouser pockets as I went. Frank stowed the greatcoat in a locker this time, because the racks were full of little macs and duffle coats in a variety of pastel shades, suggesting that somewhere in the building, Jon Tiler was up to his ears in hyperactive eight-year-olds. Good, I thought vindictively. After last night's fuck-up, he had a lot of bad karma to burn off. I hoped piously that he'd find enough suffering to get himself back into spiritual equilibrium.

I couldn't ask Alice, but that was no fault of Frank's. She'd taken advantage of Peele's trip to Bilbao to call a meeting, and all the archive staff except for the SAs and the security team (which seemed to consist of Frank all by himself) were closeted with her for the whole morning. Which left me cooling my heels.

Up in the reading room, several large boxes had appeared overnight and were now piled up in front of the librarians' station, forming an additional cordon sanitaire between the staff and the sparse sprinkling of end users. There was a young Asian woman on the desk this morning, and she gave me what seemed to be a sincere smile over the barricade of boxes. But when I asked if she could let me into the strong rooms, she gave an incredulous laugh.

"I'm not a key-holder," she said. "Sorry. I'm only a clerical assistant. I don't have any access to the collection at all."

I thanked her anyway, and we introduced ourselves. She, it turned out, was Faz, the part-timer who had the thankless task of helping out Jon Tiler. What did she think about that? "He's a little bit strange," she said cautiously. "Not very forthcoming, you know? Hard to read. But we don't have that much to say to one another, really. I just get on with it, and he gets on with it, and when he doesn't need me anymore—or when I can get him to admit it—I go and do something else. Like this. A change is as good as a rest."

I remembered that Rich had listed Faz as being there when the ghost attacked him, and I asked her about that. She was very happy to talk about the ghost, but with everyone else crowding around, she hadn't seen very much of the drama.

"I've seen her in the stacks, though," she said with a little more enthusiasm. "Three times. Once very early on, and then twice last week—two days running. I'm in the sweepstakes, but I'll need to pick up the pace a bit to be in with a chance. Elaine's seen her six times, and Andy's on eleven."

I asked her the same questions I'd asked the archivists, about what the ghost looked like and what impression she'd got of it. Faz hit the same beats as everyone else, more or less, but she had a few ideas of her own, too.

"She's young," she said judiciously. "And I think she's pretty, only you can't see because she's got that red misty stuff in front of her face. She just looks as though she'd have pretty features—I suppose because she's got such a nice, neat little chin. I thought she might be in her wedding dress at first, because she's all in white, but a wedding dress doesn't have a hood—and anyway, her hair's all wild. You'd do your hair up on your wedding day, wouldn't you?"

"What do you mean, wild?" I asked, curious. This was a new slant. My own view of the ghost, from across the street and in the dark, hadn't been clear enough for details like that.

"Like she's been standing on a hill, and it's been blown about a bit." Faz thought about this. "Only she's wearing a hood, so obviously it's not that. But you know what I mean. Like she's just woken up, maybe. I don't know."

"Did you ever hear her speak?"

Faz looked a little distressed. "Yeah," she said, unhappily. "I did the first time. She just kept saying 'roses.' Going on and on about roses. And she held out her hand to me. It was like she was begging. She's different now. Quieter. But I don't think she had a happy life, poor thing."

I changed the subject. Emotional outpourings about ghosts make me uncomfortable.

"What's in the boxes?" I asked, pointing. "New acquisitions?"

Faz glanced down as if she'd forgotten the makeshift ramparts that had been piled up around her.

"Oh," she said. "That's bunting, I think."

"Bunting?"

"And glasses, and cutlery, and stuff. For the reception on Sunday. Cheryl's mum is getting married again."

"So I hear," I said. "I'm lucky to be here at a time of such joy and laughter."

Faz looked sidelong at me to make sure I was being sarcastic, then grinned conspiratorially. "It doesn't get any better," she said in a low voice that wasn't meant to carry. "Maybe it will when Mr. Peele goes off to work for the Gug. Maybe Rich Clitheroe will take over. I reckon he'd be a bit more human."

"I heard Alice was the front-runner."

Faz made a sour face.

"That'll be it for me, then," she said. "Enough is enough."

———————

I sat up in the workroom with my feet up on Tiler's desk and waited for the meeting to break up. While I was waiting, I reached out with my mind and tried to get another whiff of the ghost—again with no results. I pondered that paradox without wringing any sense out of it; a ghost that had done the things that this one had ought to have left a stronger trail and be a hell of a lot easier to find.

Just before eleven, Cheryl ambled into the room. Her frankly lovely face lit up when she saw me. "Yo, Ghostbuster," she called, pointing at me with both hands.

"Yo, Cheryl."

She stood over me, made a comic business out of squaring up to me.

"I'm on Sylvie's side," she said. "You'll have to take both of us on."

"Necromantic troilism. That sounds like it might be fun."

"I'll smack you," she warned, grinning all over her face.

"S&M, too? It gets better."

The mild flirtation had to stop there, as everyone else filed in through the door—Rich, Tiler, Alice, and several other people I hadn't met yet.

"That's my desk!" Tiler protested indignantly. "Get your feet off it!"

I made a "mean you no harm" gesture and stood. He took possession with a warning glare.

"Alice," I said, "I need to get back into the strong room where the Russian collection is being sorted."

"Rich will take you," she said, barely sparing me a glance. "I've got a lot on today. Assuming the job isn't finished by the end of the day, you'd better come up and tell me what you've done and how it's going. When Mr. Peele comes in tomorrow, he'll want to know where things stand."

Which was masterfully understated, I thought.

"You reckon that's what it is, then?" Rich asked as he collected his keys. Cheryl waved good-bye with a cheeky grin. I waved back, but with professional gravitas. "That the ghost came in with that Russian stuff?"

"It's the most likely scenario, yeah," I said. "The ghost moves around a lot, but the biggest cluster of sightings is down on the first floor, which is in the right ballpark. It made its first appearance shortly after the Russian collection came in here, and it dresses in what you could loosely call a Russian style. I'm not ruling anything out, but that's where I'm starting today, anyway."

"Fair enough," said Rich.

We walked up hill and down dale until we reached our destination, where Rich unlocked the door.

"There's plenty of Lucozade in the fridge," he said. "In case of emergency"—he paused and shrugged.

"—break glass," I finished.

"Exactly."

"Any vodka?"

He looked a question at me.

"More authentic," I explained.

Rich grinned. "I'll have to try that one on Jeffrey."

I pulled up a chair. The massive task in front of me filled me with inertia. I glanced desultorily around the stuff that was already lying on the table, and I remembered what Cheryl had said about retroconversion. "Why the notebook?" I asked Rich, pointing. "Can't you just enter everything up directly into the computer?"

He shook his head emphatically. "Some people do, but it's a mug's game. Better to make notes by hand first, until you know what you're dealing with. Going through a load of database entries that you've already keyed in to change one piddling detail on all of them—I don't even want to think about it."

"Couldn't you get someone else to do that? A catalog editor, maybe?"

Rich looked at me as though he suspected I might be taking the piss. "If I want Cheryl to stick her boot in my face, I'll just ask her to," he said. "Anyway, the records are stored in your own personal area while they're being written up and messed about with. They don't go to the general-access catalog until they've been signed off and approved by an A2—a senior archivist." He scowled momentarily, probably at the injustices of the power structure and his own position in it. But he managed to keep his tone light when he spoke. "So what's the program for today?"

My turn to scowl. "I'm going to go through every one of these letters and envelopes and birthday cards and laundry lists until I find one—or maybe more than one—that has some kind of psychic echo of your ghost. Then I'm going to use that to sharpen up the trace I've already got."

Rich looked interested. "Like a sniffer dog?"

"That's not very flattering, but yeah, like a sniffer dog—working from an object and following the trail from that object to someone who it used to belong to."

"Cool. Is it worth watching?"

I gave a slightly sour laugh. "How many items are there in these boxes?"

"Er . . . four or five thousand. Probably more. We're not that sure."

"I leave you to imagine the thrilling and slightly depraved spectacle of me stroking and fondling every last one of them."

"I'll see you later, then."

"Sure."

He turned and left. I pulled the first box over and got started.

The spoor I get from touching an object isn't the same as the instant hot news flash I get from touching a living person. It's more subtle and less focused, and to be honest, it's a whole lot less likely to be there at all. Think how many things you touch in the course of a day and how few of them mean anything to you. Now if someone happened to pick up a hammer, say, and used it to stave your skull in, it's likely that the explosive charge of his anger and your agony would stay there in the wood or the vulcanized rubber of the hammer's handle. Then, when someone like me comes along and touches the handle—bang. The charge goes off. I feel your pain, as the saying goes.

But most of the things you touch just don't carry that same weight of significance—and to make matters worse, the same object will pass through other hands after yours. The older the thing you're dealing with, the muddier and more smeared-out the psychic trail. And then, just for gravy, while an exorcist is trying to read the thing, his own emotions are adding yet another overlay to what's already there. All in all, it's like trying to take a fingerprint off a melting ice cube.

But in the right conditions, it's something I'm pretty damn good at.

I transferred the contents of the box onto the desk and spread them out more or less evenly. Then I passed my left hand slowly over them, palm downward, as though my spread fingers were the steel loops at the business ends of five small metal detectors. I took my time over it, letting my hand wander backward and forward across the sprawled treasure trove of old letters and cards. Slowly a sense formed in my mind: a three-dimensional web, its vertical axis being time, of vague and formless feelings, bleached out and blended together almost to the point of illegibility; a tasteless soup of memory and emotion.

When I had that sense firmly in my mind, I brought my right hand into play. While the left hand still hovered, the right moved quickly, lightly touching first one sheet of paper and then another, tapping and jabbing into the stack at the points that looked most promising.

It's not rocket science. I'd encountered the ghost twice now, and it had touched my mind both times, leaving an incomplete and fuzzy impression there. I was looking for something in this mass of documents that would match that impression so that I could complete and sharpen it. When I had a psychic fix on the ghost that was vivid enough and whole enough, I could take out my whistle and finish the job; the impression I form and hold in my mind while I play is the burden of the cantrip that I weave, and music is the medium that expresses it.

After maybe ten or fifteen minutes of this, I was more or less certain that there was nothing doing, so I carefully packed the contents of the first box away again and hauled a second box up onto the table. Once again, I unpacked and spread the old documents across the space in front of me and began to read them.

That was how I went on through the rest of the morning and into the afternoon. At a steady pace, and with my own emotions carefully held in neutral, refusing to be hurried or frustrated—it's hard enough anyway without raising that kind of static.

I lost track of time, not because of the endless repetition but because the impressions I was taking from the old papers, faint as they were, exerted a sort of hypnotic pull of their own. Floating in that fuzzy palimpsest, I found it hard to stay anchored in the chilly afternoon in November that had been my starting point. It was still there, and I was still there, but my awareness of it was dulled. Gradually, I stopped hearing the gurgling of pipes and the opening and closing of distant doors. I was somewhere else, somewhere outside the normal flow.

Just once I thought I had something; the image of a weeping woman came through to me very clearly when I touched a particular photograph. She was young, and she was heartbroken—but her face was intact, her hair was ash blonde, and most of all, she wasn't here. This was just an afterimage, with no sense of presence behind it. The photo was of a street, presumably in the Eastern Bloc somewhere—a residential street in a small town, drab and anonymous and more or less timeless.

Half roused out of my trance by the effort of conscious thought, I was suddenly aware of the sound of dozens of shrill, piping voices all talking over each other and the vibrations under my feet of a beast with sixty or so short but serviceable legs. I pulled myself together— pulled myself out of the psychic web I'd been weaving and back into my own flesh—and rubbed my eyes. Then, as the noises got louder, I stepped to the door and looked out. The corridor was alive with children, all in blue blazers with red badges on the pockets, and all clutching crumpled sheets of paper in their hands. They seemed to be working in pairs and sticking very closely together, as though this was some kind of three-legged race that worked on an honor system. "That's not a plaster molding!" one little blonde girl was shouting indignantly at the boy next to her, who had a shell-shocked air. "That's just where they put the fire extinguisher! We've still got to find a plaster molding!"

They ebbed and flowed along the corridor, staring intently at walls, floor, ceiling; swept around a corner; and were gone, trailing a few stragglers as any stampede will. In the distance I heard Jon Tiler's voice shouting, "No, stay on this floor! Stay on this floor! I'll tell you when you can go up the stairs!" He sounded only a half inch away from hysteria.

One of the kids had dropped his sheet of paper, so I picked it up and examined it. THE BONNINGTON ARCHIVE ARCHITECTURAL TREA-SURE HUNT, it said in a font that declared aggressively, "This is fun you're having now—have some fun, damn you." Underneath there was a list of architectural items, with the playful challenge HOW MANY CAN YOU FIND? DADO RAIL, CEILING ROSE, GABLE, WINDOW BAY, and so on. Next to each item was a box to tick. The first item, already ticked, was MY PARTNER.

I went back to my work, satisfied that Jon was working off his guilt. Again, I became lost in the soft textures and fuzzy logic of the past, my mind suspended in a shapeless but compelling skein of my own making. Hours passed, undifferentiated, and I worked my way steadily through the boxes. Variations on a theme: the same old gruel of emotions, too thin to nourish, too bland to titillate.

The next time I surfaced, it was a change in the quality of the light that brought me back to a gloomy winter day that was already waning. I looked at my watch; it was well after five, and I still had about a half dozen boxes to go. More to the point, I'd totally failed to find what I was looking for. Nowhere in all the pages I'd touched was there a scent or a footprint of the ghost I'd met.

My instinct was just to slog on to the end of the road, but the bleakness of the place was soaking into me like a physical chill. Seeing the kids on their treasure hunt had boosted my psychic reserves a little, but the effect had worn off quickly. And anyway, it was nearing the end of the archive's opening hours; if I was going to stick around any longer, I needed to make sure someone else would be around to lock up after me. So I yawned and stretched, stood up stiffly, and with some reluctance made the pilgrimage to the workroom.

Apart from Alice herself, the gang were all there: Cheryl and Jon Tiler typing away at their computer terminals, while Rich seemed to be busy copying a list of names from an old document into his notebook. There was also a red-haired guy I didn't know, working away at the photocopier. He was another of the part-timers, and Cheryl introduced him as Will.

"Any luck?" Rich asked.

"Not so far," I admitted. "I'm still working on it. Has there been a sighting today?"

He shook his head. "All quiet on the Western Front."

"Yeah, well, sometimes when the normal routine of a place is disrupted, a haunting will stop for a while." I wasn't normally this garrulous, but I was putting off the evil moment; I wasn't anticipating much pleasure in reporting in to Alice. "Ghosts are usually very fixed on routine—some of them will hang around the same place for centuries and show themselves bang on midnight, every night. But change the wallpaper, and they're lost."

Cheryl perked up at all this talk about ghosts. "What about the violent ones?" she asked. "Have they got a routine, too? I mean, do they get into it? Are there, like, serial-killer ghosts?"

Piqued, Rich brandished his wounded arm. "Hey, this is real, Cheryl," he said. "People are getting hurt. Can we not talk about it as if it's a role-playing game?"

Cheryl was unrepentant. "All right, but it's interesting, though, isn't it? Maybe that's what sick-building syndrome is. It's just ghosts you can't see having a go at you."

Rich opened his mouth to speak, but then thought better of it and just shook his head as if to clear it. He returned to his keyboard with a scowl on his face.

"Yeah," I said to Cheryl. I was trying hard not to break into a grin. Rich had every right to feel aggrieved, but it was hard to stay serious around Cheryl when she was so determined to be sensational and flippant. I was starting to like her a lot. "Sometimes they do repeat the same sequence of behaviors, time after time. You've got to realize, though, that the sample is probably too small to count for anything. The number of ghosts that have ever actually attacked the living is tiny—when you weed out the folk tales and the compulsive liars."

I suddenly realized that they were both looking past me, at the doorway. Turning to follow their eyes, I saw that Alice had sneaked up on me again, just like she'd done the day before.

"That's the real challenge, isn't it?" she asked, mildly.

Ingratiatingly, Tiler fed her her cue. "What is, Alice?"

"Weeding." She didn't even bother to look at him; it was me she'd come in here gunning for. "Have you had better luck today, Castor?"

I could have pulled against the hook, but I think she would have enjoyed reeling me in. "None at all," I said evenly. "I've been working through that Russian collection, but I haven't found anything that's likely to be of much help."

Alice just stared at me for a moment. She'd taken a few steps into the room, but she clearly didn't feel much more comfortable in here than Peele did. Her mouth quirked, as though she was fighting down an urge to spit.

"You said that what you do depends on your obtaining an impression of the ghost? A fix on her?"

"Yes. That's right."

"But you did that yesterday, didn't you? The first time you went into the Russian room. That's what you told me. So why is it that you're still unable to dispel her?"

"It was a weak fix," I said bluntly.

"Does that mean it's useless?"

I clenched my teeth on a word that probably didn't appear in any of the archive's seventy-five miles of shelving.

To tell the truth, I was a little frustrated myself. The ghost had been right there with me twice now. The first time, I'd screwed the contact up for myself; the second time, Tiler had done it for me. If I could have held either one for just half a minute longer, I could be shaking the dust of the Bonnington off my feet and walking home with a grand in my pocket—at that moment, a consummation very fucking devoutly to be wished. Instead, I was providing sleeve notes for Alice, who I knew by now was one of those people who never stop asking until they get the answer they want.

So I did something a little stupid. I went on when I should have stopped and got out of there.

"No. I didn't say that. A weak fix is a good start—and I was lucky to get one so fast. You can turn a weak fix into a strong fix, if you know what you're doing."

I could still have walked away at that point. I was going to. I'd already decided. But she was looking at me with scorn and skepticism, clearly measuring my lackluster performance against the three hundred pounds I'd already been paid.

"In fact," I said, "there's something we could try right now, if Rich is up for it."

"Eh?" Rich had had his head down all this time, either working or pretending to. The idea that he might get drawn into the action obviously filled him with alarm.

"It's a trick I've used a couple of times," I said. "It might pull the ghost in if it's close by. And even if it doesn't do that, it should still give me a clearer sense of where the ghost is hanging out—what part of this building is its anchor, or its home."

I cleared a space on the layout table. This involved shoving aside some of Jon Tiler's pencils and worksheets, which he snatched out of my hands indignantly.

"Has she got to have an anchor?" Alice asked, stubbornly insisting on the personal pronoun.

"No," I admitted. "But most of them do. We're playing the odds." I turned to Rich.

"Rich," I said, "how would you feel about being wounded again? Just very slightly this time, and in the name of science?"

He hesitated again, searching my face for a clue to what I meant. When I took out the diabetes blood-testing kit from my pocket, he looked even more doubtful—but Tiler looked downright sick.

"It's okay," I reassured him. "It's not surgery, it's just—sympathetic magic. The ghost spilled Rich's blood. That's unusual in itself. Most ghosts, even the ones in the angry brigade, they're happy just to chuck stuff around. Smash a window or two, maybe, leave scratch marks on the furniture—that sort of number. Actual violence, though, that's rare. Wounding you is probably the most intense experience this spirit has had since it crossed over."

I had their full attention now. Opening up the test kit, I took out the disinfectant and unscrewed the lid. Then I picked up a bubble pack and tore it open. It contained a sharp—a thin strip of stainless steel with a short but keen point at one end. I anointed this end with the antiseptic.

"Nobody knows," I said, "whether ghosts are made out of emotions or just drawn to them. Either way, it's pretty much an accepted fact that they'll usually choose to hang around in places where they experienced strong emotions in life. Fear. Love. Pain. Whatever. But there's another side to the equation. If they become involved in strong emotions *after* they've died—because they've seen or been part of intense or violent events—then that's got a powerful draw for them, too. When this ghost stabbed Rich with the scissors, the experience must have been incredibly powerful. Incredibly vivid. Pleasant or unpleasant, or most likely both. What Rich felt, and what the ghost felt, would have been all tangled together, and all screwed up to a pitch of intensity—like being caught in a nail-bomb blast and having an orgasm at the same time."

Alice put on a sour, disapproving face at the sexual metaphor, but I think they all got it.

"So we can use that now," I concluded, simply. "If Rich reenacts the wound, the ghost may respond. It ought to feel the ripples from the original event stirred up again by the replay. If we're lucky, it won't be able to help itself. It might be drawn right here, in which case I'll probably be able to finish the job tonight. But whether it comes or not, it should look in this direction; it should be pulled toward us. And I'll sense it. I'll be able to triangulate on where it is."

All eyes turned to Rich, who shrugged as nonchalantly as he could.

"Okay," he said. "I'm not scared of a little prick with a needle."

In the tense, expectant atmosphere, nobody touched the straight line. Rich held out his hand, and without preamble, I jabbed him once with the sharp, on the ball of his forefinger. He had enough self-control not to wince.

"Squeeze out a drop of blood," I said. "On the desk, preferably."

"I can't authorize the cleaners to wipe up blood," Alice objected, but Rich was already doing it. Clenching his right forefinger in his left hand, he tightened his grip, and a pearl of blood welled up from the tiny wound. It reached critical mass and fell onto the desk with a slight but audible splat.

I handed Rich a swab of cotton wool from the kit, and he reached out his good hand to take it. But before he could, both the cotton wool and the sharp were swatted from my fingers by an invisible force. Rich gave a yelp of shock as his hand was flicked away, too. All the heads present, including mine, snapped around—to stare at empty air.

Then the entire room went crazy.

It was as though there was a wind—a whirlwind—that we couldn't feel: a whirlwind that flesh was immune to, but that swept all other substances before it with implacable fury. Both doors to the room slammed deafeningly shut; books and files leaned over, tumbled, and fell to the floor; and papers flew from every desk and shelf to envelop us in an instant A4 blizzard. At the same time, the floor shuddered to a series of pounding thuds, the vibrations so powerful that my jaws clacked shut on the tip of my tongue. Cheryl swore, and Alice screamed. Rich gave a choking cry, backing away from the swirl of papers and striking ineffectually at the air. Jon Tiler and the other guy whose name I'd already forgotten both hit the floor in best *Protect and Survive* style, with their arms over their heads as though they were expecting a nuclear attack.

As for me, I just stood and watched as maps and posters and fire-drill charts hauled themselves off the walls and added themselves to the general melee. It was instinctive: not arrogant, or defiant, or particularly brave. It was just that this was information, and I wanted to make sure that I didn't miss anything that might turn out to be important.

So when one small piece of paper or card came fluttering toward me, sailing against the storm, I noticed it at once. Unlike most of the diabolically animated paperwork, it was a lot smaller than A4. More to the point, it was dancing to the beat of a different drum, almost hovering, its short feints to left and right keeping it more or less directly in front of my face. I reached up and grabbed it out of the air. I couldn't look at it because file folders and envelopes and catalogs and worksheets were beating against me and wrapping around me. I closed my hand on it instead, used the other hand to shield my face until, only a few seconds later, the tempest stopped. It didn't slacken or falter, it just died, and everything that had been snatched up into the air fell simultaneously to the ground. Except for the scrap of card that I was holding—that went into my trouser pocket.

The archive staff blinked and looked around them, shell-shocked and disbelieving. Only Alice and Rich were still on their feet; Cheryl had ducked under her desk to join Jon Tiler and the other guy on the floor. Nobody said a word as they all got up again and stared around at the debris.

"Well, that was what we call a positive result," I said into the silence.

"The—the damage!" Tiler stuttered. "Look at this! What have you done, Castor? What the fuck have you done?" Alice was just staring at me, and I saw that her hands were trembling.

"I don't think anything much is broken, Jon," Cheryl offered. "It's a terrible mess, but look—most of it's just paper."

"Just paper? It's my worksheets," Tiler howled. "I'll never get them sorted out again."

"Looking on the bright side," I said, "it worked. I got a really strong line on the ghost. I can pinpoint more or less exactly where it came from."

They all looked at me expectantly.

"The first floor," I admitted. "Just as we thought."

Eight

I BEAT THE KIND OF RETREAT THAT COULD BE CALLED either hasty or strategic, depending on which side of the line you were watching it from. I was helped by the fact that Alice seemed unable even to frame, let alone speak, the many harsh words that she wanted to say to me. I assured her that I'd taken more from that brief encounter than just a confirmation of what we already knew, and I promised her definite progress tomorrow. Then I was out of there.

The lights in the corridor had already been turned off, but there was a strip light on in the stairwell. By its subliminally flickering glare, I reached into my pocket, took out the offering that the ghost had thrown at me, and examined it. It was card, not paper: a white rectangle about five inches by three, printed with pale blue lines and perforated close to one of the long edges by a single circular hole. This hole had once been about half an inch away from the edge, but was now joined to it by a ragged tear.

It was a card ripped out of a Rolodex or file-card index. On it there were four letters and seven numbers.

ICOE 7405 818.

ICOE? Was that a name? An acronym of some kind? The Institute of . . . Christ knew what. The rest of it looked to be a central London phone number, though—logical enough if this was from someone's desk directory. Leaving aside the question of what I was meant to do with it, it represented a sort of breakthrough in a job—I almost thought *case*—that had otherwise brought me nothing but a day of aggravation.

I fished out my mobile phone—no time like the present. But the battery is faulty, and the damn thing is always out of charge; this time was no exception. I thrust both the phone and the card back into my pocket and carried on down the stairs.

The security office was already locked, and there was no sign of friendly Frank. I went behind the counter to pick up my coat, but of course it was shut into one of the lockers, and I didn't have a key. I was contemplating kicking the flimsy door open when Alice came down the stairs at my back and saw me. I turned to face her, bracing myself for a bollocking, but what I read in her face wasn't anything as straightforward as anger.

"Great show," she observed, her voice tense. "Fun for all the family."

"I don't know," I countered. "I think I need some tunes you can actually hum."

"So how is it done?"

I considered tact and courtesy. Briefly. "You get a ghost. You drive it rat-arse crazy with a drop of blood. The recipe's in the *Iliad*." She didn't answer, so I tried again. "Look, I didn't expect that kind of a response. I'm sorry about the damage. I thought the ghost would come in for a low pass over the blood, but the reaction we got was completely—"

Alice wasn't listening. She came around the counter and wielded her totemic key ring to liberate my coat. I took it from her outstretched hands, nodded a curt thanks. I thought she was going to say something else, but she didn't. She just took her own coat and handbag out of the next locker along. Her hands hadn't stopped trembling, and when she unhooked her big, unwieldy key ring and tried to slide it into her bag, she couldn't manage it. With a muttered "Shit!" she thrust it into her coat pocket instead. I left her to it.

Outside, a light drizzle was falling, but the wind on my face—only a breeze, really—felt good after a day in the archive's stingily recirculated air. I could have taken a train from Euston and changed, or hopped a bus heading north through Camden Town, but I decided to walk to King's Cross and grab the Piccadilly line direct. I was two or three blocks away from the archive, walking head down along the Euston Road, when I realized that Alice was keeping pace with me—shivering despite her coat, her arms clasped around herself, her keys jangling audibly in her pocket.

I stopped and turned to face her, waiting for the other shoe to drop. She stared at me, her eyes sullen and haunted.

"I'm not happy about this," she said. "I'm not happy about where it's going."

I carried on waiting. I thought I knew what she meant, but I needed a bigger clue than that.

"I thought—" It was a difficult admission, and she had trouble getting it out. "I thought it was all bullshit. I thought Clitheroe was lying, and everyone else was hysterical. Because if there'd been anything there, I would have seen it, too—and I didn't see anything. Until tonight."

I was as careful as I could be: a neutral observation, not loaded at all. "You saw Rich getting that wound on his face."

"It wasn't the first time—Rich hurts himself a lot. He shut his hand in a drawer a few months back. And another time he tripped and fell down the main stairs. I thought it was an accident he was too embarrassed to own up to."

"But you saw—"

Alice cut in, her tone brittle and dangerous. "I saw him prancing around like an idiot, yelping, waving the scissors. Then he managed to cut his face, somehow. It wasn't like tonight."

She was staring at me, and I saw in her eyes what a heroic understatement it had been when she'd said she was not happy. I'd pigeonholed her the day before, and now I knew I was right. Alice wasn't even a vestal; she was what we refer to in the trade—often with a certain degree of contempt—as a DT, or sometimes just as a Thomas: one of the absolute nonsensitives who stood at the opposite end of the human bell curve from wherever I was. She couldn't see ghosts at all.

Funny. After her behavior up to now, seeing Alice so scared and unhappy should have been a feast of schadenfreude for me. But in fact, I felt a reluctant sympathy for her. I'd been there. We all have to go there, eventually. We all have to drop the shield of skepticism and bow our heads to the axe of that's-just-how-it-fucking-is.

"I know," I said, feeling a weight of tiredness drop onto my shoulders. "When you see one for the first time—when you realize it's all true—you have to swallow a lot of very heavy stuff all at once. It's hard."

I let the words hang in the air. Yes, I was sorry for her, but I had troubles of my own, and she was one of them. Did I really want to help her dry her eyes and square her shoulders? No.

But some things come with the job.

"I'm going home," I said gracelessly. "I've got ten minutes. If you want my version of Metaphysics 101, you can have it."

Alice nodded, probably as reluctantly as I'd made the offer.

"Better make it somewhere inside," she said. "Otherwise I don't think I'll last that long."

The nearest "somewhere inside" was Saint Pancras's church. It was open and empty. We sat down in the back row of pews. It was almost as cold as it was outside, but at least it was dry.

"Metaphysics 101," Alice prompted me, her voice shaky.

"Right. Blake hit the nail bang on the head, didn't he? '*What is now proved was once only imagined.*'" Thanks for that one, Pen. "If ghosts are real, then a whole raft of things that you were happy to think of as metaphors, or folk myths, or medieval clutter left behind in the wake of the Enlightenment turn out to be sober truth. You start wondering about Heaven. And Hell. You start asking yourself what's going to happen to *you* when you turn your toes up. Are you going to be stuck in some dismal pit of a place just because you lived there or worked there or died there? Is the afterlife like this one, only with no sex, no drugs, and no time off for good behavior?"

Alice nodded, slowly and unhappily.

"Well, the answer is nobody knows. If you're religious, you could talk to a priest about it. Or a rabbi, or whatever flavor you favor. But I'll tell you how I get through it."

She was watching me, expectantly. Someone else was watching, too. I felt that prickle again; that pressure on my skin lighter than touch. I glanced into the shadows near the door, thought that maybe I saw someone moving there.

"I stick with Blake," I said, "and I draw a line. Between what's proved and what's just jerking off—premature reification. If I see my Aunt Emily get decapitated in a freak piano-tuning accident, and then a bodiless shape that looks just like Auntie Em comes walking through my bedroom wall at three in the morning with its head tucked underneath its arm, I don't just jump for the nearest conclusion—which is that whatever is on the label has to be in the box. You know the Navajo?"

"The Navajo Indians?" Her expression was blank, nonplussed.

"Yeah, them. They see ghosts as some kind of evil force of nature. *Chindi*, they call them. They're the part of the soul that can't go on to something better—all the nasty impulses you don't usually follow up on. All your selfishness and greed and stupidity. They're not you; they're just a sort of negative afterimage you leave behind you when you trade up to eternal life."

Alice didn't look convinced; it was probably a bad example.

"All I mean is, there's no automatic assumption that ghosts are people trapped in some fuck-awful repetition of what they used to do when they were alive. We don't know what they are. We don't have any way of finding out."

Her uncertainty was hardening into something else.

"And that makes it okay for you to destroy them?" she asked, her voice almost too low to hear.

I shrugged. "Is that what I do? That's another unknown."

"Not to you."

"Yes, to me."

"I don't see that. You must know what it is you're doing."

This was novel. I was meant to be talking Alice through this very sudden existential crisis—and instead I found myself being asked to justify my own existence. It must say something profound and worrying about me that I didn't just leave her to it.

"At first necromancy was something I did by accident," I told her. It was the easiest way to put it, but *accident* was a pretty pale word for it all the same.

"Accident?"

"Yeah. I mean, without wanting to do it. Without deciding." I looked toward the door again, then back to meet her unblinking gaze. "It's easy to summon ghosts. Easier than sending them away, I mean. If you're in the right place, and there are a lot of them around, it can be enough just to start talking to them. Or look at them. Or lift your hand and beckon. With me, it's music."

"What is? How do you mean?"

"The trigger. The thing I use to bring them and then to bind them. I play a tin whistle."

She laughed incredulously.

"You don't!"

I slipped my hand into my coat and brought it out.

"Jesus," said Alice with a sort of pained wonder. "The magic flute!" I let her take it from me, and she sighted along it at my face as though it was a tiny rifle. That reminded me of Ditko pretending to fire bullets at my feet to make me dance—and then of the way the whistle felt hot in my dream after I'd played it. A shiver of genuine unease passed over me. I took the whistle back from her and replaced it where it belonged: ready to hand, and only to *my* hand.

"But exorcising the ghosts is harder?" she prompted, giving me that look again.

"Usually a lot harder. But you can't make any kind of a rule about it—each one's different." I changed my tack. "Are you good at maths?"

"Better than I am at Navajos. I took it to A level—and I can multiply four-digit numbers in my head."

"Okay, then. David Hilbert. Prussian mathematician in the late nineteenth century. He reckoned you could make a mathematical model of anything—a chair, a sentence, the swirl of cream in a coffee cup, which side your balls will hang down when you put your pants on, whatever."

"Okay."

"Well, that's a way of looking at it that sort of works. I play a tune, and the tune is a model. I'm modeling the ghost. I'm . . . *describing* it in sound. But then after that—if I've done it right—it cuts both ways. I've made a link of some kind; I've tied the ghost to the sound."

I stopped. Words weren't adequate for what I did; I always got myself twisted round and upside down when I tried to explain it. But Alice was running with the idea.

"Something like a voodoo doll," she said tentatively. "I mean, a voodoo doll is a model that's intended to work in exactly that way. You make it represent a real person, either with a spell or with a fetish, like a lock of their hair or something. Then when you stick pins in the doll, the person who the doll is meant to be feels the pain."

I was impressed. That was a much better analogy than the one I'd been aiming for.

"Right," I agreed. "Well, that's what I do. I make the tune represent the ghost. I knit them together—I make them become two parts of the same thing. Then when I *stop* playing . . ."

I let the sentence hang. Again, I'd reached the point where language couldn't take me any further. What did happen to the loose spirits I packaged up and shipped out? Where was I sending them? Did they go on to greener pastures or just stop existing? I didn't know. I'd never found an explanation that didn't sound like bullshit.

"When you stop playing?" Alice pressed.

"Then the ghost stops being there. It goes away."

"Where to?"

"Wherever music goes when it's not being played."

It wasn't what she'd expected to hear, and it left her if anything even more unhappy than before. I should have known it would.

What could I tell her? My own definition of life extended from cradle to grave, and what came after that I saw as something else. If you could find your way to Heaven or Hell, all well and good. If you couldn't, you had no damn business hanging around the local chip shop or in your wife's sock drawer. In other words, if there was a natural order at all, then I was part of it—a moving finger that never wrote anything down but was really good for canceling things out.

"Try a priest," I suggested again, all out of homespun wisdom. "Or just someone you love and trust. Try Jeffrey, maybe. Talk it through. Don't run away from it. In my experience, there's nowhere to run to."

I suddenly realized at that point that Alice was staring at me in a sort of pained bewilderment.

"Jeffrey?" she said with an incredulous emphasis.

"What?"

"'Try Jeffrey'? Is that what you said?"

I thought about it, and it was.

"I meant," I tried again, "that you should talk to someone who—"

"I know what you meant, Castor. I want to know why the hell you meant it. You think Jeffrey and I are attached? Romantically attached? Did I do or say anything that would lead you to that conclusion?"

"You seem to have a good working relationship," I temporized.

"Bullshit." Alice was really angry now. "Nobody has a good working relationship with Jeffrey. The relationship that I have with him is that I do the work, and he hides behind my skirt."

"Okay." I spread my hands, offering surrender.

It was rejected. "Not okay. Not okay at all. Some whingeing creep told you I slept my way into this job, right? I knew the rumor was circulating, but I didn't know it had reached light speed. For the record, I'm senior archivist because I do the job really efficiently. And Rich isn't, because nobody except him thought he could handle it."

"Okay," I said again. I didn't want to argue with her. It wasn't like it was any of my business, after all.

She stood up, glaring down at me. "In my opinion, it's you that needs to have that talk, not me," she said. "And I don't mean with a priest or a rabbi. I mean with yourself. God helps those who help themselves, Castor. I suggest you start by taking a good, hard look at what you do for a living."

Alice grabbed her bag and left, not exactly storming out, but certainly leaving it clear that she didn't want to be followed. And I sure as hell didn't want to follow her right then. Even Good Samaritans will give up the habit if you smack them hard enough, and I wasn't going to make the same mistake twice in one evening—of doing the wrong thing because the right one wasn't available.

But as I got up, I noticed that she'd left something behind her. The heavy key ring had fallen out of her pocket onto the wooden bench, and she hadn't noticed it in the near dark of the church's interior. I picked it up, hefted the impressive weight of it. Alice wore it like a totem. She'd be really upset when she missed it—not least because it had her ID card attached to it by a bobble-chain, and she wouldn't be able to open any of the doors at the archive without it. Changing my mind, I sprinted after her.

No sign of anyone in the doorway or outside the church. By now, the drizzle had turned into steady rain. London in the wet smells like an incontinent dog, but in other ways, it's not so endearing. I gave it up and just carried on walking down toward King's Cross. I didn't even know which direction she'd taken, and in any case, it wasn't the end of the world. I'd just have to be there when the place opened the next morning to hand the keys back to her.

As I was about to go down into the Underground by the steps outside King's Cross Station, I passed a phone booth that was miraculously both intact and unused. Well, we do live in an age of signs and wonders, after all. Remembering the card in my pocket, I stopped and fished it out. I had just enough coins on me to feed the meter and get a dial tone.

7405 818. I vaguely knew the code, and I had an idea that it was somewhere fairly central. Close to the West End, if not actually in it. I dialed, and the phone at the other end rang just once.

"Hello?" A man's voice, low and smooth—slightly bored. Music was playing in the background somewhere—louche synthetic jazz. Someone laughed loudly in a way that suggested there were a lot of other people hanging around whatever place the phone was in.

"It's me," I hazarded. The only response this got was dead silence, punctuated by the complaint of a tenor sax at being inexpertly played. "From the archive," I added for the hell of it.

More silence. "Wait a moment," the man murmured. I waited. The sax had been shut off now, which meant either there'd been a mercy killing or the guy had his hand over the phone receiver.

That was all I got. He hung up.

Discovering another few twenty-pence pieces in a trouser pocket, I made a follow-on call. This time around, nobody even answered. If there was a magic word, then "archive" wasn't it. My next line was going to be "A ghost asked me to call you. Do you know why that might be?" So on the whole, it was probably all for the best.

———

I got back to Pen's house a little after seven and found it empty. Her basement rooms were locked up, and the first and second floors where she was meant to live but didn't were as chill and damp as always. I went on up to my own room in the old house's sprawling roof space.

I was aware as I unlocked the door of a heavy, slightly musty smell. That should have alerted me that something was wrong, but then again, when you live with Pen and her magic menagerie, you have to accept that earthy smells are going to be frequent houseguests.

I threw the door open.

He was sitting on the bed, and he was heavy enough so that the springs bowed under him, making a broad hollow around his broad backside. It was the guy from the pub the night before—and he didn't look any better from this close up. Worse, in fact. His face was so deeply lined that it looked as though it had been assembled from snap-together pieces, and his pale eyes had a watery gleam in them that looked somehow unhealthy. That didn't make him any less scary, though. He might be diseased, but a diseased ox can do a lot of damage.

I took a quick look around the room. The window was open a crack, but this was three flights up, and nobody of this guy's heft had any business shinnying up a drainpipe. If he'd parachuted in from a passing plane, there should have been a hole in the ceiling. That left the obvious.

"Pretty good," I acknowledged. "But at the same time, strangely pointless. Or is this performance art? You break into people's houses and then sit around waiting for a round of applause?"

A slow, pained frown crossed his slow, pained face.

"I'm Scrub," he said, as if that explained everything. "I got a job." His voice was so throaty a growl that it was barely audible at all. He sounded like he needed surgery—or maybe like he'd just had some and it hadn't taken all that well.

"That's great." I shrugged my coat off and threw it over the back of a chair. Ordinarily, I would have hung it up on the bed, but there wasn't much room around the edges of this behemoth—and I suspected that the springs were already operating at the limits of their tolerance. "Let me guess. Ballet dancer? Manicurist? Jockey?"

It wasn't a small room, but between me and him, it definitely felt crowded. I walked around the bed to the rolltop desk that I use mainly as a liquor cabinet. I threw the top back, found a glass that wasn't too grimy to see through, and poured myself a stiff whisky. It wasn't that I really felt like drinking, it was to cut the smell, which now that I was inside the room was too strong to ignore. It was a smell of things rotten and sick and ripe, left out in the open long after they should have been buried. A smell you instinctively wanted to move a long way away from.

"I got a job," he expanded, getting garrulous now, "for you."

I slugged the whisky and let it swill around my mouth before swallowing.

"Thank you," I said, "for the thought. You don't look like you've got that many to spare."

This time the frown came quicker—the patented Castor mental workout was already bearing fruit.

"That's not polite," Scrub said.

"I tend more toward brutal honesty."

His face lit up like a baggy old armchair soaked in kerosene. "Brutal? Oh, I can do brutal." He stood up, towering over me without having to make much of a big deal out of it. The look in his pale eyes was unnervingly cheerful all of a sudden. "Brutal's what I like best. 'Specially with the likes of you."

I tallied up my options and got to two. I could play nice and save myself a spectacular beating, or I could bluff.

It was unfortunate that I tallied them up in that order. There was nothing to counter the lingering echoes of my favorite word.

"Listen, you big, thick bastard," I said harshly, tilting my head back to keep eye contact with him. "You were following me all around the West End—last night, and again tonight. You just broke into my room. And you've probably fucked up my bed beyond all hope of unfucking just by dumping your big fat arse on it. So don't think you can get away with threatening me, too. Say what you've got to say, and then sod off to the black pits of fucking Tartarus, okay?"

It took a moment for Scrub to process this much information, but in the meantime, his default options kicked in. He reached out one ham-size hand and closed it on a big fistful of my shirt. Buttons popped and fabric tore as he lifted me off the ground.

His strength was incredible. He didn't even have to brace himself. My feet dangled, and my back arched involuntarily as he dragged me in close to his face. The bunched-up cloth of the shirt rode up into my armpits and pushed my arms away from my sides so that I looked as though I was trying to fly.

"Which bits of you do you need?" he asked me, his voice rasping like a saw—which by coincidence was what his breath cut like, too. "To do your stuff, I mean?"

"Every last one of them." I got the answer out somehow, in a choking gasp, but it was a struggle to keep my debonair tone. "It's a holistic thing. I lose one body part, and I'm out of tune."

"I could beat out a tune with you on that fucking wall," Scrub growled, pointing with his free hand. Even in this embarrassing predicament, with my legs treading air and my lungs unable to fill because of the way my weight was lying on the impromptu yoke of my bunched-up shirt, I was amazed. He'd picked up my metaphor and elaborated on it. He was only as stupid as a bag full of spanners, not a hat full of arseholes.

"Do it—myself—," I wheezed with the last of my breath. I let the whistle drop out of my sleeve, where I'd palmed it when I took my coat off, and held it up in front of Scrub's smirking, lumpy face.

"Bluff" was the wrong word for it. It was an educated guess.

He smacked the whistle out of my hand so fast and so hard that he almost took the hand with it. Then in one effortless wave of motion, he lifted me and slammed me down onto the rolltop desk, where his heavy hand, with his full weight bearing down on it, held me pinned. My head slammed against the wood, which was cherry with a brass inlay. I saw stars, bells, and tweeting baby birds. Scrub's meaty forefinger prodded my cheek.

"You ever," he said with a calm that was a lot scarier than his earlier bluster, "raise that thing near me again, and you will live out your frigging life with nothing between your legs except a ragged hole."

"Just kidding," I said when I could say anything. There was a ringing in my ears, and I couldn't hear my own voice. "But now we know where we stand, eh? So what's this job you were talking about?"

"You fucking scumbag!" Scrub spat. But he lifted his hand away and took a step back, giving me room to haul myself off the desk and get on my feet again.

"Yeah, right," I agreed, wiping my mouth with the back of my hand and finding that the warmth there was blood; I must have bitten my tongue when he threw me down. There was a sharp ache across my shoulders and a dull one in my head. To make a point, though, I turned my back on him and retrieved the whistle from where it lay against the far wall. I had him taped now, although in the process, I suspected I'd made an enemy for life. I couldn't resist prodding the bruise one more time, though, for the sake of my self-respect. "What sort of a face did you have before this one, then, Scrub? And what sort of a name? Rover, was it?"

I half expected him to hit me anyway and take the consequences later, but he didn't. Just as well, because a punch from one of Scrub's hands would end most fights before they'd even got started and probably lay me out for what was left of the night—assuming I ever woke up from it at all. I think that was what stopped him, to be honest. He had his orders, and he took them very seriously.

"The gentleman who employs me wants some cleaning done," he said at last, after a range of scary emotions had passed across his face. "Couple of hours' work. Couple of ton in your hand."

"When and where?" I asked, pulling back the chair that went with the desk and sitting down—carefully, because of the pain in my upper back.

"Down Clerkenwell. Now. He's waiting."

"Not now," I said. "Can't be done. I'm finished for the night."

Scrub, in two giant steps, crossed the room.

"You want to be finished, I'll finish you," he rasped. "Otherwise, you come now."

I'd taken it as far as I could, so I gave it up. Some men have greatness thrust upon them.

Nine

THERE WAS A CAR OUTSIDE ON THE STREET, WHICH I'd seen on my way in but hadn't really registered. It was a squat, powerful BMW X5 in electric blue, with tinted windows and a showy, diamond-cut grille, so God knows I *should* have noticed it. I must have been wandering in and out of the afterlife, which isn't exactly unusual for me.

It was still raining. Scrub had given me about a tenth of a second to grab my coat before herding me down the stairs. I wished to Christ he'd stop long enough to let me put the bastard thing on.

The big man threw open the BMW's rear door and I climbed in, with a small assist from his mighty right arm. He climbed in after me, making even a car of this weight and build rock slightly on its wheelbase. There were two other men, both in the front of the car. The one in the passenger seat, who looked like he numbered weasels among his close relations, glanced round at me and gave me a nasty smile. The driver was a stolid blond with a face that looked a bit like Tom the cartoon cat's face after it's been hit with a frying pan. He peeled away from the curb with a flick of his hand on the wheel and the breathless sigh of German engineering.

They drove me back into town again, down through Stamford Hill and Dalston, then veering west through the back streets of

Shoreditch—a meandering route that had us dipping down past Old Street only to swing back and cross it again, going north. Finally the car pulled up somewhere off Myddelton Square in Clerkenwell, in a street so narrow you could hardly get the doors all the way open.

I stepped out into the rain, now a heavy downpour, with another encouraging push from Scrub to get me moving. The weasel from the front passenger seat alighted, too, and the car drove off again as soon as our feet hit the ground.

We were standing in front of a club with blacked-out windows and a gaudy sign. KISSING THE PINK. The brickwork around the windows was painted dark blue, though, and there was a gilded eagle on a rock done in haut relief above the door—the universal secret sign of old Truman Hanbury pubs bought up on the dead-cat bounce and converted into strip joints—which, of course, was Clerkenwell's boom industry these days.

I glanced up at Scrub, who caught my look and nodded brusquely. We went inside.

There was a foyer, of sorts. It was a corner room with walls slightly off the true, converging toward the street side. Polished bare boards bore the muddy paw prints of early-evening punters. A man sitting at a desk in a shallow recess off to the right glanced up as we walked in and then, seeing Scrub, ignored us completely. We passed through unmolested into the club.

It was bigger than it looked from the street, with a semicircular stage against one wall, a bar opposite, and a dozen or so circular tables in between. There were also booths around three of the walls, the lighting carefully arranged to leave them in shadow so that from inside them, you could see without being seen.

On the stage, a blonde woman who was more or less naked already was finding some tiny items of clothing she'd missed on an earlier pass and taking them off. A polished silver pole extending from stage to ceiling was her constant support and occasional stage property. A dozen or so guys in tailored suits, relaxing no doubt from a hard day in the City, and a half-dozen more, who looked like tourists, were staring at her gravity-defying breasts with a willing suspension of disbelief. Most were absorbed enough not to notice our passing, but a few who found themselves in or close to Scrub's lumbering path drew their feet in hastily and then stared at me with a slight comic double take. I didn't blame them—my torn shirt, now soaking wet, was sticking to my chest, and there was probably still a little blood on my face from where I'd bitten my tongue. I had the sartorial élan of Robinson Crusoe.

Scrub was still pushing, so I kept on moving. We walked right across to the far side of the room, to one of the booths that I now realized was occupied. A short, heavy-featured man who looked to be in his early fifties was sitting there alone, facing us, reading and scribbling in a ring-bound notebook. As far as I could tell in this light, his complexion was both florid and pockmarked. His eyebrows were the heaviest I'd ever seen, and his eyes were scrunched up and tamped down underneath them like two miniature worlds with Atlas's hairy arse-cheeks sitting right on top of them. He was wearing a royal blue suit over a shirt in some kind of paisley design, and his tie was as wide and as bright as a centurion's shield. Having been watching *Man from U.N.C.L.E.* repeats on cable TV recently, I was inescapably reminded of Mr. Waverly.

"So you're an ass man?" he said to me, glancing up. The blunt words contrasted oddly with the smooth, cultured voice; it was a voice that ought to have been introducing guest speakers or proposing loyal toasts. But that suggests a certain po-faced solemnity, and this was also a voice that smiled at its own pretensions. There was the faintest hint of an accent in it—or rather, maybe, the complete absence of an accent that only comes with learning English from a book.

I just looked at the guy with a solemn frown—as though I was considering the philosophical implications of the question.

"I watched you as you were watching the act," he said, his shoulders heaving as he chuckled throatily. "You prefer the steatopygous perspective, because that's where your eyes kept going. Ergo, you're an ass man. It's always good to know."

With these formalities now over and done with, the man turned to Scrub and the weasel, his hand flicking from one to the other in a brusque benediction. "Scrub, you stay with us. Arnold, you're back on the door—and tell one of the ladies to come round and get Mr. Castor a drink, if you please. Saffron—or Rosa. Make it Rosa. She offers a rear view that Mr. Castor should find engaging."

The weasel darted away while Scrub faded into the background— to the limited extent that a man the size of a forklift truck can do that. I stopped thinking about Mr. Waverly, and Sydney Greenstreet in *The Maltese Falcon* loomed up to fill the gap. A squat, squashed-down Sydney Greenstreet. In paisley.

"I'm Lucasz Damjohn," my host said. Luke-ash—not a name I'd ever heard before. "Please, Mr. Castor, you're putting me at a disadvantage. Sit down."

I dumped my coat, which I'd been carrying all this while, over the side wall of the booth and sat down opposite him. He nodded as if, along with my obedience, rightness and order had come back into the universe.

"Excellent," he said. "Did I call you away from anything important, or were you merely relaxing after a hard day?"

"I run a twenty-four-hour service," I said, which made him smile, very quickly on and then off.

"Yes, I'm sure. Since I started using Scrub as a messenger, *everyone* seems to run a twenty-four-hour service. And everyone makes house calls. I'm sorry if that was heavy-handed, but I'm not the kind of a man who finds it easy to wait. Quite the contrary. I belong to the lamentable breed who find that inactivity leads naturally to impatience and then to aggression. My formal education, you see, was never completed—and so I lack the inner resources that are necessary to make profitable use of idle time. I need stimulation, or boredom quickly sets in." He threw me a glance full of speculative concern. "Is that the case with you, Felix? Do you feel that you're getting enough stimulation in your life?"

Felix? I was Felix now? That came out of nowhere, and it threw me slightly, but with the massive form of Scrub still looming in my peripheral vision, I decided the better part of valor was to let it pass. "I'm not complaining," I offered by way of nonanswer.

Damjohn nodded vigorously, as if I'd said something profound. "Well, indeed. Nobody is going to listen if you do, so where's the profit in it? Where's the profit?"

He stopped and looked up as a woman approached the table. Or a girl, maybe; she didn't look much over seventeen, although presumably she'd have to have been to work in a place like this. Her face was beautiful: heart-shaped, dark-eyed, with lustrous chestnut-brown hair worn in a ponytail that extended down to the middle of her back. Her lips were sensuously full and glossily red, her skin pale except for a single overemphasized spot of blush on each cheek. Beautiful, like I said, but blank; the gaudy makeup only embellished the emptiness of her expression in the same way that the revealing costume emphasized how little she had in the way of breasts. Her eyes were dark with a natural darkness under the layers of mascara and eyeliner: more bleak than soulful, though. She didn't look like she enjoyed her job much.

"Whisky and water, please, Rosa," Damjohn said, flicking her a glance that was brief enough to count as subliminal. "And for yourself, Felix?"

"That sounds fine to me," I said.

Rosa turned to go, but Damjohn reached out a hand and touched her wrist with the tip of his index finger, which was enough to make her stop and turn back again, looking expectantly at him as if she was waiting for further orders.

"This is a very important guest we have here," he said with heavy jocularity. "Mr. Felix Castor. In case you've never heard of him, Rosa, he's a big man in the ghost business. An exorcist, I mean. An inspector of specters."

Rosa's gaze flicked to me, her face as inscrutable as a death mask. Damjohn looked over at me, too, as though somehow he was making this ham-fisted joke for my benefit. I stayed deadpan. God knew, I didn't want to give him any encouragement.

"When we've finished our little chat, Felix will go upstairs and give our premises a thorough examination," Damjohn continued after a pause that seemed significant in a way I didn't quite get. "Tell the girls to keep their backs to the wall, please. You see, Felix is an ass man."

He lifted his finger from the back of Rosa's hand, and she left without a backward glance. Damjohn returned his attention to me—although to be honest, it seemed as though he'd been watching me all the time.

"So, as you will have gathered, I need to have the place cleaned," he said. "You can do that, I presume? Put down the vermin? Caulk and seal, so that nothing untoward pops its head up and scares the girls when they ought to be working?"

I played stupid for the hell of it—and because I always like the client to spell out exactly what it is he wants. "Do you mean cockroaches, or—"

"Please," Damjohn said with an impatient horizontal slash of his stubby hand—an erasure mark hanging in the air between us. "I mean ghosts, Felix. Ghosts. I'm perfectly capable of stamping on cockroaches without instruction or assistance."

"And what makes you think you've got a haunting, Mr. Damjohn?" I asked, bedside manner kicking in again hard.

He grimaced disapprovingly. The woman on stage slid down the pole into a precarious position, sitting back on her haunches with her legs spread wide, and the scattershot applause forced a momentary silence on us. "I don't believe I told you what I thought," Damjohn said when the clapping had died down again and the woman had departed. Incongruously, a wide-screen TV slid down from the ceiling over the center of the stage area, showing highlights from what looked to be a Manchester City game. "But women," Damjohn mused, "have a very delicate sensibility. A curtain blows open or a pipe gurgles, and they think they've received a message from the other side." He tapped the spine of his book, frowning momentarily as if he was pursuing that thought a little further. "For my own part, I've never knowingly received a message of that kind. But then, it would be a matter of complete indifference to me if I ever did. Certainly I don't think a vengeful ghost would intimidate me at all. If some man had a grudge against me, it would be my personal preference to have him dead rather than alive, you understand? I'd see that more as a convenience than as anything else." He looked at me again, solemn-eyed. Eyebrows like that could provide a lot of solemnity.

"A convenience," I echoed cautiously. "Right." I was missing a lot here, enough so I was beginning to feel irritated and hard-done-by. Rosa came back with the drinks and set them in front of us. I watched her with a certain curiosity, but this time she kept her gaze fixed on her tray and walked away briskly as soon as she was done. She did have a cute bum, despite her slim build. But she wasn't even close to being my type. I don't go much for the "imagine me in a school uniform" look.

I took a sip of the whisky. Single malt, and good single malt, at that. I wished I'd passed on the water.

"So you just want me to inspect the premises and see whether I can find any sign of ghost or poltergeist activity," I summed up.

"Yes."

"Because the girls don't like it."

"Again, yes."

"Then how do they cope with Scrub?" I asked, hooking my thumb over my shoulder at the big man, who was standing behind me as impassively as one of the guards at Buck House.

Damjohn gave me a look of puzzled innocence. "Scrub? You think that Scrub is a ghost, Felix? He looks solid enough to me."

He evidently wanted me to tell him what he already knew. "Scrub is a *loup-garou*," I said. "They used to be called werewolves, although I doubt whether the animal part of Scrub is a wolf. It would have to be something the size of a bull." I took another sip of the whisky. If the wardrobe that walked like a man decided to take offence at my tone, it would be a shame for this fine liquor to go to waste as well as my head getting broken. "You see, what happens is that a human ghost possesses an animal host, and then it sort of moves in and redecorates. The ghost reshapes the animal body according to its memories of its own original form. It sheds fur, shifts muscle tissue around . . . makes itself look more or less human again.

"It was a French scientist—Nicole David—who first nailed this, and that's how come we use the French word for it. It's sort of an open question how long the human shape can be maintained—depends on the strength of the ghost's will, mainly—but the animal is always going to reassert itself whenever it can. Dark of the moon seems to be the time when the human side is weakest and the animal side is strongest. Hell of a thing. Once you've seen a *loup-garou* make the change, you never forget it. You can try, but you never forget it."

Damjohn had been watching me keenly all the way through this speech, and I was about halfway into it before I realized that Scrub was a sort of audition piece—a hurdle for me to jump. Well, I'd jumped it, and now I sat back and waited to see what my prize was going to be.

Damjohn smiled and nodded, visibly pleased.

"That was very good," he said. "Very good indeed. I know another man in your line of business, and he didn't make that identification straight away—or without prompting. I can see that you're a man of some intellect, Felix."

"Thank you, Lucasz."

What was sauce for the goose came near to choking the gander. Damjohn's eyes, already screwed up almost invisibly small, disappeared for a moment in their own intricate folds as he digested this small touch of warmth and familiarity. But he bounced back again and didn't stoop so low as to make a whole thing out of it. He changed the subject instead. "In terms of remuneration," he said, "I can offer you an arrangement that I think you'll find to your liking."

I didn't like the sound of that. When you've previously heard a precise sum, and then you hear the words "an arrangement," or "sweet deal," or for that matter "undying gratitude," in my experience, any movement you're making is in the wrong direction. "The sum of two hundred pounds was mentioned," I pointed out.

"Of course it was. It was I who mentioned it. But if you wanted to factor in some time with Rosa or one of my other girls, then that could also be arranged. Pari passu."

So Damjohn was a pimp as well as a club owner. He had very refined manners for a pimp—but then a pimp with a public-school accent could have ended up as a lawyer; you had to give him credit for his moral integrity. I saw what he was doing, though, and I didn't like it.

"Pari passu?" I repeated, sitting back. "And pro bono publico? Very laudable. But given that we only just met, we should probably keep this on a cash-and-carry basis."

Damjohn's manner became a little less cordial, but on the credit side, he didn't bitch-slap me. "As you wish. But you'll do the job? Now? Tonight?"

There's a time and a place for the lecture that I gave to Peele, about how slow and steady wins the race. This wasn't it. I could take a look around, and I could lay down some wards if it turned out they were necessary. If he had a real problem on his hands, we'd have to renegotiate. I shrugged. "Well, now that I'm here . . ."

"Good. Scrub, take Mr. Castor upstairs."

My audience was over. Damjohn gave me a slightly austere nod and returned to his figures. Scrub lumbered forward as I stood up, then waited at my shoulder as I drained the whisky in a sacrilegiously quick swallow. He led the way, off to the far right, where an unmarked door stood open in a corner of the room, left strategically unlit. Like the main door that led from the foyer into the club, this one, too, had its own Saint Peter: a slab-face Saint Peter in a rumpled tux. He gave Scrub a respectful nod and stood aside to let him pass through. I followed in his wake.

On the other side of the door there was a staircase, and at the top of the staircase there was another bar. Nobody was dancing up here, or at least not vertically and not anywhere I could see. About a dozen women in unfeasible underwear sat at the bar in small groups, talking in low voices. They all looked me over as I walked in, but seeing that I was with Scrub, they lost whatever interest they'd had in turning a trick and went back to their conversations.

"The members' lounge," Scrub rumbled.

Some old jokes rise from the dead often enough to arouse my professional concern, but there was nothing in Scrub's imperturbable grimace to suggest that he saw the funny side of that phrase. I looked from him to the little clusters of working girls, then back again.

"How does Damjohn want me to do this?" I demanded. The thought of looking under the beds while these good ladies were earning their keep on top of them didn't delight me.

"Check the knobs," said Scrub.

Oh lord. I looked at him with pained interest, deciding that there had to be more.

He held his hand out in front of my face, fingers together, palm vertical—the "paper" position from rock/paper/scissors. "If the knob's like that, the room's empty. If it's like this"—he rotated his hand through ninety degrees—"then there's someone in there."

"And what do I do with the occupied ones?"

"Miss them out," rumbled Scrub. "Unless you want to look through the keyholes."

I let that pass and started on my rounds. I'd been in three brothels in my life—one in Karachi (looking for beer), one on the Mile End Road (in my professional capacity), and the third in Nevada in a moment of weakness I regretted afterward and even during. All three

had had a lot of things in common, and this one was cut from the
same cloth. The rooms were all one degree more desolate even than
hotel rooms. Each one just had the bed, the functional center of the
room, a table with a few girly magazines strewn across it like holiday
brochures ("you're going to Brighton again this year, but would you
like to see Paris, Rome, and the Algarve?") and a small pedal bin with
a thick plastic bag as a liner. There were no pictures on the walls and
no ornaments on the bedside tables. No Gideon Bibles, either—this
wasn't the sort of place where either clients or employees let the distant prospect of salvation get in the way of the job in hand.

They were all clean, too. Not physically clean (although in fact
they were that, too), but *meta*physically clean. To tell the truth, I was
a little spooked by it. It wasn't just that there were no ghosts—a lot of
places get away without being actively haunted. But any place that's
lived in ought to have a few psychic fingerprints on it: echoes of old
emotions held in the stones or the air or the dust on the windowsill.
This place had nothing. It felt like it had been scrubbed clean.

In other words, it didn't need an exorcist because one had been
through there already and done an immaculate job.

The rooms were on two floors, thirty-eight in all and twenty-one
that were empty—still early, I suppose. I was as thorough as I know
how to be. I even ventured into the bathrooms, which being the backstage area, so to speak, were a fair bit less polished than the bedrooms.
But here too there was nothing to make my antennae quiver, unless
the absence of anything suspicious is suspicious in its own right.

I reported back to Scrub. He was leaning against the bar at one
end, and all of the whores had casually gravitated to the other end. It
wasn't just me who found the big man's presence unsettling. When
he saw me coming, he stood up, straightened his jacket with a shrug,
and led the way back down the stairs.

"Felix!" Damjohn exclaimed, as if I'd been gone for hours and he'd
started to get worried about me. He laid down his pen and closed his

ledger, gesturing me once again to sit down facing him, but this time I didn't bother.

"You're spotless," I told him. "Whiter than white. Under the circumstances, I'll be happy to settle for half of what we agreed, since I didn't have to do anything besides—"

He waved me silent.

"Nonsense," he said. "Nonsense, Felix. I'm only too grateful you were able to come." This was overlooking the fact that he'd sent Scrub along to make sure that I did. "Scrub, please take Mr. Castor through to the front desk and tell Arnold to pay him out of petty cash. Felix, a pleasure."

He held out his hand, and reflexively I took it. That was a mistake.

FLASH. *They're all lined up on the concrete apron behind the factory's loading bay. Men in green overalls, almost like those that doctors wear in the west, but darker; women in dirty smocks, their hair bound up in scarves. They all smell faintly of vinegar, because what the factory does, in the autumn months at least, is bottle pickles. The captain is happy and strokes my hair. He has to lean down, because even for my age, I'm small. "Which one is Bozin?" he murmurs, and I show him just by looking. He nods. Bozin evidently looks as the captain thinks he should. He gestures to the soldiers, who haul the man out of the line. A middle-age man like all the others, his face stolid and stupid. The captain puts away his pistol, which he has been waving, and borrows a rifle from one of the soldiers. Then he drives the butt of the rifle three times into that stupid, belligerent face while two of the soldiers hold Bozin upright. The blows are hard. The man's nose is smashed, his teeth driven into his throat, one eye caved in. But when he falls to the ground, he isn't yet dead. He's still making liquid gurgling noises in his throat. The captain turns to me, makes a gesture that means "help yourself." I kick Bozin in the balls.*

FLASH. *The woman, Mercedes, has become a point of pride with me, a badge that I wear when I go out at night. Her beauty, her sophistication, the expensive gloss that covers her like a sheath, these are the signs that I'm not a boy anymore. They say to everyone who sees us "Look at me and respect me." Her very name is the name of a luxury car, a possession that screams out your status to the world. I'm sorry, sometimes, that I have to treat her with such cold contempt, but that's the very heart of the matter. For me to win respect, I have to show that she needs and merits none. The more I belittle her, the greater I am. At first this is hard. But then one night we quarrel. She tries to leave me, and I beat her. That beating—the inflicting of terrible and unnecessary pain on someone who has brought me so much pleasure—is an annunciation. It's so hard to stop.*

FLASH. *The houses that still stand are burning. I walk through the streets at my leisure, because no more shells will fall. I had property here, but nothing that I couldn't afford to lose; I may even be compensated when the United Nations arrives with all its democratic fanfares and its bureaucratic paraphernalia. I contemplate a house that is about to fall, and I draw this moral. Yugoslavia itself was a house, precariously built and supported by only one beam. When that beam—Tito's Communist party—was kicked away, it was inevitable that the boisterous children fighting and playing inside would bring the house down on their heads. Their heads, not mine. The house collapses in a shower of sparks and a billowing gust of ash and smoke that envelops me and blinds me for a moment. In the wreckage, a slender hand and arm, burned black—a child's arm, perhaps, or the arm of a woman of slender build. Of course. That was what I was smelling. I wipe a smut of ash from my alpaca coat and am annoyed to find that it smears greasily rather than flaking off. This has become an uncivilized and tainted place. I walk on, but without hurry. There's twelve hours yet before the plane leaves.*

I jerked my hand away fast, my teeth coming together with an audible *clack*. That touch—that subliminal data-squirt of impressions—had taken less than a second.

Damjohn stared at me for a long, wordless moment. He knew from my face that something had just happened; he wasn't sure what. He considered asking, weighing curiosity against the loss of authority he might suffer. I saw him make up his mind.

"I'm sure we'll meet again," he said at last, smiling a bland, meaningless smile. Just as he'd done before, he signaled that I was dismissed by lowering his eyes to his book. Scrub, who had missed the whole thing, was already lumbering back across the stage area toward the street door. A new blonde was dancing her way through a new set of lingerie, and the ranks of the mug punters had grown mighty.

Snatching up my coat, I crossed the room in Scrub's broad wake. I had to fight against the bitter bile that was coming up in my throat. I kept it down. I wished I could do the same with the crawling tide of images and impressions that was still washing around inside my brain. I swore to myself that I was never coming here again, even if that hairy-eyed bastard sent the French Foreign Legion to pick me up.

The weasel man, Arnold, was now sitting at the desk in the foyer. Scrub muttered the words "Two ton" as he walked by, then took up his station on the pavement outside. I found it hard to believe that his presence would encourage the passing trade, although the club didn't seem to be having any trouble in that regard. The rain had slackened off now, and the evening was once again fresh and blustery. Maybe that helped.

Arnold paid me out in fives and tens with silent, laborious concentration, his lips moving as he counted. I took it in silence and stuffed it into my back pocket. I'm not averse to dirty money, up to a point, but I wasn't feeling very happy with myself right then. I came out onto the street, hoping but not expecting to see the BMW roll smoothly around the corner and pull up right in front of me. No such luck; there wasn't the same urgency about getting me home as there had been about bringing me here. Scrub's heavy hand fell on my shoulder.

I turned. He was looking down at me with a sort of ponderous calculation.

"You use music," he pointed out, basso profundo.

I knew what he meant. "Yeah, I use music."

"You play a little tune."

"Right."

He touched me lightly on the Adam's apple with the tip of his forefinger.

"I could rip your throat out before you got to the second note."

His point made, he lumbered back inside.

I headed off into the night, the chill wind cutting into me and a writhing nest of worms inside my head. I was restless, I was wet, and I was a long way from home. Okay, not geographically, maybe, but psychologically. The weird encounter with Damjohn had got to me and unsettled me—the contents of his head clinging to me like half-dried vomit. In pure self-defence, I pulled my thoughts around to the situation at the Bonnington. That didn't make me any happier, but at least it exercised my mind in a different way.

I was down to the last knockings of the Russian collection, and if I came up blank, I'd have nothing to cover my embarrassment. Could I be wrong about the ghost being linked to those documents? I'd taken a few swipes with Occam's razor, and that was what I'd ended up with, but that didn't make it so. I really didn't want to have to retreat and regroup with Peele and Alice breathing down my neck on either side.

There were still those last few boxes, though. It was possible that Sod's Law was operating, and that the ghost's anchor was just going to turn out to be one of the documents at the very bottom of the stack.

I shrugged into my coat, slid my hand into the pocket by reflex, and felt the spiky, angular mass of Alice's keys.

Ten

I GOT INTERESTED IN LOCKS BACK WHEN I WAS working up the magic act at university. I had the idea that I could build in some escapology as well, so I went down to London looking for a shop that would sell me a pair of handcuffs. I learned a lot from that exercise, but more about the outer limits of consensual sex than about escapology.

Then Jimmy, the barman at the Welsh Pony on Gloucester Green, mentioned a guy he knew: Tom Wilke, the Banbury Bandit, who'd just finished a two-year stretch for breaking and entering. "They did him on two dozen specimen counts, with about a hundred more taken into consideration. He'd be your man," Jimmy said. "Any kind of lock. He says he can do them blindfolded."

I was young enough to find the thought of chatting to a career criminal appealing, so I asked Jimmy for the guy's address. Jimmy said he'd have to set it up first and left me to stew for about a week. I went in there every night to ask him if he'd seen Wilke and if he'd asked him, but the answer was always no.

Then one night, there was a different answer; it was sod off.

"Sorry, Fix," Jimmy said apologetically. "He's not himself since he got out of Bullingdon. He's gone very quiet. Doesn't want to talk to anyone or have anyone round. Maybe it's just something he's going through. I'll ask him again in a few months."

But I couldn't wait that long; I had to be doing it now. I worked on Jimmy until he gave me Wilke's address just to get rid of me, and I went round to see him myself.

Tom Wilke lived in a flat on some grubby estate off the ring road, three floors up with no lift. It was eerily silent, as if the whole place was empty: no kids on the stairs, no music blaring out of open windows, even though it was high summer. I knocked on the door and waited, knocked and waited some more. When it was clear that no one was going to answer, I turned around to leave.

Just as I got to the stairs, I heard a sound that made me turn.

A sob. Somebody crying. I listened for a minute or so and it came again, from behind the door I'd just knocked on. A heartbroken, strangled sob.

I went back and tried the door. It opened. Fortune favors the pure of heart and the brassy of bollock.

Inside, a hallway just two steps wide, then an open door that led through into a poky living room—cramped despite the fact that there was almost no furniture there. A middle-age man with a shock of white hair and a build so spare he looked malnourished was sitting in a spavined G-plan chair by the light of a bare bulb, with tears running down his cheeks.

I thought at first that the curtains were drawn, but they weren't. It was just that the windows were covered in smeary black ash so thick that even the light from a streetlamp right outside could barely filter through them. Floor, walls, furniture—everything else in the room except for the man himself was all similarly covered.

Tom Wilke was so drunk that he couldn't even stand up, and when I knelt down next to the chair, his eyes could barely focus on me. He had no idea who I was, but my sudden appearance didn't seem to faze or anger him. He pleaded with me, his free hand pawing at my sleeve.

In the other hand he was gripping a bottle of Grant's with about a quarter of its contents left. His breath stank like a distillery.

"I always lock the door," he said, "so they don't notice I've been. Takes them longer. Always lock the door . . ."

Since his own door hadn't been locked or bolted, that puzzled me for a moment. Then I realized he wasn't talking about his own door.

"Never hurt anyone," Wilke was mumbling now, shaking his head in pained disbelief. "Never carry a knife, a gun, anything. Colin said keep five quids' worth of change in a sock. Tap them on the head if they get bolshie. No. Never did it. Never needed to. In and out, me. Every time."

I ran my hand along the arm of the chair, which was as greasily filthy with ash as everything else in the room. Then I looked at the tips of my fingers. Clean.

I went and made some coffee, but it was for me, not for Wilke. He finished off the whisky, and I pieced together the story from his stop-start ramblings, although sometimes his tears made him completely incomprehensible.

One of the houses he'd done, just before he'd gone inside, had been a semi down on Blackbird Leys. A shabby-looking place, but a mate who worked for UPS had told him the bloke who lived there took orders for his hi-fi shop at home sometimes. There was a chance of a good take, and he'd borrowed a van for the night.

It took Wilke ages to find the place. It was on one of those godforsaken estates that seem to be built on some sort of fractal system, with endless identical streets opening off each other and feeding into each other so that you're lost before you start.

But he found it at last, and getting inside was a piece of cake. It would have been sweet as a nut after all, except that there was nothing there; not just no hi-fi kit, nothing worth taking at all. In one of the bedrooms, a kid in a cot, heavily asleep all by itself—no jewelry, no money, no portable electronic stuff. Even the TV had a cracked casing, so nobody was going to touch it.

So he left again, as quietly as he'd come, pissed off and bitter and rehearsing the words he was going to have with this UPS wallah. He was basically running on automatic. He locked the front door behind him, forgetting that it had been unlocked when he arrived. He wrote the night off. He went home. He went to bed.

The next morning, in the *Oxford Mail*, he read that a two-year-old had burned to death in a house on Blackbird Leys. The address, which he'd spent so long trying to find the night before, jumped out at him from the page. There couldn't be any possibility of a mistake.

"They couldn't get in," Wilke mumbled, his rambling despair going on and on in an endless loop. "They came back, and the house was on fire. How the fuck? Nothing. Don't understand it. I didn't touch anything, did I? They couldn't get in. Door was locked, and nobody had the key. When they got there, it was all burned down . . ."

He whined like a wounded animal. The whisky bottle fell out of his hand and rolled across the floor as Wilke covered his eyes and rocked and moaned through clenched teeth.

It was about a week—maybe as long as two—before it started to happen. He wasn't even in his own place the first time; he was at a café, eating a bacon sandwich and talking to a couple of likely lads about a possible warehouse job. Pretending it was business as usual, when inside he kept hearing a kid crying in an empty house, and he couldn't concentrate on what anyone was saying for more than a sentence or two at a time.

Black ash began to settle on the table, on his plate, on the men he was talking to. He jumped up with a shouted curse, which made the two men he was dealing with stare at him as if he was insane. He responded aggressively—were they blind or something?—and things got unpleasant. Wilke realized that nobody except him could see the ash. Then he ran a hand through it and realized why that was.

The haunting had continued ever since. He'd never seen an actual ghost. It was just that wherever he was, the ash would start to fall, and the longer he stayed anywhere, the thicker it got. It was even in his dreams, so that avenue of escape was barred.

After a few weeks, he was thinking about suicide. After talking to a priest, he gave himself up instead. He provided the police with a list of the houses, offices, and warehouses he'd burgled, with the Blackbird Leys address at the top of the list. He told them everything they needed to know to bring a case, and when they did, standing in the dock in a rain of ash that nobody else could see, he pleaded guilty on all counts.

Wilke thought it would stop then. He thought he'd done enough to atone. But nothing changed. He knew now that nothing ever would. He was using alcohol to blunt the horror, and when alcohol stopped working, he'd probably go back to option A and top himself.

My emotions as I listened to this were ricocheting around like rubber bullets inside a Dumpster. What the man had done was horrendous. Unforgivable. Everything he'd suffered he'd deserved, ten times over. But he hadn't set out to kill anybody. He'd just done something stupid and then tried his best to pay for it, only to discover that he was facing a life sentence without appeal. I stood over him and judged him—guilty, then innocent, then guilty again—before finally reaching the only conclusion I could: that it wasn't my call.

"I think there's another way out of this, Tom," I told him. "I think we can help each other."

It took about a week of sleeping on his floor and sitting in his death-dark room every day before I finally got a scent of the little ghost that was hiding in all that sifting ash. Such a huge weight of fear and despair from such a tiny source. I caught its attention with nursery rhymes: "The Grand Old Duke of York," "The Old Woman Tossed Up in a Basket," "Boys and Girls Come Out to Play." After that, it was easy. The light broke through the ash as I played, and the room resumed its normal colors. When I finished, all that greasy, granular pain was gone. A scream that had addressed itself to the eye instead of the ear had stopped echoing at last.

I felt exhausted. I felt compromised, and sleazy, and black with ash that couldn't be seen anymore. I got up to go, but Wilke wouldn't let me. He was in my debt, and with gratitude as extreme as his earlier grief, he insisted on paying. He took me through every kind of lock there was, starting with simple levers and wards, then working through every kind of tumbler, pin, wafer, and disc, before finishing off with ultramodern master-keyed systems that are about as relevant to normal escapology as depleted uranium shells are to the game of darts.

I lapped it up. I was the best pupil he ever had. And the first, and the last; he got religion after that and took holy orders. I never saw him again.

———————

I mention all this only to make a point, and the point is this: I didn't need Alice's keys. With enough time and with the tools I'd inherited from Tom Wilke, I could have got into any room in the archive. No, what I needed was Alice's ID card, because the locks were all wired up to the readers on each door. A key alone would open them, but would also sound an alarm. This way, I could slip in and out with nobody the wiser. I hoped.

The place felt different at night.

I mean that in a literal sense; it had a different set of resonances, a different tonality. And since it was empty—since there was no other human presence there to dilute the effect with feelings and associations of its own—I felt the full weight of it as I walked through the darkened corridors.

It was a sad weight, even a sinister one. There was a flavor in the air like cruelty and pointless anger. Obviously, unless you're in the business, you'll have to just imagine that those things have flavors—for me they do.

I found my way to the Russian room, swiped myself in as Alice Gascoigne, and got stuck into the boxes again. There were only seven left, so a couple of hours at most would see me through to the end. I turned one bank of lights on; the strong room had no windows, so there was no chance of being seen from the street. After a minute or so of treading water, I got back into the flow, and time soon became suspended again in the murky laminations of the past.

On some level I was aware of a motorcycle driving by in the street outside, setting up a sympathetic vibration in the floor beneath my feet. Then there was silence again, even deeper for having been broken.

I was back in the rhythm of the psychic trawl, my fingers flicking across the papers, tapping out a pianissimo signature that nobody but me could disentangle. I took it slowly, very slowly, because as I neared the bottom of the stack, I was lingering longer over each sprawl of papers, more and more reluctant to take no for an answer.

But I got to the final handful at last, and I had to admit it to myself.

Nothing. Nothing at all. Not one out of all these voices speaking faintly through faded ink and yellowed paper was the voice of the Bonnington ghost.

I stared at the last clutch of documents in dumb chagrin. I'd been so certain that the thread would be there for me to pick up; the logic of it was so clear. But logic had let me down.

For a moment I thought about going back and starting again. It was a grisly prospect, but I had no other leads to pick up. If the ghost wouldn't appear to me directly, I'd have to rely on something it had touched while it was still alive. Something that still held the imprint of its mind and personality . . .

Sometimes I miss a trick that's so obvious, I wonder if there's any hope for me at all. I came bolt upright in the chair, swearing at my own stupidity. Then I reached across for my coat and started to rummage in the pockets.

I didn't have anything that the ghost had touched during its lifetime. But I had one thing that it had definitely touched since.

I pulled out the crumpled Rolodex card and held it up to examine it in the none-too-bright BS 5454 light.

I'd never tried this before, but there was no reason why it shouldn't work. Okay, a ghost throwing its weight around isn't quite the same proposition as a living human being touching something, but on the other hand, the trail was that much more recent. At any rate, it had to be worth a try.

Gripping the card firmly in both hands, I closed my eyes and listened with my mind. There was nothing there, but since this was the turning after the last-chance saloon, I held on. Still nothing. But after a long, strained moment, in the dead center of the nothing, a different *kind* of nothing opened up—the pregnant pause of dense, focused attention. It was as though I was holding a telephone receiver and I'd made a weak connection. Now someone on the other end was waiting for me to speak.

It wasn't what I was expecting, but like I've always said, if life gives you lemmings, jump off a cliff.

"Hello," I said.

No answer. I wasn't really expecting any; I was just showing willing. But if the link that had opened up between me and the ghost wasn't verbal, there had to be some other way to use it.

For a while I just waited, hoping that something might come into my mind without me reaching for it—some idea or emotion flowing from the ghost into me, bringing with it the pinpoint fix that I needed for the cantrip. But it seemed like the ghost was waiting, too.

I'm not sure where inspiration came from, but it came suddenly, and in spite of the sheer ludicrousness of the idea, I went for it: twenty questions. In that game, you zero in on the answer by asking broad, general questions first and then getting more and more specific. Maybe I could coax the ghost into playing a quick round with me.

I let my mind go blank, my emotions drift back down to neutral— like tapping a compass with your thumbnail to make sure the needle is floating free.

Then I started to think without thinking.

I'd like to say that this was an eastern discipline I'd picked up in an ashram in Puna, but the truth is that I'd first learned how to do it back at Alsop Comprehensive School for Boys, when I'd been introduced to acid. I used to think of it then as turning my mind into a slide projector; I'd just allow images to form behind my eyes and watch them glide past in sequence, accompanied by whatever feelings the drug high was giving me.

The beauty of it was that I didn't have to select the images. Once I'd got the process started, they just kept coming. Actually, it was less like a slide show, more like a DVD in fast-forward, giving microsecond stills extracted from the continuous flow of memory. They weren't random; nothing with a human mind as the operating system ever can be. But they were random enough.

Flick. Flick. Flick. No sound, no movement, no idea, no context. Just pictures, forming and fading in my mind so quickly that I could barely identify them myself in the brief time that each one was there in front of me.

Pictures of London first: Marble Arch, the Jerusalem Tavern, a back street in Soho where I'd been mugged. And parts of places: a door I didn't recognize, with green paint peeling from bleached wood; an aerial view of two large Dumpsters with some kid sitting in between them, sniffing glue out of a Waitrose bag; the tracks of two tires on a gravel drive, like waves in a Zen garden. Then people: faces, hands, shoulders, smiling and snarling mouths, the curve of a thigh with a hand (my hand?) touching it—abstract flesh against abstract fabric.

It was working—or at least it seemed to be. The needle turned, and the ghost was the force that pulled it. I surrendered totally to that pull, letting the images that the ghost responded to linger just that bit longer in my mind, and letting each of those pull the next picture along behind it in a sort of themed cascade. The bare thigh became a man's chest, a well-muscled arm, an erect cock, and then, inexplicably, the wheel arch of a car against a curb, with fat raindrops sitting on it. More cars, on roads, on driveways, in garages full of junk, their wheels up on makeshift brick pilings.

Roads. Cities. Houses. Rooms. Another pull from the ghost, stronger this time. It didn't like the rooms so much, so the pictures veered back out into daylight: parks, trees, a bench in some garden, the outhouse behind a pub.

The link was flowing now with frictionless ease, and with it came a sense of being a machine in someone else's hands. If my mind was a projector, the ghost was holding the remote and clicking me on. I let it happen: no resistance, no recoil. More pub scenes, men laughing, men puking, men talking shit with messianic fervor. Another tug: take me somewhere else.

A pavement by the Thames, just down from the Oak; postpub stations of the cross in Soho, Covent Garden, Bounds Green, Spitalfields, the Albert Dock, Porte d'Orléans, Mala Strana under Prague Castle. A huge tug on that one, and now I was seeing a bridge with snow on it, spotless except for the clear double line of my footprints; an open-air smithy in some town square I'd wandered through in northern France, the owner dipping a slender ingot of red-hot metal into black, oil-slicked water; a dirt road in some place I couldn't put a name to, wet with new rain and a little blood.

A shed door, seen from the inside, the wood splintered and torn in vertical lines as though an animal had been clawing at it; a man's arm, gripping a shot glass and raised in salute; a piece of paper, held up to the window of a car by a much smaller and slimmer hand, and almost transparent because of the condensation on the glass, so I could see the smudged writing on the other side: ПОМОГИТЕ МНЕ.

I wasn't feeding into this process at all anymore, and these weren't any memories of mine. Somewhere along the way, the ghost had taken my slides out of the projector and slipped in some of its own. I didn't know what she was getting out of it, but for me it was working—helping me to triangulate on that weak trace and build it up into a clear sense of her that I could use in an exorcism.

Meanwhile, the images kept coming. A frozen lake with the chimneys of some kind of factory rising behind it. A room with no windows and no furniture except for a shapeless sofa covered in a bright orange fabric with suspect stains on it. The curve of a woman's shoulders and back, the woman turned away from me, her hand up as though to hide her face from my eyes. A book with a page torn out of it, held in the heavy grip of a man's hand, his finger tracing the tear, the herringbone tracks of a stainless-steel watchband written in red across his wrist. The edge of some kind of patterned fabric, red and yellow check. A row of plastic bottles, some empty, some full of clear liquid, standing at the foot of a wall. A man's face, cold and hard, behind his back a snowcapped mountain, one hand raised beside his head with the fingers spread wide.

That was the one that did it for me, because I knew that face—knew it better than I wanted to. My body arched backward, and the shift in balance was enough to topple the chair I was sitting in. I went crashing to the floor, and a second later, the sound was echoed in another crash from somewhere far above me.

I was so groggy and dazed for a moment as I came up from the half trance that I didn't realize what that meant. But a single thought cut through the shit and fog that filled my brain. I'd lost her again. I'd been so close that another few seconds would have been enough to nail her down for good, and then I'd jolted myself out of the receptive state and lost her.

Then a second thought dropped into place next to the first.

There was someone else as well as me in the building.

I mean, someone else who was still alive.

Further thoughts crowded in on those first two, muddying the waters. There were any number of explanations for the noise. It could just have been the echo of my own fall or a sound from the street outside that had bounced in a weird way and come back to my ears from inside the building. And if it was another live human being, five would get you plenty it would only be Jon Tiler popping back in for his bag again, even later than last night.

My mind was pulled back to the images that had just flicked through it. They were still vividly there, hanging in front of my eyes in the dark—vivid enough to obliterate my dim surroundings if I let them. The car, the factories, the wristwatch—these were things from the modern world, so they shot to pieces any idea that the ghost was a turn-of-the-century Russian whose spirit had become entangled in some old love letters or a promissory note.

And with that realization came another. Bare arms with a hood? The ghost wasn't wearing any kind of full-length cloak or ecclesiastical robe; it was most likely to be a hoodie. Like I said, sometimes I'm so corkscrew sly and subtle that I miss what's right in front of my face.

But it was the last image that had left me reeling. Like I said, I knew the man, and if he'd been here at the archive before me, then I needed to have words with Peele sooner than soon—some of which would be of the kind that you're not liable to read in the Bible.

I pulled myself together, which took a bit of an effort. Wherever I went next, I was all done here. The room didn't have any more revelations to offer me, because the ghost had nothing to do with any of the stuff in these boxes. In the chagrin and frustration of that moment, my thoughts went back to the crash, which was a welcome diversion from the clutter and confusion that the rest of my mind was now filled with.

There was another explanation for that sound. It could be the ghost itself, stirred up by our little two-handed game and throwing another tantrum. If it was, then I might have a chance of collecting the last coffin nail, the last tiny sliver of her psychic fingerprint that would allow me to do my stuff. Something to report to Alice—besides "I've been barking up the wrong tree and now I've got splinters"—would be very useful.

Well, I sure as hell had nothing to lose. I picked myself up off the floor, stepped out of the room, and headed on down the hallway. I'd been through this maze a few times now, but in the dark, I still managed to miss my way. Somehow when I should have come to the bottom of the first set of stairs, I came to a dead end instead and had to retrace my steps. Strange. That blind-ended corridor had the worst vibes of all: a headache-inducing sludge of sorrow. Something really unpleasant must have happened there once, or maybe it was just that the tumble I'd taken had bent my psychic tuning fork all out of shape.

Second time lucky. I found my way to the stairs and walked up quickly, my footsteps filling the unpeopled silence like the marching of a clumsy ghost army. Up, down, in, out. I threaded my way through the nearly dark corridors by feel, with the occasional help of a patch of dirty yellow white light from the street outside. I passed the workroom, which was silent and empty, Alice's office, then Peele's. Everything here was silent, dark, and deserted. If it was the ghost who'd made the sound, it seemed she was taking a breather.

I walked on until I came to the main stairwell—the stone one that led down to the lobby—and there I stopped and listened. This place was an echo chamber; if anything moved in the building, my best chance of hearing it was probably from right there.

But there was nothing to hear except for the blood drumming in my own ears. Perhaps I'd got it wrong in the first place; that thunderous bang that had followed the sound of my chair falling over could have come from almost anywhere. I was about to give up on it when suddenly there was a quick rustle of movement from the dark above me, instantly stilled. I waited, but nothing followed on from this flurry of sound. Interesting. There's a kind of silence that just has the overwhelming feel of someone trying desperately not to break it, and that was the kind of silence I was breathing in right then. From my earlier wanderings, I remembered that the fourth floor was mainly additional office space and nonsecure storage, and above that there

were the empty shells of rooms where the building work was still going on.

I climbed up the next flight of steps slowly, with laborious stealth.
There was no sign of anyone or anything there. I waited for another
long, uneventful while and was rewarded by another microscopic
fragment of sound from just above my head: a floorboard protesting
as someone shifted his weight. I climbed again, into the attic level,
where the palletloads of bricks waited in the dark like the ghosts of
strong rooms yet to be born. I trod carefully here; the ropes of the
block and tackle hanging down into the stairwell had reminded me
that the railings had been removed from the top landing. One foot
out of place, and I'd be doing a vertical quick step.

The building got less extensive horizontally the farther up you
went; most of the extensions had been to the first and second floors.
Up here in the roof space, there was a single straight corridor with
half a dozen rooms leading off it, three to each side. The great rose
window was directly over my head here, and through it I could see
a few stars breaking cover as a mass of black cloud shifted off west-
ward. They did nothing to relieve the darkness, though; it was even
more dense and opaque up here than it had been on the floor below.
I squinted down the corridor. Nothing to see, but that didn't mean
there was nothing there.

I walked down the corridor, trying each door in turn. They all
opened, and they all gave onto empty rooms. Those on the right-
hand side were completely bare, just dusty floorboards and nailed-up
plasterboard, without even electric sockets or lights. Those on the left
were in a more finished state, but turned out, when I flicked on the
shadeless lights, to hold nothing more interesting than a few boxes
and stacks of old papers.

But the last door on the left was already slightly ajar. I pushed the
door fully open and scanned the room from the corridor without trying to walk in. I found the light switch to the right of the door and
pressed it. Nothing happened. Either the bulb had given out already,

or more likely nobody had bothered to put one in the socket yet. It was too dark to see much, but the room seemed to be little more than a cupboard; shelves extended from floor to ceiling on the wall facing me, which was only about six feet away. More box files and stacked papers: a smell of sour, unbreathed air.

I took a single step forward, over the threshold. I just about had time to take a paranoid glance behind the door before someone barged me hard from behind, sending me staggering forward into the room. I slammed painfully into the shelving before I could even fall. One of the shelves tipped under my weight, but I got my balance back and turned around.

The light from a torch dazzled me momentarily—and then the torch itself, wielded in a more blunt-instrument kind of way, smacked me on the side of the head. But since the light of the torch telegraphed the movement, I was moving with it; instead of being brained, I just got a clip to the side of the head, and then I was up and fighting.

Fighting someone who seemed a fair bit more solid than me and who took my body punch in his stride. He hit me again, with his fist this time instead of the torch, and I went down on my back.

I heard the door slam to; that got me up again fast. If my attacker had a key, I could be locked in here. I got both hands around the door handle and leaned down and in. I pulled, and he pulled back against me. I braced myself with one foot on the wall, the other on the floor, and pulled harder.

When the door flew inward, I staggered back and almost went down again—but for the second time I hit the shelves and managed to stay upright. As my attacker's footsteps retreated along the corridor, I was out of the door and after him. I couldn't see him up ahead, but I could hear him, his feet crashing on the bare boards. I came out onto the landing at a flat run, registering about a second too late that those pounding footfalls had stopped.

I just about caught a blur of movement from off to my right-hand side, and I started to turn. His shoulder hit me midchest, knocking the breath right out of me and sending me backward in a drunken, flailing stagger. One step, two . . . I would probably have managed to get my balance back if there'd been anything under me on step three. Instead, my trailing foot stepped out into nothingness, and I tipped and fell without a sound off the edge of the landing.

I'm too introspective, maybe, to make a good man of action. Certainly on that short fall, I didn't have enough time even to react to what was happening. I remember throwing out my arms as if there might be something conveniently placed for me to catch hold of. Only empty air rushed through my fingers, and I closed my eyes, bracing myself—metaphorically speaking—for a solid chunk of marble tiling to rush through my head.

But something writhed out of the shadows to one side of me like the business end of a lash, thwacking solidly against my chest and the side of my head and then snaking around me once, twice, three times. Along the line where it touched me, fire ate its way inward from my skin to my core, and I opened my mouth to scream.

The sickening jolt as I stopped falling turned the scream into a voiceless bullet of breath that shot through my clenched teeth and ricocheted away into the darkness. I dangled for a moment like the bob on the end of a pendulum telling borrowed time. Then the rope loosened and unraveled from around me, and I fell the remaining few feet to the ground.

I landed heavily on the cold tiles, unable for a moment even to suck breath back into my lungs. Someone ran past me, and I got a blurry view of his back as he sped through the open door.

By the time I could get back on my feet and stagger to the door, there was no sign of anybody out on Churchway. A sudden gust of cold wind blew newspaper pages and Styrofoam burger boxes along the pavement, and that was the only movement. After a few moments to get my breath back to normal, I went back inside and climbed the stairs back up to the attic. This time, though, I turned on the lights—so this time, I saw the short dogleg at the end of the corridor, off to the left, that I'd missed the first time around.

There was another door there, too, off the end of the dogleg, and so on the same line as the other left-hand rooms, but maybe slightly smaller. This was where my attacker had hidden—after pushing open another door on the main corridor so that I'd be that bit more likely to turn my back on him before I reached him. Clever guy. Clever and scared and just a bit desperate. Someone who had taken advantage of the archive being open after hours to slip back inside and . . . well, and what?

I tried the door. It opened like all the others, and there was a functional light switch just inside. It showed me a room no different from any of the ones I'd already seen. No shelves this time, but a big bundle of flat-packed storage boxes tied with string stood propped against one wall. On the floor there was a roll of brown parcel tape and a plastic supermarket bag that, on inspection, proved to be stuffed with a great many other plastic supermarket bags. No big revelations here. Maybe the guy had just retreated in front of me as I came up the stairs until he ran out of space to retreat into and came out fighting. They say you ought to be careful when you corner rats.

But there was a cupboard. I only saw it as I turned to leave, because it was a low, squat sort of cupboard, and it was completely hidden behind the door. I pulled on the handle: locked. I probably had the key that would open it sitting right there on Alice's key ring, but my hands were shaking from my recent air-miss, and it could take me a long time to find it—with the risk that someone down below would see the light where no light should be and draw the wrong conclusion. All in all, it was probably better to wait.

I went downstairs, let myself out, and locked up. I was about to post Alice's keys and ID card back through the mail slot, but I yielded to a wicked temptation and put them back in my pocket instead. You never knew.

I was intending to go home, but somehow I found myself heading south instead of north. Just down from Russell Square, I found a late-night bar that was still open, went in, and ordered a whisky sour.

I was bone weary, and I wasn't thinking all that straight, but coming to the archive by night had succeeded beyond my wildest dreams. It wasn't some freak accident that had tangled me up in the ropes of the builders' pulley. It wasn't the air that had held me and stopped me from falling. It was her. And in wrapping herself around me like that, she'd come in so close that I couldn't possibly fail to get what I needed. I had her now, had her mapped out in my mind in many dimensions—a vivid sensory snapshot of her essence and her parameters that was untranslatable except into music and that I could no more forget than I could forget my own name.

I toasted myself in silence. They think it's all over, said Ken Wolstenholme's voice from deep within the dusty archive of my head.

Well, it is now.

Eleven

OVER THERE," WHISPERED JOHN GITTINGS. "IN THE corner, behind the hedge."

I looked where he was pointing and saw nothing. But then a second later, the leaves of the box hedge rustled again, although there wasn't the slightest breath of wind. One of the keepers raised his rifle, and I pushed it right back down again.

"You don't even know what you'd be hitting," I muttered. "You'd look pretty bloody stupid if it was a peacock."

John and I exchanged a glance as the keeper shipped his rifle again with obvious resentment. "Pincer movement?" John asked.

"Makes sense," I said. "I'm going to go around the zebra house and use the back wall for cover. You come in along the line of the hedge on this side, but don't get in too close. When I round that corner, we should see each other. I'll give you the high sign, and we both start playing at once."

John nodded tersely. I turned to the head keeper, a guy named Savage. He wasn't carrying a rifle, and he seemed to be the only one of the zoo staff who didn't want to play Buffalo Bill. "The music should drive him out toward you," I said. "He won't be able to stick to the hedge because he'll be hurting too much. If we're lucky, he'll just break across the grass, and you can pop him at your leisure."

"That seems easy enough," Savage acknowledged.

"Yeah, it does, doesn't it? Only if we hit the wrong key, he'll turn around and tear our throats out."

"He" was a *loup-garou*, and I was moonlighting. John's call had come in at seven in the morning, when I was just surfacing from shallow sleep and another set of very nasty dreams. Pen had relayed the message, expecting me to say some pithier equivalent of "No, thank you"—and was amazed when I passed back the answer that I'd be there inside of an hour.

It's a character flaw, I know. When I'm unhappy about something, I pick a fight, and that morning, I was in such a lousy mood, I'd have taken a swing at John "The Quietman" Ruiz. So all things considered, the other John's invitation to come and help him corner a werewolf at Dunstable Zoo had come as something of a relief.

Were-something, anyway. They didn't know exactly what they had, because all they'd seen were the savaged carcasses of five animals: three wallabies, a zebra, and most recently a lion. So we were talking about something vicious and fast that didn't care what it killed, and now they thought they had it cornered in a stand of trees at the back of the site between the rhino enclosure and a high wall that backed onto the main A-road beyond. The keepers had closed in with tranquilizer guns, but they couldn't flush the *loup-garou*, and they didn't want to go in blind.

So here I was. It was therapy, really—a way of keeping busy without facing the things that were really bugging me. If it left me alive and in one piece, I'd be laughing.

I skirted the back of the zebra house, staying in close. I wasn't worried that he'd see me—there wouldn't be any line of sight until I got to the corner—but the rank zebra-shit smell ought to hide my scent from him while I got in closer.

When I got to the corner, I peered cautiously around it, scanning the distant line of the hedge. After a moment or two, I made out

Gittings; he was padding silently along, zeroing in on the area where we'd seen the suspicious rustling of leaves.

I waved to him, and he waved back. But when I started the countdown on my raised fingers, he made a negative sign with his left hand, the right gripping his tabor. John's a music man, like me: strictly percussion, but it still puts us close enough in our exorcism technique that we can work well together. Now he was signaling that he wanted to get in closer. I shook my head emphatically. We were only trying to flush the beast with generalized psychic static, not to exorcise the spirit that was animating whatever flesh we had here. We didn't need to be right on top of the damned thing.

But John had other ideas, obviously. Ignoring my vote of no confidence, he took another few steps forward along the hedge. Then he went down on one knee, pointed to me, and indicated that he'd do the countdown himself. I wasn't happy about it, but I didn't have any choice. I shrugged and nodded.

On zero, I started to pipe. I opened low and soft, let the wind pick it up, and then started to layer in the dips and rises that ought to get the *loup-garou's* ghost-passenger hurting.

For a minute, and then a minute more, nothing. But patience was the key. I glided up and down the scale, confident that sooner or later, I was going to hit a nerve. John knelt, nodding encouragement to me, his left hand dancing like a conductor's baton. But he still hadn't started to play.

There was movement in the box hedge: branches trembling, then bending, seemingly only a foot away from where John was kneeling.

I was expecting something to burst out of the hedge. The thing leapt over it and hit the ground already running—running toward me. Rifles popped, but the keepers had been aiming low to the ground; I could actually see the scatter and swirl of leaves as most of the darts ripped harmlessly into the hedge.

The beast was a nightmare. Even now that it was out in the daylight, I couldn't see what animal it had been. The ghost inside it had bulked out the torso and the legs and turned the gape-mouthed head into a tooth-bristling, mythical obscenity. Of course it didn't help that I was seeing it full-on; teeth filled most of my line of sight.

Gittings was standing now, and his fingers on the tabor made a loud, rapid stutter of sound like machine-gun fire. The beast didn't slow, and it was coming in so quickly, it would be on me in seconds. I had two choices: run and be brought down from behind, or stand my ground and get my throat ripped out.

I went for option C. Since the thing could jump like a flea, that was probably what it was going to do. When its upper body came down low to the ground, tensing for the spring, I dropped and rolled forward. Its flying leap took it over me while I finished my roll on my back and got in a lucky kick that caught its hind leg and made a mess of its landing trajectory.

Didn't do me much good, though. Okay, I was up and running before it could get all its legs in their right places again and turn around, but the bastard thing went from zero to sixty in three seconds. With me these days, it's more like three weeks' notice and a friendly push-start. The thing's whole weight hit me solidly in the middle of the back, and my feet went out from under me. I hit the ground heavily, face slamming hard into the grass. Stenching furnace breath billowed over me, and I ducked and covered only just in time to hear massive jaws snapping closed an inch from my ear.

They only closed once, I'm happy to say. Five sharp cracks sounded closely enough together to be mistaken for one, and the thing collapsed on top of me. A moment later, the keepers were hauling me out from underneath the *loup-garou*'s stinking, slumbering mass.

God, it was even worse this close up. The basic shape was canine, but the claws were recurved like sickle blades, and there were additional spurs of bone at elbows and haunches. Splotchy fur like a hyena's covered its overmuscled shoulders, but its hind quarters were bare and leprous. It must have massed about two hundred and fifty pounds.

"Old soul," said Savage with something like respect. He meant that this was a ghost that had been around the track a few times and had picked up some neat tricks where the molding of its host flesh was concerned. Even now, it was impossible to tell what kind of dog this monster had started out as.

"Have you got a cage to put it in?" I asked.

He shot me a glance; shook his head. "We couldn't keep this here. The smell of it would make the other animals run mad. No, this goes to Professor Mulbridge down in London. And good riddance."

Gittings came up panting. "Sorry, Fix," he said. "I thought this way would work better."

I gave him a high-octane glare. "What way is that?" I demanded. "You sit on your hands, I lose my head?"

"No. I wanted you to get its attention and then, while it was focused on you, I thought I'd have time to do a full exorcism. That's why I got in so close. Rip the ghost out of the flesh, and you've just got an animal, after all. Much easier to deal with."

I poked him in the chest. "Don't change the plan on the ground when it's me that's in the line of fire, John. Next time, you find another piece of raw meat to dangle, okay?"

He was contrite. "Sorry, Fix. You're right. It just seemed like a good idea."

I simmered down. It had been a bad call, but it wasn't really Gittings that was jangling my nerves, and taking it out on him wouldn't make me feel any better.

"Let's get out of here," I said.

"Breakfast's on me," said John recklessly. But my churned-up stomach wouldn't let me eat, so that was a really cheap round.

———

Driving back into London, I thought about the various reversals that last night had brought. I asked myself why the hell I was out in the Bedfordshire sticks doing a good impersonation of live bait instead of in the Bonnington, whistling the faceless lady back to her grave.

And the only answer I could come up with was that I was still unhappy.

Pen needed the car, so I dropped it back around to her. Walking down Turnpike Lane, I called Peele to tell him I had some things to do that would keep me away from the archive for most of the day.

"What's left of the day, you mean," he corrected me prissily. "It's almost noon now."

Time flies when you're enjoying yourself. "I had some other matters to attend to," I said.

"Other matters?" He was suitably scandalized. "You mean you're taking on more commissions before you've finished here?"

"No, I went to the zoo."

"Very amusing, Mr. Castor. The things that you're doing today, can you honestly tell me that they relate to us? To our problem here?"

"Yes," I said, which was true enough. "A lot of it is about getting more background information. I'm on the case. I feel like I'm really moving forward." And now I was stretching the truth more or less to breaking point. "But if I can use a military metaphor, Mr. Peele, sometimes when you move forward too fast, you leave your flanks exposed. I just want to make sure that I'm not missing something."

He gave in sullenly and indicated that there was a conversation that needed to be had about an incident in the workroom the day before. I told him I'd be at his disposal either later that day or first thing tomorrow. Then, before he could hang up, I hit him with the little sting in the tail I'd been holding back all this time.

"Oh, just one more thing before you go, Mr. Peele," I said like Columbo's understudy. "Why didn't you tell me I was the second name on your list?"

"I'm sorry?" Peele sounded surprised and coldly affronted—as if I'd accused him of marital infidelity.

I rephrased. "Why didn't you tell me you'd already used another exorcist? Gabriel McClennan has been in the Bonnington, and he's met your ghost. I like to know if I'm unpicking someone else's work rather than doing a job from scratch."

There was a long silence. "I don't understand," Peele said at last. "Who told you that? Nobody else has been at the archive. I came to you first."

He sounded sincere, but I couldn't let it go. I knew what I'd seen when the ghost was flashing pictures into my head. "You came to me first. Okay. Why was that, exactly? You said it was a personal referral. Who from?" I should have asked him before. Nothing to plead in my own defence there except ego, because it was an obvious question.

"I did say that," Peele admitted, sounding annoyed now. "I'm afraid it was an overstatement. What I meant to say was that I'd done the research myself—chosen you on the basis of my own efforts, rather than—"

"You saw one of my ads," I suggested.

"Yes." Reluctantly, with a slightly sullen undertone—the voice of an honest man who's been caught out in a trivial lie. "I believe it was in the classified section of the *Hendon Times* . . ."

My ad had been in the *Wembley Times*, but all of the North London free sheets are basically the same paper with a different masthead. After what had happened with Rafi, though, I'd never renewed the standing order. The ad wouldn't have been in there for over a year.

Bachelor flat. Stack of newspapers getting taller and taller in a corner of the kitchen or a hall cupboard.

"This was an old copy, right?"

"Perhaps. I looked through several issues, but more or less at random."

It made sense, but I was still suspicious.

"My office is in Harlesden. This other man, Gabriel McClennan, he's local talent. You've probably walked past his office on your way to work—"

"I told you, I've never heard of an exorcist named McClennan!"

Peele sounded irritated and indignant now—and it didn't have the hallmarks of the anger you use to cover up a lie, with which I'm more than familiar. But I couldn't have mistaken that face. The archive ghost had met Gabe McClennan at close quarters. Another exorcist had already worked the place, and yet she was still there. So if it wasn't Peele, somebody else was trying to exorcise the ghost. Now why would that be?

"Okay, skip it," I told Peele brusquely. I'd follow up in my own sweet time, but it didn't look as though I was going to find out any more right then—and I knew better than to clutch at straws purely so that I could flog dead horses with them. "How did your meeting in Bilbao go?" I asked to change the subject.

Peele was aware of the discontinuity but unable to resist the red herring. "Very well, thank you. Very successfully indeed. I hope to hear good news within the next few days—news that will strengthen the links between the Bonnington and the Guggenheim Museum and be good for both institutions. But Mr. Castor, I need to know more about the progress you've made. Alice says—"

"Excellent progress, Mr. Peele. Better than I'd expected. In fact, I've just been able to eliminate a false trail that might have tied up a lesser exorcist for two whole days. Sorry to disrupt your morning. I'll check in with you later on."

"A false trail?" he echoed, bemused. But I hung up before he could shape that into an actual question.

The cloud had set in again thicker than ever, stone gray buttresses hanging over the city like masonry suspended in midfall. I took the Tube to Leicester Square and then headed up Charing Cross Road before turning west into Soho.

There was something going on at the archive that I was being kept in the dark about—I didn't like that much. And I'd been pulled back from the brink of a broken neck, or worse, like a toddler wandering in traffic—I liked that even less.

Worst of all, I knew what it was that had saved me. And that was a pill so bitter, I almost couldn't get it down.

Gabe McClennan has an office on Greek Street, and he calls it that with a straight face. The signs at street level read NEW MODEL IN TOWN, INDIAN HEAD MASSAGE, and GABRIEL P. MCCLENNAN, SPIRITUAL SERVICES. The street door was open, so I went in, but Gabe's door was locked, and there was a damp, heavy silence. The model and masseuse probably did most of their work on the night shift, but Gabe's shingle ought to be open now if it ever was. On the other hand, let him who keeps regular office hours cast the first stone. I knocked a few times just in case, but got no answer.

Later, then. Because I was damn well going to finish this jigsaw off now that I'd started it—even if I had to knock some of the pieces into place with a ball-peen hammer. Yeah, I could just have played the tune and taken the money, like the Pied Piper, but I guess I'm not as pied as I make myself out to be. In any case, and for reasons I wasn't keen to explore, it had suddenly become important for me to get at least some idea of what the hell I was dealing with here. Call it professional pride. Or call it what you like.

I had three places on my itinerary, and I'd budgeted the whole day. That may sound a bit pessimistic, given that they were all in North London, but my first port of call was the Camden Town Hall planning department. You don't exactly abandon hope, but you certainly slip it into a back pocket.

Back at King's Cross again; it felt like I'd never left. The town hall building looks like a set from an old *Doctor Who* episode, and to some extent, that gives a fair impression of the experience you're likely to have when you go in there: meeting strange, not-quite-human creatures, burning your way through vast swathes of time, that sort of thing. I went in through the Judd Street entrance and was sent straight back out again; planning was at the other end of the building and was entered via Argyle Street. The gods of local government would be angry if I walked straight through, and I'd end up with my resident's parking permit revoked and a council-tax bill for seven grand and my immortal soul.

Actually, the system worked surprisingly well, at least to begin with. I knew I was being set up for a fall, but I took it for what it was worth. The planning department had partly gone over to computerized records. There were half a dozen terminals set up in the foyer where you could just sit down, type in an address, and get a planning history. Thinking about Cheryl, I spared a brief moment of pity for whoever was sitting in the bowels of the building, retroconverting.

"You won't get everything," I was told by an arrogant, acned young clerk who looked less like a *Doctor Who* villain and more like the kid in a teen gross-out comedy who doesn't get the girl but does lose his trousers at the graduation ceremony. "There'll only be an entry where there've been changes to the building since the late 1940s—that's when the planning-application system came in. If you don't know your dates, you could be here for a long time."

But I wasn't choosy, and it turned out that there were a whole fistful of documents on file for 3 Churchway, Somers Town, one of them going all the way back to 1949. That one was an application to repair bomb damage to the roof, frontage, and right exterior wall. Back then, the building was listed as belonging to the war office, but by the mid-1950s, when an application was put in to extend it to the rear, it had become an "annex to the British Library." Then nothing until 1983, when there was a further extension and a change-of-use certificate; now number 23 was going to come under local authority control and house an unemployment claims office and a job center. Well, that was the Thatcher era—unemployment was a growth industry. One final application, from 1991, was for interior works. I suppose that was when they put in all the bare, brutalist staircases, the fake walls, and the dead ends. Nothing on file for the work that was going on now, but maybe current work was filed elsewhere.

That was as far as I could get online. Now I had to fill in some request slips and hand them in at a small counter in the main planning office. This was a large room on the second floor, cut in two by a long Formica counter, and it was as busy as a cattle auction. Most of the people there were men in overalls who were looking to get official stamps on hastily scrawled documents, but there was also a leavening of clerks from other parts of the building filing forms or retrieving forms or maybe just exchanging pheromones like worker ants.

I waited for almost an hour and a half before a stern, middle-age lady with a face out of a *Far Side* cartoon came back with a package for me. It was a set of photocopies of the oldest plans they had for 23 Churchway—the ones that had been filed back in 1949—and the newest ones from the 1990s. I figured that with those fixed points to work from, I could fill in the gaps.

So far so good. I genuflected to the dark gods and got out of there fast. My next stop was the British Newspaper Library, out in Colindale. A Thameslink train from King's Cross took me to Mill Hill, and on the way out there, I took a look at the building plans. As I'd expected, the ones from 1991 had all the new staircases and corridors and fire doors marked in and were so small and so complicated, they looked like a maze in a kids' puzzle book: *help Uncle Felix get from the office to the haunted strong room—but look out for that nasty Mr. Peele.* By contrast, the 1949 plans were austere and simple and clear, and showed fewer than half as many rooms. The place had grown and mutated to the point where the original architect would probably need the plans just to find the street door.

I didn't know the building well enough yet to pinpoint the room where the Russian stuff was being kept, but the first floor as a whole seemed to have been made over according to a crude but workable plan. Each of the original rooms had been split down the middle, so every second wall was a new plasterboard partition. The original doors, too wide for the new, smaller rooms, had been bricked in, and new, narrower doorways had been put through. A secondary staircase that showed on the original plans had been torn down, the space cannibalized to make small cubicles that were probably toilets or store cupboards. At the same time, the cramped stairways that I'd seen in situ had been created, wedged into the new ground plan wherever there was a gap too narrow to become an actual room. The overall effect was really depressing—it was like reading the tactical projections for the rape of a corpse.

From Mill Hill overground, I walked the rest of the way—but then I overshot and found myself walking past the grounds of the Metropolitan Police Training Academy, which were filled with primary-school kids learning how to ride bikes. A young woman was looking wistfully through the chain-link fence at all the children zooming and zigzagging through a maze sketched out in orange plastic bollards. She turned to look at me; there was an unhealthy bloom to her skin, and I caught the faint sweet-sour whiff of decay wafting off her. She was one of the returned. Her mud-stained jeans and sweatshirt and the occasional strand of dry grass in her hair gave a fairly clear indication of where she'd slept last night.

"I'm still waiting," she said.

I should have just walked on by, but her face had that Ancient Mariner quality. I was the one in three.

"Waiting for what?" I asked her.

"For the children. I said I'd be here when they got back." A spasm passed across her slack face—annoyance, or unease, or maybe something purely physiological. "Mark said something about a car. There was a car. They didn't get the number." A leaden pause. "I told them I'd wait here."

With the sound of happy shouts and laughter ringing in my ears, I trudged on my way. I looked back once. She was staring through the fence again, her arms hanging at her sides, her face a solemn mask, trying to read the runes of a life that wasn't hers anymore.

Two minutes later, I entered the cathedral-like silence of the Newspaper Library, which smells like a worldful of armpits and is illuminated by five-watt strip lights guaranteed not to damage old newsprint by allowing it to be read.

I was probably wasting my time here, but I needed to rule out the obvious before I started looking for more esoteric answers. If the Bonnington Archive was built on an old Indian burying ground, or if someone had slaughtered the entire staff in an obscene necromantic ritual back in the 1960s, when that stuff counted as hip, I'd feel pretty damn stupid to have missed it.

You can get most of this material from other, more salubrious places now, but the Colindale Library has still got the fullest index of anywhere I know and a stack of old papers on microfiche that goes way back into the mists of antiquity—probably to headlines like ONE IN THE EYE FOR HAROLD.

But Churchway, Somers Town, hadn't made the headlines once in all those many years. It seemed to be a place where nothing much had ever happened. No penny dreadfuls. No Victorian melodramas. No threads to follow, which only helped insofar as it offered no more blind alleys for me to walk down—and threw me back on my own resources. That was okay. I still had some.

When I came back out onto the sunlit street, blinking in a brightness that seemed somehow unreal after that half-lit world, the risen woman I'd met on my way in was loitering on the well-tended patch of lawn just outside the library's side door. Her eyes were closed, and her lips were working silently.

I had to pass her, but I gave her a wide berth this time; I didn't want to get sucked into her private world of unresolved crises and suspended time. I got about ten yards farther down the street.

"Felix." The hairs on the back of my neck prickled. I spun round. Nothing in the zombie's expression or posture had changed. It might not even have been her voice; one congealed mumble sounds much like another.

But then her eyes flicked open. She looked up and around, fixed me with a slightly dazed stare.

"He says you're closer now than you were," she whispered. "Even though you think you're lost. He says this is where it starts getting hot."

Another spasm crossed her sallow face. Her eyes closed again, and she went back to her silent recital. There was nothing to say, so I didn't say it.

One more stop to make, and it wasn't exactly on my way.

Nicky's current place of residence is the old EMD cinema in Walthamstow. That gives him loads of room—more than he actually needs, if he's honest. The place has been closed and boarded up since 1986. Entrance is via a second-floor window, but that's less inconvenient than it sounds, because there's a shed at the back of the building with a flat roof. It's just a case of shinnying up a drainpipe, which, if you've learned it as a kid, is a trick you never really forget.

Nicky was in the projection room, as always, at his computer, as always. And, as always, the cold bit into me right through my tightly buttoned-up coat. The air-conditioning units are standard industrial ones, but Nicky has been over them himself, taken them to pieces and rebuilt them to his own more exacting specifications. The blast they put out now is like a wind sweeping off the South Pole across the Larsen B ice shelf.

Nicky was pleased to see me, because I usually bring him something to feed two of his three addictions—say, a bottle of some really good French red and a couple of jazz singles of 1940s vintage. Today I was short-changing him slightly; I only had the wine. All the same, he was cordial. He'd noticed some new pattern in the ephemeral ripples that stir the surface of the material world, and he wanted someone to bounce it off.

"Here, Fix," he said eagerly, swiveling his monitor to face me. "Check this out. Look where it spikes."

With his Mediterranean tan and his extensive (if largely shoplifted) wardrobe, Nicky doesn't look like a walking corpse; he looks like a fashion model who's hit hard times. That's a tribute to his absolute dedication—his obsessive attention to detail. Most of the dead who've risen in the body tend to wander around in an unhappy and aimless way, getting further and further past their sell-by date, until the battle between decomposition and willpower shifts inexorably past a certain balance point. Then they fall down and don't get up. In rare cases, the spirit freed from its flesh-house will find another vacant cadaver and start all over again. Mostly they just give up the ghost, as it were.

But that wasn't Nicky's style. Back when he was still alive—which was when I'd first met him—he'd been one of the most dangerous lunatics I'd ever met outside of a secure institution, and what made him dangerous was his ability to focus on one idea and squeeze it until it bled. He was a tech-head conspiracy theorist who cut open the Internet to read its entrails; a paranoiac who thought every message ever sent, every word ever written was ultimately about him. He thought of the world in terms of a web—a communal web devised by a great agglomeration of spiders. If you were a fly, he said, the only way to stay alive was to avoid touching any of the sticky threads, to leave no trail that anyone could follow back to you. Of course, he wasn't alive anymore—a heart attack at the ripe young age of thirty-six had taken care of that—but his opinions were unchanged.

"Right. What am I looking at?" I demanded, stalling for time as I looked at the graph on his computer monitor. There was a red line, and there was a green line. There was a horizontal axis, marked out in years, and a vertical axis not marked at all. The two lines did seem to be in rough synchrony.

"This is the FTSE 100 share index," Nicky said, tracing the green line with the tip of his finger. His fingernail was caked with black dirt. It was probably oil; he had his own generator, which he'd half-inched from a building site. He didn't like drawing power directly from the national grid for reasons given above. In Nicky's world, invisibility is the great, maybe the only, virtue.

"And the red line?" I asked, setting down the bottle of Margaux

I'd picked up for him at Oddbins. Nicky doesn't drink the wine. He doesn't manufacture any stomach enzymes anymore, so he wouldn't be able to metabolize it. He says he can still smell it, though—and he's built up a nose for the expensive stuff.

He shot me a slightly defensive look. "The red line is a bit of an artifact," he admitted. "It plots the first and final readings of pro-EU legislation, or a statement by any government front-bencher in favor of greater European integration."

I bent low to get a better look. Nicky smelled of Old Spice and embalming fluid—not of decay, because his body was not so much a temple as a fortress, and no crack in a fortress can be considered small. All the same, I liked it better when he had his rig set up down in the cinema's main auditorium, which has better through-drafts.

"Okay," I said. "The red line is a little out of phase. It spikes earlier."

"Earlier, right, right," Nicky agreed, nodding excitedly. "Two to three days earlier in most cases. Up to a week, sometimes. If you plot the recession line, the correspondence is even closer. Every time, Fix. Every fucking hail-Mary-full-of-grace time."

I tried to get my head around this. "So you're saying—"

"That there's a causal link. Obviously."

I frowned, trying to look like I was giving this serious thought. Nicky was watching me, hairy-eyed and eager. "How does that work?" I asked.

He was only too happy to explain. "It works like this. Satan is in favor of federalism, because that's his preferred method of working. It's like, you know"—he gestured vaguely but emphatically—"engineering the Fall of Man just by corrupting Adam and Eve. The more the nations of the world are brought under one rule, the easier it is for the infernal powers to assert direct control over the whole show—just by attacking and subduing one soul. Or a couple of hundred souls, if we're talking about the EU Council of Ministers. So when the government pushes a European agenda, it's because they're in thrall to Satan and they're doing his will."

I chewed this over. "And the share prices?"

"That's their reward from Satan for obeying orders. Whenever they push the whole plan forward, he makes their shares go up in value. He gives them the earthly paradise he's always promised his servants."

He was still looking at me, waiting for a reaction. "I don't know, Nicky," I said, temporizing. "The FTSE—that's a composite figure, isn't it? You've got a lot of companies there, with their own chief execs and their own business plans. And you've got a lot of investors with their own axes to grind . . ."

Nicky was disgusted. "Oh for fuck's sake, Fix. Of course it's a composite figure. I'm not saying that Satan can just wave his hand and make the share index go up and down. Obviously he works through human proxies. That's why the lag time varies. If it was a perfect, frictionless system, it would be immediate, wouldn't it? You're proving my point."

"I hadn't thought it through that far," I said cautiously. I sat down on the table where the printer rested; it was a heavy, old-fashioned laser jobbie, and I had to balance my buttocks precariously on about an inch of free space. "Nicky, I was wondering if you could help me with something."

"With what?" He was instantly suspicious. He knows I don't come around just to sniff wine and swap gossip, but he hates the fact that our relationship is mutually abusive. Like all conspiracy nuts, he's a romantic at heart.

"A job I'm doing."

"What kind of job?"

"The usual kind."

Very pointedly, Nicky picked up the bottle of wine and examined the label. It was a '97, and it wasn't anything like cheap.

"Thought you'd given up that ghost-toasting shit," he observed.

"I'm back."

"Obviously." The wine had mollified him, but only up to a point. "I'll need another two of these," he said. "And you mentioned some guy in Portobello Road who had Al Bowlly and Jimmy Reese together on some old Berliner hard rubber?"

I winced. "Yeah, I did say that, Nicky, but I'm not in the government, and Satan isn't sexing up my share options just yet. The wine or the disk—not both."

Nicky played hard to get. "Tell me what you're looking for," he said.

"A young woman. In her early twenties, most likely. Dark-haired. Possibly Russian or East European. The area around Euston Station. Murder or accident, could've been either, but violent. And sudden."

"Time frame?"

"I don't really know. Maybe summer. July or August."

He snorted. "Congratulations, Fix. That's probably the vaguest brief you've ever given me. Toss me a bone, here. Eye color? Complexion? Distinguishing marks?"

I thought about the blurry red veil that stood in for the ghost's face. "That's all I've got," I said. And then, more to myself than to him, "Maybe . . . maybe her face was injured in some way."

"The disk."

"What?"

"I'll go for the Berliner disk. But it better be fucking genuine. And it better be fucking Al Bowlly, not Keppard doing an Al Bowlly impression. I'll know."

"It's the real thing," I assured him. They were just names to me; my tastes run to classical, home-grown punk, and the raw end of alt dot country. I've got exactly enough savvy about jazz to know what to look for when I'm in need of a bribe.

"You know what your sin is, Fix?" Nicky asked me, already tapping some terms into a nameless metasearch engine that displayed in black on dark gray. "The particular thing you'll go to Hell for?"

"Self-abuse?" I hazarded.

"Blasphemy. The last days are coming, and He writes it in the Heavens and on the Earth. The rising of the dead is a sign—I'm a sign, but you don't want to read me. You don't even want to accept that there's a point to all this. A plan. You treat the Book of Revelation as if it's a book of police mug shots. That's why God turns His face from you. That's why you'll burn, in the end."

"Right, Nicky," I said, already walking away. "I'll burn, and you'll tan. For so it is written. Call me if you get anything."

I think I was in a fairly somber mood as I walked back along Hoe Street. Something about Nicky's tirade had brought another recent memory to the surface of my mind—Asmodeus, telling me that I was going to miss the boat because I wasn't asking the right questions.

Everyone's a fucking critic.

Suddenly I was dragged out of my profitless thoughts. Passing a shop, I caught my own reflection in the window, at an odd angle, and someone else was moving behind me—someone I thought for a moment that I recognized. But when I turned, she was nowhere in sight. It had looked like Rosa—the girl at Damjohn's club, Kissing the Pink, for whom Damjohn had sent because he thought I'd like to admire her backside. Pretty unlikely that she'd be here, I had to admit, but the impression had been a really strong one all the same.

Visiting Nicky is dangerous. You can catch paranoia as easily as you can catch a cold.

———

By the time I got back into Central London, it was the gloomy, smoky dog-end of the afternoon. Thus runs the day away. I tried Gabe McClennan's office again, but this time even the street door was locked.

Well then, that encounter was postponed—but not canceled. And I was left full of a restless impatience that had me striding down Charing Cross Road as though there was actually somewhere I needed to be. If it had been a few months before, I would have taken a cab over to Castlebar Hill—to the Oriflamme, which for exorcists in London is home away from home. But the Oriflamme had burned down a while back when some cocky youngblood had tried to demonstrate tantric pain control in the main bar and had set fire to himself and the curtains. There was talk of reopening elsewhere, but for the time being, it was just talk.

So I retired to a pub just off Leicester Square that used to be the Moon Under Water and was now something else, where I downed a pint of 6X and a whisky chaser to fuel my righteous wrath. Nothing was adding up here—and a job that should have been textbook-simple was developing the sort of baroque twiddles that I'd come to loathe and mistrust.

The ghost was recent. She'd lived and died in a world that already had factories, cars, and wristwatches. Okay, in theory, that could still have placed her at the turn of the century, but that wasn't the impression I'd got. The interior trim of that car had looked very modern and very luxurious, and watches with stainless-steel bands probably didn't even exist before the 1940s. So she didn't come into the archive with the Russian collection. And so the thing that tied her to the building in Churchway was something different—something I'd missed in the general rush to judgment.

Of course, I didn't really need to know who she was or who she *had* been—not to do the job I was being paid for. All I needed was enough of a psychic snapshot to form the basis of a cantrip, and after last night's adventures, I already had that. So why wasn't I breaking out the *méthode champenoise* round at Pen's instead of brooding in a loud bar in Soho?

Because I was being played for an idiot—and I never did learn to take to that.

If Gabe McClennan had been at the archive, this ghost had a history that I wasn't being told about. And if someone was scampering around the building after hours, it seemed a fair bet that they were there to keep tabs on me. Either that, or it was somebody conducting some kind of business that they didn't want daylight to look upon. I chased my thoughts around in decreasing circles for a while before getting back to the point—which I'd been avoiding pretty strenuously.

I'd told Peele that I'd do the exorcism by the end of the week. That gave me two more days, not counting today. But I had a strong enough fix on the ghost now to weave a cantrip anytime I wanted to. The job was effectively done. I could go in tomorrow, whistle a few bars, and walk away with the rest of that grand in my pocket.

And I'd be alive and in one piece and able to do this only because the ghost had stepped in to stop me before I made that fatal misstep in the dark.

There's a good reason why I don't think too much about the afterlife, and it's not squeamishness. Or at least, it's not the kind of squeamishness that would make you swerve aside from thinking about your brakes failing when you're driving down a one-in-three cliff road—or shut off thoughts of sharks when you're bathing in the sea off Bondi Beach.

It's my job. Can I put it any simpler than that? It's what I do. I send ghosts on to whatever comes next. Which means that if there's a Heaven, say, then I'm doing a good thing, because I'm opening the door to their eternal reward. And on the other hand, if there's no world after this one—nothing at all aside from the life we know—then I'm just erasing them. I've always had my own way of getting around the problem, which is by refusing to think of the ghosts themselves as human. If they're just psychic recordings—the residues of strong emotions, left on play-and-repeat in the places where they were first experienced—then where's the harm?

Now I could feel that particular defence crumbling and water leaking through more holes than I had fingers to plug them with.

I nursed the whisky for half an hour, then ordered another and brooded on that. And I was about to order a third when a glass appeared in front of me. It was black sambuca, and it had been served in that showy way that normally annoys the hell out of me—set on fire, with a coffee bean floating on the top—but when the woman eased herself in on the stool next to mine and leaned forward to blow out the flames, I forgot all about that.

The phrase "drop-dead gorgeous" is overused, in my opinion. Did you ever seriously look at a woman and think that your heart would stop? That the sheer intensity of her beauty threatened to burn a hole through your skull so that your brains would bleed out?

I was looking at her now.

She was tall and statuesque, where normally I go for petite and cute, but you could tell at one glance that she was the sort of woman that categories would crash and founder on. Her hair was a coal black waterfall, and her eyes were of a matching color, so intensely dark that they seemed to be all pupil. If the eyes are the windows of the soul, then her soul had an event horizon. She would have looked good with a Lady d'Arbanville snow-white pallor—good but Gothic. She was every shade in white's spectrum, which I'd never appreciated before. Her skin was the palest ivory, her lips a darker and richer color, like churned cream. The black shirt she wore seemed to be made of many layers of some almost-sheer material, so that as she moved, it offered microsecond glimpses of the flesh beneath. By contrast, her black leather trousers showed nothing but surface contours and talked to me entirely in terms of textures. A silver chain, entirely plain, decorated her left ankle, which was crossed over her right. Black stilettos sheathed her feet.

But it was her smell that was having the strongest effect on me. For a moment, when she first sat down, it had hit me as a hot wave of rankness like the stink of a henhouse after a fox has been busy in there. Then a second later I realized I was wrong, because the smell had opened up into a thousand shades of meaning: subtle harmonies of musk and cinnamon and dew-wet summer air overlaid on sweet rose; heavy, seductive lily; and undisguised human sweat. There was even a hint of chocolate in there, and those hot, sticky boiled sweets called aniseed twists. The total effect was indescribable—the smell of a woman in heat lying in a pleasure garden that you had visited as a child.

Then those astonishing eyes blinked, slowly and languorously, and I realized that my appraisal had taken several seconds—seconds in which I had just been staring at her with my mouth slightly open.

"You had a certain look about you," she said, as if to explain the free drink and her presence. Her voice was a deep and husky contralto; the equivalent in sound of her face. "Like a man who was reliving the past—and not really getting a lot out of it."

I managed a shrug and then raised the sambuca in a salute. "You're good," I admitted, and took a long sip. The rim of the glass was still hot, and it burned into my lower lip. Good. That gave me some point of contact with reality.

"Good?" she repeated, seeming to give that a moment's thought. "No, I'm not. Not really. You can take that as a warning."

She'd brought her own drink over with her, too—something in a tall glass and bright red that could have been a Bloody Mary or plain tomato juice. She clinked glasses with me now and drank off half of it in one gulp.

"Given how short life is likely to be," she said, setting the glass down and favoring me with another high-octane stare, "and how full of pain and loss and uncertainty, it's my opinion that a man should live for the moment."

If this was a chat-up line, it was a new one on me. I took another mouthful of her smell; I was disconcerted to find that I had an erection.

I groped for a bantering tone. "Yeah, well, normally I do. Most of the moments I've had today haven't been up to all that much."

She smiled. "But now I'm here."

Her name was Juliet. More than that she wasn't interested in telling me, except that it came out that she wasn't from London. I could have told that from her accent; or rather—as with Lucasz Damjohn—

her lack of one. She spoke with a kind of diamond-edged clarity, as though she was setting syllables down next to one another in line with a pattern she'd already memorized. It might have made her sound like a Eurovision Song Contest presenter, but when did Eurovision ever make you stand inside your pants?

She wasn't interested in finding out about me, either, which was great. The less I talked shop right then, the more I liked it. Whatever the hell we did talk about, I don't remember it now. All I remember was the absolute certainty that we were going to walk out of that bar and find somewhere where we could fuck like demented rabbits.

In the meantime, another glass of black booze arrived, and then another, and another. I drank them all without tasting them. Everything seemed to be black when you looked at it properly; Juliet's eyes were black kaleidoscopes that stole the world away from you and then gave it back again translated into subtle, midnight shades.

We tumbled out of the bar into the black night, lit by the thinnest sliver of moon, and then into a black cab that drove away without needing to be told where we were going. Or maybe I did mention a destination, some part of my brain still trying to deal with the mundane realities while I groped at Juliet's shadowy curves and she fended me off without effort.

"Not here, lover," she whispered. "Take me somewhere no one can see."

Then the cab was receding into the distance, and we were standing on the pavement outside Pen's house. The windows all black except for one; Pen was in the basement, and I remembered vaguely that I hadn't seen her for two days. It didn't seem important right then; nothing was important except getting into my room with Juliet and locking the door. Once that was done, the whole damn world could end, and I wouldn't care.

I couldn't get the key into the lock. Juliet spoke a word, and the door sprang open of its own accord. What a useful trick! She was leading me by the hand up the stairs, and there was a bubble of perfect silence around us, so that when I spoke her name in a drunken slur, I couldn't even hear it myself. She looked around at me and smiled, a smile full of almost unbearable promise.

My own door opened just as easily as the street door. She drew me inside and closed it behind us. "Oh Jesus, you're so—" I blurted, but she shushed me with a finger on my lips. This wasn't the sort of occasion where you had to flatter and cozen your partner with clumsy words that didn't even fit. Her blouse fell away without her touching it; so did her trousers and her shoes. Her flesh was uniformly pale, a dazzling contrast to her dark hair and eyes. Even her nipples, and the area around them, were all as pure and perfectly white as if they were carved from bone. Naked except for the slender chain tinkling out its seductive, silvery tune on her ankle, she pressed me to her, and her lips sought mine, one strong hand on the back of my neck, holding me in place.

"Now," she growled. "Give it to me. All of it."

She was tearing at my clothes with her other hand, and it didn't surprise or alarm me that her long nails shredded cloth like paper, making deep lacerations in my flesh along the way. She fumbled briefly between my thighs, until with her help, I tore free of what was left of my trousers and pants. Our mouths fused, then our groins. We merged at last, Juliet holding the contact as she drew the breath from my lungs into hers, and heat expanded from my heart and crotch to fill the world.

I thought it was true love. But then the heat grew more intense, went in an instant from blood-warm to blistering, and, opening my eyes, I saw that the two of us were wreathed in red fire that hid the room from my sight.

Twelve

I WAS IN AGONY. THE TERRIBLE HEAT WAS RUNNING through the rooms of my body like a monster too big to be contained in me, searching for doors and windows by which it could escape, looking to be joined with the greater heat that enveloped me. I tried to pull back from it, but it was as though I was welded into place: crucified on some twisted tree that wound around and around me and held me tight. I couldn't even scream; my mouth was already open, but something was locked onto it, stifling me so that I couldn't make a sound as I was devoured.

There are two ways in which pain can take you. Most times, if it's bad enough, it will just throw your wits out of the window. But if you're panicking already, then pain can be an anchor to cling to—something you can use to get yourself focused again. That's how it was with me. The agony of the fire shrilled through me like an alarm bell, waking me out of the trance that the succubus had lulled me into.

That's what she had to be, of course. Her black-on-black eyes and her natural perfume should have warned me, but I was inside her orbit before I knew what I was dealing with. After that, I was thinking only with my dick and no more capable of rationalizing what was happening to me than I was of dancing the cancan with my legs sewn together.

So I was going to die. And it was going to hurt.

Succubi consume your soul, and they take their time because—well, putting it as delicately as I can, because the orifice that they use for the job doesn't have any teeth. I could already feel myself weakening, sliding away, and the hell of it was that the feeling was one of febrile, throbbing pleasure. She was killing me, and she was making me enjoy it.

But at least I was thinking again, thinking through the pain and the arousal, like trying to tune into my own voice on a radio through wave after wave of howling static. And because I was thinking, I saw that I had a chance—an outside chance, somewhere between slim and snowball-in-Hell.

My mind was saturated with the succubus's subliminal scream of love, with the intoxicating, stupefying presence of her, expressed in smell and taste and texture, all urging me onward and inward. That was how she worked.

And as an exorcist, I could use that presence, that vivid, perfect sense of her. That was how *I* worked.

With my hands free and my whistle to my lips, it would have been easy. Well, it would have been three or four degrees farther away from impossible. With my whistle somewhere on the floor in the shredded remnants of my coat and my mouth locked tight against hers, I had to improvise.

I reached out with my left hand, flailed blindly for a moment, and then found a hard surface: the slatted cover of the rolltop desk. The pain was excruciating, and so was the pleasure, but I did my best to ignore them both. I started to tap out a rhythm.

It wasn't a full cantrip, but it was the start of one. When I play the pipe, I use pitch and tempo and slur and every damn thing else to turn the endless involutions of what I'm seeing in my mind into something ephemeral floating in the air in front of me. Compared to that, what I was doing now was like trying to make a functioning revolver out of prechewed wood pulp, and then aim and fire it. All I had was the one ingredient to cook with, the one dimension to work in.

It was never going to dispel the succubus, but I was hoping it would throw her a curveball. It did. A tremor went through her as the rhythm built and hit, and then for a moment or two she froze, some of the terrible strength going out of her sinuous limbs. I used those moments to push my head back, against the pressure of her cupped hand, and get my mouth away from hers.

I gulped in a lungful of air. By contrast with the searing heat that raged through me, it felt like swallowing a bucket full of ice splinters. No time to dwell on the agony, no time to go for a second, deeper breath. Instead I started to whistle, in quick but halting counterpoint to the rhythm I was still beating out with my fingers.

The effect on Juliet was spectacular. Her implausibly perfect face convulsed, her features seeming for a blurred instant to melt and run into some other configuration. She screamed in rage, and it was such a terrible sound that I almost lost the tune. Her grip tightened on me, threatening to crush my chest, but only for a moment. The shrill staccato of the cantrip bit into her, and she let me go, staggering back against the wall.

As Juliet went down in a fetal crouch, I crashed to my knees on the floor. The impact jarred me enough to make the breath hiccup out of me, and although it was only for a moment, the succubus drew strength enough from the brief stammer of silence to recover and straighten up again. I caught the tune at the head of the next bar and quickened the rhythm. She froze in place again, glaring down at me.

That was when a metallic glint from under the bed caught my eye. I scrambled down on all fours and came up holding my whistle. Juliet's eyes widened. Still whistling through my teeth, I set the mouthpiece of the tin whistle to my lips and came up on one knee in a Jon Anderson battle stance.

We were balanced on the cusp of a catastrophe curve. Freed from her suffocating embrace, I was able to get more range and more volume. But I didn't dare to stop for an in-breath, and in spite of the chains of the exorcism tightening around her, Juliet was still managing to stay both on her feet and on the mortal plane. She was a demon, not a ghost, and as I'd found to my cost with Rafi, it takes more than "Sing Something Simple" to take one of these bastards out.

She took a step toward me—a step, and then another. Her arms were reaching out for me, and fuzzy flowers of darkness were opening behind my eyes. I was going to run out of oxygen, the music would stop, and then that would be that.

Then, in silent-comedy style, the door flew open, and Pen charged in. She was holding a rifle with a five-pointed sheriff's star on the stock, which had the disastrous effect of making me laugh. I lost what was left of my wind, and the last breathy note of the cantrip dissolved into a whooping hiccup just as Pen aimed and fired.

She was a lousy shot. The first slug hit me in the shoulder, stinging like hell. The second went wide and blew a tiny, perfect hole in the lower left pane of the window. The third, fourth, and fifth hit the succubus in the stomach, chest, and forehead.

Juliet howled—a long, drawn-out bellow of agony and rage. Then she leaped over my head, and I heard the window smash into fragments, showering me with shards of broken glass and slivers of wood.

That was the last thing I remember, unless the quick fade to black counts as a memory in itself.

Drifting in and out of consciousness, I was vaguely aware of a voice intoning solemnly against my ear. Something about sin, something about light, then back to sin again. It made it hard to get any sleep, but then again, so did the tight band of pain across my chest and the ringing bells of agony in my head. I turned onto my other side, stifling a groan, and sank into the dark again.

The next thing I knew, there was a bright light pressing against my eyelids like a hot poultice and a less than gentle breeze on my face. Opening my gummed-shut eyes with a great act of will, I found myself staring straight up into the hundred-watt bulb of the antique Anglepoise next to my bed. I raised one hand—which was surprisingly hard because it seemed to weigh a lot more than usual—and pushed the lamp aside. When the afterimage faded out, I was looking at the gaping hole in the wall where the window had previously been and the moonless darkness beyond. The succubus had torn out the entire frame as she went through it and had even knocked loose a small section of the brickwork. I like rough sex as much as the next man, but Jesus, there has to be a limit.

I sat up slowly, taking care not to put too much strain on muscles that were already trembling and waving little flags of surrender.

"Good to have you back, Felix," said a voice from very close by, on my right-hand side. "I hope you feel as bad as you look."

With a sinking heart, I turned my head. The man sitting at the edge of the bed closed the book he was reading—a Bible, of course; I didn't need to check the spine—and gave me a watery smile. He was wearing his professional blacks, but he was the sort of man who would have looked better in a suit of armor: like, for argument's sake, Joan of Arc's. Maybe that was because his midbrown hair had copper blond highlights in it, and his blue eyes flecks of paler, colder silver. Or maybe it was just the hard, combative set of his broad shoulders, which neatly gave the lie to the half smile on his handsome face. *Suffer the little children to come unto me: the rest of you bastards I'll get to later.* He was five years older than me—five years and three months, to be more exact—and he never ever let me forget it. That was the root of his claim to know better than me where my life should be going, and the moral high ground was always his preferred battlefield.

"Hello, Matty," I said, my voice coming out as an emasculated croak. "How's the God business?"

"Better than the devil business, apparently," my brother answered dryly. "Do you know what day it is?"

"What day it—"

"The day of the week, Felix. Where are we in the week?"

"Oh for Christ's sake!" I protested weakly, but Matt was implacable. "It's Wednesday night," I said at last, giving up because my head was hurting and because giving up was easier than arguing about it. "Unbelievably, and appallingly, it is still Wednesday fucking night. I mean, unless I was out for twenty-four hours. Queen Elizabeth is on the throne, Posh and Becks are on the skids, and it's a rollover week in the National Lottery. Succubi go for the balls, not the brains."

Matt nodded. "In your case, though," he said austerely, "it would be easy to aim for the one and hit the other."

I opened my mouth for an equally smart-arsed rejoinder, but by now, some of the empty windows in my memory were filling up with very unpleasant images. I examined my hands, which were shaking slightly, my forearms, and then (wincing as the movement of my neck made the headache come back full force) my chest. There was no damage that I could see, despite my very vivid memories of being consumed in flames.

"Soul fires," said Matt. Lucky guess, I told myself, irritated as always by his ability to read my mind. "The succubus's heat is of the spirit, not the body. You're bruised all over, there's a bullet hole in your shoulder, and you've got scratches in some very intimate places, but you're not burned."

I nodded. It was what the textbooks said, but I'd never met a succubus in the flesh (I remembered Juliet's flesh with a reminiscent tremor of horror and arousal) or felt that kind of pain before. God knows, it had seemed real enough at the time, like turning on a rotisserie over a barbecue pit while the devil pricked my crisping skin to let out the juices.

The rest of the last twenty-four hours was swimming back into focus now, and none of it looked much better than the fiasco it had ended on. The ghost's snapshots of life and death and Gabriel McClennan; the intruder at the archive and my forestalled attempt to take a long walk off a short stairwell; a day spent chasing my own tail in various scenic locations in North London; and then an unlikely encounter with a predatory demon who was cruising the lower end of Charing Cross Road looking for a square meal and a bed—not necessarily in that order.

I looked at my watch. Just after three o'clock, which meant I'd been unconscious for more than two hours. I felt a sudden, almost physically painful sense of urgency: a feeling that I had a lot to do, and it was already almost too late to start. In fact, I wasn't sure if I could even walk, but if you don't try, you never find out. I threw the covers aside and swung my legs off the bed.

"You'll need to rest," Matt said, a slight edge of warning in his voice. "Your system has taken a huge shock. And if you could bring yourself to pray—"

I waved away that suggestion. I was trying to stand, but my body wasn't cooperating.

"What are you even doing here?" I demanded irritably. "Did the Holy Spirit come and wag its tail at you to tell you there was a soul in danger?"

Matt frowned. "Your landlady called me. When she tried to wake you up and couldn't get any response, she became afraid. And since she knew that what had fled out of that window was something other than human, she chose to put her faith in an agency that is itself more than human." I didn't answer; I was still trying to get my legs under me and my balance straight. I was naked apart from my socks, which somehow is a lot more undignified than being all the way there, and my body was marked all over with shallow cuts that looked as though they could spell out a hidden message in Mandarin Chinese. "You ought to be grateful," Matt went on. "To her, if not to me. Without the holy water and the blessings I put on you, you'd be sinking into coma by now."

I gave a humorless laugh, but it was a straw in the wind. Annoyingly, the church's armory of waters, oils, and sing-alongs did have some efficacy over ghosts and demons—only sometimes, and only if they were wielded with genuine faith, but Matty had that in spades. I couldn't deny that he'd probably saved me from much worse damage. After Pen had come riding to my rescue like Davy Crockett and . . .

I put a hand to my shoulder. There was a small, raised welt there with a perfectly circular wound in the center of it. The mark left by Pen's rifle. Except that it wasn't a rifle at all. It was a kid's air gun, and I realized abruptly what it was that it had been loaded with—what it was that had made the succubus fuck and run like a traveling salesman in a bad old joke.

"Rosary beads," I muttered with mixed admiration and disgust. Rosary beads filed down to the size of BB shot. She'd said she was worried about me—and that Rafi had given her a warning. Evidently it had been a fair bit more circumstantial than the one he'd given to me.

Matt stood up and walked around the bed to stand over me. He looked down at me, his mouth set into a stern line. "Felix," he said quietly, "you can't go on like this. You've turned a gift from God into a stock-in-trade—and it's a debased trade at that—one you can't follow with a clear conscience. Exorcism is the Church's business, not a game for amateurs or a get-rich-quick scheme."

"Do I look rich?" I demanded, throwing out my arms to indicate my modest surroundings—more modest than ever, now that they'd been trashed by the demon. "Or were you thinking of the seven-figure deal I'm going to sign for my memoirs?"

Matt didn't give an inch; he wasn't capable of it. "You can't banish ghosts without shriving them," he pointed out with the same dogged calm. "Otherwise you could be sending innocent souls to Hell. You don't understand what any of this is about. You're like a blind man wandering down a busy street and firing a handgun at random into the crowd—except that the harm you're doing is enormously, incomparably greater."

With the help of the bedpost I did manage to get on my feet this time, so our faces were only a few inches apart as I gave him my answer, with as much quiet dignity as I could manage given the whole stark-bollock-naked thing.

"Thanks for the sermon, Matty. But you'll have to bear in mind that I don't believe in Heaven, or Jesus, or papal infallibility. And all that stuff about fighting the good fight and serving God instead of mammon—well, it's inspiring, but let's be honest. Your crowd are no better at poverty than they are at chastity, are they?"

Matt was silent for a moment, but not because my eloquence had struck him dumb. He just wanted to make sure that he didn't talk back in anger; that would probably be a sin.

"You don't believe in anything, Felix," he said at last, composing his face into an absolute deadpan. "And that's precisely why you shouldn't have anything to do with the final disposition of human souls. You don't know where you're sending them, or by what authority, or how the power that God has placed in your hands works."

"Whereas you'd like to slot it into a convenient schematic that has unbaptised babies going to Hell," I shot back. "You're in a pyramid-selling scheme—the biggest one in history. And maybe a thousand million people bought into it, but that doesn't make you right."

"Limbo," said Matt. "Unbaptised babies go to Limbo. But you knew that." He turned his back on me and crossed to the gaping window; Matt never did like staring contests. "Nobody in this world can know whether or not they're right," he murmured. "We see as through a glass, darkly. We can only do our best. But when the choice is between doing nothing and doing harm, surely nothing is the wiser option?"

I took a step after him, which was almost a serious mistake; I was still weak enough to need the bedpost's support and solidarity. "The Gospel according to Cool Hand Luke? Sweet, Matty—and lowdown. Because the alternative to freelance exorcism isn't nothing. I mean, what your people do, that's a sod of a long way from nothing, isn't it?" I saw his shoulders tense slightly at that. "You think I don't know that the Church has got its own exorcists? You think I don't know there's a recruitment drive on? Sorting out the sheep from the ghosts on behalf of Mother Church—I wouldn't call that nothing. And the ones who meet your stringent quality standards—well, I assume they get the blessing, the whistle, and the wave. Fuck knows what you do with the others, but I've heard some ugly rumors, and it's obvious you don't want anyone to see you doing it. At least with me it's one size fits all. I don't pretend to be God—or to be on first-name terms with the bastard."

I didn't realize how loud my voice had got until I saw Pen standing in the open doorway—this time holding a tea tray with a single mug on it, and so looking less like Annie Oakley, more like one of Toulouse-Lautrec's busty waitresses. In the sudden silence, Matt turned to face me, and there was a gleam in his eyes that could almost have been called threatening if my brother hadn't been above such unworthy emotions.

"One size fits all is what the devil says, Felix," he said in a tone of mild and sad reproof. "One size only fits all if you've got nothing to measure by. But you *do* have something to measure by. If you remember nothing else, remember dear Katie, God rest her. And your poor friend Rafi. Remember what you did to him. You see how dangerous it is when good intentions—"

The contents of the mug hit Matt full in the face. From the smell of it, it was gunpowder green tea laced with something herbal and potent. It was warm rather than hot, though, and it didn't do much damage. The tray did; it smacked edge-on into his nose and made him stagger back. He turned to stare at Pen in absolute astonishment. She was standing with the tray gripped tightly in both hands, clearly ready to deal out more retribution as soon as he opened his mouth again.

Two thick trickles of blood were oozing from Matt's nostrils to combine on his upper lip. He felt the bridge of his nose gingerly with one slightly shaky hand, still staring at Pen. She lowered the tray, suddenly self-conscious as the berserker moment passed. "Sorry, Fix," she mumbled. "I'll make you up some more." She went out of the room, and a moment later, I heard her footsteps stomping heavily down the stairs.

I found that Pen's act of cathartic violence had purged my own anger at Matt pretty effectively. "You shouldn't talk about Rafi when she's around," I told him. "She was his—" I hesitated. There wasn't an easy way to describe the way Rafi and Pen had circled each other, the intricacies of their sometime-never mating dance. "She loved him," I said. "She still does."

"And does she know what you did to him?" Matt snapped back, cradling his nose. It was already beginning to swell, the skin at the bridge not yet bruised but flushed dark red.

"Pretty much," I said. "Yeah."

Matt shot me one last look of exasperation, then followed Pen out of the room.

I got dressed, which was a complicated operation, because every move I made caused another set of muscles to report in unfit for duty. Mournfully consigning the remains of my many-pocketed greatcoat to the wastebasket, I shrugged on an antique trench coat that gave me an entirely misleading air of retro-chic.

I felt sick and sore, but also restless and uneasy. I couldn't leave it alone, but I couldn't make it go anywhere useful. Raising a succubus wasn't an easy thing to do, or a safe one. Okay, it was true that she didn't need to have been called and bound for any one particular purpose; it could just be coincidence. I tried that idea on for size. The thing that called itself Juliet had picked me at random from the slow-moving river of unaccompanied men that flowed through the West End of an evening. She didn't know who I was, and she didn't care.

Yeah, it was possible. Obviously, it was possible. She belonged to a predatory species, and although they lived somewhere else, they were known to use the Earth as a hunting ground. But Asmodeus had warned me—and warned Pen, too, telling her enough so that she could arm herself in advance. *You're going to take this case, and it's going to kill you.* Unless there were even worse horrors waiting in the wings, Juliet had to be what he was talking about—and this attack had to be related in some way to the archive ghost.

I found Pen down in the basement, which was where I expected her to be. She was feeding Arthur and Edgar when I knocked and came in. The birds ate liver, which Pen bought in industrial-size freezer packs and thawed one piece at a time. Her hands were stained red brown with watery blood. She looked around, then nodded her head at a fresh mug of milkless tea that was steaming on the mantelpiece. I picked it up and took a long slug; I knew enough about Pen's herbal remedies to take it with fervent gratitude.

"Where's Matty?" I asked, my voice still creaking slightly.

"He left," she said, sliding another sliver of meat into Arthur's clashing beak as Edgar cawed loudly for parity. "I'm sorry I hit him. Especially after he came out in the middle of the night to make sure you were all right. It was just—I think I was on edge after"—the pause stretched—"after seeing that thing."

"It's okay," I said. "My brother believes in the mortification of the flesh. He should have thanked you."

She made no answer.

"And I am," I added. "Thanking you, I mean. When you barged in and did your *Reservoir Dogs* number, I was running out of breath. A few moments later, and I'd probably have been running out of internal organs, too."

Pen was staring at me with troubled eyes.

"I'll pay for the window," I went on, conscious of the fact that I was only speaking to fill up the silence. "I'm wrapping up a job right now, so I'll have seven hundred quid coming through in a day or so. That should more or less cover it, wouldn't you say?"

She shook her head, but it wasn't an answer to my question. "Fix," she said woefully, "what the fuck have you got yourself into?"

"I don't know," I admitted. "I don't know what I've got myself into. But I'd like to start finding out."

"It's just a straight exorcism, isn't it? What's the problem?"

I opened my empty hands—a minimalistic shrug. "I think it got personal."

"Oh Christ, don't say that!" Pen looked genuinely unhappy, and I could guess what she was thinking.

"Not like with Rafi," I said. "It's just—I almost fell down forty feet of stairwell last night, only this ghost waded in to stop me."

"The ghost—"

"Right. And tonight, some bastard lets a succubus off the leash and gives it my scent. I want to know what I'm doing and who I'm doing it to. I want to know what else is at stake here."

She nodded slowly. "All right," she said. "I can understand that."

I pressed my advantage. "Pen, I hate to ask this, but would you be up to driving me somewhere? I don't think I'd be safe behind a wheel right now."

———————

The discreet door on Greek Street was closed and locked, but there was a light on in a third-floor window. Right now, at four in the morning, someone was doing a photo shoot, or having their head massaged, or being spiritually healed. There's a whole lot of sterling work that goes on while the city sleeps.

"And this Gabe McClennan is an exorcist," Pen demanded. "Like you?"

"He's an exorcist," I allowed. "The rest of what you just said was actionable slander."

In fact, in a profession not much known for its ethical probity or compassion, McClennan stood out as a twisting, weaseling, backstabbing bastard. I knew two or three guys from whom he'd stolen clients, money, or equipment, and half a dozen stories about people he'd screwed over. Someone even told me once that Gabe took a huge wad of cash from Peckham Steiner, the sanity-deficient granddaddy of all Ghostbusters, just before he died, on the pretext of building him a "safe house" where ghosts wouldn't be able to touch him. But Steiner is likely to turn up sooner or later in any story that exorcists tell. I don't normally listen to tattletale stuff like that unless I've got some personal experience to weigh it up against, so I'd been professionally courteous toward Gabe the first few times we'd met—and on one job, he'd actually sought me out because I had firsthand experience of a factory in Deptford he'd been asked to disinfect.

I'd agreed to help him and had offered him a thirty-seventy split, which he'd cheerfully accepted. Bearing the stories in mind, I asked for cash on the nose, and he counted it out into my hand underneath the green and yellow overpass at the Queen Mary's end of the Mile End Road. Then we walked off in opposite directions, and before I'd gone a hundred yards, I was jumped and rolled by two guys who came at me from behind. They might have had nothing at all to do with McClennan, but it sure as hell looked like he was renegotiating the deal on the fly. At any rate, that was the last time we ever collaborated.

"Wait for me here," I told Pen. "With the doors locked. Keep the keys in the ignition, and drive away if anybody comes."

"Anybody but you, you mean?"

I gave her a solemn nod. "You're on the ball, chief," I said. "I like that in a woman."

"After tonight, Felix, I think I know more than I ever wanted to know about what you like in a woman."

I let that one pass. It was too close for comfort.

"What are you going to do if he's not there?" she demanded.

By way of answer, I showed her the balding black velvet bag that held my lock picks. She shook her head in tired disapproval, but said nothing. She knows all about Tom Wilke and how I obtained my indefensible skills. She fervently disapproves, but right then I could see that it paled into insignificance next to all the other murky shit that was flying around.

I got out of the car and crossed the street. There were three bells over on the left-hand side of the door that roughly corresponded with the three signs. I pressed the one marked MCCLENNAN. Nobody answered. I pressed again and looked around me as I waited.

Greek Street is an after-midnight kind of place, but most of the nightlife had already rolled over and turned out the lights; we were only a couple of hours away from dawn.

But after a few moments, I heard footsteps from inside, accompanied by the atonal creak of badly warped floorboards. A bolt was drawn, then another, then a key turned, and the door opened a crack. Gabe McClennan, in his shirtsleeves and with a heavy stubble on his face, stood in the gap.

He stared at me for a few moments, looking totally nonplussed. It was clear that I was the last person he expected to see on his doorstep at four in the morning. Actually, it was one step beyond nonplussed, into the related domain of baffled and hacked-off.

"Castor," he muttered. "What the fuck?"

"I wanted to consult with you on a job I'm doing, Gabe."

"In the middle of the night?"

"Well, since you're still up . . ."

He rubbed his eyes with the heel of his hand.

"Castor," he said again. He laughed and shook his head as if he couldn't believe it. "Yeah, whatever. Come on in."

McClennan turned and walked back inside, and I followed. The light on the third floor clearly wasn't anything to do with Gabe; the door he opened was right off the first-floor landing, next to a doorless cupboard full of electric meters and half-bald mops lying drunkenly against the wall.

Despite the shabby frontage and the dubious location, Gabe's office was a hell of a step up from mine. It was dominated by a huge antique desk with ball-and-claw feet that was big enough to split the room in two. His filing cabinet had four drawers, a cherrywood veneer, and a vase full of chrysanthemums on top. He even had a diploma on the wall, although Christ only knew what it said. Two-hundred-meter swimming certificate, most likely.

"So what can I do for you?" he demanded as he walked around the desk. It wasn't just the stubble; he was looking pretty rough in other ways, too. The bags under his eyes were so dark, it looked as though someone had given him a combination punch when he had his guard down, and if his shirt had had a map of the Lake District on it, the sweat stains under his armpits would have been Windermere and Coniston Water. It was an unusual sight. McClennan has an aquiline face, a spare build, and a thick bow wave of snow-white hair that he wears in a style intentionally reminiscent of Richard Harris. Normally he has a style that can best be described as dapper. To-night—like me—he'd clearly been overworking.

He rummaged in his pockets, ignoring me for a moment until he'd found a small pill bottle that was about half full. He shook out two black tabs and popped them. Then, in the expansiveness of the hit, he remembered his manners and held the bottle out to me. "Mollies," he explained unnecessarily. "You want some?"

I shook my head. A lot of exorcists have an amphetamine habit, occasional or chronic. They say—or some of them do, anyway—that it makes them more sensitive to the presence of the dead: lets them receive on a wider range of frequencies. There's something in that, too, but I've always found I lose as much on the comedown as I gain on the rush. So usually I pass.

"The Bonnington Archive," I said, parking myself on the edge of the desk. I didn't want to take the client's chair; it would only give Gabe an unwarranted sense of power and authority.

"Never heard of it," he shot back, quick and easy. I glanced at his face, but he was looking down right then—searching in his desk drawers this time. Then he found what he was looking for and hauled it out—a bottle of Johnny Walker Red Label, about two-thirds empty.

"You sure about that?"

McClennan stared at me, then shrugged; all ease and edges now that the mollies had kicked in.

"Yeah, I'm sure. Ghost-toasting may be easy money, Castor, but I don't do it in my sleep. Why? What's the skin?"

"Nothing, probably. But I'm doing a burn there, and your name came up."

He was opening the drawers on the other side of the desk, bent over again so I was just getting the top of his head.

"My name came up? How? Who mentioned me?"

"I don't even remember," I lied. "But someone said you'd been there. Or maybe I saw your name on a receipt or something. So I just wanted to touch base with you, see what you made of the place."

He slammed a drawer shut and straightened up. He looked the same as he'd looked when he'd opened the door—half blitzed with exhaustion, but not particularly fazed by anything I'd said.

"You didn't see my name on any receipt," he said, "because I was never there. If someone mentioned me, then I must have worked for them somewhere else."

"Yeah," I said, sounding regretful. "That must be it. Just my luck. It's a tough nut, and I wanted to bounce some ideas off you."

"You can still do that," said Gabe. "Why not? We're both professionals, right? I stroke your dick, you stroke mine. Shit, I can't find any glasses. Give me a second, will you?"

He came back around the desk, past me, and on out of the room. I leaned forward so I could look through the open doorway and saw him heading up the stairs. Maybe he was going to borrow some crockery from the Indian head masseuse.

In the meantime, the devil finds work for idle hands to do. I crossed to the filing cabinet and gave the top drawer a tug. Locked. But three quick steps took me round to the driver's side of the desk, where Gabe had left the top drawer open. It was full of the usual strata of desk-drawer shit, and I could have excavated for five minutes without finding anything more useful than pencil shavings and paper clips. But I got lucky. A small ring with two identical keys was lying against the bottom right-hand corner of the drawer, where it would always be ready to hand in spite of the apparent chaos.

I went back to the filing cabinet and tried one of the keys. It turned, and the drawer slid open with only the smallest squeal of reproach.

A to something or other: Gabe filed his cases in alphabetical order, and most of them even had file tags attached, all written out with the same sputtery black biro.

Armitage

Ascot

Avebury

Balham

Beasley

Bentham

Brooks

Damn. I went back and checked again, but there was nothing there. No Bonnington file, no smoking pistol.

But there were no footsteps on the stairs, either, and I suddenly noticed that the file right at the back of the drawer was a *D:* Drucker. I don't even know where the inspiration came from, but I back-tracked from there through Dimmock, De Vere, Dean, Dascombe . . . Crowther.

Two strikes. Damn again.

I wasn't expecting anything now, but for the hell of it, I slid a finger in between Dascombe and Crowther and pushed them apart. There was another folder hanging in between them that had no file tag. Instead, the name DAMJOHN was written on the inside edge in black felt-tip. Gabe must have run out of the little plastic tag holders.

The wonderful thing about a Russian army greatcoat is that you can carry a Kalashnikov, a samovar, and a dead pig underneath it without making any noticeable bulge. It's not so easy with a trench coat, because it's a thinner and more figure-hugging sort of garment. But it was a thin file, and it just about fit in. I slid the drawer closed and made it back to the desk just as I heard Gabe's footsteps coming down the stairs.

"You okay taking it straight?" he asked, setting two cut-glass tumblers down on the desktop. "I don't have any soda."

"Straight is fine," I said. He poured me a stiff measure, another for himself.

"So tell me about the case," he said.

I turned the glass in my hand, watched the facets catch the light. "Ghost takes the form of a young woman with most of her face hidden behind a red veil. Multiple sightings, persistent over time—about three months, give or take—but spread out over the building, so there's no locus where I can easily read her from."

Gabe shrugged with his eyebrows. "So you hang around until she shows up. Doesn't sound like she's particularly shy."

"No, she's not," I admitted. "To be honest, I think I've got a hook halfway into her already. That's not the problem."

"Then what is?"

I took a tentative sip of the whisky, swirled it on my tongue. "The furniture," I said—furniture being exorcists' slang for any aspect of a haunting that's not directly tied in to the ghost itself.

Gabe snorted. "Spend too long looking at the furniture, you'll end up tripping over your own feet. Didn't you tell me that?"

"No. Can't say I did."

"Well, it's true anyway. Just do the job and draw your pay. Fuck do you care?"

"I'm starting to care." I put the glass down. Whatever cheap-ass generic whisky Gabe had decanted into it, the only time Johnny Walker had seen that bottle was if he ever used it to piss in. "And I'm starting to see complications. Did you ever meet a man named Lucasz Damjohn?"

Not a flicker. Gabe consulted his memory, then shook his head. "Nope. Don't think so. Does he work at this archive place?"

"He runs a strip joint off Clerkenwell Green. With a different kind of establishment over the top, in case fancy begotten in the eyes wants to take a quick stroll elsewhere."

Gabe looked a question. I ask you, what's the point of an Oxford education if nobody gets your Shakespearean references? "He's a pimp," I clarified.

"Okay. So how is he connected to your ghost?"

"I'm not sure yet. I think maybe he killed her."

Gabe's jaw dropped. Only for a second, then he reeled it in again and tried to look unconcerned, which was interesting to watch. "How do you even know you've got a murder?" he asked. "What, is she wearing wounds or something?"

"Or something," I said. Then I glanced casually at my watch, did a double take, and stood quickly. "Oh shit, Gabe, this is going to have to wait. I just realized I've got to meet someone at five."

"You've got to meet someone?" Gabe repeated. "What, you set up appointments in the middle of the night? Sit. Have another drink. I can't help you unless you tell me the whole thing."

He tried to refill my glass, which was already mostly full. I moved it out of his reach. "I'll catch you another time," I said, and headed for the door.

He jerked to his feet. It was clear that some idea of stopping me was going through his mind. But I kept on going, out into the hall and then into the street, crossing over to where Pen was parked. Seeing me coming, she threw open the passenger door and started the engine.

As we drove away, I saw McClennan standing in his doorway, watching us go. For the first time, it occurred to me to wonder what he had been doing to get himself so wasted.

"Take a left," I directed Pen. "Then another." While she drove, I opened the file and took a look inside.

The contents were meager. There was a letter, not from Damjohn but from a firm of solicitors, discussing the terms on which Gabriel McClennan would be placed on retainer to Zabava Ltd., "a company incorporated in the United Kingdom for the provision of leisure facilities in the Central London area." A copy of the contract was stapled to the letter. It said that McClennan would provide "services of exorcism and spiritual prophylaxis" to all of Zabava's premises for a fixed fee of a grand a month. The contract was signed by McClennan and by someone named Daniel Hill.

Then there was a sheet of paper with a list of addresses on it—most of them in the East End—and another with dates printed on it in columns (all except the last one had been checked through with yellow marker), a scrawled note on half of a torn sheet of A4, which read *Change to Friday 6:30*, and a matchbook from Kissing the Pink, the club where I'd met Damjohn the other night. Very tastefully done—the name of the club was balanced on either side by the silhouette of a woman's upper body, in profile so that her erect nipples were given the prominence the designer thought they deserved.

I was hoping for a smoking pistol. This didn't even qualify as a spud gun.

Pen had us heading back to Soho Square now. I told her to pull over, kissed her lightly on the cheek, and dived out of the car. "I'll see you later," I promised.

"You bloody well be careful, Fix," she called after me, but I was already sprinting for the corner and back around onto Greek Street. I walked about a third of the way along, then, when I was about twenty yards from Gabe's place on the other side of the street, I found a doorway to loiter in.

It didn't take as long as I thought it would—but then I guess there's not much traffic at that time of night. About ten minutes later, a car pulled up outside Gabe's door—an electric blue BMW X5. Arnold the Weasel Man climbed out of the front passenger door, and a huge, shapeless object wearing a suit edged and wedged its way out of the back. Scrub—there couldn't be two like him in the whole damn world. He held the door open, and Damjohn himself stepped out after him. Must have been a tight fit. Damjohn led the way inside, Scrub followed, and Arnold brought up the rear, pulling the door to with a decisive slam.

So it was official. They were all in it together. I just wished I had the faintest clue what "it" actually was.

Thirteen

THERE'S A PLACE WHERE I GO SOMETIMES TO retrench and regroup—to dredge up a bit of strength when I'm feeling weak and to find some silence in the city's remorseless polyphonic shit-storm. Bizarrely enough, it's a cemetery: Bunhill Fields, off the City Road close to Old Street Station. It ought to be the last place in the world I'd want to be, but somehow it suits me down to the ground—and then about six feet farther.

One factor is just that it's old and disused. The last burial there was more than a century ago; all the original ghosts clocked off and headed elsewhere long before I ever found the place, and no newer spirits have come along to set up shop. There's a quiet and a peace there that I've never found anywhere else.

And then again, there's the fact that it's not hallowed ground. It's a dissenters' graveyard, full of all the bolshie bastards who played the game by their own rules back when doing that could get you the pre-Enlightenment equivalent of cement overshoes. William Blake is dreaming of Jerusalem under that sod, and Daniel Defoe is probably dreaming about something a fair bit earthier. You've also got John Owen and Isaac Watts, the reservoir dogs of eighteenth-century theology. What can I tell you? I just feel at ease in their company.

So that's where I was, and that's why. I needed to think. When I walked back into the Bonnington, I wanted to feel that I wasn't going in there completely naked, without any kind of a plan.

Disengage and reassess, I told myself. Go through what you already know, and see if it builds up into a picture of what you thought you didn't.

I take on this job, and on the first day I'm already being followed by Scrub. Bearing in mind the toolbox that Lucasz Damjohn must have at his command, it said a lot that he'd pick out such a big and powerful item. Scrub must normally be reserved for putting the frighteners on rival whoremasters; applied to me, he was just overkill.

Damjohn then goes out of his way to get to meet me, but doesn't try to lean on me in any way or even particularly pump me for information about what I'm doing.

Then it turns out that McClennan and Damjohn are old cronies.

And the archive ghost has met Gabe McClennan—a shit-hot exorcist, whatever else he might be. So why the hell is she still there?

That was the sixty-four-thousand-dollar question. I'd really started to sell myself on the idea that Damjohn might have something to hide, but that kite just wouldn't fly. If McClennan had been sent in to burn the Bonnington ghost, she'd be toast. Like he said, he would have gone in, done the job, and drawn his pay. But he hadn't, unless the job he'd been sent in to do was something different.

And someone had raised a succubus to burn me out—an exotic and dangerous weapon, but one that wouldn't raise an eyebrow with the police or anyone else, given what I did for a living. What had I done that was worth that kind of attention? Or what was I doing now?

Answers on a postcard. None of it made any sense at all, and the more you looked at it, the more it fell apart. Pretty much the only thing I was certain of was that I wasn't going to be playing any tunes at the Bonnington until I had some answers.

I gave it up at last. Whatever power Bunhill Fields normally exerts on my highly suggestible mind, it wasn't working right then. I was feeling as though my eyeballs had been scooped out, roughly polished with a sanding wheel, and then shoved back more or less into their right places. My head was full of gray cheese instead of brains. If I'd had brains, I would have gone back home to Pen's, boarded up the window with yesterday's *Independent*, and slept for twelve hours.

Gray cheese took me to the Bonnington instead.

Frank looked at me with grave concern. "You look rough," he said as I dumped my coat down on the counter—and his face as he said it was slightly awestruck. "What happened to you?"

"You should see the other guy," I said, falling back on cliché.

"Was he a professional wrestler?"

"No, he was a girl. Where's Jeffrey?"

"I believe Mr. Peele is in his office. I'll call him and tell him you're—"

"I prefer to come as a surprise," I said, and walked on toward the stairs. Frank could have stopped me, but he didn't. I guess having been chewed up, spat out, and left for dead had some sort of meaning in his moral framework. Cheers, Frank. I owe you one.

I made a point of looking in at the workroom. Rich, Jon, and Cheryl and a couple of people I didn't know all glanced up as I appeared in the doorway—glanced, and then kept looking.

"Mate, you should be in bed," Rich said after a pause so heavy it wasn't just pregnant but ready to break its waters and deliver.

"Yeah," Cheryl agreed. "A *hospital* bed. You look like you picked your teeth with a chainsaw, man."

Jon Tiler said nothing, but he suddenly seemed to be sitting very still. He'd been reaching for a pen; now both of his hands were flat on the desk, and he was just staring at my face. He looked unhappy. I opened a mental file drawer and dropped that look right into it.

"I used to juggle chainsaws," I said conversationally. "It looks dangerous, but you just have to keep at it. Rich, have you got a pen and paper?"

"Yeah, sure," he said. He found the pen in his desk tidy and a sheet of scrap lying next to his printer. He pushed them across the desk to me.

Taking the pen, I wrote down the symbols that the ghost had shown me in that remembered image—scrawled on the torn-out page of a book and held up to the inside of a car window. ПОМОГИТЕ МНЕ.

I reversed it and pushed it back across to Rich.

"That's Russian?" I asked.

He stared at it, his eyes widening slightly. "Yeah," he said.

"What does it mean?"

He looked up at me—a puzzled, searching look. "SOS," he said. "It means 'Help me.'"

"Thanks. That's what I needed to know."

I gave them all a nod and walked back out, then on down the hall to Peele's office.

————

Peele was on the phone when I walked in, talking about productivity and different ways of defining it. I sat down opposite him and stared at him in silence as he went on. The stare and the silence did their job; he wasn't looking directly at me, of course, but a good stare communicates itself by means other than sight. After less than a minute, he made a clumsy excuse and said that he'd call back. Then he hung up and shot me an exasperated microsecond glare.

"You've got a problem," I said. "And I think it might be a different problem from the one you think you've got."

"Mr. Castor!" he blurted. "That was the Joint Museums Trust! I was taking an important—I was engaged on"—words momentarily failed him, and he almost met my stare—"I don't appreciate you coming in here unannounced and simply presuming on my time!"

"Well, I'm really sorry," I said with nothing in my voice that could be read as sincerity. "I assumed you'd want an update on the ghost situation."

If I thought that would stop his mouth, I was wrong. Peele was full of indignation, and it needed to find a vent.

"This isn't proceeding as I expected," he said, sounding near-terminally agitated. "Jon Tiler was in here yesterday morning, determined to file a formal complaint against you after the damage you caused on Tuesday night. I persuaded him not to, but it was a very unpleasant interview. I hope you have some positive progress to report."

"No," I said. "But I do have some *negative* progress to report—in other words, I've been able to rule a few things out. You see, I was operating under some mistaken assumptions about your ghost. Like that she had to be tied to the Russian collection in some way. But that's not true, is it?"

Now Peele really did look at me—for the barest fraction of a second, then his gaze fell to his desktop again. "Isn't it?" he asked, after a pause long enough to count to three in.

"No, it isn't. She dates from a much later period—viz the present day—and that puts a whole new complexion on her being here. I'm looking for a different kind of explanation now."

That was meant to sound vaguely threatening and maybe to sweat some additional information out of Peele, if there was anything there to be sweated. But as strategies go, it sort of blew up in my face. His lips set in a tight line. "Mr. Castor," he demanded, "why are you looking for an explanation at all?"

I tried to parry that question rather than answer it. "I'm a professional," I said, deadpan. "I don't just come in and clean up. I have to understand the context for—"

Peele cut across me. "You made no mention of context when I took you on," he pointed out coldly. "You promised to carry out a specific service, and now you're making caveats that seem to me to have nothing to do with the matter in hand. I also have to ask, since you raise the issue of professional standards, whether your objectivity has been compromised in some way."

It was my turn to look blank. "My objectivity?" I repeated. "Do you want to explain that?"

"Certainly. On every occasion up to now, when we've talked about ghosts, you have used the impersonal pronoun—'it'—to refer to them.

This has been consistent and at times almost aggressive—as though you felt a need to establish a point of some kind. Now, overnight, the ghost you're meant to be exorcising for us here has become a 'she.' I have to ask why that is."

Damn. Fairly caught. I could dodge the kick, but the stable door was already down—and I hadn't even realized it until I saw the splinters.

"You're an academic," I said in a good imitation of offhand. "Words matter a lot to you; they're part of your stock-in-trade. I don't have the leisure to look for nuances like that. I just get the job done."

"That, Mr. Castor," Peele answered scathingly, "is what I should very much like to see."

I leaned across the desk. The best defence is a good smack in the face. "Then work with me," I snapped. "You can start by showing me your incident book again. If the ghost didn't come in with the Russian stuff, then where did she come from? What else was happening back in early September that could explain her popping up here?"

Peele didn't answer for a moment. It was clear that he was asking himself the same question and not getting any good answers.

"And finding this out will help you to complete the exorcism?" he demanded at last.

"Of course," I said, not even flinching at the flat lie. I wasn't about to explain that I could do the exorcism right there and then—probably while standing on my head and juggling three oranges.

With obvious reluctance, Peele opened his desk drawer and took out the ledger that I'd seen a few days previously. He started leafing through the pages himself, but I reached over and blocked him by putting a hand on the cover and closing the book again.

"You'd better let me," I said. "I may not know what I'm looking for, but I've got more chance of recognizing it if I see it for myself."

Peele handed me the book with a look on his face that said he was keen to get rid of it—that he was sick of the entire subject of the haunting. Funny. For me, now that someone was apparently trying to kill me because of it, it was starting to develop a visceral fascination.

The book fell open at Tuesday, September 13, which I took to be just a happy coincidence. That was the date of the first sighting, I remembered. And I also remembered how long the entry had looked when I'd last seen it. It looked even longer now, and Peele's tiny handwriting even more impenetrable. To put off the moment, I flicked ahead through the pages to the most recent entry, which of course was only two days old; it concerned Jon Tiler's complaint about the indoor tornado I'd whipped up when I'd tried to use Rich's blood to raise the ghost.

Going back through November, there seemed to be an entry for every day—most of them fairly terse. "Richard Clitheroe saw the ghost in stack room 3." "Farhat Zaheer saw the ghost in the first-floor corridor." Nothing in October after the first week, though; there was a lull, Peele had said. There was a lull and then when she came back, she didn't talk anymore.

But as I continued to flick through the pages, I saw the pattern start up again: dozens of sightings, scarcely a day without at least something, going all the way back through September to the thirteenth. Okay, not everything that was going on was ghost-related. On September 30, there'd been a leak in the women's toilet: "Petra Gleeson slipped in the water but seems not to have been injured." And on September 21, someone named Gordon Batty had had "another migraine headache."

I was so lost in this fascinating saga of everyday life among archiving folk that when I got to the dense block of text for September 13, I carried on turning the pages. That was when I realized why the book had fallen open at that particular page in the first place—it was because the previous one had been torn out.

I reversed the book and showed the gap to Peele.

"Did you make a blot?" I asked.

He stared in astonishment at the mismatched dates and then at me.

"That's impossible," he protested, bemused. "I'd never take a page out of the incident book. It's an official record. It's audited every year by the JMT. I don't know how this could possibly have happened . . ."

Better try to rule out the obvious, in any case. I pulled the book open in the center of a signature and showed Peele that they were stitched in already folded. "Sometimes with a book that's stitched like this, you tear a page out from the back to write a note or something, and then its partner falls out from the front a while later. Could that have happened here?"

"Of course not," he insisted a little shrilly. "I would never do that. Not from the incident book. It would show up the next time—"

"—the next time the auditors did their rounds. It's okay, Mr. Peele, I'm not accusing you of anything. I just wanted to make sure we weren't dealing with a random accident. Assuming we're not, the other working hypothesis is that someone came in here and tore the page out on purpose, to remove some reference that he or she didn't want to become common knowledge."

"But if I wrote it up in the book, it was *already* common knowledge!"

"Then perhaps what they wanted to avoid was someone drawing a link between two things that happened around the same time."

"Such as?"

"Such as I have to say I don't have the faintest idea." I looked at the point where the incident book's dry narrative line was broken. The last entry that was present in full was for July 29; August must have been a slow month. Then the dates resumed with a brief entry for September 12 (Gordon Batty's first migraine, chronologically speaking), followed by the epic details of September 13.

"Something in August," I prompted Peele. "Or it could have been around the start of September. Maybe even just a few days before the ghost was first seen. What else was happening then? Does anything stick in your mind?"

"August is slow," Peele said, ruminating. "The school visits stop altogether, so all we do is collate, repair, catalog new acquisitions . . ." He shook his head. "I don't remember anything. Nothing that stands out."

"Well, do you mind if I question your staff again?"

He flared up again. "Yes, Mr. Castor. To be honest, I do. Why would that be necessary?"

"Like I said—to establish a context for the haunting."

Peele thought for a while, then shook his head firmly.

"No. I'm sorry, but no. I don't want any further disruption to the running of the archive. If you can do your job without getting in the way of the people who actually work here, then do it. If you can't, then give me back the deposit I've already paid you, and I'll bring in somebody who *can* do it."

"The deposit is nonrefundable, Mr. Peele."

"Now see here, Castor—"

"Those were the terms you agreed to. But I don't think the issue here is whether or not you get your money back. You've got a dead woman in your archive, and she didn't die all that long ago. You need to know why she's here and why she's so full of rage and misery that she's attacking the living. If you don't get answers to those questions, exorcising her could be just the *start* of your problems."

"I don't understand the logic of that statement."

"Then think about it. It'll come to you."

I left him fulminating. There seemed no point in staying. In fact, the longer I hung around, the bigger the risk that he might actually talk himself into throwing me out. And I wasn't ready to go, not yet.

I stuck my head into the workroom. "Peele wants someone to open doors for me," I said. "Any volunteers?" This lying thing—once you got into it, it was really a fantastic labor-saving device.

Rich opened his mouth to speak, but Cheryl got there first. "I'll go," she said. "Sign the keys over, Rich." Rich closed his mouth again and shrugged. There was a brief transaction in which Cheryl swapped her signature for a turn with the big key ring. Then we headed for the door.

I walked on down the corridor, and Cheryl fell in beside me. "The Russian room?" she asked.

"No. The attic."

"The attic? But there's nothing up there."

"I know. My brother says nothing can be a real cool hand."

Two nights ago, dressed in opaque shadows, the attic had looked numinous and threatening. By daylight, it just looked empty.

We went to the end room, and Cheryl followed me inside. I pointed to the cupboard.

"What's in there?" I asked.

Cheryl shook her head. "I haven't got a clue," she confessed. "Why?"

"I'm just curious. Would there be a key to that cupboard on Rich's ring?"

Cheryl flashed me a wicked grin. "Hey, smutty innuendo aside, if it's got a hole, Rich has got a key."

She went down on one knee and squinted at the lock on the cupboard door. Then she nodded, satisfied, and started to sort through the heavy ring of keys. "Silverline 276," she said. "It's the same as the ones downstairs. Here you go."

She slid a key into the lock, turned it, and pulled the door open with a flourish.

The cupboard was empty.

"Maybe it's got a false bottom," said Cheryl without much conviction. She bent over to examine it, and I found myself staring at hers—which was indisputably real. My body reacted of its own accord; blood rushed to my face and to other outlying parts. Arousal exploded in me like a signal flare.

When Cheryl straightened, she could see the sudden change in my mood at once. It must have been written all over my face.

"You didn't bring me up here to open cupboard doors at all, did you?" she demanded, reprovingly but with no real heat. "You dirty bugger."

It was the succubus, Juliet. She'd reached inside me, which was her mystery and her power, and turned the dial on the outer casing of my libido from "normal" to "seismic." Evidently, that wasn't something that just went away—and being in such close proximity to Cheryl had triggered an aftershock. I braced myself for a smack in the face, but Cheryl was looking at me with a quizzical and contemplative expression on her face. I opened my mouth to explain, but she shook her head briskly to stop me from saying anything.

"I've never had sex at work before," she murmured at last. "And you are pretty attractive—in a sleazy, government-health-warning-on-the-packet sort of way. You know what I always say, yeah?"

I'd forgotten, but I remembered now. "If you've never tried something, you've got no right saying you don't like it."

"Exactly. But are you sure you're not letting your eyes make promises your trousers can't keep, Castor?"

"That's a valid question," I said, trying to reengage the parts of my brain that weren't connected with panting and sweating. "Cheryl, this isn't me. This is just a sort of hangover from—"

She stopped my mouth with a kiss, which tasted very faintly of coffee and cinnamon. I had ample opportunity to taste.

When we broke off, she smiled at me again—a smile with a world of promise in it.

"Someone could just walk in," I reminded her, making one last doomed effort to be the voice of reason.

"That's where the keys come in handy," Cheryl said. She crossed to the door, closed it, and locked it. Then she came back over and began to unbutton my shirt.

"I've got cuts and lacerations," I warned her. "In some of the parts you may be planning to use."

"Poor boy. Let Auntie Cheryl have a look."

She had very gentle hands—which she used to do a number of things that were highly prejudicial to the exorcist/client relationship. I responded in kind, and things went from bad to wonderfully bad.

But even as Cheryl drew me into her with a wordless murmur of approbation, I was thinking of the parcel tape and the plastic bags. Where did they go?

Fourteen

W E SAT UP IN THE ATTIC IN A COMPANIONABLE POST-coital languor, leaning against the bare wall. We'd already made ourselves decent again, and anyone clattering up the bare stone stairs would announce themselves from a good way off, so we didn't have to worry about being caught in a compromising position.

"You never suggested using a condom," I commented.

"Have you got a condom?"

"No."

"There you go, then."

"Are you always this happy-go-lucky?"

"I got carried away. So did you. But I'm on the pill. Are you saying I should still be worried?"

I shook my head. I steer clear of relationships. I've always been afraid of someone I love turning up dead, and then—having to live with that or having to deal with it. Having to face the choice. So although I'm not entirely celibate, I think I count as chaste.

"And no more should you. Word. Let's change the subject."

"Okay," I conceded. "Can we talk shop?"

"Sure. Go on."

"Have you ever heard of a strip club called Kissing the Pink?"

Cheryl laughed; she had a dirty laugh that I liked very much. "I'm glad we're talking shop now," she said. "I'd hate to think you were gonna ask me out on a date. No, I don't know it. I've never been in a strip club in my life. I saw the Chippendales once, if that's any good."

"Have you ever met a man named Lucasz Damjohn?"

"Nope."

"Or Gabriel McClennan?"

"Nope again. Felix, what's any of this got to do with my Sylvie? You're sounding like a private detective."

"It's all tied together somewhere," I said, aware of how lame that sounded. "Cheryl, what about these rooms? Do they ever get used for anything?"

"Not yet. We're gonna expand into them eventually. Some bits of stuff get stored up here, but not much. Why?"

Instead of answering, I got up, breaking what was left of the drowsy, intimate mood. I crossed to the window and looked out. Then down. Three floors below was the flat roof of the first-floor extension. A plastic bag lay on the gray roofing felt, the wind making it jerk and flurry, but not shifting it.

"What's underneath us on this side of the building?" I called over my shoulder.

"Strong rooms," said Cheryl.

"Just strong rooms?"

"Yeah, just strong rooms."

"With no windows?"

"Right. Why d'you want to know? What's going on?"

"I thought I heard someone up here," I told her, going for a half truth. "When there shouldn't have been anyone."

"That'd be Frank, then," said Cheryl.

"Sorry?" I said, turning back to face her. "Why would it?"

"He does his meditating up here. Jeffrey said he could."

"Frank meditates?"

She grinned. "How'd you think he got that laid-back? We've got the only Zen security guard in London. Only he's really a butterfly dreaming he's a security guard."

"This was at night. When the archive was closed."

"Yeah?" She blinked. "Okay, I take it back, then. Frank only comes up in his lunch hours. But—what were you doing up here after the place was shut?"

"Long story," I said. "Would you mind keeping it a secret for now?"

"You'll have to buy my silence."

"With what, exactly?"

She waggled her eyebrows suggestively.

"I'm just a plaything to you, aren't I?" I complained with mock bitterness.

"Too right, boy. Let's say six o'clock tonight—give me time to get out of here. I'll meet you at Costella's. You're gonna have to work hard to keep me happy."

"Will I get time off for bad behavior?"

"We'll see. Depends how bad you can be, I suppose."

"Cheryl, is there an alley off to the side of the new annex?"

"Yeah, that's where the wheely bins are. Why?"

"I'm going to go down there and shinny up on that flat roof."

"As an aftermath to sex? A lot of people would just smoke a cigarette or something."

I kissed her on the lips. "Smoking's bad for you," I pointed out.

"So am I, boy. I'll do your back in."

"I'm looking forward to it. Wait for me—I'll only be a minute."

I left her there and descended the stairs. Frank gave me an amiable nod as I went by. For the first time, there was a second guard on duty with him—a younger man with a military crew cut who gave me a fish-eyed stare. I smiled a smile of good-natured idiocy and kept on going.

The alley was a cul-de-sac, lined on both sides as Cheryl had said with the wheely bins of the adjacent buildings—each standing black plastic coffin bearing a number in white paint that had dripped while it was drying.

Everything looked different from ground level. Judging the spot as best I could, I climbed on top of a Dumpster and then used the horizontal bar of a closed steel gate. It was an easy climb, which didn't surprise me in the least. Someone at the archive was doing it on a regular basis, after all. But I was too far over, and I was looking into a builder's yard. The flat roof of the Bonnington annex ended ten feet to my left. I tightrope-walked along the wall until I got to the roof. I could see the plastic bag lying close to the sheer wall of the main building—which, apart from the attic skylights at the very top, was an eyeless cliff face.

I went over to the bag and picked it up. *Good Food Tastes Better at Sainsbury's*, it said. But whatever was inside it, it wasn't food. It was heavy and rectangular. I tore open one corner and looked inside.

The words От всей души поздравляю и желаю всего наилучшего looked back at me, but that was a coincidence. More than half the letters and documents in the bag were in English.

A whistle made me look up. Cheryl was leaning out of the attic window. She waved at me, and I waved back. I mimed "stay there," palm out like a policeman's stop sign. She nodded.

I went back inside and headed for the attic, but she met me half-way.

"What was in the bag?" she asked.

"A selection of good wholesome produce at reasonable prices," I said. "Cheryl, will you let me into the Russian room again?"

"I thought you said it was a dead end. What was in the bag?"

"Stuff. I did say that, and I might even be right. But there's something I want to take a look at."

Everything in the strong room was just as I'd left it the other night. The boxes were still stacked up on the floor, Rich's laptop was still on the table, and the place still had the same sour, dispiriting smell as it'd had the first time I'd walked in, four days ago now.

"Six o'clock," Cheryl reminded me.

"I'll be there," I promised.

We kissed and parted.

As soon as she'd left, I turned the computer on. Then, while it warmed up, I went looking for the other thing I needed. It should have been on the table, but since it wasn't, I must have shoved it into one of the boxes along with an armload of papers.

It took me about ten minutes to find it, but at least it was still there: the ring-bound reporter's notebook with Rich's handwritten notes in it. Armed with that, I opened the database program on the computer and tried to figure out which end of it was up. There was a file named RUSSIAN1, which seemed to be a reasonable place to start. The program said it contained about 4,800 records.

I opened a few at random. Like the boxes, there wasn't a lot to choose between them.

> LETTER. 12/12/1903. SENDER MIKHAIL S. RECIPIENT IRINA ALEXOVNA. PERSONAL. RUSSIAN.
> LETTER. 14/12/1903. SENDER MIKHAIL S. RECIPIENT PETER MOLINUE. PERSONAL. ENGLISH.
> LETTER. 14/12/1903. SENDER MIKHAIL S. RECIPIENT RUSSIAN EMBASSY "TO WHOM IT MAY CONCERN." BUSINESS/FORMAL. RUSSIAN.

I flipped through the pages of the notebook, looking for something that would be a bit more distinctive. In the end I settled for a Valentine's Day card and typed in some of the search fields that Rich had jotted down. RECIPIENT CARLA. DESIGN HEART WITH WINGS.

Yeah, there it was: item number 2838. The next document I tried, a birth certificate, was number 1211. The third was a book of wedding photos, and it showed up as number 832.

It was no use. Even if I was right, it could take me days to find what I was looking for. There had to be another way of doing this. I thought about it for a long while. Then I picked up the phone and placed a call to Nicky.

He answered in his usual guarded way—making sure he knew who I was before he owned up to being who he was. Normally I take that in my stride, but not today. "Nicky, enough of the bullshit," I said testily, cutting him off. "I need another favor. If it comes to anything, I'll buy you a whole crate of that overpriced French mouthwash. Meet me at Euston Station. At the Burger King on the main concourse, okay? That way, you'll be able to see me from a hundred yards away, and you'll know it's me, rather than some weird branch of the government pulling a sting. It's goddamn urgent, okay? Someone's trying to kill me, and I'd like to know why."

Taking that kind of tone with Nicky was a high-risk strategy. I waited to see if he'd cave in or tell me to go fuck myself. He did neither. "Trying to kill you with what?" he demanded tersely.

"A stairwell. And then a succubus."

That got a response, at any rate. "Holy shit. A fuck-demon? What did it look like? Did you get pictures?"

"Did I get pictures? Nicky, I was lucky to get out with my wedding tackle still attached. No, I didn't get pictures."

"Then what was its name? Was it one of the steganographics?"

"I'm not an expert. She said her name was Juliet. She had black hair and black eyes."

"Anything else? Markings? Nonhuman features? What were her sexual organs like? Any teeth down there?"

"Nicky, for the love of Christ—they were like a woman's—she was normal. Stupendously high-end normal." Something popped up in my mind, like conceptual toast. "Except for her breasts."

"Which were?"

"She didn't have any areolae around her nipples. All of her skin was pure white."

"Got you. Okay, I'll do some looking around."

"That's not what I want you to do."

"I'll do it anyway. The hell-kin fascinate me."

"Just meet me, okay?"

"Euston Station. I'll be there—but twenty minutes is all you're getting, and you can pay for the taxi."

I went looking for Rich. I found him in the public reading area, watching over a florid, preoccupied woman who was leafing through what looked like the catalog from some ancient exhibition of chamber pots and toilet furniture. He looked up when I came in and gave me a nod.

"Alice is looking for you," he said. "She didn't look happy."

"I'd probably be more worried if she did. Listen, Rich, there was something I wanted to ask you about."

"Go on."

"The first week in September. Maybe the last week in August. Do you remember anything out of the ordinary happening around then?"

He looked blank.

"Can you give me a hint?" he asked. "What kind of anything?"

"The kind of anything that would end up being written into the incident book."

"So . . . an accident? Or a breakage? Someone going home sick?"

"Sounds like the right sort of territory, yeah."

Rich frowned thoughtfully, but I suspected that was just to show willing. "Nothing that springs to mind," he admitted. "The trouble is, those things happen all the time. Unless you've got something to pin it to—something that definitely happened at the same time—you don't remember it well enough to say when it was."

"The first appearance of the ghost," I said. "It was almost exactly at that time. Does that help?"

He shrugged helplessly. "Sorry, mate."

"Never mind. It was a long shot. If you do come up with anything, though, let me know. Ask Cheryl, too. And any of the part-timers you see."

"And Jon?"

I had to mull that one over for a moment. "Yeah, and Jon," I said at last. "Anyone you bump into. It doesn't do any harm to ask."

"Doesn't do any good either, most of the time," he observed cynically.

"I'm noticing that, brother," I admitted. "But hope springs eternal, eh?"

———————

I slipped out of the archive at lunchtime and crossed the road to Euston Station. I've never liked the place; it looks like a scaled-up model of something run up by a *Blue Peter* presenter out of the slatted interiors of fruit boxes. But it teems with people around the clock, which made it an ideal place for a private meeting. Feeling guilty and hunted because of what I was carrying under my shirt, I glanced around behind me. The crowds parted for a moment, and a female figure ten paces or so behind me turned and took a sudden interest in a newspaper display. I wasn't sure, but again I thought I recognized her as Damjohn's girl. Rosa. I hesitated. I had to meet Nicky, and I knew he wouldn't wait, but I was in a maze, and any Ariadne would do. I took a few steps toward her, but then a few more clusters of people eddied past, and when I got to the newsstand, there was no sign of her.

With a grimace of annoyance, I moved on to the Burger King. It doesn't have any doors; it just opens out directly onto the concourse, which was why I'd chosen it. Nicky likes to have a clear field of vision in all directions.

As soon as I sat down in the coffee shop, he was pulling out a chair and slipping in next to me. He must have been circling around for a while, waiting for me to show, but it would go against the grain for him to sit down first. I felt the chill coming off him; he'd be wearing freezer packs under his bulky fleece, and probably a thermos of dry ice somewhere to freshen them up. Unlike most of the risen dead, Nicky was always pragmatic and prepared.

From his pocket he produced a thin sheaf of A4 pages, folded in half and then in quarters. He handed them to me, and I looked a question.

"Dead girls," he said. "The stuff you were asking about."

"Quick work," I said, impressed.

"Easy work. But like I said, you gave me a sloppy brief; there's a lot of stuff there. You've still got *your* work cut out. Now, what's today's crisis?"

I took the small but heavy bundle out of my shirt and slid it across the table to him: hard, rectangular, wrapped in newsprint from that morning's *Guardian*. He unwrapped it and stared at it as though he'd never seen one before.

It had taken a lot of nerve to walk past Frank with that stuffed up my shirt. I'd thought of asking him for my coat, but I didn't want to risk drawing any more attention to myself. "I need it looked at," I told Nicky. "Looked at properly. Dissected, autopsied, and written up in excessive detail. The file you're particularly looking at is called RUSSIAN1. It's a database file. I want to know if it's been tampered with—if anything unusual has been done to it anywhere along the line."

"This is somebody's laptop," Nicky said.

"Yeah."

"Not yours?"

"No."

"Stolen, Castor?"

"Borrowed. It'll get back to its rightful owners in due course."

"And you've got the brass balls to pass it on to me?"

"Sure, Nicky. They're *already* out to get you, remember? And you're dead. You don't have a damn thing to lose."

Nicky wasn't amused. "The work I do," he muttered, glaring at me,

"I try to keep it as low profile as I can. I try not to disturb the grid. Because the grid"—he gestured with his hands, fingers spread—"is like a great, flowing river. And along the banks of the river, a whole army of guys are sitting on folding chairs with rods and lines all set up. Everything you touch, Castor—everything you touch is a hook. There are people out there who want to know everything there is to know about you. So they can control you. So they can neutralize you. So they can kill you whenever they want to. You think I don't know that paranoia is a clinical condition? I know better than anyone. But you embrace it when it becomes a survival trait."

"And the scariest thing is that you're making sense to me," I observed sourly. "Listen. I swear to you, your name never gets mentioned. Nothing you do for me goes any further—even to the guy who hired me. I just use it to corroborate what I already know or think I know. And afterward, I'll owe you a favor. A really big one."

Nicky nodded slowly, more or less satisfied. "I like people owing me favors," he said. "Okay, Castor, I'll shag your laptop."

"Do you think you'll be able to tell if someone's doctored that file?"

He laughed mirthlessly at that. "Are you joking? I'll be able to tell if anyone farted in the same room as this machine. And what they ate beforehand. I've got my methods, Castor—and my resources. Your succubus, by the way, she's been around for a while."

The body swerve left me standing. "What?"

"There are descriptions of her in some of the grimoires. The black eyes. The dead white skin. The name."

"Juliet?"

"Ajulutsikael. *She is of Baphomet the sister and the youngest of her line, though puissant still and not easily to be taken with words or symbols of art. But with silver will you bind her and with her name, anagrammatized, appease her.*"

"How do you know she's the one?"

"Because she used a name that's made up out of some of the letters of her real name. She always does. Don't ask me why. I guess it's just a demon thing. Was she wearing silver, by the way?"

"A chain. On her ankle."

"There you go. You're lucky to be alive, Castor. She's fast and she's mean. Gerald Gardner—Crowley's old mate—talks about someone he knew who summoned her to impress his friends at a stag party. She played all coy, got him to put one foot over the edge of his magic circle, then she ripped off his cock and balls and ate them. Not quite the hot oral action he was hoping for, I'm guessing.

"Oh, and she doesn't give up. That's the other thing the occultist crowd all insist on. Once she's got your scent, she keeps coming. Watch your back."

There was no answer to that apart from the involuntary wince I gave. "Thanks, Nicky," I said. "I was feeling bad about the whole thing, but not nearly bad enough, obviously. You've raised my game."

"Sorry. I thought you should know."

I got up.

"ASAP for this, Nicky," I said, pointing down at the laptop. "Call me today, if you can. I need to get that back before anyone notices it's gone."

"I'll be in touch," he said. Then, as I turned to leave, he stopped me with a raised hand. "You're aware you've got a shadow?" he said.

"What, still? I saw her as I was coming in, but—"

"She's walked past three times. Checking you out. Waiting for you to leave, maybe."

I was impressed by the sensitivity of his radar—and happy to have the corroboration. "Yeah, I'm aware."

"Is she anybody I need to know about?"

"No, she's strictly personal."

"You're kidding." Nicky looked disgusted. "She's too young for you, Fix. She's too young for anybody."

"Call me," I said.

I headed back across the concourse and out through one of the many sets of doors that lead through to the bus station. There was a flight of concrete steps ahead of me, going down into an underpass that crossed the Euston Road. I took it. At the bottom, I turned a corner. Then I waited.

I heard her before I saw her: clip-clapping clumsily down the steps on tall, precarious heels. She turned the corner and almost ran straight into me. Her brown eyes, made pandalike by inexpertly applied makeup, opened wide with shock. It was Rosa. Now that I saw her full-on, there was no mistaking.

"Was there something you wanted to talk to me about?" I asked her.

I'm not sure what I expected, but it wasn't what I got. Rosa reached into her coat and pulled out a steak knife; it looked alarming and incongruous in this setting.

A moment later, it looked a whole lot worse as she lunged forward and tried to embed it in my chest. I leaped back, and the blade sliced empty air in front of me. Rosa almost overbalanced, but recovered and took another swipe.

"You did it to her!" she shouted in a thick accent that sounded Czech or Russian. "Again! You did it to her again! It was you! He told me it was you!"

On the third pass I tried to grab her wrist, but she twisted free and almost caught me with a backhanded slash that came out of nowhere. She was so thin! My hand had closed for a moment around her forearm, and there was almost nothing there. But the hate she was obviously feeling for me had given her a hectic strength, and she closed in again with a scream of anger.

This time, I didn't try to hold her. I just knocked the knife out of her hand with a vertical swipe of my arm. I hadn't meant to hurt her, but she gave a gasping sob and staggered back, clutching her wrist. I kicked the knife away to the other side of the tunnel and then threw my arms out, fingers spread and palms up, to indicate that I didn't mean her any harm.

"I didn't do anything to anybody," I said. "But I'd love to know what it is I'm supposed to have done. And who told you I did it. If you explain that to me, maybe we'll know where we stand."

She glared at me, still clutching her wrist. She cast one longing glance at the knife, then sprinted for the stairs. I caught her in two steps, my hands around her waist. I leaned to the side as she flailed and kicked, because I needed to keep my legs out of the way of those deadly heels.

"Please," I said. "Rosa. Just tell me what you're so angry about. Tell me what I'm being accused of."

She froze suddenly and then went limp in my arms. She half turned, her head lolling sideways onto my shoulder. At the same time she gave a trembling sob of exhaled breath. She slumped against me, making me take her weight as her body pressed against mine.

Disconcerted, I relaxed my hold—and she jackknifed at the optimum moment, the back of her head slamming with sickening force into the bridge of my nose. I fell backward against the wall of the tunnel, and she was away. By the time I could see through my watering eyes, there was no sign of her.

With my head throbbing and my pride hurting a damn sight worse, I climbed the steps back up to street level and took a look in both directions. Nothing. Even in six-inch heels, the kid had a good turn of speed on her.

The pain in my head was getting worse, making my stomach churn with nausea. I sat down on a low wall to regroup and re-equip. Being beaten up by women seemed to be one of the hazards of this particular job. At least Cheryl had been gentle with me.

One thing surfaced through the throbbing ache and bobbed around on top of it, cheerful as only an abstract fact can be in a world of intense physical pain. *She just kept saying roses,* Farhat had told me when I had asked her about the ghost, *going on and on about roses.* And Cheryl had said the same thing, back in that first interview. But they were both wrong. I was willing to bet that what the ghost was talking about was *Rosa*.

I reviewed my options. There were some ideas I wanted to follow up at the archive now—ideas about plastic bags and flat roofs. And Rosa was suddenly looking like someone I needed to talk to urgently the next time I caught her without a kitchen implement in her hand. But the immediate priority was Nicky's notes—and if I took them back to the Bonnington, I was risking a run-in with Alice.

So I took them down into the Underground instead. Not as good as Bunhill Fields, but it was a lot closer, and it did the same trick, to some extent. Fast-moving vehicles act as a kind of block or damper on my psychic antennae—so in spite of the engine noise, the vibration and the rocking, the nonexistent air-conditioning, the smell of used food and the proximity of other people's armpits, for me the place has a haze of contemplative calm hanging over it like an angel's protective wing. I often ride the Circle Line when I need to think long and deep.

Uncomfortably ensconced in a seat that had had one of its plastic arms ripped out at the root, and therefore sharing rather too deeply in the personal space of a burly guy in a Scissor Sisters T-shirt who smelled strongly of acetone, I took the notes out of my pocket and looked them over. There was a lot more there than I'd thought at first—about ten sheets of deceptively thin onionskin printout paper, all full of dense, unformatted type with the occasional "your guess is as good as mine" percentage sign. God alone knew where Nicky had dug this stuff up.

They were database entries for suspicious deaths, and they were made slightly impenetrable by the fact that the fields were all run together without headings or even spaces. The first entry began:

MARYPAULINEGLEESON2BROWNBLUE5BLUNT-
INSTRUMENTTRAUMAIMPACTED12NOTDETER-
MINED7SKULLCLAVICLELEFTHUMERUSPAVE-

MENTOUTSIDEOLDBARRELHEADPUBLICHOUS-
EYESWITNESSACCOUNT2253YES12MINMULTIPLE-
SEEATTACHED1ST2ND3RD4TH5TH6TH7THSEEAT-
TACHED8TH9TH10THSEEATTACHED11TH12THAB-
RADEDCLEARABRADED

It went on for a long while in this grim, deadpan tone. Then there was a second name, KATHERINE LYLE, followed by another cascade of words and numbers. It occurred to me as I scanned it that I should probably make a point of never handling the original document; the black emotions locked up in it would probably clothesline me straight out.

In some ways the printout was completely impenetrable; in others, it told a lot of depressing variations on a bleak and familiar story. Mindful of my limitations, Nicky had included on some of the later sheets material of a different kind—downloads from news-agency summaries or other less telegraphically terse sources. With the help of these crib notes, I was able to work my way through the main list a lot more quickly.

It was mostly a case of weeding out the ones that were impossible, and after that, the ones that were possible but didn't feel right. Straightforward accidents with lots of witnesses; domestic manslaughters where the victim lived in the area and would have far stronger links to her own home than to the Bonnington, which after all was only a refrigerated warehouse full of moldering paper; heart attacks and strokes and all the banal tragedies of human existence that normally let you slip into the afterlife without raising too much of a splash.

I got it down to a short list of three, but I realized that I'd need a bit more information to tell me which if any of the three was actually the archive ghost. And at that point, an inspiration equivalent in weight and momentum to a half brick neatly aimed hit me smartly at the base of the brain.

I had a contact, one I could bring in on this. He wouldn't like it a whole lot, but that which doesn't kill us makes us strong.

I looked up at the electronic display strip on the wall of the carriage: THE NEXT STATION IS MOORGATE, it read. The train had almost finished its circuit of the Circle Line. After Moorgate came the Barbican and then Farringdon, from where it was an easy step to Damjohn's club. Two stops after that and I'd be back in Euston Square, at the archive. But Alice was gunning for me at the archive—according to Rich, anyway. And I didn't really have anything I could usefully do there until Nicky finished interrogating the laptop and got back to me.

So Kissing the Pink was where I went first. The idea in my head was that I'd make my peace with Rosa and find out how she was connected to the archive ghost. I was pretty vague on details after that, but I hoped that something would present itself.

As I was walking there, I took out my mobile phone, which for once I'd remembered to recharge, and placed a call to a Hampstead number. I got through on the first try. James Dodson wasn't happy to hear from me again, and when he heard that I wanted to come over and visit, it pretty near spoiled his day. I had to insist. Things might have got ugly if we'd been talking face to face. But that was a treat I still had to look forward to.

There was no sign of Rosa in the downstairs area of the club, and my courage failed me at the thought of questioning the whores upstairs. I did ask one of the waitresses, though. Yes, Rosa had been around earlier in the day, but her shift was finished now. She might possibly come in again tomorrow; she usually did on a Friday. I bought myself an overpriced gin and tonic and drank it slowly in the club area downstairs, staring glumly at a parade of beautiful, naked, emphatically alive women who somehow seemed a lot less real and tangible to me right then than a single dead one.

There was a small, decorous commotion over to my right as two men were settled at one of the tables by a very deferential waitress. I squinted into the half dark and without any surprise at all identified the pair of them by their build: the squat, hairy-browed Damjohn and the tall, patrician Gabe McClennan.

They were oblivious to the room, continuing some intense conversation that had already been under way when they sat down. Intense on Gabe's part, anyway—he was talking with his hands as much as with his mouth, and his face was working with anger and frustration. Damjohn responded with imperturbable calm, or perhaps with the very mildest irritation.

I'd already made up my mind that I'd bail out if Damjohn showed up; there wasn't anything to be gained by letting him know that I was looking for Rosa, and it might even get her into trouble. But somehow retreat seemed like a very unpalatable option right then—and sometimes whacking the nest with a stick is the best way of finding out what kind of insect you're dealing with—the downside being that sometimes you get stung.

So without consciously thinking about it or making anything that would count as a decision, I found myself crossing the room, putting my half-finished drink down on their table, and pulling out a chair in between the two of them.

"Afternoon, gents," I said. "Mind if I join you?"

Gabe stared at me as if he'd just bitten into an apple and found me squirming around inside it. Damjohn's expression was impassive for the space of about two seconds and then broke into a smile that you couldn't have told from the real thing with aqua regia.

"Mr. Castor," he said. "Of course not. Please, sit." He gestured expansively, and I dumped myself down with an exaggerated sigh of satisfaction. McClennan looked like he was going to choke.

"How's business, Gabe?" I asked, flashing him a smile.

"You stole from me, you little fuck!" His voice was a low, venomous snarl. "You came into my office with your bullshit story and then you—" Damjohn stopped him dead with a raised hand—a neat trick that I almost felt like applauding.

"We were just talking about you," he clarified blandly, turning to me.

I bowed my head coquettishly. "Only good things, I hope."

"A mixture of good and bad. But then, I wouldn't expect a man in your profession to be an angel. I have, I must tell you, been surprised by your—resilience. Your unimpressive frame and build belie you, Mr. Castor. They give a false impression of vulnerability."

"I'm a weed," I said amiably. "The more poison you put down, the more I spring up again."

"Yeah? Well, I'll fucking poison—"

"McClennan," Damjohn said, "if you speak again, I'll become aggravated with you. Do you really want that to happen?"

Gabe left that question hanging, and Damjohn went on as if he hadn't been interrupted by either of us. "In point of fact," he mused, giving me a thoughtful stare, "I believe you may have the right skills and the right temperament to fit in well in one of my little enterprises."

"You're offering me a job?" I had to ask, because I didn't believe what I was hearing. Bribery was the last thing I'd been expecting.

"These things are never offered unless they've already been accepted, Mr. Castor. I'm sure you understand. Are you *looking* for a permanent position?"

Gabe was going a very scary color, fetchingly set off by his snow-white hair. It looked as though the effort of not speaking was going to cost him a major blood vessel.

"You've already got an exorcist," I pointed out with a nod in his direction.

"My table is long and wide. It's all a question of what good things you bring to it."

"And that's where I stick," I said. "I mean, all I can do are the basics. I can't raise demons, for example."

"No." Damjohn's eyes flicked over to Gabe for the merest instant.

"But for dangerous and marginal activities of that nature, one uses the reckless and the stupid. For you I'd have other tasks."

I shook my head, not in refusal but in lingering disbelief. This was surreal. Damjohn was between me and the stage; from where I was sitting, a hugely pneumatic redhead was spreading her legs right behind his head, giving him a most unusual—but somehow appropriate—halo. "How much would you be looking to pay?" I asked, just for something to say.

"As a starting salary? Let's say two thousand pounds a month. With a lump sum to cover moving expenses and any possible friction on the more tender areas of your conscience. And it goes without saying, but I will say it anyway, that any of my girls would be delighted to receive a visit from you at any time. More than delighted—because you'd be coming to them as my personal friend and associate. If you have any unusual needs of a sexual kind, they would be well catered for."

Damjohn looked at me shrewdly, and I got the feeling that I was being weighed and assessed by a very skilled fisher of men. "I can see," he said, "that I've still failed to find the measure of you, Mr. Castor. But I do have one other inducement to offer you."

He stopped and waited for a response. I shrugged to indicate that I was still listening. On the stage, the redheaded woman was gone. In her place, a sax player was laying down some very lazy and half-hearted licks to a recorded backing, no doubt making the sex tourists feel like real urban sophisticates.

"You must have wondered—a man who does what you do for a living and who has been gifted by nature as you have would *have* to wonder—what conceivable scheme of things would allow the dead both to return as they do, in the forms that they do, and then to be sent away again by the likes of yourself and Mr. McClennan here. You must, in other words, have questions about the structure and logic of the invisible world—its geography, for want of a better word. You must have asked yourself what it all means."

I'm sure that Damjohn saw me tense. Up to now, I'd been feeling pretty much on top of this conversation, because I knew that there was nothing he could offer me that I'd want. Me and love— even me and sex—is a complicated equation, and you can wear empty pockets with a certain chic, like a badge of integrity. But answers? Oh yeah. I'd gone halfway around the fucking world looking for answers.

Damjohn smiled, and this time he meant it—not as an expression of any warm feelings toward me, but from the pure and simple pleasure of having found my weak point.

"And you'd know?" was all I could find to say. "How's that, then? I heard that Jesus walked among the prostitutes, but that was a while ago now. You're not telling me the two of you met?"

The smile curdled slightly, but Damjohn's tone stayed light and relaxed. "No. I've not had that pleasure. But I have spoken to his opposite number, as it were. I have knowledge that comes with a price many would consider too high. Of course," he glanced across at Gabe again, this time with undisguised contempt, "I've usually been able to persuade others to pay it on my behalf."

He leaned forward, his stare spearing me. "I know where they come from, and I know where you send them to. I imagine that information would pique your curiosity. Am I wrong?"

The look on his face was the overintense benevolence of a man who's just invited you into the deep woods to look at some puppy dogs. I stared back at him, my feelings for a moment in too great a turmoil to allow me to speak. While that moment lasted, I was a six-year-old boy again, the remains of my birthday cake still in a Tupperware box in the bottom of the fridge, screaming at my kid sister to get out of my bed because she was dead already and she was scaring me. I saw her fade into nothing, her sad face last of all like the fucking Cheshire Cat in *Alice in Wonderland*.

"But you understand," said Damjohn, sitting back, "the offer hasn't been made. Not officially. Because the answer comes first." He looked at me expectantly, really enjoying himself. McClennan was staring at me, too, with so pure and incandescent a hatred that he reminded me of one of those South American frogs that sweat venom. That wasn't because I'd rifled his filing cabinet; it was because Damjohn was trying to seduce me instead of just getting some heavies in to make my arms and legs bend the wrong way.

And that made it easier, in a way. So did Katie, in another way, but that's more than I can explain. I stood up.

"The offer hasn't been made?" I repeated.

Damjohn shook his head reassuringly, imperturbably.

"Then I'm not telling you to shove it up your arse and tamp it in with a polo mallet. I'll stick with the devils I know. Until next time, eh?"

I left my drink unfinished on the table. Gargling it and spitting it in Damjohn's face would probably have counted as rude.

As I was walking through the foyer, heading for the street door, the phone rang in the little alcove, and the duty bouncer picked up. At the same time, a burst of louche jazz sounded from behind me and made a synapse connect somewhere in my memory.

It took only a second to try it out. I stepped outside and stood to one side of the door. On my mobile phone, I flicked through the last dozen calls or so until I found the number I was looking for: 7405 818. When I dialed, I got the engaged signal. I waited about thirty seconds; tried again.

From inside the club, I heard the phone ring. On my cell, I heard the gravelly voice of the bouncer. "Hello?"

"Wrong number," I said. "Sorry."

ICOE 7405 818. Someone at the Bonnington Archive had the number of a brothel in his Rolodex. Not sinister in itself, maybe—but given Damjohn's touching interest in me, it was another link in the chain.

Then, when I was heading west toward the Bonnington, I made another connection. I'd been thinking about that missing page in the incident book, and suddenly I saw a way that the book could help me even in its maimed form.

So despite almost being carved up with a steak knife and failing to find hide or hair of Rosa, I was in a pretty good mood when I got back to the archive. I'd resisted temptation, discomfited my enemies, and started to put the pieces of this sad-ass puzzle together in a new order. All in all, I was feeling the smug satisfaction of a job well begun and therefore half done.

Right up until Alice told me I was fired.

Fifteen

I JUST NEED ANOTHER DAY," I SAID, AMAZED TO HEAR a tone in my voice that sounded like pleading. "Honest to God. One more day will do it. Peele said I could have until the end of the week."

Alice's stony face didn't soften by so much as a muscle. She was holding my trench coat in her hands, and now she thrust it back at me.

"Is this yours?" she demanded in an overemphatic, "this is for the record" voice.

"Yeah. It's mine. Look, Alice, I'm serious. All I need to do now is nail down a few more bits and pieces. I'm there. Really."

"Frank stowed your coat on one of the racks," Alice said, ignoring me completely. "Then he needed to leave the desk, so he decided to put it up in a locker, where it would be safer. When he folded it up, these fell out of the pocket."

She brandished her keys in my face.

Shit. I'd had a fuzzy half memory of transferring the damn things to my trouser pocket. That probably didn't count as extenuating circumstances, though.

"You left them behind in the church the other night," I said. "I was going to give them back to you, but it slipped my mind." Come to think of it, that didn't sound a whole lot better.

"Did it?" she inquired with biting sarcasm. "Castor, the first conversation we ever had was about the value of the collection and how seriously we take our security. Since then, you've been in and out of here for the best part of a week, having to be swiped through card readers, having to wait while doors were unlocked for you and then locked again behind you. I find it hard to believe that none of that made any impression on you. That it all just . . . slipped your mind."

"Is all of this aggression intended to cover your embarrassment at losing the things in the first place?" I asked.

If I thought candor would disarm Alice, I was wrong. She unleashed a torrent of profanity that surprised me not so much by its vehemence as by its breadth. Her face flushed first deep pink, then red, and although she wasn't entirely coherent, a few key points did stand out of the rushing tide of invective. One, I was a thief; two, I'd compromised the archive's security; three, Peele had agreed I shouldn't be allowed back inside the building.

"You're out!" she yelled at me. "You're out of here, Castor. Now! And we'll expect our deposit back tomorrow. Otherwise, we'll get it back through the courts! Get him out of my bloody sight, Frank."

Frank gestured toward the door—an action that fell a long way short of pitching me out on my ear and probably left Alice feeling a certain sense of coitus interruptus. But there was no getting around it, all the same.

I made one last try. "I think your ghost is a murder victim," I told her, laying my cards on the table. "I also think you've got a thief on the staff. Someone who's been systematically pilfering stuff from the collection over months, or maybe years. If you'll just let me—"

Alice turned her back on me and walked away. Frank touched my shoulder very lightly, but his face was set hard. "We don't want any trouble, do we, Mr. Castor?" he said.

"No," I answered with glum resignation. "We don't. But it's a hell of a thing, Frank. We always seem to get it anyway."

———————

"You've got everyone well pissed off with you, Felix," Cheryl said cheerfully as she threw herself down on the seat opposite me in the Costella Café. She tossed a lick of hair back from her forehead, stifling her broad grin with some difficulty. "Sorry, I know it's not funny. I just can't help laughing when Alice loses it like that. It's like seeing Nelson get down off his column to have a punch-up with a cabbie."

"You were watching from the balcony when she chewed me out," I accused her.

"Yeah, I was—and I could've sold seats, easy. She'd been after you all day. When she asked me if I'd seen you, I lied and said I thought you'd left already—then it turned out you had. If I had your mobile number, I would've warned you. But you've got some other jobs lined up, yeah?" By the end of this speech, she was managing to sound solicitous rather than on the verge of giggles.

Instead of answering, I took her hand in mine. "Cheryl," I said, staring solemnly into her eyes, "there's something very important I want to ask you."

That made her lips quirk in alarm. "Hey, it was a good bang, Felix, and I like you and everything. But you don't want to get the wrong idea . . ."

"I want you to steal something for me."

Cheryl's face lit up. "Black ops! You star! What do you need?"

"The incident book. Peele keeps it in his desk drawer."

The light went out again. "Don't be stupid! How am I gonna get it out past Frank? If I get caught, I'll be out on my arse—and probably on a charge, too. I thought you meant secret information or something."

I nodded. "I do mean information—but I need the hard copy, as they say. And you *don't* bring it out past Frank."

"There's only one way out of the—"

"You wrap it in a plastic bag and throw it out of the window of that room where we had our brief encounter this morning—just like someone else is doing. I'll climb up and get it later on tonight."

Cheryl blinked. "Someone's stealing from the archive?"

"Yes. That's what was inside the bag. A whole bunch of letters and papers and at least one bound book. Some of it comes from the Russian collection—but there's a fair bit that looks older. A lot older."

She stared at me hard. "Why haven't you called the police?" she asked.

"Because I've still got a job to do, and there's a lot more at stake here than a few old papers. I want to find out how Sylvie died and what her connection to the archive is. Calling in a load of plods who'll lock the place down will just make that harder. Plus, if Alice has her way, they'll arrest me, too. No, I'll go to the cop shop when I'm good and ready."

"And in the meantime, you want to knock some stuff off on your own account."

"Imitation is the sincerest form of flattery. Look, Cheryl, I'm onto something. Something a lot bigger than stolen papers—big enough that whatever happened to Sylvie was just collateral damage. But I need that book. I was about to ask Peele to lend it to me when Alice put the boot in."

Cheryl looked puzzled now. "So you're pitching for Sylvie now?"

"Pitching. Batting. Fielding. Working the scoreboard."

"But you're supposed to disappear her. That's why they brought you in, isn't it?"

I hated saying it; I knew damn well how ridiculous it sounded. "She saved my life the other night, so I sort of owe her one."

"One you can't exactly pay back to a dead person," Cheryl observed, widening and then narrowing her eyes at me in a way that conveyed a world of meaning. "You lead a fucking weird life, Felix."

"It's Fix. Everyone who can stand me calls me Fix."

She looked at her watch. "Frank will still be around," she mused. "I could say I needed to go back up for my purse."

I waited, watching a big psychomachia play itself out on her face: duty versus mischief. It was enthralling theater, and I would have enjoyed it for its own sake if I'd had less at stake.

"Yeah, all right," she said at last. "I'll give it a go."

Twenty minutes later, I was standing in the alley to the side of the Bonnington, more or less invisible in the early-evening gloom, and I saw the bag come sailing out of the attic window, flying wide. There was a muffled thud as it hit the flat roof. I climbed up onto the wheely bin again and hiked myself up with my arms. This was getting to be a habit. I retrieved the bag and got down again as quickly as I could. I wasn't overlooked from the Bonnington, but there were buildings on all sides, behind whose dust-smeared windows there could be any number of prurient onlookers.

Cheryl met me at the corner of the street, and we walked on together.

"I'm an accomplice now," she observed.

"That's right. You are."

"I could lose my job if anyone finds out."

"Yeah, you said."

"So I get to know what's going on. That's fair."

"That is fair."

A silence fell between us, expectant on her side, deeply thoughtful on mine.

"So are you going to—"

"Come and meet my landlady," I said. "You'll like her."

—————

Pen doesn't cook much, but when she does, three things happen. The first is that the kitchen becomes a sort of domestic vision of Hell, complete with roiling smoke and acrid smells, in which pans have their bottoms burned out of them, glasses are shattered by casual immersion in boiling water, and gravel-voiced harpies (or Edgar and Arthur, anyway) mock the whole endeavor from the tops of various cupboards while Pen curses them with bitter imprecations. The second is that you get a meal that emerges from this Vulcanic stithy looking like a photo in *Good Housekeeping* and tasting like something Albert Roux would knock up to impress the neighbors. The third is that Pen herself is purged by the ordeal, refined in the fire, and radiates a Zen-like calm for hours or even days afterward.

Tonight's effort—in Cheryl's honor—was a lamb cassoulet. Hugely impressed, Cheryl worked her way through seconds and then through thirds.

"This is amazing," she enthused. "You gotta give me the recipe, Pam!"

"Call me Pen, love," said Pen warmly. "I'm afraid there isn't a recipe. I cook holistically—and half pissed—so nothing ever comes out the same way twice."

She refilled Cheryl's glass. It was something Australian with an eagle on the label. The Aussies always seem to go for raptors rather than marsupials on their wine bottles; if it was me, I'd be pushing the unique selling point. I held out my own glass for a top-up. As a party piece, I can sometimes be persuaded to recite the whole of that Monty Python routine about Australian table wines. *"A lot of people in this country . . ."* The hard part is finding anyone to do the persuading.

"So you live with Felix?" Cheryl asked, arching an eyebrow.

"Not in the Biblical sense," said Pen, shaking her head. "Although there is something a bit Old Testament about him, isn't there?"

"Like, something out of Sodom and Gomorrah, you mean?"

"I *am* still sitting here, you know," I interjected.

"No," said Pen, ignoring me, "I was thinking Noah. Very fond of himself. Big, insane projects that he always drags everyone else into. Chasing after anything in a skirt . . ."

"I didn't hear that about Noah."

"Oh yeah, he was a horny old bugger. They all were. Never turn your back on a patriarch."

For our unjust desserts, she wheeled out a supermarket chocolate torte. She also got the brandy out, but I wrested it from her hands and put it back in the boot locker where she keeps it. "We're going to need clear heads for this next bit," I admonished her.

"What next bit?"

"We've got work to do."

"'Big, insane projects,'" Cheryl quoted.

"I warned you," Pen said, shaking her head. Cheated of her brandy, she poured herself another glass of wine.

I cleared all the dirty dishes to one end of the massive farmhouse table and spread open the plans that I'd copied at the town hall. Then I went and got the incident book, which had landed flat when Cheryl had bunged it out of the window and so had survived its fall without visible damage. I cracked it open at September 13, the missing page again making it easy to find.

"What are we gonna do?" Cheryl asked.

"Well, seeing as Jeffrey has gone to the trouble of specifying the time, place, and date for each of the ghost's appearances, we're going to plot them against the building plans."

Cheryl's expression said that wasn't much of an answer. "Because I need to know what exactly it is that she's haunting," I explained. "I thought it was the Russian artifacts, but it isn't. So it's something else."

"Does it have to be that specific?"

"No, but it usually is. Most ghosts have a physical anchor. It can be a place or it can be an object—from time to time it can even be another person. But there's nearly always something. Some specific thing that they're clinging to."

Neither of them looked convinced. "This archive of yours counts as a place, doesn't it?" Pen demanded. "Can't she just be haunting the whole building?"

"I'm talking more specific than that, Pen. *Within* the building, or maybe close by, there should be an area that's uniquely hers. An area that she associates herself with and that she hangs around in most of the time. Or a particular thing that she owned in life, maybe, and still has strong feelings for."

"How is that gonna help you?" asked Cheryl.

"Because once I know what it is, I may have a better idea who she was and how she died."

Cheryl nodded. She got it. So now I could tell her the bad news.

"And *you're* going to have to put the crosses in, because you're the resident expert."

I handed her a magic marker. It took two tries, because she didn't want to take it. She was looking at the plans with a deeply pained expression. "I suck at this stuff," she wailed. "This is almost maths. I'm a humanities graduate, yeah?"

"We'll work it out together," I promised. "Pen, you read aloud from the book. Not all the entries—just the ones that mention the ghost."

"Should I add voices?" Pen asked hopefully.

"There's just the one voice. Think of Sourdust from *Titus Groan*, and you'll be on the right lines."

That seemed to appeal to her. "I can do that," she said approvingly.

"Then let's go."

We made a start, but Cheryl was right—it wasn't easy. The building had changed so damn much over the years, and the plans—even the recent ones—looked so different from the baroque, three-dimensional maze that the archive had become. But on the other hand, Peele's notes were meticulous, and he always gave chapter and verse. I felt a grudging respect for the man. After two dozen ghost sightings, a lot of people would have started using ditto marks, but not Jeffrey. Every damn time, he recorded the when and the where and the who in the same amount of rich, unnecessary detail.

And one by one, we plotted them out on the plans.

As we worked, I thought about that missing page—a blank space surrounded by information—information that up to now I hadn't even tried to use. But there was a pattern hidden in the random flux of things going bump in the tail end of the afternoon. There had to be. And the incident book was still the key.

Every sighting became a cross, and the plans slowly took on a fly-specked appearance as Cheryl marked each one down. Basement. First floor. Second floor. Basement. First floor. Third. Fourth. She'd almost never shown up on the fourth floor—only twice in eighty or so appearances—and never in the attic. Visits to the third floor were rare, too, and they were always in strong room K or the corridor outside. On the second floor, she'd turned up in half a dozen rooms and in the corridor, and on the first floor and in the basement, she was even more ubiquitous.

We sat back, staring at the fruits of our labors. The silence was the silence of revelations not arriving. In droves.

"She's all over the place," said Cheryl.

"Yeah," I agreed in a slightly dead tone. "She is."

"No, she's not." Pen's voice was a little slurred, but there was a weight of certainty in it. We both looked at her.

She shrugged. "She's on a running rope."

"Explain," I said.

Pen bent over the plans. "Okay," she said, "suppose this cross here was a bit farther over—I mean, suppose she was in the corner of this room, not out in the middle. And this one—she could easily have been ten yards or so farther down the corridor."

She rubbed out two of the crosses as she spoke; drew in two more. A third she moved only half an inch or so, to place it closer to a cluster that was already there. She looked at me expectantly.

"Straight lines," I said. "She works in straight lines."

Pen tutted. "They're not straight, Fix. They're curved!"

I started to feel a tingling in the back of my neck as my hairs rose—

not from a ghostly visitation but from the gathering, inescapable sense of something opaque becoming obvious.

"Fuck me sideways," I murmured.

Cheryl was looking from one of us to the other and back again. "Is someone gonna tell me the news?"

My eyes flicked backward and forward, from basement, to first floor, to second floor, third, fourth.

"Okay," I said, "so I'm an idiot. I don't have a good visual imagination. It's like—the Milky Way."

"It's like *what*?" Cheryl demanded. But Pen was nodding excitedly.

"The Milky Way. We see it as a line in the sky because we're looking at it from the wrong angle. But it's not a line, it's a disc. And these aren't lines, either. Put the vertical dimension back in, and it's right there. It's—"

"—a running rope," Pen finished.

"I'm gonna sulk," Cheryl warned.

I put the plans one on top of another and held them up to show her. She squinted at them doubtfully. Now that I'd seen what Pen was driving at, I couldn't believe that Cheryl was still missing it.

"Look—on each floor, she turns up in a whole lot of different places, but they make a rough circle. A really big circle in the basement, then a slightly smaller one on the first floor. Smaller still on the second, but still with more or less the same center. On the third floor, you've just got a scattering of points, all very close together. But suppose you mapped all of this in three dimensions. What would you get?"

"A headache," said Cheryl bitterly.

"You'd get a hollow hemisphere."

"The higher she gets in the building," I said, pointing, "the less room she's got to move in horizontally. Don't you get it? Think of a dog on a leash. If its owner beats it with a stick, what's it going to do?"

"Run away," said Cheryl. "I think I'm being patronized now."

"No, you're not. Just see it in your mind. The dog will run away as far as the leash will let it. And then it will keep running, but it will only be able to go in a circle, right? A circle with the owner—and the stick—right in the middle."

"Okay."

"But suppose it was a space dog. With a jet pack. It would still go out to the full extent of the leash, but it wouldn't be a circle any-more—because the dog would be free to move up and down and all around . . ."

"So it'd be a sphere."

"Exactly!"

Cheryl looked again at the overlaid plans. The black crosses showed clearly through: concentric circles, narrowing as they went up through the building.

"There *is* a fixed place," I said. "A tether of some kind—but she's not haunting it. She's getting as far away from it as she can. She's run-ning on the end of a leash."

"And the man with the stick—"

"Is at the center. The place where she doesn't want to go. The place where she's never been seen."

Cheryl took the plans from me and laid them down on the ta-ble again. "It's got to be on the first floor," she murmured. Then she glanced at Pen and me to double-check her logic. "The first floor or the basement. I mean, she'll have the widest circle where she's on the same level as . . . the thing. The place. Whatever."

Pen nodded emphatically. "So where is it?" I asked. "What's at the center of the sphere?"

Cheryl traced the line of the main corridor, muttering to herself. "That's the front desk. These are the first-floor strong rooms. A, B, C. Ladies' toilet . . ."

She tailed off into silence, but her fingers still moved over the map. Finally she looked up at me, her face a picture of bemusement. "It doesn't work," she said. "You're wrong."

"Why?" I demanded.

"Well, this room here—that's the dead center, right? That's smack in the middle of the circle, in the basement. That's what she's avoiding. It's called SECOND CONFERENCE ROOM on here."

"Yes? So?" I pressed her with a slight sense of unease. "What's it called now?"

"It's not called anything now, Felix." Cheryl's tone was flat. "Because it isn't bloody there."

Sixteen

TWENTY-FOUR FEET IS EIGHT PACES, ROUGHLY, SO COUNT them off. One. Two. Three. Four. Five. Six. Seven. Eight. Good. Then do a ninety-degree turn and count again, to ten this time. One. Two. Three. Four. Five. Six. Seven.

Then I bumped into the wall and whistled softly and tunelessly in the dark.

Cheryl was right.

Despite my earlier fears, it had been easy enough to break into the Bonnington with my lock picks. Their internal security was as spiky as hell, but the front door rolled over and played dead for me after only a modicum of manual stimulation. All the alarms were on the strong room doors, thank God, and I wouldn't be visiting any of those. The reinforced door at the back of the reading room that led through into the staff-only part of the building was a lot harder and took me ten anxious, sweaty minutes. As a fallback, I had Cheryl's ID card in my back pocket, but I was hoping not to have to use it, because the card readers on the doors probably had some kind of an internal memory.

I'd come alone. Pen was going to be my alibi in case things got nasty, and Cheryl didn't need to be anywhere nearby while I was breaking into her place of work. But it would have been useful to have her all the same. It was hard enough making sense of the plans in a well-lit kitchen; standing in a dark corridor, working by filtered moonlight, it was frankly a bit of a bastard.

But all I was doing was pacing out distances, after all; once you got past the logistical problems, it wasn't exactly complicated. Fifteen minutes bumping and shambling in the dark brought me to the only conclusion that made any sense.

There *was* a room missing. The corridor doglegged around it in a way that made it obvious, once you knew that something had been there and had been excised.

I tried again in the basement floor and found the same thing—another lacuna, more or less exactly underneath the first—now with the added mystery of a staircase that had been moved six yards along the corridor. Why would anyone go to that degree of trouble to take a modest-size slice out of a huge public building?

When the answer came to me, I went back up to the first floor and let myself out as carefully as I'd entered. Back on the street, I counted my steps again, but I already knew where I was going to end up.

Which was at the other door: the one I'd walked past on the first day, because it was silted up with old rubbish and covered with a crudely hewn slice of hardboard. Because it was so obviously disused and didn't lead anywhere. It was an appendix, a forgotten and useless by-product of the building's inorganic evolution. And that was what I found myself staring at now—with new eyes.

The rubbish cleared away really easily—suspiciously easily, if you were already in that frame of mind. It was basically only a couple of empty boxes and an old blanket—the minimalist signifiers for a stage set of "a place where homeless people sleep at night."

The plywood sheet that had been nailed to the door had a cut-out rectangle where the keyholes were—another sign that this place wasn't quite as disused as it looked. The two locks here were a Falcon and a Schlage, and they made the archive's front door look like a bead curtain. I struggled with the Schlage for half an hour, and I was about half a breath away from quitting when I finally heard the click that meant the cylinders were all in a line.

I pushed the door, and it opened. Beyond was a sort of lobby space about four feet square with what looked like a folded blanket for a doormat, and beyond that was another door that was also locked. Its wood looked a lot flimsier than its metal bits, and my patience had worn out a while back, so I just kicked it open.

I stepped into a completely dark room that had a sharp-sour, organic smell to it—a smell of sweat and piss and I didn't want to know what else. I groped on the near wall for a light switch, found one, and flicked it on. A naked hundred-watt bulb cast a harsh, clinical spotlight on a room that Mr. Bleaney would have turned down flat. Three of the walls were painted a sad shade of hospital green, while the fourth had been covered over with oppressively dark wood paneling, relieved by a few vertical slats of a lighter color. The floor was covered by a strip of paisley-patterned linoleum that had been cut for another room and didn't reach all the way to the edges. The glass of the window was intact, but all you could see through it was the inside face of another plywood board.

The room itself was bare enough to count as empty, the only item of furniture a stained, fluorescent-orange sofa with a sort of 1970s lack of shame about itself. Against the base of one wall was a row of a dozen or so liter and two-liter bottles, some full of clear liquid, some empty. That was all.

I let the inner door fall closed behind me and advanced a little farther into the room. The shock of recognition had already hit me, followed by the reflection that it really wasn't any shock at all. This was the room I'd seen when I'd played twenty questions with the ghost—the room she'd showed to me in the slide show of her memories. She'd remembered it and communicated it to me faithfully in every detail—except that maybe there were a couple more empty bottles now and a couple fewer full ones.

I searched the room. It took no time at all, because there was nothing to look at. Nothing under the sofa, nothing behind it. There might have been something down the back of its the cushions, but I was reluctant to touch the thing—it looked as if even casual contact could pass on communicable diseases. I unscrewed one of the bottles and sniffed, then tentatively tasted. As far as I could tell, it was just water.

What did that leave? There was a shelf above the door, but it was empty apart from a thick deposit of dust. The paneling could be covering a multitude of sins, so I pressed it in a few places to see how determined it was to stay attached to the wall. On the third push, something gave and rattled slightly. I looked closer and saw the door that was set into the wood, its verticals hidden by two of the decorative slats. Closer still, and I saw the keyhole.

This one was a Chubb of about 1960s vintage—easy enough in this context to count as wide open.

Beyond the door, a flight of stairs going down. This was the original one from the plans, which was no longer part of the archive itself—and that in turn explained why there was a newer staircase a few yards farther on from where the original had been.

The acrid smell was a lot sharper now.

Most likely this space had been separated from the building while it was government-owned, perhaps as some sort of grace-and-favor apartment for a civil servant who wasn't senior enough to merit anything over by Admiralty Arch. Or maybe it had been hived off from the rest of the house when two ministries fought each other for lebensraum. Either way, it seemed to have been forgotten since—but clearly not by everybody.

There was another light switch on the stairwell, but when I pressed it, the light went on in the downstairs room, rather than in the stairwell itself. I went down carefully, afraid of tripping in the inadequate light.

The basement room was even bleaker than the first-floor one.

Again, there was just the one item of furniture—a mattress, even fouler than the sofa, and naked except for a single checked blanket in bright red and yellow—well, *formerly* bright would be closer to the truth. In one corner of the room, there was a bucket full of murky liquid, which was the source of the smell. It had been used as a latrine. So, at some point, had the floor around it. On the floor right next to the bucket was an iron ring that had been inexpertly set in messily poured cement—obviously not a feature of the original room. There was a coil of rope there, too, thrown into a corner.

I know a prison cell when I see one. Someone had lived here, fairly recently, and not because they wanted to. Some of the other memories I'd absorbed from my brief psychic contact with the ghost surfaced again. The blanket had featured in there, I was damn sure of that. And Gabe McClennan's face. What had been behind it? Snowy peaks . . . I turned and saw on the far wall, only a few feet away in this claustrophobic space, a ragged-edged poster of Mont Blanc bearing the legend *L'Empire du Ski*. Déjà vu ran through me like a tide of needles.

And turning my head had made me catch a near-subliminal glimpse of something else. A splash of red, under the near end of the mattress, almost at my feet. I squatted down on my haunches, feeling a mixture of reluctance and grim triumph. I was close to the answer now—the source of everything. I slid my hand under the mattress to lift it up.

And a jolt of pain slammed through me as if I'd touched a bare electric cable. From hand, to arm, to heart, to all points of the compass.

I snatched my hand back and spat out a curse.

Or rather, I tried to spit it out, but it wouldn't come. Silence took root in my mouth, my throat, my lungs. Silence fell on me like the grubby blanket, like a bell jar slipped over my head and shoulders, like a handkerchief soaked in chloroform.

No, that was panic and overreaction. I wasn't dizzy. I wasn't losing consciousness. I was just completely unable to make a sound. I mouthed words, and I tried to push breath through them to bring them into the world, but nothing happened. My voice had gone.

Lifting the corner of the mattress more carefully this time, from above, I was able to see why. The red wasn't congealed blood, after all; it was a circle, inscribed in dark red chalk, with a five-pointed star inside it and a series of painstakingly inscribed marks at each point of the star. In other words, a ward put there by an exorcist. Normally, the text written in the center of a ward like this would be *ekpiptein*—dismiss—or *hoc fugere*—get out of town. Here it was *aphthegtos*—speechless.

I straightened up, feeling a little shaky. I knew what Gabe McClennan had been doing here now and why nobody at the archive had reacted to the name. He'd never visited the archive itself at all. This was where he'd come, and this was what he'd been brought in to do.

But why silence the ghost instead of sending her away? That made no sense at all. It wasn't as though McClennan would have offered a discount. If anything, the binding spell was harder than a straight exorcism.

Whatever the answer was, one thing was now explained. This was why it had been so hard for me to get a fix on the ghost, even when I'd been so close to her. She was bound by this ward, and its strictures hemmed her in like a straitjacket—a straitjacket sewn onto her soul. The change in her behavior made sense now, too—the sudden flare into what had seemed like motiveless violence. She was responding to this necromantic assault.

The ward ought to have had no power over a living human being, but the psychic sensitivity I was born with had left me wide open to it. What I was suffering now was like snow blindness or like the deadened hearing that follows after an explosion. My voice would come back, but it could take minutes or even hours.

A feeling of claustrophobia crashed down on me and made my heart race. Even my breath was making no sound in my chest or in my mouth. A voiceless pall hung over and around me. I turned the other corners of the mattress over, not expecting to find anything. But at the far end, closest to the wall, there was a broad, dark brown stain on the underside. The color was pretty much unmistakable. So was the bitter almond smell of stale blood, which had been masked until I got this close by the sharper ammonial reek of the piss bucket.

I was conscious that anyone finding the upstairs door open could cross the room above me, see the light on down here, and lock me in with a single turn of the key—assuming that this was an anyone who had the key in his pocket. It wasn't an idea I liked all that much. I retreated to the stairs, cast one more look around the grim place, and headed back up to street level.

The upper door had swung to. I opened it and stepped out into the first-floor room. Just the one step, then I stopped dead. The room was dark; the light from the basement cell barely made it up the stairwell, creating only a strip of fuzzy gray in front of me, sandwiched between broader areas of indelible black. While I was in the basement, someone had turned the upstairs light off.

All I had by way of a weapon was my dagger. It was intended for exorcisms, not for self-defense, and I didn't bother to keep it sharp, but it might make someone think twice if I waved it around. Standing stock-still in the dark, and grateful now for the absolute silence of my breath, I slid it out of my pocket and held it down at waist height, ready.

Then I smelled her perfume—that terrible, polecat's-arse musk that bullied its way into your brain and reprogrammed you so that you loved it.

And I heard her laugh—soft, mocking, utterly without mercy.

"It won't help you," Ajulutsikael murmured almost caressingly, and I knew she was right. She was faster than me, and stronger. She could see in the dark. She could take the knife out of my hand and pick her teeth with it before slamming it back into my guts, and there wouldn't be a damn thing I could do about it.

Hoping to throw her off balance and maybe postpone the inevitable, I tossed the knife casually away into the dark and took out my whistle. It wouldn't work; the *aphthegtos* ward would stop any sound at all from coming from my mouth. But such as it was, the pathetic bluff was all I had.

She wasn't fooled. Either she could sense the magic of McClennan's sigils hanging on me or she could just tell from my face that it was a bluff. I heard her heels click on the floor as she strolled unhurriedly toward me. She knew there was nothing to fear from the whistle this time.

"There was a woman chained here," Ajulutsikael said. Her voice was the same throaty murmur, but it was from a lot closer this time. She was a couple of steps away from me and just right of center. If I ducked her first charge, I could fake left and make a run for the door. But there was no way I'd ever reach it. There was a moment of terrifying silence during which I tensed and got ready to move. Then she spoke again, from even closer. "Did you chain her?"

I shook my head.

"Did you keep her as your pet until you tired of her? Alone? In the dark? Was the stink of her fear sweet to you?"

All I could do was shake my head again, more urgently. Who rips my head off gets trash, more or less, or at least takes their own chances with the resale value—but dead or alive, I didn't want to be associated with this hell-hole.

"A pity. It would have been more enjoyable then. But I'm going to eat you anyway." A kind of anger came growling and graveling up from under the feline playfulness. "I'm going to make you pay, man, for the indignity of this summoning. For being made to dance on a chain at the whim of these stinking bags of meat. I'm going to take you slowly. You will love me as you die, and you will despair."

I could actually see her now; my eyes had adjusted to the point where she showed as a darker splodge of shape against the background darkness. A fluid blur of black, as deep as midnight.

I threw out my arms in a sort of shrug—the closest I could get to pleading for my life. Her hand fell on my shoulder, turned me round to face her. I hit out, and my fist was caught. I pulled away, and she drew me close—then threw me effortlessly across the room so that I slammed into the sofa, toppling it, and rolled over and over across the floor until I hit the base of the wall beyond.

"Let's make ourselves comfortable," she whispered.

I was winded and stunned, but I braced myself to make some kind of a fight of it. I got up on one knee, which was as much as I could manage.

What happened next I can only describe in sound, because that was all that I was aware of. There was a series of heavy impacts, as though a bunch of guys with hammers had hit the far wall on the same command, but slightly out of synch. Ajulutsikael grunted in surprise and pain, and the window shattered. Not just the window, in fact. With a loud, indiscreet crash, a corner of the plywood panel snapped clean away and tumbled out into the street. Yellow light from a streetlamp flooded into the room.

It showed Ajulutsikael in a defensive crouch, hands raised in front of her face. A bottle came whipping through the air toward her, and her right arm came across in a blur of motion. She smashed it out of the air in an explosion of glinting glass and incandescent drops. It didn't help her. The jagged shards of glass slowed as they fell, turned and leapt back up at her, slicing at her flesh, stinging her like brittle bees. As I stared, trying to process what I was seeing into some kind of sense, a shard from the broken window, a triangular wedge about eight inches long, parted the air like a dart and buried itself in her back.

Spasmodically, only marginally under my conscious control, my head jerked around. The ghost was standing at the head of the stairs, the scarlet veils of her face billowing and rippling like sheets left out to dry in a stiff wind. She didn't move, and her head was slightly bowed, but she faced Ajulutsikael full-on. Her head turned, and her gaze swept the room from left to right, right to left—and the storm of shattered glass danced in time.

Ajulutsikael had seen her, too. She moved toward the ghost, fingers curved into claws. But the storm of glass moved with her, arced around her, broke on her like a wave, only to bend and recurve almost instantly for another pass. Her clothes hung off her in shreds—her clothes and strips of her flesh. Black streaks of blood crisscrossed her face, and her eyes were wide and mad.

A feral growl began deep in her throat, built to an ear-hurting bellow in which consonants I couldn't have reproduced even if I hadn't been gagged by McClennan's ward smashed against each other like calving icebergs. The ghost trembled and flickered. The glass fragments fell to the floor like prismatic rain.

Discretion is the better part of staying alive. I lurched to my feet, crunched and staggered through broken glass to the door, and fled into the night.

When I was a hundred yards down the street, my feet pumping like pistons, I heard a rending crash from behind me. I risked one glance over my shoulder. Ajulutsikael was out on the street, straddling the saw-edged wreckage of the hardwood door. Then she saw me and came after me at a dead run. With each loping stride, her stiletto heels struck sparks from the cold stones she ran on.

I came out onto Euston Road and tacked left. Traffic was still heavy and fast enough to form a serious blockade, so getting across the road and losing myself in the alleys around Judd Street wasn't going to be an option. She'd be on me before I found a gap. But up ahead there was a skip truck stopped at a red light, with a loaded skip on board.

I didn't have time to make a conscious decision. If I had, I might have hesitated—it was chancing everything on one throw of the dice. And if I'd hesitated, she would have punched my heart out through my ribs as I ran.

As it was, I grabbed for a loop of chain that was hanging off the back of the skip and missed it as the light went green and the truck lurched forward. Hearing the rasp of the succubus's heels behind me, like a knife on a strop, I forced myself into one last spurt of speed and snatched at the chain again. This time, I just managed to snag it as the truck's gathering momentum made the trailing end of it snake out toward me. Dragged half off my feet, I staggered, righted myself, got one foot back under me, and jumped.

Ajulutsikael jumped, too, and something whipped past my trailing leg before I could pull it in. The sudden chill of its passing was followed instantly by a sudden wash of warmth. She'd drawn blood.

For a moment I was braced by one foot against the back of the truck. Then it slipped, and I was just dangling on the chain like an overlarge air freshener whimsically hung up on the outside of the vehicle instead of in the cab. The chain whipped around on its pivot, unbalanced by my weight, so that I saw the road behind me in quick, dizzying glimpses. Ajulutsikael was still pounding along behind the truck tirelessly, not gaining but keeping pace with it. The next time we hit a light that was against us, I was dead meat.

With a desperate effort, I hauled myself up the chain until I could hook one hand over the rim of the skip. At the same time, my feet got a purchase on the edge of the truck's bed, so my hands weren't carrying my full weight by themselves anymore. That was as secure a perch as I could get, but it left me one hand free to grope around inside the skip. After a moment or two, I found and pulled free a jagged piece of white porcelain from a sink or a toilet. It was about the right weight and heft, but unless I chose my moment, Ajulutsikael would see it coming.

We got to an underpass, and we went down. The succubus's view of me was momentarily eclipsed by the rising edge of the road's surface. I counted down from three and lobbed the chunk of bathroom debris just as we took a sharp right turn.

It was perfect. The sudden angular momentum as we turned made my arm into a kind of slingshot. The porcelain payload hit the succubus squarely in the chest, and she went down in a skidding tangle of limbs. A human would have been killed outright. But then, a human wouldn't have been able to hit that speed in the first place.

I kept staring back along the road as we bumped onward in case she reappeared, but there was no sign of her. After that, the ride felt almost luxurious. I'd recommend it to anyone who wants to see split-second, disconnected glimpses of London while freezing half to death and fighting off clinical shock.

Of course, it was a long walk back from Brixton. But you can't have everything.

———————

It's a logical inference that I made it home in one piece, because I can remember Pen cleaning the messy wound on my leg with antiseptic while Cheryl stood behind her, fist pressed to her mouth, saying "Shit" often enough for it to have become a meaningless sound.

"You stink," Pen said severely.

"I'll shower," I said groggily. I didn't know what I meant by it. It was just sounds, but it was still a novelty to be able to make sounds again after my brush with McClennan's ward of silence. And Pen wasn't listening anyway, so I was under no obligation to make any sense.

"It's the same smell that was in your room after that thing ripped the window out," she said. "You've seen her again, haven't you?"

I winced involuntarily as I thought back to the dark room, the overpowering smell, the mocking voice from the deep shadows. "I didn't see all that much of her, to be honest."

"He's always been attracted to the wrong kind of women," Pen said acidly, over my head, to Cheryl.

"Yeah, I'm the same with blokes," Cheryl answered morosely. "You think you know what you're getting into, but you never do."

They carried on talking, but my mind slipped onto another frequency, and I wasn't really hearing them anymore. The ghost couldn't talk. She'd been silenced—deliberately, sorcerously silenced by Gabe

McClennan, presumably acting on orders from—Damjohn? Why? What could she have said that represented a danger to him? If he'd had her killed, if she could incriminate him in any way at all, then why not just exorcise her and have done with it?

And how was Damjohn linked to the archive? What blindingly obvious point was I missing? Did the pimp and sleaze-king have a sideline in stolen artifacts?

ICOE 7405 818. That was the only solid thing I had to go on. Someone at the Bonnington had the number of Damjohn's club, Kissing the Pink, in his Rolodex, ready to hand in the event of—what? Was it just intended as a last resort? For regular briefings and progress reviews? To cover some unforeseen crisis, like an outsider nosing around in places where he wasn't meant to?

I probably got a glimpse of it then. Not the who and certainly not the why, but the broad shape of what the answer had to be. I couldn't articulate it yet, but I think I could have played the tune of it, as though it was a ghost I was going to raise and then render. Right then, that wasn't much of a consolation.

Seventeen

Bᴀᴄᴋ ɪɴ ʜᴀᴍᴘꜱᴛᴇᴀᴅ ᴡᴀʏ ʙᴇꜰᴏʀᴇ ɪ ᴡᴀꜱ ʀᴇᴀᴅʏ ᴛᴏ be. Hauling off on that lion-head knocker again in the bright stillness of a very early Saturday morning. I'd taken Friday off to recover, but I was still stiff and aching and feeling like I might shed limbs if I moved too fast. I asked myself bleakly if I was living right. The answer came when the door opened, letting out a sweet smell of sandalwood and revealing Barbara Dodson in jeans and tight T-shirt.

"He's in the study," she said, standing back to let me walk past her. "You can go straight through."

I stepped inside. "How's Sebastian?" I asked.

She gave me a long, thoughtful look. "Sebastian's on great form. Happier than he's been since we moved in here. Peter's been feeling a little sorry for himself, though. We can't get a word out of him."

"Probably a phase he's going through," I suggested.

She nodded slowly. "Probably."

I walked on down the hall into the study, limping only slightly.

Supercop James was standing just inside the door, steeling himself to tackle me as soon as I came in. He went straight for the jugular, predictably enough. "I'm assuming you came over to apologize," he snarled. "For your sake, I *hope* that's why you're here."

I was too tired for games. "No," I told him, "you're not assuming that at all. You're assuming I came here to blackmail you. You're hoping you can buy me off cheap or scare me into changing my mind."

His eyes widened by an infinitesimal fraction, and his lips parted to show his clenched teeth. He was wound up very tight indeed—tight enough so that he might even break, without careful handling. But I didn't know him well enough to tailor my approach to his tender sensibilities, so I gave it to him straight.

"You're right," I told him. "This is a shakedown. But contrary to everything you've ever been told about blackmailers, if you give me what I want, I'll go away and leave you alone. And it's not money, it's just information. I want you to pull some police records for me. Three, to be precise. Do you think you can do that?"

Dodson gave a short laugh that sounded like it must have hurt coming out.

"Just information? You want me to steal files from the Met? Go against everything my job is about? Can you think of a single good reason why I shouldn't punch you in the mouth for resisting arrest, and then arrest you?"

I nodded stonily. "Yeah," I said. "Just the one. Davey Simmons. According to all the newspaper reports I could get my hands on, he asphyxiated after inhaling a cocktail of superglue and antifreeze from a plastic ASDA bag. Not a nice way to go."

The color drained out of Dodson's face, leaving it gray and slightly glistening, like wet cement. He sat down in the black leather office chair. I could tell he was staring death in the face. Not his own death—he looked as though he could probably have coped with that a fair bit better—but someone else's. "Davey Simmons was a human train wreck," he said without conviction.

"Yeah. I read that, too. Broken home, in and out of trouble, psychiatric problems, couple of convictions. But the police thought it was a bloody odd setup, all the same. Did any of your mates ever talk over the finer points of it with you?"

Dodson shot me a look full of hate. "No," he said tightly. "They didn't."

"You see, there was glue in his hair. And on his right cheek. It was as though the bag had been held over his whole head, rather than just over his mouth and nose—which I believe is the preferred mode of delivery for fans of recreational Bostick. The bruises on his wrists got them thinking, too. Could someone have held him down and shoved a bag over his head, then held it there until he died? That'd be a pretty shitty thing to do to someone, wouldn't it?"

There was a long silence, tense at first, but becoming slacker as Dodson's fury surrendered to despair. "It was a joke," he muttered, almost too low to hear.

"Yeah?" I said unsympathetically. "What's the punch line?"

Dodson didn't seem to hear. "Peter and his friends found . . . Simmons . . . in a toilet cubicle. He'd mixed the stuff up in the bag, and he was already inhaling it. They wanted to scare him. For a joke. Maybe teach him a lesson."

I let the silence lie for a bit longer this time. Then I put the little sheaf of paper I'd got from Nicky down on the desk in front of him. He stared at it dully.

"These three," I said, pointing. "The ones I've gone over in highlighter. They're the only ones I'm interested in. I want autopsy reports, witness statements, and anything else you can lay your hands on. By tonight."

He shook his head. "Impossible," he said. "That amount of material—" Then he started to read the stuff and shook his head again, even more emphatically. "I'm not in Murder anymore. I don't have access to any of this stuff."

"I'm sure you can call in some favors from old friends, you being a big man in SOCA these days. And photocopies will be fine. Hell, at a pinch, even a disk will be fine. Just get me the stuff, and then we can walk out of each other's lives again. For good, this time."

I took a step toward the door. Dodson came jerkily to his feet. His arm shot out and he blocked me, stepped in close, and stared down at me from his full, imposing height.

"Peter didn't mean for the boy to die," he said with a menacing emphasis. "You understand me?"

"I wouldn't have an opinion about that," I said evenly, meeting his wide-eyed stare with a narrower one of my own.

"I've already punished him. I think his own guilt would have been enough, but I've grounded him for the rest of the school term, and I've canceled a holiday we had planned in Switzerland. It's not as though I just let this pass. It's not as though he doesn't understand what he's done."

"Davey Simmons is dead," I said in the same level tone. "So fuck you and the squad car you rode in on."

I thought Dodson was going to hit me, but he just let his arms drop to his sides and looked away.

"Tonight," he said.

"Yeah."

"And then we never hear from you again."

"Exactly."

"I could make life very difficult for you, too, Castor."

"I don't doubt it. But let's make each other happy instead, eh?"

I let myself out. Barbara had very sensibly made herself scarce.

What now? No word from Nicky about the laptop. No way I was going anywhere near the archive again, in case Ajulutsikael the sex demon was still staking the place out. What did that leave?

It left Rosa. I knew the odds were stacked fairly heavily against me finding her, but she could make this so much easier. I was certain she knew the dead woman—reasonably certain that she could fill in the last few gaps for me and give me what I needed to make sense of this mess.

Of course, I had to assume that Damjohn knew that, too. If he was as heavily mixed up in all of this as I thought he was, he'd have put

Rosa somewhere where I couldn't get close to her, so Kissing the Pink was probably a nonstarter. All the same, that was where I had to go.

It was the dead time of midafternoon, when the lunchtime City crowd had evaporated away like a bead of sweat on a pole dancer's cleavage, and the sex tourists were still sleeping off the debaucheries of the night before. I walked in off the street to find the doorman—not Arnold, fortunately—half asleep in his cubicle and the club itself three-quarters empty. Evidently we were in between dances—the wide-screen TV was showing a soft-core porn movie so old and so labored that it had to count as kitsch rather than titillation.

I was a little afraid of running into Damjohn himself or, even worse, into Scrub, but there was no sign of either of them. A guy I didn't know from Adam was guarding the inner door that led up to the brothel, and he nodded me through without a look.

"You've got a girl named Rosa," I said to the blonde apparition who was serving behind the upstairs bar. She looked like a centerfold, which is to say that her tan was carotene-poisoned orange, and I was nearly certain she had two staples through her midriff. She flashed me a nonjudgmental smile and nodded vigorously, but the nod didn't mean anything. "That's right, darling," she said. "Only she's not in today. We've got some girls who are just as young, though. We've got Jasmine, who's five foot six and very busty—only just turned eighteen, and you can help her celebrate—"

I cut her off before she could start taking me through Jasmine's tariff in detail. "I'd really love to see Rosa again," I said, hoping the implied lie would be taken at face value. "When is she here next?"

"She does Fridays and Saturdays," the woman said, the smile slipping almost imperceptibly.

"Today is Saturday," I pointed out helpfully.

She nodded again. "That's right, sweetheart. Only she's not in today. She took a day off on flextime."

Flextime. Right. I kept my face straight because I'm a professional, God damn it. But I knew the next kite wouldn't fly.

"Do you have her home number?" I asked.

The smile was folded away abruptly and put back into storage for a more fitting occasion.

"I can't give out personal details, dear, you know that. I've got lots of other girls here. You have a look around and see if there's anyone you like the look of."

I took the brush-off with moronic good humor, which seemed to be the safest way to go. And then I took my leave as soon as I could without drawing attention to myself.

So Rosa had disappeared. Nothing more I could do there for the time being. Nothing much I could do anywhere until Nicky called. Probably the best thing I could do would be to go back to bed and sleep, because I'd probably need the energy later.

But there was something else nagging at the edges of my mind— something I'd dismissed as coincidence, once and then again. It's funny how coincidences look less and less coincidental as they pile up against each other. So I called Rich, who was surprised to hear that I was still on the job. "I dunno, Castor," he said, only half joking. "After that business with Alice's keys, you're sort of a leper."

I rubbed absently at one of the scratches on my arm. "Yeah, I'm feeling like one," I said. "Keep losing bits and pieces of myself. Rich, remember when you told me about the Russian documents? You said they'd come from somewhere down around Bishopsgate. And you said that you were the one who found them. How did that happen, exactly?"

Like Cheryl, Rich seemed surprised that I was still harping on about the Russian collection. "It was a friend-of-a-friend-of-a-friend sort of deal," he said. "One of my old lecturers at the Royal Holloway knew a guy whose grandad came here just before the Revolution. He had suitcases full of this stuff, and he didn't even speak enough Russian himself to make sense of them. But I thought you said you drew a blank on all that stuff in the boxes. How can it be relevant now?"

"It probably can't," I admitted. "But the coincidence worries me.

The ghost turning up so hot on the heels of the collection, and speaking in Russian." And the weeping woman I saw when I was touch-sifting the stuff but I didn't mention that. "Have you still got the address?"

"I might have. I don't even know if the bloke is still there, though."

"Doesn't matter. I thought I might go over and take a look around. If there's nobody there, I don't lose anything except time."

"Hang on a minute, then. I'll go take a look."

It took a lot longer than a minute; I was close to hanging up and dialing again when Rich finally got back to the phone.

"Found it," he said cheerfully. "I knew it was around here somewhere. Most of the correspondence went through Peele, but I found the guy's first letter to me. Number 14 Oak Court, Folgate Street. That's right off Bishopsgate, up the Shoreditch end."

"Thanks, Rich."

"Let me know how it comes out. You've got me interested now."

"I will."

I hung up and headed east.

Nobody remembers the name of the medieval bishop who built the bishop's gate and gave it its name. But then again, he was a lazy bugger and deserved to be forgotten. All he was doing was building himself a back door through the city wall so he could commute from his gaff in sunny Southwark to St. Helen's Church without having to walk around to Aldgate or Moorgate—and maybe so he could have a pint at the Catherine Wheel on Petticoat Lane on the way.

There's precious little of either sanctity or idleness about Bishopsgate these days. It's all banks and offices and finance houses most of the way up from Cheapside, having been homogenized and beaten flat by the slow historical tidal wave of monopoly capitalism. But if you're lucky or persistent, you can step off that old main drag into a maze of courts and alleys that date from when London's wall still stood and her gates were locked at night in case unwelcome guests should come calling. Hand Alley. Catherine Wheel Alley. Sandys Row. Petticoat Lane itself. Old names for old places. That weight of time hangs over you when you walk them.

But Oak Court was postwar and carried no weight except for a few gallons of ink and paint squandered in uninspired graffiti. Three stories of yellow brick, with external walkways on each level and a blind eye here and there where a window had been covered over with rain-swollen hardboard. Three staircases, too, one at each end and one in the middle, separated by two squares of dead-and-alive lawn with a wrought-iron bench in the center of each. It was a dispiriting place. You wouldn't want to be one of the people who had to call it home.

I climbed the central stairwell. The sharp stink of piss cut the duller but more pervasive scent of mildew, and the brickwork was stained brown-black close to the ground—stained and still wet, as if the building bore wounds that had only half healed.

Number 14 was on the top floor. I rang the bell and, when I heard no sound, knocked on the door as well, but the place looked deserted. At the bottom of the full-length glass panel, there was a sill of dust, and through it I could see an untidy avalanche of old circulars from Pizza Hut and campaign fliers from the local Conservative Party. Counting back to the general election, I decided it had been a while since anyone was in residence here.

I turned away and headed for the stairs. When I got to them, the force of very old habit made me glance back over my shoulder one last time to make sure that nobody had come to the door just as I left. Nobody had, but as I turned, I felt a familiar prickling of the hairs at the base of my neck—the familiar pressure of eyes against my skin and my psyche.

I was being watched—by something that was already dead.

I couldn't tell whether my watcher was close by or far away. Out on the walkway like this, thirty feet above the street, I could be seen from a fair distance. But forewarned is forearmed. I kept on going down the stairs, and as I went, I unshipped my whistle and transferred it into my sleeve.

There was no sign of anyone down on the street. I headed back toward Liverpool Street, using windows where I could to glance behind me without turning my head. There was no sign that I was being followed.

As soon as I got around the corner, I broke into a sprint, made it to the next turning, and sprinted again, heading for a sign fifty yards away that said MATTHEW'S SANDWICH BAR. It was a narrow place, only just wide enough to take the counter and the queue, which was surprisingly long, given that this was the middle of a Saturday afternoon. I got through the door at a dead run and joined the end of the line, turning my back to the street. A window behind the counter allowed me to look back toward the corner without seeming to.

About a minute later, a man turned the corner, then hesitated and looked to left and right, at a loss. He was followed a second or two after that by a second man, who loomed over the first like a bulldozer over a kid's bike. The first man was Gabe McClennan. The second was Scrub.

They looked around a little more, then conferred briefly. It was clear even from this distance that Scrub was angry, and McClennan was defensive. The big man prodded the chest of the smaller one with a thick, stubby finger, and his face worked as he presumably chewed Gabe out for losing me. Gabe threw out his arms, pleaded his case, and was prodded again. Then there was a little more subdued pantomime of pointing fingers and anxious, searching glances, including several back the way they'd come. Finally they parted, McClennan going on down Bishopsgate, while Scrub retraced his steps.

I gave them thirty seconds or so to get clear, then set off after McClennan. It wasn't a hard choice. He wouldn't be able to squeeze my skull into a pile of loose chippings if he turned around and saw me.

I caught sight of him almost immediately because he was still looking restlessly left and right as he walked along, hoping to pick up my trail again. In case he decided to look behind him, too, I hung back and made sure there were always at least a couple of people between us. His white hair made a handy beacon, so I was unlikely to lose him.

He walked the length of Bishopsgate. Every so often he turned off along one of the side streets, but when he saw no sign of me there, he doubled back onto the thoroughfare itself, heading south toward Houndsditch. When he got there, he hailed a cab and shot off toward the river.

I swore an oath and legged it after him, since there was no other cab in sight. At Cornhill I got lucky, as one pulled out onto Gracechurch Street right in front of me and stopped in response to my frantic hail. "Follow the guy in front," I panted.

"Lovely," the cabbie enthused. He was a tubby Asian guy with the broadest cockney accent I'd ever heard. "I've always wanted to do a number like that. You leave it to me, squire, and I'll see you right."

He was as good as his word. As we turned right onto Upper Thames Street and fed into the dense stream of traffic along the Embankment, he faked and wove his way from lane to lane to keep McClennan's cab in sight. In the process he earned himself a few blasts of the horn and at least one "Drive in a straight line, you fucking arsehole!" but I could see the back of Gabe's head framed in the window, and he didn't turn around.

We followed the river through Westminster and Pimlico, and I began to wonder where the hell we were heading. I'd only followed Gabe on a whim, hoping that he might lead me to Rosa—which required a long chain of hopeful assumptions, starting with the one where Damjohn had taken Rosa out of circulation in the first place. If she'd just had it away on her own two heels, then I was wasting my time.

That conclusion looked more and more likely as McClennan's cab took a right at Oakley Street and drove on up toward the King's

Road. It was stretching credibility past breaking point to believe that Damjohn might have an establishment up here. As far as my understanding goes, the brothels of Kensington and Chelsea are very much a closed shop and, good manners aside, any East End lags trying to get into that particular game would be slit up a treat.

Gabe jumped ship at last just before Sands End, paid off the cab, and continued on foot. I did the same.

"That good enough for you?" my cabbie asked, deservedly smug.

"You could write the book, mate," I said, tipping him a fiver. Then I was off after Gabe before he could get too much of a lead on me.

He didn't go far, though. He stopped at the next street corner— Lots Road—under a pub sign that showed a horse leaping a brook, took out his mobile, and had an intense conversation with someone. He glanced up at the sign, said something into the phone, nodded. Then he put the phone away and walked on into the pub—the Runagate.

I debated with myself whether I should give this up as a bad job. It would be useful to see who Gabe was meeting up with—more useful still to be able to eavesdrop, but that was probably asking too much. In any case, having come this far, it seemed a bit ridiculous just to jump into another cab and go back into the City.

Cautiously, I followed Gabe inside. The place was reassuringly crowded, and I was able to pause on the threshold and get my bearings. I couldn't see Gabe at first, but that was because his highly visible hair was momentarily eclipsed behind a row of tankards hanging up on the far side of the bar. A few seconds later, he turned away from me with a pint in his hand to walk over toward the side door—and out through it. As the door opened and then closed, I had a glimpse of a beer garden beyond, with small wooden picnic tables and bright green parasols.

That made life a bit more problematic. If I followed him through that door, I might be walking right into his line of sight, and there'd be no crowd to hide behind. It would probably be better to go around the outside of the building and at least see the lay of the land before I moved in.

I stepped back out onto the street. Barely ten feet away, Scrub was squeezing his huge bulk out of a minicab, making it rock wildly on its suspension.

I ducked back inside before he could see me and looked around for somewhere to hide. No upstairs. No saloon. The gents. I crossed the bar in three strides, threw the door open, and ducked inside.

The only other occupant, who was waving his hands under a hot-air drier, glanced around at me and then gawped in disbelief. Fortunately, I already knew that the deck of fate was stacked against me, so the fact that the other man was Weasel-Face Arnold didn't faze me in the slightest. I hauled off and kicked him as hard as I could where a kick was likely to have the most immediate and dramatic effect. Then, as he doubled over, I got a good, solid grip on his neck and rammed his head sideways into the unyielding white ceramic of a sink. He folded without a sound.

Damn! Taken on its own merits, the violence had been quite ca-thartic, but I had nothing to tie him up with, and as soon as he was found, the whole place would be up in arms. Whatever was going on here, it was probably a bad idea to try getting any closer to it right then.

On an impulse, I went through Arnold's pockets. Nothing par-ticularly exciting there, but I took his wallet and his mobile phone just in case either of them might prove to be useful later on.

I opened the door a crack, checked out as much of the bar as I could see, and then stepped out. No sign of Scrub, for which I was devoutly grateful. Most likely he was already out in the beer garden with McClennan.

I went back out onto the street again, which immediately made me feel a little bit safer. At least I was away from the epicenter of whatever alarums and excursions would follow on when Arnold was found—so there was probably nothing to lose by taking a look around the side, so long as I kept my head down.

I rounded the building. The approach looked good, because there was a fence around the beer garden that came up almost to head height. Peering around the corner of the building, I caught sight of Scrub's unmistakable back on a bench in the far corner, his enormous frame almost completely hiding McClennan from view. They were talking earnestly, but I was too far away to hear a word.

By bending over like an old man, I was able to shuffle my way around the outside of the fence without being seen. I knew when I was in the right place, because I could hear McClennan's voice, raised in complaint.

". . . never told us what the hell was going on. That's all I object to. If I'm told up front what the risks are, I'll take them. But this—this just isn't what I signed up for, and I—"

Scrub's basso-profundo rumble cut through McClennan's feeble-sounding litany of grievances with three terse words.

"You're on retainer."

"Yes. Yes, thank you for reminding me of that fact. I'm on retainer. As an exorcist. Nobody mentioned raising hell-kin. Nobody mentioned performing necromantic surgery on a ghost with too much mouth to it. Why didn't he just let me toast the fucking thing? Then we wouldn't be having any of these problems."

"Castor?" Scrub growled. "Castor isn't a problem. First of all, he couldn't find his arse with a map. Secondly, there's no evidence anywhere that he can get his hands on. And thirdly, I'm going to kill him as soon as Mr. D gets tired of using your fuck-pig demon."

"I half killed myself raising that thing." Gabe spat the words out, bitterly angry. "Just the effort of bringing it up from Hell—you don't have any fucking idea! And then I had to do the binding while I was still weak and sick from calling her, and if I hadn't got every last detail down right, she would've torn me apart."

"Mr. D assumes you're competent to do your job."

"Oh, thanks." Gabe's laugh sounded like it must have left welts coming out. "Thanks so fucking much. Am I supposed to be flattered?"

"You're supposed to do what you're told."

"Right, right. And if Castor gets his hands on the other little trollop?"

"He won't."

"Why doesn't Damjohn just kill her and be done with it?"

"Why don't you ask him?"

Gabe didn't seem to have any answer to that. The silence lengthened and was followed by a change of subject.

"What's keeping that fucking moron?" Scrub's voice, rumbling like a train passing under your feet.

"He said he had to piss."

"Well, go and get him."

Which was my cue to leave.

———————

Rosa. Rosa was the key. But I didn't have any idea how to find her or even where to start looking.

Actually, that wasn't strictly true. It was just that nosing around the only starting point I had—the strip club—felt uncomfortably like sticking my head into the muzzle of a cannon and striking a match to see what was in there.

I was honestly amazed at my own stupidity.

The blonde on the upstairs bar shot me a look that conveyed a lot of dislike and mistrust with great economy. But my opening words were calculated to disarm her suspicions and make her love me like a long-lost brother.

"You know," I said, smiling cheerfully, "I don't think I've ever stood a round in here."

The blonde's lower jaw went through a cataclysmic plunge. She did her best to reel it back in.

"The drinks are on me," I clarified helpfully. "Let's have champagne all 'round, shall we?" I took out my wallet and slapped my credit card down on the bar. Well, okay, it was Arnold's wallet and Arnold's credit card, but I know he would have been happy at the thought of giving pleasure to so many people.

The barmaid recovered from her surprise and hurriedly went diving for bottles, in case I unexpectedly recovered my sanity. I took the first one from her, ripped off the foil, and popped the cork as she was setting up the glasses. The girls at the end of the bar had gotten wind of what was going on by now, and they all crowded around. I knew that the markup on the drinks was colossal and that they were probably on a percentage of bar takings as well as what they took in the bedrooms; persuading a punter to buy them a glass of champagne was an easy earner compared to the regular daily grind, if that's the right expression.

I handed each glass out as soon as I'd poured it, pressing it into an outstretched hand happily and clumsily—and with the maximum of skin-to-skin contact. My psychic antenna was fully alert, but it only works by touch. I knew what I was looking for, but I also knew I'd have to take whatever I could get.

I struck gold around about number eight or nine. She was a pouty, slightly emaciated brunette dressed in a fire-engine red bra and panties (the panties bearing a sequined love heart at front and center), a gauzy see-through top, and a pair of black stockings adorned with fleur-de-lys.

"We've never met," I said to her, taking her hand in both of mine and getting a stronger psychic fix on her. "What's your name?"

"It's Jasmine," she said, giving me what she probably thought was a sultry look. "What's yours?"

"I'm John," I said, because it was the first thing that came to mind.

"And would you like to go upstairs with me, John?"

"Yeah," I said. "That'd be great."

She smiled warmly. "What sort of thing do you like?"

"I'd like a full body-to-body massage," I hazarded. And then, to forestall more detailed questioning, "Do you do Glaswegian?"

Jasmine bluffed like a trouper. "Of course I do, you naughty boy," she purred. She took a key that the blonde woman handed to her, glanced perfunctorily at the number, and led me away with her arm crooked proprietorially in mine. After all, I was the only John in the place.

I couldn't tell if I'd actually been into the room she took me to, but it was identical to all the ones I'd seen—a bleak, clean little box, and in its way as perfect a triumph of function over form as a battery cell on a chicken farm.

"So you tell me exactly how you'd like me to do it," Jasmine coaxed, sitting me down on the bed, "and I'll tell you how much it's going to be."

I put on a crestfallen face. "Actually, Jasmine," I admitted, "I was hoping we could just talk—since it's my first time with you, and all. So what's the price for missionary with no trimmings?"

I was expecting ructions, but she took it in her stride; it must be more common than I'd imagined for punters to get this far and then lose their nerve.

"It's sixty, John. Let's get that sorted now, and then we've got all the time in the world just to get to know each other."

Docilely, I counted three twenties into Jasmine's hand. She slipped out of the room, presumably to hand it over to the duty madam, and then came back in again a few seconds later and closed the door behind her.

"Do you want me to take my clothes off?" she asked, standing over me and smiling down at me with her hands cupping her breasts.

It seemed a token gesture, given how skimpy her outfit was to start with—and it wouldn't do anything to establish the necessary mood of calm consultation. "No, thanks," I assured her. "What you're wearing now is fine. Absolutely fine."

She sat down next to me, put a hand on my knee, and snuggled in close. She had a floral smell that was sweet and delicate, but it reminded me—unfairly—of Juliet, a.k.a. Ajulutsikael. I fought the urge to pull away.

"So what would you like to talk about, John?" she cooed little-girlishly.

I went for broke. "You've got a colleague named Rosa," I said. "And I guess you work some of the same nights, so I was hoping you might know her."

It wasn't what she expected or wanted to hear, but she rolled with it.

"Is Rosa your favorite?" she asked in the same Shirley Temple tone.

I thought about the steak knife. "Rosa leaves a very powerful impression," I acknowledged, genuflecting at the secret altar of my conscience in penance for such a cheesy line. "And ever since I saw her, I've been wanting to meet up with her again. But she's not in today."

"That's right. She's not." Jasmine was still playing the game by the house rules, but there was a guarded edge to her voice. "Do you want me to pretend to *be* her? You can call me Rosa, if that makes it better for you."

I shook my head brusquely. "I want to make sure she's all right. And I want to talk to her again."

Jasmine didn't answer. Either I'd struck a nerve, or she was just wondering if my obsession might spill over into actual violence. I was hoping for the former, because when I'd touched her hand, I'd got a fleeting glimpse of Rosa's face on the surface of her mind. At the very least, she knew the girl; and, perhaps, if my luck was in, she was concerned about her already.

But her first reaction wasn't promising. "Rosa's fine," she said. Her voice had changed now, closed down to a flat monotone. She took her hand off my knee.

"How do you know that?"

A pause. "Because I saw her yesterday. She's fine."

"When yesterday?"

Anger flared in her eyes. "Look, if you're social services or someone, you can kiss my sodding arse!"

"I only paid for missionary, remember? I'm not social services. And I'm not a cop, either, but then you probably have pretty good radar for cops. I really do just need to talk to her. And I really am worried about her. If you tell me she's okay, then that's great. But when did you see her?"

Bowing to the inevitable, I took out my dwindling roll of cash and held out another twenty for her to take. She didn't make a move for it. She just scowled at me, but not in aggression. It was more like her flexing her facial muscles as she came back out of role and took off the mask. My luck was holding. It looked as though I'd guessed right, and Jasmine was worried about Rosa on her own account. At least, that was the only reason I could think of for her not either whistling for the bouncer or helping herself to the extra twenty.

She still had to decide how far to trust me, though, and I could see it was going to be someway short of the full distance. "In the afternoon," she said. "About two. She came in late, and Patty had words with her. Then Scrub"—she stumbled slightly on the name; I could see there was no love lost there—"Scrub came in and took her to see Mr. Damjohn."

The pause lengthened.

"And?" I prompted.

Jasmine looked unhappy. "And she never came back in again after that."

"Do you know where Scrub took her?"

Jasmine rolled her eyes, then shook her head once, tersely. How would she know? Why would she want to find out? This clearly wasn't the kind of place where you asked too many questions. But that was still what I had to do.

"Does it happen often?" I asked. "Scrub taking the girls off for a talk with the boss? Does Damjohn give you a quarterly review or something?"

Another head shake. "If he needs to see us, he sees us here. But mostly he leaves it to Patty to sort out the girls. He takes care of the downstairs stuff."

"Well, did Scrub say anything about why Damjohn needed to talk to Rosa?"

Jasmine didn't answer at first, so I waited. Sometimes waiting works a lot better than asking again.

"He said—she'd been told before. She'd been warned. That was all. He didn't say about what. Then she said she'd just been out for a walk. She hadn't met anyone on the way, she just needed a walk."

It seemed blindingly obvious that what Rosa had been warned about was tailing me. But she'd done it anyway—not to talk to me, but to take a swipe at me with a kitchen cleaver borrowed for the occasion. *You did it to her. You did it to her again.*

"Did they leave in a car?" I asked.

"Yeah."

"A BMW?"

"I didn't see. But I heard it pull away."

"Do you have any idea where Damjohn lives?"

Jasmine laughed without a trace of humor. "A long way away from here, I'll bet. No. Nobody knows where he lives. This is the only place where we ever see him."

"He never takes a couple of the girls back home for some unpaid overtime? Droit du seigneur sort of thing."

"No. Not that I've ever heard of. Carole reckons he's gay."

I didn't agree. From my brief acquaintance with Damjohn—and especially from that unwanted flash of images and ideas when I'd shaken his hand—I suspected that he got his kicks in some other way that only touched on sex at an odd tangent.

"Nothing else?" I asked, just to make sure.

She thought hard, frowned, looked at me doubtfully.

"I think Scrub said—but it doesn't make any sense."

"Said what?"

"Well—what I heard was 'It's the nice lady for you.'"

"The nice lady?"

"Yeah. Or maybe 'the kind lady.' Something like that. I don't know. It just sounded funny, so it stayed in my mind."

"Thanks, Jasmine," I said, meaning it. "Thanks for trusting me."

She wasn't much consoled, but this time, when I held out the twenty, she took it and slipped it into her stocking top. "Do you think you can find her?" she asked. Her professional polish had all faded away in the space of a minute; she looked close to tears now.

"I don't know. But I'm going to try."

"Will Scrub—will she be okay?"

There was no point in sweetening the pill; whores know self-deceiving bullshit better than priests do. "I don't know that, either," I admitted. "I think she might be okay for a while, at least. If there's something Damjohn doesn't want her talking about, there's no point in going over the top to keep her quiet if it's only going to come out another way."

Jasmine didn't ask what I meant by that, and I didn't explain. She probably wouldn't have understood in any case, but to me it was looking like one of those logic problems that end up with the proposition that all men are Socrates, and Socrates is a rubber chicken. Thesis: I was the one who was nosing around where he shouldn't be and asking all the awkward questions. Antithesis: Rosa was only dangerous if she told me something I wasn't supposed to know. Synthesis: They only needed to keep her out of circulation until they'd succeeded in nailing me.

Fucking wonderful.

———

It felt like a long day. I went back to Pen's place around four and killed some time recording a tune on a Walkman I'd picked up at Camden Market last year. It's an old one—cassettes only—but it comes with its own plug-in mike and speakers, which makes it handy in all sorts of ways. It took a while to get the tune exactly right, and I was far from sure that I'd ever need it, but I had nothing better to do until either Dodson or Nicky called me and gave me the green light. I had John Gittings's pincer movement in my mind—it had nearly got me killed the first time we'd tried it, but that was no reason to ditch a good idea. I worked steadily for an hour and a half and got a certain amount of relief from my turbulent thoughts.

Nicky didn't call in the end; he just appeared, out of nowhere, in the accepted conspiracy-theorist style. I went downstairs looking for coffee and realized as I was pouring a generous scoopful into the moka pot that he was there, behind me, sitting at the kitchen table in the dark. He hadn't moved at all since I came in. I could have gone right back out again without noticing him—and when I did notice him, I thought for a second that he was a visitant from some other plane entirely.

When I saw that it was just Nicky, I swore at him vehemently. He took the abuse with stoical indifference.

"I've done enough talking on the phone for one week," he said quietly. "I work hard on my footprint, Felix. I keep it small for good reasons."

"Your footprint?" I echoed sardonically.

"The traceable, recordable, visible part of my life," he paraphrased, deadpan. "If I wanted to be visible, I'd sign onto the electoral register, wouldn't I?"

"Whatever," I said, giving it up. I pulled up a chair and sat down opposite him. "Have you got anything for me?"

He nodded and unfolded his arms, revealing the laptop sitting between them on the table. He pushed it across to me, and I took it.

"And—some kind of written summary?" I hazarded hopefully.

"No need for one. One folder—RUSSIAN; one file—RUSSIAN1; three thousand, two hundred records in an unbroken numerical sequence with the prefix BATR1038. Data entry in every case is by one user—the system gives him a handle of 017—and all amendments are by the same user. There's only one conclusion a reasonable mind could draw."

"And that is?"

"017 was the only man-slash-woman-slash-data-processing-entity to have any contact with this folder at any point."

I absorbed this in silence, cast into momentary depression, until I saw the bolt-hole in Nicky's wording. "You said a reasonable mind," I pointed out.

He nodded. "Absolutely. A mind like mine, that welcomes paranoia as a way of maintaining a critical edge, comes out somewhere quite different."

"Come on, Nicky," I said. "Give me the punch line."

"In a hundred and fifty-three cases, user 017 suddenly and for no apparent reason switches to a different data-input method. I found it in config.sys, because the log entry had actually been rewritten to allow it."

"Layman's English."

"He ditched his keyboard and overwrote selected fields from a handheld Bluetooth keypad—probably that diNovo thing that Logitech were trailing in Houston a while back. The beauty of that is— well, I'm assuming that this is a dongle system. Keyboards are connected via an individually coded hardware key."

"Right."

"So a Bluetooth device wouldn't physically connect to the computer at all. It wouldn't have to fit the keyhole, because it wouldn't be going in through the keyhole. It's a completely wireless system."

I chewed this over for a moment or two.

"But it was still user 017?" I said. "Same guy, different keyboard?"

Nicky grinned evilly. He was enjoying this. "It was someone telling the *system* he was user 017. But he had to use his own handle when he altered that config file. Even when you pull yourself up by your bootstraps, you still cast a shadow. He's user 020."

"Got you, you bastard," I muttered. "Nicky, that's brilliant—

thanks. I'll be wrapping this up in the next day or so, and then you can expect Christmas to come early."

Nicky took the praise as stoically as he'd taken the curses earlier; it would have been beneath his dignity to take a bow. But he didn't move. "There's one other thing, Felix," he said.

"Go on."

"While I was in there anyway, I took a look around some of the other folders. There were a couple of dozen of them, going back about six or seven years. The older ones are fine—no tampering, no anomalous entries. But for three years or so now, user 020 has been keeping really busy. The earliest Bluetooth-fed entry was last March. Before that, he was using an IRF widget, but the principle was the same— using the back door that the system keeps open so that you can dock your laptop or your Palm Pilot with your main machine and update address books and the like."

He stood up.

"About two thousand records were affected," he said. "On this drive, anyway. Assuming there are other self-contained input machines, there's no saying what else Mr. Twenty has been getting up to."

As he walked to the door, I called out after him, "Nicky, what's he doing to the records? Just so I'm absolutely clear. What's he falsifying?"

"You already know that, Felix," Nicky chided me.

"He's deleting them," I said. "He's wiping items off the system."

"Exactly. Hey, I was never here, which is why you didn't see me. Have a nice evening."

Eighteen

SUNDAY. THE DAY OF REST. BUT AS SOME CLEVER bastard once wittily remarked, there's no rest for the wicked—which must make me a very nasty piece of work indeed.

I don't know where policemen go to unwind and spend their precious limited leisure time. You can sort of picture it, though. Some bar where everyone checks the pint line on their glass before they take a sip, where you can leave your coat on the back of the chair when you go to take a piss, and where Paki jokes never go out of fashion.

For obvious reasons, that wasn't where James Dodson arranged to meet me. He chose Bar Italia on Old Compton Street instead, and he was sitting at the far end when I arrived, trying hard to blend in with the decor. As soon as I sat down, cinnamon latte in hand, he slapped a manila folder down on the bar top and stood up.

"Everything you need is in there," he said. "Now, unless drinking with you is a deal-breaker, I'm leaving. And I'm keeping you to your word, Castor. If I ever hear from you again—if I ever even see your face—I've got some friends who'll be only too happy to make you cry tears of blood."

I shot him a pained glance, the cliché offending me more than the threat. "Yeah, but then I'd just die, Dodson, and I'd have to come back and haunt you. Better quit while you're behind."

He stalked out, either deciding that I wasn't worth the effort of verbal swordplay or remembering that he'd come out unarmed. I turned my attention to the folder.

Like the man said, it had everything I needed. The cinnamon latte went cold and formed an unhealthy-looking skin like a badly healed wound while I dived deep into the phantasmagoria of signed and sealed plodology that Dodson had dredged up for me.

You can say what you like about our police force, but their paperwork is immaculate. Autopsy reports were cross-referenced to X-ray prints, path results, explanatory diagrams, and in one case even a T-shirt—or at least a photograph of a T-shirt. That was included because some fibers from the shirt were found down the throat of the woman in question, indicating some attempt to asphyxiate her "after her clothing had been removed at an earlier stage in the assault."

Being what I am makes me morbidly sensitive in a lot of ways, obnoxiously hard-assed in others. On this occasion, it was the first trait that was dominant, and I had to work to keep my breathing regular as I pieced together the nightmare circumstances in which these three women's lives had hit the buffers.

Jenny Southey was a hit-and-run victim, but it hadn't been clean or quick. She was a prostitute working the streets around King's Cross. Barely eighteen. A car had crushed her against a wall, breaking her pelvis and rupturing her liver. The accompanying file notes said they'd brought in a suspect, and he'd made an incoherent confession. The whole thing seemed to be an accidental result of overenthusiastic curb-crawling with a vast amount of alcohol thrown in. Whatever sentence they eventually gave the guy, I wished him a lifetime's supply of brewer's droop to go along with it.

Caroline Beck was even younger, but her death was just as brutal and arbitrary. She died of a methadone overdose at a party, three streets away from the Bonnington in the evocatively named Polygon Road. That would have been par for the course if she'd been a user, but she wasn't; some high-as-a-kite arsehole had come up to her while

she was dancing and injected her before she even knew what was going on. He'd just wanted to spread the good vibes, but since he chose
the carotid artery and since she'd never injected before, the effect was
spectacularly enhanced. The girl had died about half an hour later,
when her muscles went into spasm, and her breathing stopped.

Both of those sounded plausible enough to me—the sort of fucked-
up, messy deaths that leave a little piece of your spirit trapped in the
mesh of agonizing, unresolved emotions. But when I turned to number three, I knew I'd found my ghost.

Unlike the other two, she didn't have a name—just a case number
and a clinical description. One hundred and fifty-nine centimeters in
height; hair brunette; eyes brown; build slender; age approximately
mid-twenties. Naked, but a T-shirt found near the body provided
samples of her blood and sloughed skin cells when tested. She'd been
found in a skip on a builder's yard in the hinterland beyond the Amp-
thill Estate, dead for at least three days. The date on the incident
report was Wednesday, September 14—the day after the ghost was
first sighted at the Bonnington Archive.

The details were grim. The girl had been sexually assaulted, both
vaginally and anally, with traces of semen only in the vagina but
trauma to both areas consistent with rape. Her face had been exten-
sively slashed with some sharp and irregular metal implement that
had caused massive laceration and blood loss. The police pathologist
had spent a lot of time cataloging those facial injuries: *"a multitude of
shallow, irregular cuts and gouges, widely varied in depth and profile,"*
he noted, deadpan, before going on to list the position and extent of
each and every one of them. *"The instrument used in the attack had a
number of different surfaces and edges that moved independently of each
other,"* he concluded. But the cause of death was asphyxiation—that
T-shirt, jammed tight down into her throat until she couldn't breathe
around it.

The facial injuries were a dead giveaway. So was the T-shirt. In the
photo you could clearly read the motif Открыто. I had no idea what

it meant, but even I could tell that it was Cyrillic. And it wasn't a T-shirt, as such; it was a white, sleeveless hoodie.

In among the rest of the documentation, I found a photograph of the girl's head and shoulders. The dry description of those wounds did nothing to convey the reality, and I flinched as I stared at the bloodied scrape of raw flesh that was all that was left of her upper face. I knew the first time I saw her that it wasn't a veil she was wearing; I just hadn't wanted to think too much about what it really was.

So it's you, I thought. Somebody raped you. Somebody murdered you. Somebody tied your soul up in a magical straitjacket.

And then they brought me in to finish you off.

Anger bubbled up from my chest into my throat, sublimed out from between my clenched teeth. It took some of the edge off the horror and helplessness, so I welcomed it. But something odd happened to it when it reached the atavistic lumber rooms of my brain. The face of my sister, Katie, kept coming in between me and the ravaged face in the photo, and I was momentarily blinded by tears. Not tears of blood, just the ordinary variety, but they felt hot enough to scald. Grief and bitter shame filled me. I didn't try to analyze either emotion; I just endured them until they subsided and I could see the shape of the rage again under that dead black pall.

Someone was going to pay. It helped a little to be able to say that to myself and mean it. Someone was going to pay with extortionate, punishing interest.

I went back to the records that Dodson had given me. None of the later file notes indicated that the dead woman had been identified at any stage in the investigation. In fact, "investigation" was probably too grandiose a word for it. The police had done a little doorstepping to see if anyone had heard anything, despite the pathologist's clear note that there was *no evidence of trauma or sexual congress in situ.* They'd taken a statement from the site manager, who'd confirmed that the skip was unused and unattended for at least a week before the body was found. They'd done a little tiptoe through the missing-persons list, put in a routine information request to Interpol, then sat back and brewed up. It was immaculate autopilot policing; nobody cared, and nobody was going to chase their own tails over some Eastern European whore found naked and used up on a building site. Even with the immigration quotas down, it was still a case of some for everyone, and more coming.

I paid for the coffee I hadn't touched, left the café, and headed off down Old Compton Street. I was still missing something, but I sort of knew the shape of it now. I could fill it in by looking at the pieces that surrounded it.

Damjohn was a pimp. He ran strip clubs and brothels in the Clerkenwell triangle, and someone at the Bonnington knew him well.

Gabe McClennan was an exorcist. He'd been to the archive, but whatever he went for, he'd been firing blanks that day. He'd silenced the archive ghost, but he hadn't killed her.

Rosa was a whore. She worked for Damjohn. Damjohn had gone out of his way, it seemed now, to make sure I got to see her—and then she'd tried to kill me with a steak knife because of something she thought I'd done to some other woman.

The ghost was from somewhere in Eastern Europe—probably Russia, since Russian seemed to be her native language. But she'd died in Somers Town, raped and murdered, and her spirit was trapped in the basement of a public building where she had no compelling reason to be in the first place.

Some one thing joined all of these things together and made sense out of them. But the closest I had was the card the ghost had given me on my second day at the archive, with its cryptic inscription ICOE 7405 818. The more I chewed it over, the less it seemed to mean.

Under the circumstances, the last thing I was in the mood for was a wedding. But that was where I was going to go.

The Brompton Oratory, immortalized in song by Nick Cave & the Bad Seeds, which was another set of associations I could have done without. But I had to admit, speaking as an atheist, that it was a hell of a place of worship—all vertical vistas and baroque flounces. If you got married here, you wouldn't need a wedding cake.

Three white limousines were parked out in front of the building, the lead one decked out with white ribbons. Two ushers in immaculate morning suits standing in the portico stared aghast at my trench coat and my general air of walking in out of a storm. They were a matched pair in one respect only—they both had exactly Cheryl's complexion. But one was a barge pole stood on its end, while the other was both an inch shorter than me and six inches broader—muscle, from the look of it, not fat. It was this handy-looking gentleman who rolled into my path, like one of those kids' trucks that Tonka used to make out of stainless steel, that you could drop off a cliff without even scratching the paintwork. I warned him off with an admonitory raised finger. "I'm on the bride's side," I told him. "Let's not do anything to spoil the mood."

"*We*'re on the bride's side," the barge pole said sternly, stepping up on my other side. "Let's see your invitation."

I made a show of going through my pockets, hoping that some other late arrival would roll up and distract their attention. No such luck.

"It's here somewhere," I offered. "Can I go in now and show it to you later?"

"What's the name of the bride?" Barge Pole demanded by way of a compromise.

Bugger. "I've always called her by a nickname," I hedged.

"What nickname?" Tonka Toy getting in on the act now.

I tried to think of a nickname. His fist closed hard on a handful of my shirt, and his face creased in a stern frown. Inspiration struck just in time to stop me going arse over tip down the steps.

"Oh, I remember now," I said, smacking my brow to punish my

brain for its erratic performance. "Cheryl's got my invitation. Cheryl Telemaque. My fiancée."

"Fiancée?" The barge pole sounded appalled, and the burly guy looked stricken enough to make me wonder if he was carrying a torch for Cheryl himself. Either way, that seemed to do the trick. I slipped between them and was in through the door before they could react. Neither of them followed me.

Inside, I found Herbert Gribble's great masterwork of devotional plagiarism filled to bursting with rows of people wearing suits and dresses that were probably mortgaged rather than bought outright, all sitting docilely and waiting for the bride to show. The groom was up at the altar, looking as cool and collected as a man tied to train tracks and hearing the distant whistle.

Cheryl was in the fifth row back, dressed to match the architecture in a beige dress with enough lacy froth to make "baroque" seem an appropriate word for her, too. Her cream leather shoes with nickel silvered roses on them fitted in with the Italianate charm of the place. Farther away I could see Alice Gascoigne and Jeffrey Peele, side by side, and Jon Tiler looking like a partially trained orangutan in a suit that had been made to measure. For a chimp.

I sat down next to Cheryl. She glanced up, away, back, her eyes widening in horror—a double take worthy of Norman Wisdom.

"Felix!" she whispered hoarsely. "What are you doing here?"

"I was in the neighborhood."

She wasn't amused, and I didn't blame her. "I don't mind you coming, but you look like something the cat dragged in. Are you mad?" She waved agitated hands at my shirtfront. "Look, you've not even ironed your shirt. You're all crumpled up like you've been rolling on the ground."

"That was the ushers outside," I said as a meager gesture toward self-defense. "They were going to rough me over. Where the hell did you dig them up from?"

"They're my cousin Andrew and my cousin Stephen," she snapped.

"And they're really, really, nice so don't you say another bloody word."

Time to find a less loaded subject, perhaps. "I thought you grew up rough in Kilburn," I said, looking around at all the silk and silver.

"Yeah, I did," she said, flashing me a grim look. "And I can still do rough if the need arises."

"I don't doubt it. But where does your mum get the chops to swing a gig like this?"

People were turning to look at us. Cheryl blushed a richer, darker brown that clashed with the dress and made me want to take it off her. "It's not my mum," she muttered fiercely. "It's my Aunt Felicia. She's a member of the order."

"The order?"

"The Catholic Oratorians. They own this place, yeah? Now, what are you bloody well doing here? Stop changing the subject."

"I want an invite."

"You've just invited your sodding self, haven't you?"

"Not to this. To the reception. It's at the Bonnington, isn't it? Can you get me in through the door?"

She just stared at me for a moment, nonplussed. "Are you gonna cause trouble at my mum's wedding?" she demanded.

Time to duck again. "It's about Sylvie," I said.

Cheryl was still suspicious; she had good Castor-radar already, despite having known me for less than a week. "What about her?"

"I know who she was. I know what was done to her. She was raped and murdered, and her body was dumped in a skip. I owe it to her not to let go of this."

That gave Cheryl pause. Quite a long pause, as it turned out. Before she spoke again, she blinked three times, staring at me with wounded, tearful eyes.

"Murdered?"

"Gouged in the face with something sharp and jagged. Choked with her own—"

"Don't!"

"I'm not going to cause a ruckus, Cheryl. I promise you. I won't be any bother. But I have to try this."

More heads were turning in our direction. Our hissed conversation was now causing as much of a stir as my scruffy casuals and giving the lie to my promise to be discreet.

"Try what?" Cheryl asked weakly, like someone who knows they're in a fight that they're going to lose.

"The laying on of hands."

First she didn't get it. Then she did, and she was appalled.

"What, you think it was someone at the archive who did it?"

"No. I'm a hundred percent certain it was."

"And what, you're gonna go around feeling people up to see if any of them's a murderer? Not at my mum's effing wedding reception, you're not!"

"Everyone shakes hands at a wedding. Nobody will even notice."

The organist broke into "Here Comes the Bride," and all heads turned.

Cheryl's mum looked very much like Cheryl, only taller and more statuesque. Her dark face under the white veil was austerely beautiful, and she walked like an empress. It was something of a revelation—if heredity counted for anything, Cheryl was going to grow old very gracefully indeed.

The bride proceeded up the aisle in stately fashion, and various elderly women on both sides of the aisle made good use of their handkerchiefs. Alice Gascoigne kept hers firmly in its holster; she'd seen me by now, and she was staring at me with an expression like the one Banquo's ghost must have used on Macbeth.

"You said she was sad," I reminded Cheryl. "Now you know why. Do you want the bastard who did that to her to get away with it?"

She didn't answer.

Cheryl's mum was making her vows now. They sounded as though she'd run them up herself, because they went from "With my body I thee worship" into some pretty explicit subclauses.

Cheryl looked away. "Okay," she said, sounding miserable and flat. She opened her purse, which was made of cream-colored leather and just about big enough to hold a handkerchief and a tampon. By some alchemy she took out of it a large rectangle of card with a gold border. She handed it to me without a word. It began *You are cordially invited to the wedding of Eileen Telemaque to Russell Clarke, on Sunday, November 27, 2005.* With a whispered thanks to Cheryl, I shoved it into my pocket.

More vows from the groom, who sounded as though he was reading from a crib sheet and seeing some of them for the first time. Well, if you don't read the small print, you haven't got a leg to stand on.

"When does the reception start?" I whispered to Cheryl.

"At three. It's on the invite. Felix, don't fuck this up, okay? Don't do something awful."

I went through some hurried mental calculations. There was some stuff I needed to do first. I squeezed Cheryl's hand and slid back along the pew. "Catch you later," I promised.

"You're gonna catch *something*," Cheryl prophesied bitterly.

It's hard to leave a wedding discreetly while it's still in progress. The ushers glared at me as I strolled past them and out the door, trying to look as though I'd only popped in to read the gas meter. Behind me, the swelling organ chords worked their way through to a very impressive diapason that hung in the air like floating furniture.

———

I got to the Bonnington first, broke into the secret rooms all over again, and did what I had to do. The atmosphere down in the basement room was so oppressive, I felt as though I was sipping the dank air rather than breathing it. I took care not to touch McClennan's ward of silence with my bare skin again. To be honest, I could barely bring myself to look at it. It struck me right then as the most purely evil thing I'd come across in a long and eventful life.

When I was finished, there was nothing left for me to do but loiter. I let myself back out onto the street, locked up carefully behind myself, and retired to the Rocket on Euston Road. One side of the pub looks out toward Ossulston Street, which is where those sleek white limousines would turn to go into the one-way system before parking out in front of the Bonnington. I'd have plenty of warning and plenty of time in the meantime to sink a pint and steady my nerves.

I hadn't lied to Cheryl. Not exactly. But I hadn't told her the whole truth, either. There was no point at all in me shaking hands with the archive staff if all they were thinking about was the cost of the canapés and how big the bride's arse looked. I had to get their emotions stirred up and their thoughts turning toward the dead woman. Well, I'd come up with a way of doing that. And it was going to make Mrs. Telemaque's fourth wedding one that everyone would remember.

The cars rolled up about half an hour later. I gave them a quarter of an hour after that and then went sauntering along after them.

The doors of the Bonnington were open. No sign of the ushers from the Oratory, but an MC in a red tux gave me a welcoming smile that congealed into something a lot less cordial when he saw how I was dressed. I flashed the invite at him and walked on by.

There was no receiving line, so when I got up to the reading room, my entrance went unnoticed. I looked around at a scene of untrammeled joy and innocent celebration; it made me feel just a little bit awkward about what I was going to do next.

Some trestle tables had been set up at one end of the room and draped with long white tablecloths that trailed to the floor. Champagne cocktails were being served, and waitresses dressed in vaguely period black and white were tacking around the room with silver trays full of elegant finger foods. All very refined. More annoyingly, the shelving units and the librarians' station had all been pushed back against the wall and camouflaged with white sheeting; there was no natural cover that I could use for the next stage of the proceedings, which was the truly fiddly one.

It didn't help that I stuck out like a rabbi at a hoedown. The only reason nobody had noticed me so far was because there was a speech going on, and all eyes were turned on the man—a complete stranger to me—who was giving it. I scanned the crowd, saw Rich dressed in an immaculate gray morning suit with a sky blue waistcoat, talking with Jon Tiler off at the edge of the crowd on the far side of the room from me. Cheryl was up at the front, her arm linked in her mother's. After a little casting around, I located Alice and Jeffrey by the drinks table, Alice holding out her champagne flute to be refreshed while Jeffrey talked to a fat woman in a voluminous red dress. His face set in a tight, pained smile, he looked like a man trying hard to have a good time at his own lynching party.

I looked around for somewhere I could play undisturbed, but nothing much suggested itself. Just as the speech wrapped up to loud applause, I ducked behind a pillar that at least would shield me from a casual glance. I slipped my whistle out of my pocket and put it to my lips.

Right here in the heart of her territory, my sense of the ghost was as sharp and as clear as it was ever going to be, but this still wasn't going to be easy. Too much going on, too many competing sounds and stimuli. I closed my eyes to block out at least one source of distraction and tried to focus only on the feel of her in my mind—the sense that for me was more like hearing than anything else, but still impossible to dissect or describe.

The groom was speaking now, and all other conversation in the room had stilled. I waited, seething with impatience, for the background hum to start up again. He talked for what seemed like an hour—about what a difference Eileen had made to his life, about how lucky he was, about how much he was looking forward to being a father to Cheryl. I wondered if he'd seen the job description.

When the applause came again, I squeezed out the first notes. I tried to keep it low, and I managed at first, but the tune goes where it wants to go. If you push it into a different pattern, you get a different result.

My mind narrowed to the succession of notes, the inscape of the ghost's music. Part of it was "The Bonny Swans," but most of it was new, hers and nobody else's, the sound that was the space she occupied in the world, the song that sang her.

Suggestive gaps in the skein of voices from around me told me that the guests closest to me had heard the music now. They were probably looking around for its source. I carried on playing, not hurrying, not slowing—I was tied to the wheel now, and I had to go where it took me.

The silence spread, and footsteps were coming toward me, but it was almost done. A few more bars would take me there. A hand clamped on my shoulder. Eyes tight shut, I ignored it, wound down through a plaintive diminuendo to a single note, which bounced up again into an unexpectedly defiant closing trill.

The whistle was snatched out of my hand. I opened my eyes to find myself staring into the eyes of the Tonka Toy—the burly one of Cheryl's two cousins. He held the whistle up in front of me, his face a scowling mask. Other faces clustered behind him, looking at me curiously or resentfully.

"Is this a joke?" the thickset man demanded aggressively.

"No," I answered. "It's an invitation."

There were gasps from the back of the crowd and then a scream. All heads turned in that direction, including the Tonka Toy's. As he gawped along with the rest of them, I took my whistle back from his hand and pocketed it carefully. All hell was about to break loose, so I wanted the instrument safely stowed.

The archive ghost was walking through the center of the room and through the people in the room, who scrambled to get some distance from her. Ghosts may be fairly common phenomena now, but some ghosts have more presence than others, and the faceless woman had a grimness of purpose about her that saturated the room.

She stopped and stared about her without eyes. She was more solid now, and you could see that the white garment she wore ended at the waist. From the waist down, she wore a plain black skirt, and her arms were bare.

"Gdyeh Rosa?" she said with a keening, complaining emphasis. *"Ya nye znayo gdyeh ona. Vi dolzhni pomogitye menya naiti yeyo."*

At various points in the crowd, people cried out.

"Ya potrevozhnao Rosa."

I shoved the usher aside and plunged into the crowd, my head darting from side to side as I went. It had to be now, while the shock of the ghost's speaking aloud was still fresh and raw in people's minds. I'd gone to a lot of trouble to set this up, and I was damned if I was going to let it go to waste.

Alice and Jeffrey were still over by the drinks table, but they were heading for the door as quickly as they could without Jeffrey actually being forced to touch somebody. Alice was leading the way, savagely determined, with Peele enclitically lodged just behind her. I stepped into their path, and she came to an abrupt halt, staring at me in affronted astonishment.

"Now this is what I call a party," I said with bumpkin jocularity.

"Castor," Alice said, and there was a hard catch in her voice that took me by surprise—a look in her eye that was something like hatred.

I put out my hand and took hers, and though she pulled back sharply, I kept hold. The first time I'd touched her, I'd listened pretty hard, but I hadn't picked up a damn thing. But this was different. She was angry and shaken, and any guard she had was down. If I couldn't get a reading from her now, I never would.

"You're looking radiant, Alice," I said, squeezing her hand and smiling inanely into her face. "You must be pregnant."

FLASH. I felt the stab of her fury and indignation, followed by an all-but-submerged twinge of real fear. Fear of the ghost, certainly, but another fear rising out of that so steeply that all perspective was lost. Alice really didn't want to be pregnant. And she really didn't want me pawing at her. As she wrestled to get her hand free, I saw in quick succession within her mind a child's-eye view of a huge, looming man shaving at an oval mirror; a dead daffodil in a slender rose vase, the last inch of water turned to brown ullage; her desk at the archive, pristine and empty, the mail trays lined up hospital-corner fashion with the desk's far right-hand edge. It took me a moment to realize that although it was her desk, it was in Peele's narrow, oddly shaped office. The boss's desk, in other words, but with her name on the door instead of his.

Alice got her hand free from mine with some effort. I thought she was going to use it to slap me, but she only swore at me under her breath—a word I wouldn't have expected her to know, the last two syllables of which were "bubble." I ignored her and lunged past her at Jeffrey.

Being autistic, Jeffrey had a much stronger and more deeply rooted objection to being touched by me than Alice did. Where she was merely fastidious, he was pathological. So I didn't have to do anything to raise the emotional temperature. He stiffened as I grabbed his wrist, and then he actually jumped, his feet leaving the ground momentarily.

"Don't!" he yelped. "Mr. Castor!"

FLASH. I got a microsecond glimpse of a corridor in the archive— the ghost standing there, sideways on but with her face turned to- ward him—before raw, flaring panic obliterated all images and left his mind pure white: the white of white noise.

Peele was physically struggling to get away from me, and people were staring at us in amazement. I let go too suddenly, and he stum- bled backward, crashing into the people behind him and sending them sprawling. Alice did slap me now—a stinging backhander that would probably leave a visible mark. Jon Tiler loomed up out of no- where to help Jeffrey get back on his feet. As he reached forward, I intercepted him and grabbed both his wrists, making him stop and stare at me in astonishment.

A moment later, I arced backward like an epileptic suffering from a grand mal seizure. I hit the ground like a badly packed sack of ballast.

I hadn't touched Tiler at all on my first day at the archive. It was probably just as well. He was a supersender—an emotional foghorn—and I would have made a bad first impression, losing control of my limbs in front of a whole lot of people I'd only just been introduced to.

I fell heavily but somehow managed to keep one hand in contact with Tiler's wrist as I hit the ground and jackknifed. The images and impressions I was getting were sluicing and scouring their way through my mind as though they'd come from a high-pressure hose. I couldn't keep them out, and I couldn't sort them. Visions of the ghost came through strongest, in all the rooms and hallways where he'd seen her—but the floodgates were open, and the rising tide of recollection broke over them, washed them away. I saw most of Tiler's childhood, got to know his mother from a baby's-eye view (his interest at that age had centered mainly on her left breast), relived potty training and bedtime stories and an abusive relationship with the family cat, and Christ knew what else. It wasn't chronological, though. I saw him sitting in a cinema, crying at *Gone With the Wind*; at home, pouring boiling water into a Pot Noodle; and at the archive, carefully swathing an old leather-bound book in bubble wrap. It was a parish register, labeled March to June 1840. He looked over his shoulder as he worked to make sure nobody saw. He protected the corners with cardboard brackets, laboriously cut out and taped together. He knew what he was doing; he'd done it a thousand times before, always with the same warm tingle in his lower abdomen. It was like ascending toward an orgasm that never came—and that feeling, that endless rising scale, was the anchor of his life.

"I think he's dead."

"Don't be stupid, Jon. He just fainted."

"Yeah, but did you hear that crack when his head hit the ground?"

"That wasn't his head. It was a metallic sound. It was something in his pocket."

"Tin whistle. Look. It's bent into an L shape."

Oh no. No fucking way. A cold gust of sorrow and remorse brought me the rest of the way up into full consciousness. My whistle. My sword and my shield through all the half-arsed vicissitudes of life. It was the same as a million others, and it was absolutely unique. And all that was left of it now was the jagged pain in my side where the broken end of it was digging into my third rib.

I opened my eyes halfway and found myself staring up into a wide range of startled, suspicious, and resentful faces. Cheryl's was right in the middle of them, and although she looked relieved to see me conscious again, I could tell from the hard set of her mouth that her membership in the Felix Castor fan club had lapsed forever. That was two body blows inside of twenty seconds.

A silver hip flask was pressed into my hand. Feeling numb and cold and strangely removed from myself, I took a swig without checking what it was and found myself coughing noisily on some raw but excellent bourbon. A lot of it went down the front of my coat, but the rest of it did the trick. I turned to see who it was I had to thank; Rich Clitheroe was looking down at me with a surreptitious eyebrow flash of sympathy and solidarity. I handed the flask back to him with a nod, flashing back to his secret stash of Lucozade in the traveling fridge down in the strong room. Well, "Be Prepared" is the Boy Scouts' marching song, and some things just stay with you. But that wasn't the phrase he'd used in any case; it was something like that, only different.

In case of emergency . . .

Domino nudged domino nudged domino, and everything fell into a pattern that had been there all along, unseen. I sat up, feeling an odd sense of weightlessness. I was like a thrown ball at the top of its arc, when it's stopped rising but hasn't begun to fall—freed from gravity, freed from the necessity of choice. Cheryl helped me to my feet, and our gazes met, furiously accusing on her side, God only knew what on mine. There was no sign of the ghost now. The summons I'd sent out to her would have broken when I lost consciousness, and there was nothing to keep her in this confusing, exposed, overbright space.

"I'm sorry," I told Cheryl, leaning in close so that nobody else could hear.

She didn't bend. "I bet you always are, afterward. I bet it even works sometimes."

"I hope it will work with Sylvie," I murmured. "I owe her the biggest apology of all."

Other voices were breaking in now, and other hands were taking hold of me. Jeffrey Peele was saying, "I can't, I can't, I can't," and Alice was interjecting comments like "It's all right" and "You're fine now" without any noticeable effect. Someone else—a woman—was asking whether she should call the police, and one of the ushers—the barge pole this time—muscled in between me and Cheryl to suggest that I might want to go out into the street and get some fresh air. His nose wrinkled, no doubt smelling the booze.

I let myself be shepherded away toward the door with his hand gripping my collar, but then I stopped again before he could get any real momentum going. I turned back, found Rich in the crowd. He stared at me, a little startled, as I made the universally recognizable gesture that meant he should phone me. I pointed to Jeffrey, meaning that Jeffrey had my phone number.

Rich hesitated for a moment—probably trying to work out what the hell I was trying to say—then nodded. The thickset usher loomed up on my other side, hooked one hand under my arm, and I was off, my feet barely touching the floor as I went.

It was probably just as well. I get all emotional at weddings.

Nineteen

Y OU'RE LOADING UP YOUR SIX-GUNS, AREN'T YOU?"
Pen said, standing in the doorway of my room. A chill wind was
blowing around the plastic sheeting she'd nailed across the splintered,
gap-toothed window frame, like a reminder that winter was on its
way. I didn't need reminding, and I didn't appreciate it much.

"Yeah," I said tersely. "I think it's going to be a bad one."

I was rummaging through the top shelf in my wardrobe, looking
for a spare whistle. There should have been at least one there—older
than the little beauty I'd just destroyed, and brassy rather than black
in color, but in the same key and with something of the same feel to
hand and mouth. I was damned if I could see it, though. The best I
could come up with was a cone-bore flute. I'd almost forgotten my
brief flirtation with that well-mannered instrument. It hadn't done
the job for me at all—something about the tone, maybe, or the tapering body. It shouldn't have made that big a difference, because tin
whistles have a conical bore, too, but every pattern I tried to weave on
it got screwed up and thrown out somewhere along the line. Still, it
was better than nothing by some small but measurable margin.

"Maybe you should get some help, then," Pen suggested. "John
Gittings?"

"Never again."

"Pac-Man?"

"Still in jail. He doesn't get out until next October."

"Me?"

I turned to stare at her. "Usual strictures apply," I said, sounding colder than I meant to; and then, more gently, "I don't have any idea how this is going to come out, Pen. But I do know it will leave you with dirty hands—by your definition and probably even by mine."

Pen looked very unhappy, but she didn't try to argue anymore. I slipped a couple of new batteries into the Walkman, wrapped the flex around the two tiny speakers, and stuffed the whole bundle into my pocket. Then I reached into the back of the wardrobe and took down a single silver handcuff that was hanging on a hook there. Pen blanched when she saw it.

"You weren't kidding, were you?" she asked bleakly.

"It'll probably be fine," I lied. "When you take out car insurance, it doesn't mean you're planning to drive off a cliff."

"Are you?"

"Am I what?"

"Planning to drive off a cliff."

"No. I'm looking to push someone else off. The insurance is in case he keeps hold of me on the way down."

I headed for the door, which she was still blocking. She hugged me briefly but fiercely. "Rafi had another message for you," she muttered, her voice not quite level.

"Rafi?"

"All right. Asmodeus, then."

"Go on."

"Ajulutsikael. He said it's not personal with her—it's the very opposite of personal. But it's not just because they're making her do it, either. What was it he said?" Pen frowned, delving into her memory. "'She hates a proud man more than a humble one. A strong man more than a weak one. A master more than a slave.'"

"He should write fortune cookies," I said and kissed her on the cheek. "He's about as much fucking use."

She stood aside and let me pass.

———

This was going to be complicated. There were so many things that had to fall right, and the first one might not fall at all. In which case all my preparations were going to be unnecessary, the ghost's unfinished business was going to stay unfinished, and I was probably going to be dead in short order—either succubus fodder or just organic landfill.

But I preferred to look on the bright side. I was going to make a hell of a noise on the way down.

Rich had called at nine, having come home from the reception, taken a shower, and thought long and hard about whether he was going to call me at all.

"What the fuck were you thinking of, Castor?" he asked me, sounding genuinely mystified. "The ghost didn't just turn up, did she? You brought her. Cheryl said she'll split you if she ever sees you again, and Alice—well, you don't want to know. She's going to get the police in, she said. The only reason she didn't do it today was because she didn't want to spoil what was left of the occasion."

I let him wind down, and then I told him that I'd cracked the whole thing.

"What thing?" The puzzlement was turning into annoyance. "You were just supposed to get rid of the ghost, weren't you? What's to crack?"

"How she got that way," I said tersely.

Rich digested that for a few seconds.

"All right," he said at last. "How did she?"

"Not now. Meet me at Euston, okay? On the concourse outside the station, at the Eversholt Street end. Eleven o'clock should be okay. And I'll tell you all about it."

"Why me?" The obvious question. I was surprised it had taken him so long to get to it.

"Because there were two crimes committed at the Bonnington," I told him. "One of them was a theft, and since you were the victim, I thought you might want to hear about it."

Rich played hard to get for a little while longer, then said he'd be there. I hung up and started to get my shit together.

So here I was, ten minutes early. The concrete piazza outside the station was as quiet as it ever gets, and it was easy to make sure that neither of us had been followed—or at least not by enthusiastic amateurs. Ajulutsikael was a different kettle of fish altogether; she had my scent now, and I had to assume that she could track me without ever coming in close enough for me to see her.

I found a secluded corner and loitered with intent. A phone kiosk and an advertising hoarding gave me a certain amount of cover, but left my line of sight clear both to the main exit from the station and to the stairs that came up from the Underground. There was almost nobody there: a small party of Japanese students with oversized backpacks, clustered just outside one set of automatic doors and taking turns to look anxiously at their watches; a homeless guy clutching a huge grubby sports bag and drinking White Lightning out of a can that he'd just broken from a four-pack; a couple of girls in pink tracksuits, too young to be out that late, sitting on a bench right across from me, back to back, sharing the one pair of headphones. None of them looked like part of an ambush, but I kept an open mind. I was clearly drifting into Nicky territory here: *you embrace paranoia when it becomes a survival trait.*

Rich came up the steps at a quarter past eleven, looked around, and didn't see me. He'd changed out of his wedding gear and was dressed in black jeans, a Quiksilver sweatshirt, trainers.

I stepped out of hiding and started walking toward him. He turned, saw me, came to meet me halfway.

"Have you got your keys?" I asked him without any preamble.

"My what?" He was startled.

"Your keys to the archive. Do you have them on you?"

"Yeah," he said. "I brought them." He stared straight at me, looking wary and tense—a man who wanted it to be known that he'd need some convincing before he went along with any funny business. "What's this about?"

"It's about a lot of things, Rich. But for starters, let's say it's about a kleptomaniac who's not averse to the occasional White Russian."

Rich's lips quirked downward, almost comically hangdog.

"Fuck," he said, nonplussed. "You mean . . . you know, I thought once or twice that—fuck."

"The Head of Steam's still open," I said. "Let me lay it all out for you."

He followed me docilely across the concrete arena to the bizarre little theme pub they've squeezed into a corner there, but we'd missed the towel by five minutes and sat down dry. I took the laptop out of my pocket and pushed it across to him. Rich stared at it, then at me. "You're one to watch, aren't you, Castor?" he said a little grimly. "I was shitting bricks over this. Half the entries on here haven't even been uploaded to the system yet. I was still trying to figure out how to break the news to Alice without catching the edge of her temper myself."

He pulled the loosely wrapped package over to his own side of the table, as if he felt the need to assert his ownership of it.

"I didn't have too many options," I said. "I knew something odd was going on, but I couldn't prove it. I needed to pass this on to a friend of mine who I thought might have a better chance of nailing it all down for me."

"And?"

"It's Jon Tiler," I said.

Rich just laughed. "No way," he protested.

"Way," I insisted, deadpan. "He uses a wireless media pad to get around the fact that he can't use his own keyboard on your machine."

"What, a media pad? You're joking." Rich was still incredulous. "That's just a remote for DVDs and stuff. It doesn't even have full alphanumerics."

"He's not adding in any data or amending it. Only deleting."

He absorbed this in silence, a number of expressions following each other across his face. When he finally spoke, it was terse and to the point.

"The bastard!"

"You get it?"

"Of course I get it. If he deletes my records before I upload, there's no system entry to cross-check against. Nobody would ever know there was anything missing."

"And that's probably what tempted him to swipe so many items in such a short space of time."

"*How* many, exactly?"

"A couple of thousand, give or take."

Rich winced. "That's taking the piss," he muttered. Then another thought visibly occurred to him; two thoughts, as it turned out. "But how's he getting the stuff out of the archive? And what's any of this got to do with the ghost?"

"I'm going to duck that second question for now. As to the first one, an ounce of bare-arsed cheek is worth a ton and a half of cunning. He's just taking it up to the attic and dropping it out of the window onto the flat roof. Then I presume he comes around sometime in the night and collects it. All the strong rooms are on that side of the building, so there are no windows below the attic that overlook that area."

"Jesus." Rich's expression was torn between annoyance and admiration. "I thought you were going to say he had a hollow wooden leg or something. Frank's going to be sick. When Jeffrey starts looking for someone to blame, he's going to start right at the front desk."

"Wait, there's more. I said the Russian collection tempted him to up his game, but he's been doing this for three years. Whenever anything new comes into the archive, he skims a little something off the top. When did Tiler start work at the Bonnington, by the way?"

Rich laughed hollowly. "2002," he said. "Fairly late in the year, I think, because they timed his appointment to start with the school year." He shook his head. "Son of a bitch."

I stood up, hands in pockets, and he looked up at me quizzically.

"Feel a burning desire for justice?" I asked.

He blew out his cheeks and thought about it. "Not really," he said. "You'll tell Jeffrey, right? And it'll all get sorted. I mean, I'm pissed off, don't get me wrong, but it's not really any of my business. Not especially."

"I don't work for Peele anymore. I was sacked, remember? Yeah, I could go straight to the police—but to be honest, there's another question I want answered first. There's something I'd like to show you. And I'd like you to see it cold. Okay?"

It took him a while to make up his mind, but in the end he nodded and got up. I led the way out of the bar, back across the concourse, and out onto the street. We crossed the road, Rich still trailing me by about three steps. It was obvious where we were heading for.

"There's no way we can go inside at this time of night," Rich said, sounding anxious. "The alarms will be on."

"Only the strong room doors are alarmed. But we're not going into the archive, anyway. Not technically speaking."

We turned onto Churchway. "You never explained about the ghost," Rich said.

"You're right. I didn't. That's what I want to show you."

We stopped at the other door—the door that looked like it didn't lead anywhere much at all, let alone to one of the gates of Hell.

"What's this?" Rich asked.

I climbed the three steps and pointed to the locks in their cutaway box. "This is why I asked you to bring your keys," I told him.

He looked confused and a little scared. "But—my keys are for the archive."

"Take a good look through the bunch. You're looking for one that has a picture of a bird on the fob and a big, squared-off barrel. And another that says Schlage. Take your time. They'll be there."

Rich hauled out the big key ring and started sorting through it. In the dim light, it must have been hard for him to see what any of the keys looked like. It took him close to two minutes, but eventually he found them: first the Falcon, then the Schlage.

"Try them in these locks," I said.

He slid the Falcon in first, turned it. We both heard the click. Then he tried the Schlage. No sound this time, but the door, loose in its frame, slid inward an inch or so under its own weight.

"I don't get it," said Rich, turning his head to stare at me with a guarded, questioning look.

"All the key rings are the same, right? All of them handed down from archivist to archivist through the colonnades of time? You, Alice, and Jeffrey—everyone holding a full set, and nobody using more than half of them. That's what you told me the first day I came here."

"Yeah, that's true, but—"

"Take a look inside," I suggested. "Someone's been using these two fairly recently."

He pushed open the door, stepped over the threshold. I followed and turned on the light. Rich cast his gaze around the squalid little room, now carpeted with shards of glass and colder than ever because of the broken windows.

"Christ on a bike," he said. Then he sniffed and winced at the acrid smell.

"You're not telling me Tiler keeps the stuff down here?" he asked, his voice tight. "It smells like"—his voice faltered.

"Like what?"

"Like—I don't know."

I walked past him into the center of the room, turned to face him. His face was pale. "This is going to sound incredible," I said. "Crazy, crazy story. Crazy and sick. A woman died here. Not accidentally. Murdered. Before that, she was kept here for a long time—days, maybe even weeks."

Rich's stare went from left to right, measuring. "But this is—" he said.

"Yeah. It's a chunk of the Bonnington, hived off maybe forty or fifty years ago. Nobody even remembers it's here or knows who owns it. It's not part of the real world anymore; it's virtual geography. Terra incognita."

Rich's face had gone beyond pale into ashen.

"I can't believe someone died here," he muttered, shaking his head.

"Not here, exactly. In the downstairs room."

His eyes flicked left, toward the wooden paneling. An instant later, they flared with alarm and looked back toward me.

The handcuff isn't really silver; it's ordinary stainless steel with a silver coating. It was sold as a sex toy in Hamburg, but when I use it (not all that often, thank God), I use it as a knuckle-duster. I caught Rich on the point of the chin with it—a really satisfying punch that made an audible smack, hooked him an inch into the air, and made him jackknife from the hips so that he landed heavily on his back with an impact that knocked what was left of his breath out of him.

He tried to get up, but fell back.

"Yeah," I said grimly. "Made you look."

Twenty

Rich TRIED TO GET UP, BUT HE DIDN'T MAKE IT VERY far, because his body wouldn't cooperate. He gawped up at me, blood trickling down his chin from where he'd bitten his lip when the handcuff impacted on his jaw.

"F-fuck!" he protested thickly, saliva frothing out to join the blood.

"Don't get up, Rich," I advised him, meaning it. "If you get up, I'm only going to knock you down again. You might end up breaking something."

He wiped his mouth with the back of his hand, staring at me with eyes that were having to work at the moment just to focus.

"You're frigging insane," he bubbled.

"Yeah, Cheryl thinks so, too. But Cheryl's no expert on sanity—not coming from that family. And Cheryl doesn't know you like I do, does she, Rich?"

He tried again, and this time he made it into a sitting position, one arm raised protectively in case I hit him again, exploring his thickening lower lip gingerly with fingers that seemed to be shaking. He shot me another look, scared but angrily defiant. "I didn't steal anything," he said. "Tiler was all on his own. If you think I'm in on his bloody pilfering—"

I cut in. I didn't have any patience for this. "Tiler doesn't matter," I snapped. "When I found out about his thieving, I thought it might be relevant in some way. I suppose I wanted it to be relevant, because I'd just come up empty-handed from the Russian collection, and I was desperate for anything that might point me in the right direction. Then Tiler whacked me in the face with an electric torch and threw me headfirst down a sodding stairwell, so I had something of a stake in him being guilty. But he isn't. As far as I can tell, what he does is just a weird hobby. He loves old documents. I've been inside his head, so I know. He's papered his bloody bedroom with them.

"No, I know you didn't steal anything, Rich. But you *did* kill somebody. How many nineteenth-century parish record books is that worth, karmically speaking?"

Rich had been gathering his strength for a big effort. He rolled to his left and made a break for the door. I'd seen it coming; I got my foot in between his legs and rammed him squarely in the back with my shoulder, adding my own momentum to his. He went down more heavily this time with a grunt of pain.

I hauled him to his feet while he was still limp and groggy from the impact, dragged him across the room, and shoved him hard against the paneled wall. He started to slump toward the floor again, but I kept him more or less upright by leaning my shoulder against him, at the same time helping myself to his keys. There was only one Chubb in the bunch. I put it into the lock and turned. The click was loud in the bare, silent room.

Hooking the door open with my foot, I took two handfuls of his shirt, around about chest height, and half pushed, half slid him onto the stairwell. He mewled in panic. "No! No! Not down there!" He fought against me, which was a bad decision on his part, because we were both off balance. Breaking free from my grip, he tumbled arse over tip down the stairs.

I lunged out and found the wall, which just saved me from falling down after him. I took a moment to get my breath back and slammed the upper door securely behind us before following him down at my leisure. So long as we had Rich's keys, we could get out anytime we liked, and in the meantime, we wouldn't be disturbed.

Rich had fetched up on his side, sprawled against the bottom edge of the mattress. Standing over him, I took a rectangular card out of my pocket, opened my fingers, and let it fall. It fluttered down to land next to his head. He stared at it woozily. The card read ICOE 7405 818.

"In case of emergency," I translated. "You said it to me last Monday when you offered me a bottle of Lucozade from the fridge. Then you started to say it again the next day, but you stopped yourself, and I filled in the gap for you. It had slipped my mind, to be honest. I was still thinking ICOE must be somebody's nickname or something. But then you offered me your hip flask today at the wedding, and it clicked."

Rich levered his upper body groggily off the floor. He shook his head, said something that was impossible to make out through his painful, hitching breath.

"Not much in the way of hard evidence?" I interpreted. "No, you're probably right, there. But you knew where to look, didn't you, Rich? When I said there was a downstairs room, your eyes went right to the door. Only the door's camouflaged against that foul wood paneling, so there was no way you could have known it was there. No clean way, anyway."

I was warming up now—and I was also goading him to answer me. I wanted the story. I wanted to hear out of his own mouth what had been done down here.

"So that's strike one and strike two, yeah? Then there's the fact that you're shit-hot at Eastern European languages, and the ghost speaks in Russian. Only you never heard her speak, did you, Rich? Everybody else in the place did, but you—the only guy who could have definitively identified the language and told us all what she was talking about—you were stricken magically deaf.

"But strike four is my favorite. That was when you sneaked into Peele's office and tore a page out of the incident book. I was straining my brain trying to think about *why* that was done—what anyone could possibly have to gain from it. And I finally came up with an answer. I finally realized what it was that was missing.

"This girl died sometime around the tenth of September—maybe a day or so before, give or take, but certainly not after. And the first sighting of the ghost was on Tuesday the thirteenth. But it wasn't the first sighting that had been ripped out of the book. That was still there, written out in agonizing detail. Because the ghost couldn't be hidden, obviously—everyone was seeing her by then. So what was being hidden was something else, something that our mystery guest didn't want to have associated with the ghost, if questions were asked later."

"Nothing"—Rich managed, his voice coming out as a breathy grunt—"to do with . . . me."

I smiled bleakly at that. "Ah, but you see, I think it was," I told him, standing over him in case he decided to make another run for it. "I think it was that famous time when you jammed your hand in a drawer. Proving what an amiable klutz you are. Proving that you don't mind having a laugh at your own expense. Only it wasn't a drawer, was it, Rich? You got that injury when she got hers. I'm guessing it was a scratch. Maybe a puncture wound of some kind, to the side of your hand. You're the first-aid man, so nobody else had to see—and you made bloody sure they didn't. But I'm pretty well convinced that was what it was, all the same."

I paused not for effect but because I felt a lurch of nausea as I imagined the scene in my mind. Down here, where it had actually happened, the very words had a miasmic sense of weight and solidity. It was hard to get them out of my mouth.

" '*The instrument used in the attack had a number of different surfaces and edges that moved independently of each other,*'" I quoted from recent, unpleasant memory.

Rich took a deep, shuddering breath. He ducked his head as though he was flinching away from a blow.

"It was your keys you used, wasn't it, you bastard? No wonder you did your own hand in while you were turning her face into hamburger."

To my amazement, Rich started to cry. Just a dry sob at first, and then another. Then he trembled again, and the tremble turned into the first in a series of great, racking heaves as the tears welled up in his eyes and spilled down his face.

"I didn't—want to" he quavered, shooting me a look of desperate pleading. "Oh God, please, Castor, I didn't want to! It was—it was"—his voice was lost in another wave of broken sobs. "I'm not a murderer," he managed at last. "I'm not a murderer!"

"No? Well, neither am I," I told him, my own self-disgust rising in me now like heartburn. "I'm just the bloke who comes in and clears up after the murderer. And I nearly did it, Rich. I was that close." I held up my hand, finger and thumb a fraction of an inch apart. But he was folded in on his own pain and fear, and he didn't look up. "I would have done it. I would have blasted that poor, screwed up little ghost into the void. All that stopped me was that Damjohn paid me a compliment I didn't deserve and tried to kill me because he thought I must be trying to find out the truth. The truth! All I was interested in was getting paid!"

I knelt down at the foot of the wall, deliberately avoiding the mattress. I put my hand on the back of Rich's neck and gripped hard. With skin-to-skin contact, and with his emotions as churned up as they were, he wouldn't be able to lie to me without me knowing. He tried to pull away, but his heart wasn't in it. He radiated self-pity and surrender.

"Tell me about it," I suggested, and if he read an "or else" into my tone of voice, he was exactly right.

It was a few minutes before he could formulate a sentence. Then—

with a few more pauses along the way for tears and hand-wringing—
it all came spilling out.

———————

It wasn't Rich's fault. It was Damjohn's fault. Peele's fault. The
girl's own fault, for panicking and making everything so much worse
than it should have been. But not Rich's fault. Fuck, no.

I sat and watched his matey persona dissolve under pressure into a
stinking mulch of misery and denial.

It all started with Peele—or at least, that's the best I can do by way
of summary. It wasn't as though Rich was telling this in a way that
made any real sense. But it had been Peele who'd stabbed him in the
back when he was looking for a promotion, and so it was Peele who'd
kick-started the whole sorry chain of events.

Rich had been at the Bonnington for five years by this time—"five
bloody years"—and it was no secret that he was after the senior archivist job. When Derek Watkins retired on ill-health grounds, who else
was there besides Rich who was qualified to step in? Who else knew
the whole system and had the personality to be able to handle the
reading-room side of things as well as the organizational skills needed
to keep things ticking over backstage?

But Peele had brought in an outsider. He'd poached Alice from
Keats House, Alice who was—these things need to be spelled out
clearly—younger than Rich biologically, his junior in terms of years
served, and a woman.

He was choked. Well, you would be, wouldn't you? To see your
contribution undervalued like that, the rights of your case set aside,
and not even to get an explanation, still less an apology. Rich had
gone in to see Jeffrey as soon as he'd heard and had lodged a formal
protest. He was told that the decision had been taken at JMT level.
They wanted someone with more of a managerial background. He
indicated that it might be difficult for him to work on a team under
someone who'd swiped a promotion from under his nose. Jeffrey said

that if Rich felt that strongly, his resignation would be reluctantly accepted, and his reference would be very positive.

He was fucked, in other words.

So Rich became fairly cynical and embittered about the archive job. He still needed it for the regular salary, but he decided to give it no more of his time and energies than he could possibly help. And since the only way up was dead man's shoes, he'd look for some other way to supplement his income and give him the lifestyle he felt he was owed.

"I never wanted to be a millionaire," he protested, snuffling as he massaged his eyes with the heel of his hand. "I just didn't want to be stuck in the same fucking hole for the rest of my life. You need a few luxuries, just to keep yourself sane."

He'd been frequenting one of Damjohn's brothels for as long as he'd lived in London—not Kissing the Pink, but another place out in Edmonton that made no bones about what it was and didn't bother with niceties like liquor licences or twinkly neon lights. Damjohn himself put in an appearance every Thursday night to collect the takings, and the ice had broken between them when Rich had recognized Damjohn's Serbian accent and had been able to tell him wassup, or the equivalent, in his native tongue.

Damjohn had been very interested in Rich's language skills. He invited Rich out to dinner at a fancy hotel and put the moves on him. He had, he intimated, a possible opening for a handsome young westerner with a clean British passport who could talk Russian, Czech, and Serbian at need. It would be easy work, too—occasional, well paid, and not impossible to fit in around a regular job. Rich took the bait.

It was hard to say no, he told me. Damjohn's personality was so intense and powerful, he just swept you along. Rich looked at me defiantly, as if I was about to disagree. "He's not Serbian, you know," he told me truculently. "He was part of all that Kosovo shit, but only because he was caught in the middle of it. His family were all Slovenes—and after Slovenia decided to fly solo, the Slovenes in Kosovo had almost as fuck-awful a time as the Albanians. But he was in Vlasenica when the Serbian army came through, and he was lucky enough to fall in with a colonel, Nikolic, who was trying to update the census records for the area. Nikolic didn't know his arse from his elbow, so Damjohn helped him out. Told him where people lived and if they were still around."

"People?" I echoed. "What people, Rich? Albanians? Muslims?"

Rich shrugged. "People," he repeated stubbornly. "The point is that Damjohn was a survivor. He could have been rounded up himself, but instead he made himself useful. And then he made himself indispensable. When they set up the concent—the transit camp at Susica, he was on staff. He was actually on staff. A Slovene! They used him to handle initial interviews. Triage. Only he didn't bother with interviews—he had a better way. When a new truckload came in, he'd go in and sit with them, as if he was just another sheep-shagger caught out by a Serbian patrol, and if anyone spoke to him, he'd just shrug—no speakee. Then he'd listen to them talking among themselves, and within a few minutes, he'd know exactly who was who and what was what. He had an agreed signal to give to the guards—when he was ready, he'd give them the wink, or whatever, and they'd take him out as if they were going to interrogate him. So then he could give them the lowdown on everyone else in the batch, and sometimes—depending on what he'd overheard—leads on other people who were still hiding out up in the hills. Fucking incredible. If the war had gone on for another year, he'd probably have been running the place."

Rich was looking intently at me as he said all this. He wanted me to understand why he couldn't just say no to Damjohn—wanted me to share his awe, which clearly went beyond conventional morality. I found myself thinking back to the images I'd seen when I'd touched Damjohn's hand. I knew from that brief flash that the man's skills as an informer had been learned at a much earlier age; the war in Kosovo had just been another career opportunity for him.

Rich had been horrified, of course, when he found out what the work was. He only took it on a one-off basis, at first, because his car had just died, and he didn't have any money for a deposit on a new one. And he was still fuming over the shit that had gone down at the archive, so he probably wasn't thinking too straight. He just hadn't thought enough about what he was getting into. If he had, he would never have gone on that initial run for Damjohn, and none of the rest of it would ever have—

"Just tell me what he asked you to do, for the love of Christ," I interjected harshly. "And put the bullshit in an appendix at the end."

Rich went on holiday to the Czech Republic. And while he was there, he went into a lot of city-center bars in Prague and Brno. Young people's bars. He was looking for girls, and he wasn't very good at it, at first. Oh, he could run a chat-up line as well as the next guy, and he knew how to trade on his well-heeled-westerner chic, but he didn't know how to segue from that into doing the recruitment pitch.

Come to London right now, was roughly how it went. Leave your family and your friends behind, and you can get yourself a new life like you'd never even believe. You can do a secretarial course— government-funded—and after six weeks, you'll be walking into a twenty-grand-a-year job. And you'll be living in a flat with your rent and utilities paid, because everyone in London claims state benefit even if they're working, so your only expenses will be food and clothes. Even if you only do it for a couple of years, you can come back with a stake. Stick to it for five years, you can come back rich. Or say fuck it and don't come back at all.

Rich learned quickly, though. Part of the trick was to choose the right girl in the first place. The "leave your friends and family behind" line played best with women who didn't have a big share of either, and he came to be good at spotting them. Young was good.

Stupid was good. Ambitious was best of all; a girl with a hunger for the bright lights would tell herself bigger lies than you'd have the balls to tell her yourself and then invest more effort into believing them.

The reality behind the pitch was as squalid as you'd imagine it to be. Rich would help the girls to fill in a passport application and give them their traveling money from the Czech Republic to Sweden. In Sweden, they were looked over by an associate of Damjohn's, a German named Dieter—no second name that Rich ever heard of, just Dieter. And if Dieter liked what he saw, he sent the girls on to London.

That was where they disappeared from the official statistics, though. They didn't come into the UK by plane, and they didn't come in on their own passports. If there was a trail, Sweden was where it ended. Rich himself came home alone and didn't trouble himself with the unpleasant details.

"But you knew where the girls were going?" I demanded.

Rich hesitated, then nodded his head just once. "The flats," he muttered. "I'm not saying I'm proud of myself. But all I was doing was talent-spotting. No rough stuff, Castor. I never hurt anybody!"

The flats were the bargain-basement end of Damjohn's operation. The girls there weren't whores by choice, they were co-opted. It was a matter of horses for courses, Rich explained morosely. In the West End and the City, you could charge a premium price for a premium product: beautiful girls with some personality and imagination who'd throw themselves into it—play games, dress up, talk the talk. The flats were a different approach for a different demographic: men who had very little in the way of disposable income, but who'd still pay for sex if the price point was low enough. In the clubs, the girls took 50 percent of whatever the john paid. In the flats, they worked for food. And they didn't get to choose who they went with or what was on the menu. They just did what they were told.

Needless to say, the girls that Rich was recruiting couldn't just be put to work as soon as they arrived in the UK. There was a certain amount of—not training, maybe, but conditioning—that had to be got through first. They had to be broken in, taught what was expected of them and what the rules were. Like never say no to anything. Never cry when you're with a john. Never ask for help. And they needed to know the names of things—parts of the body, for example, and certain kinds of physical acts. After a little while, Rich got involved on that end of the operation, too. It wasn't so glamorous—no exotic foreign travel, no expense account—but the perks were amazing.

His mind filled with images: flesh grinding against flesh like the cogs in a surreal and horrible machine.

"You got to screw them first," I paraphrased.

He flinched. "No!" he protested. "Well, sometimes, yeah, but—if I wanted to, I could—I was mainly just talking them through it, but yeah, there were times. Jesus, Castor, they were prostitutes. The only difference was that with me, it was on the house. And it was a lot better if they did it with me than with Scrub, say. At least I didn't hurt them."

I didn't want to argue about it. I was already deeper inside his head than I ever wanted to be. The thought of Scrub having sex with anybody was one I wished I could edit out of my brain forever. "You did hurt one of them," I reminded him, and he groaned in anguish, squeezing his eyes tight shut.

Damjohn, it turned out, was a much better seducer than Rich would ever be. He'd reeled Rich in with the usual banal, irresistible inducements of money and sex and then worked systematically to compromise him to the point where he couldn't say no to anything. Listening to Rich talk about it, I realized that there was nothing particularly personal about this; it was something Damjohn did automatically, partly because it was useful for business but mainly because it gave him pleasure. He'd even made a casual attempt to do it to me, just in passing, when he'd offered me time with the girls in lieu of cash money. And then once more, with feeling, when he'd offered me the same deal that Mephistopheles offered Faust. I wondered if it came from being an informer and agent provocateur in a former life. Maybe it helped you to feel good about yourself if you proved to your own satisfaction that every man had a price, and most had one that was lower than yours.

In Rich's case, Damjohn had seen that the man's true Achilles heel had more to do with security than with sex. Being a procurer of young girls for London brothels tickled Rich's *nostalgie de la boue*, but he never once dreamed of quitting his job at the Bonnington; he clung to the steady pay and the safe shallows of the nine-to-five. So that was the area that Damjohn worked on. Every time they talked, he brought the conversation back around to what Rich did for a living and where he did it. He mused about paying a visit to the archive himself, which Rich tried hard to discourage him from. He asked Rich how much the collection was worth, how it was stored, how it was protected.

And on one occasion, Rich had mentioned the bizarre little suite of forgotten rooms tacked on at the side. He'd discovered it himself more or less by accident, on an idle afternoon in the summer, when Peele and Alice were off on holiday together in the Norfolk Broads, and the place was pretty much ticking over by itself. Rich was bored and restless, counting the days until his next trip to Eastern Europe, and there was nothing much to do, so he wandered around the building, trying out his keys on doors he'd never seen open, and in the process, he'd noticed the missing slice out of the first floor and wondered what the hell it was. It hadn't taken him long after that to find the answer.

As soon as he told Damjohn about it, Damjohn wanted to see it. Again, Rich tried hard to talk him out of the idea, but there was never any way of saying no to the man and making it stick. He kept on at Rich until Rich finally brought him and Scrub over late one night and opened the door for them. They'd paced the place out, talking in murmurs between themselves whenever Rich was more than a few feet away from them. Then they'd sent him into the archive proper and shouted through the wall to him to test the acoustics. He'd barely heard a thing, even when Scrub was bellowing like a bull. Double-skin brickwork, combined with the state-of-the-art insulation that the strong rooms had to have: BS 5454 rearing its ugly head again.

Damjohn told Rich that he had plans for the secret rooms. He was always in need of places where some of his girls could be lodged for a few days or weeks when they first arrived in London, before they were moved out to his various premises elsewhere around the country. Damjohn owned some London properties himself, obviously—a lot of them—but he preferred to keep Chinese walls up between the legal and illegal aspects of his business life. The rooms at the Bonnington would make a great place for "breaking in" new girls for the flats.

Rich didn't think so, and he pleaded with Damjohn to change his mind. He didn't much mind about the girls, but Jesus, the risk to him—if it was found out, he'd lose his job. He'd probably go to jail. "And where do you imagine you'd go if it came out that you'd been involved in people trafficking, Mr. Clitheroe?" Damjohn had asked him mildly. "Sex slavery? Grooming of underage girls for prostitution?" Rich had almost broken down at that point. He hadn't even known that one of the girls he'd helped to reel in was under age. She'd lied to him and used a fake ID to get her passport. Now he saw the legal parameters of what he'd done and realized how bad it might look to an unsympathetic eye. He begged Damjohn to let him off the hook—to drop him from the books. He wanted to go back to what he knew and forget this other world, with its hidden depths and reefs.

He could have saved his breath. Damjohn had made up his mind, and it came to pass exactly as he'd said. It's a nasty feeling to discover that you're in over your head when you thought you were only paddling. Rich had cried himself to sleep that night. My heart pumped lumpy custard for him.

He'd made stipulations, of course—insisted that the rooms were only to be visited at night, and that only one girl at a time could stay there. And when Scrub and a couple of silent men with toolboxes had come in one night to refit the place, Rich had asserted the right to be there and look over their shoulders, bugging them with suggestions while they worked. The restraint ring cemented to the floor was his idea; all the soundproofing in the world wouldn't do a damn bit of good if one of the girls got into the upstairs room and started banging on the street door.

The room went into regular use a month or two after that. Rich was only told afterward, when the first girl—a Croatian recruited by one of Damjohn's other talent scouts—had already been installed. He'd suffered terribly at first just from knowing she was there. The fear had lessened a little with time, but he still found himself finding excuses to wander close to the inner wall that corresponded to the basement room on the Bonnington side (that was the blind corridor where I'd found such a thick, fetid concentration of unhappiness) and straining his ears to check that the soundproofing was working okay. He slept fitfully, woken often by gut-wrenching dreams of being arrested and thrown into a police cell that somehow became the basement room, with its bare mattress.

But the girl had only stayed for two weeks before being moved on to one of the flats. Damjohn had continued to send Rich off on new Eastern European jaunts. A second and then a third girl had been rotated through the secret rooms, and the sheer relentlessness of the routine took the edge off his unease, gradually acclimated him to the new setup.

It was the fourth time that brought the problems. It was the fourth time that had made everything unravel. If three times is a charm, four is a curse. Rich fell silent again, his mind pulling almost tangibly against the undertow of memory. His breathing became fast and shallow, and he started to shake worse than ever.

"What was her name?" I asked him softly. He didn't answer, but at that moment I felt her arrival at the edges of my perception. Not in the room, not yet. But close, and getting closer. "What was her name, Rich?"

"There were two of them," he mumbled, shrinking in on himself. "Sisters. Snezhna and Rosa. Two at once! I couldn't believe my fucking luck. Oh God, I wish I'd never seen them! I wish to Christ—"

He'd been working for Damjohn for almost two years by this time. He was an old hand and such an integral part of the operation that he had his own bank accounts to draw on—one at a Czech bank, another at a Russian one. He'd honed his skills in Moscow, Vilnius, and St. Petersburg, and he'd learned by experience that country mice were easier to catch than town mice. So this time he'd gone farther afield than ever, to Vladivostok, home of the Siberian fleet and of the Far Eastern National University. He'd read about how the economy there was imploding, and he was expecting to find and tap rich seams of desperation.

But Vladivostok was scary. As soon as he stepped off the tourist routes, he was surrounded by gangsters and pimps a hell of a lot harder and more serious about their work than he was. It felt like a place where he might accidentally and insensibly toggle from predator to prey.

Rich debated with himself. He felt vulnerable and exposed, but he didn't want to go back empty-handed—Damjohn didn't like paying for trips that brought him no tangible returns. In the end, Rich took a bus ride into the much smaller town of Oktyabrskiy, and that was a different animal altogether. Here was the Siberia he'd been expecting—the shops all boarded up, the damp misery of the people who hadn't been able to buy or fight or work their way out. True, a tourist blended in here about as well as a candy-striped hippopotamus, but most of the people he was looking at now were whipped dogs rather than sharks. This was a place where he felt it was safe for him to operate.

Oktyabrskiy was where he'd met Snezhna—not in a club or a bar but behind the counter in an all-night grocery shop. She was very pretty and had a sort of naive grace to her. Definitely the sort of girl who'd bring in the passing trade in one of Damjohn's flats.

But at the same time, Rich had an uneasy suspicion that she wasn't the sort of woman who was likely to fall for his usual spiel. She answered his casual questions with deadpan solemnity, failed to laugh at a single one of his little jokes, and wrapped parcels of groceries with a stolid precision that suggested she wasn't in the habit of fantasizing about the possibility of doing anything else. Rich started in on the hard sell anyway, because another lesson he'd learned by this time was that you take your opportunities where you find them. Someone like Snezhna was wasted in Siberia, he told her. In the West, she could live a life of luxury, have anything she wanted, never have to worry about money again.

Surprisingly, she fell for it so enthusiastically that he didn't even have to try all that hard. She asked him all kinds of questions about the work, the place, the logistics of getting there. She didn't have a passport, but if she could get one for herself, would Rich be able to give her any advice on the best way to travel to England? She'd perhaps come out just to see, at first, and then make her mind up once she was there.

Instead of having to hook Snezhna and play her, Rich found himself swept along by her momentum and having to slow her down. He couldn't ship her out to Stockholm until he'd e-mailed Dieter to tell him she was coming, and sorting out the passport would take a few days at least, even working through channels already lubricated by regular bribes. First things first—he told her to come to the passport office the next morning to get things moving. Then she'd have all the time in the world to wrap up her affairs while the bureaucrats did their stately waltz.

And then Snezhna had turned up at the passport office with Rosa in tow. Seeing the two of them together—seeing how Snezhna's arm had stayed protectively around her younger sister's shoulders the whole time, and how she'd glared at any man who even cast a glance in Rosa's direction—Rich had understood. Snezhna might lack ambition and imagination on her own behalf, but for Rosa, she wanted the world.

And he could understand the protectiveness, too. Where Snezhna was fetching, Rosa was beautiful—or at least, she pushed all of Rich's buttons. He got briefly lyrical as he described her, not knowing that I'd already met her at the strip club. Rosa was gorgeous, he said: improbably huge brown eyes, chestnut hair falling halfway down her back, and understated curves that seemed to have a kind of Platonic perfection about them. As Rich put it, she was the kind of girl who'd still look like a virgin even while you were screwing her—an absolute must-have, in every sleazy double sense.

So he carried on promising Snezhna the moon on a silver platter as he booked tickets to Stockholm for the pair of them and dropped Dieter a line with the terse message that this was a two-for-one deal. He saw Snezhna three more times, with no greater intimacy passing between them than a kiss on the cheek. The girl genuinely thought that everything Rich had done was out of disinterested friendship. She wasn't even cynical enough to conclude that he was trying to buy his way into her pants, let alone to guess at the truth.

So Rich went back to London feeling slightly frustrated and horny but with the satisfaction of a job well done—and with the happy prospect of having a little more spending money than usual that month. He went back to work in good spirits.

They evaporated a little a week later, when Damjohn told him in passing that there was a new girl coming to stay in the secret rooms. A new girl? Rich asked, getting interested. Maybe he could work off some of the sexual tension he'd been feeling ever since he met Rosa.

But the girl now locked in the basement under the Bonnington's strong rooms was Snezhna.

Rich experienced hugely mixed feelings about that. On the one hand, just thinking about Snezhna made him think about her sister, too, and brought back with those memories a powerful feeling composed of two parts nostalgia to three parts lust. On the other hand, Snezhna must know by now that he had set her up for this—sold her and her sister into prostitution—and he didn't relish meeting her again. Okay, the whole point of the "breaking in" was to take the fight out of the new girls, to make them docile and pliable. But the thought of looking Snezhna in the eye made him flinch.

So he begged off. He told Damjohn he'd prefer not to take part in the breaking-in. Damjohn asked him why, and he made up a story about a discharge from his penis that he was having looked at. Obviously Damjohn wouldn't want the goods soiled at this early stage, so he curtly accepted Rich's apologies and made other arrangements.

What about Rosa? Rich asked as casually as he could. "Nothing about Rosa," Damjohn said. "At least as far as you're concerned." She was too good for the flats. After she'd had a few weeks to get used to the idea, he was going to try her out at Kissing the Pink. Possibly he'd take a personal interest in her training.

Rich dropped the subject and went back to work. But his libido wouldn't let him rest. He kept thinking about Rosa and wishing he could see her again, perhaps even be the one who taught her her new trade. No use. Damjohn would laugh in his face if he asked, then use the information that he was besotted with the girl against him somehow. That was just how he was. And Rich had too strong a sense of self-preservation to fuck up this nice little earner for the sake of a sexual infatuation.

But with Rosa out of his reach, Snezhna began to seem like a more and more attractive prospect. He toyed with the idea of paying her a visit down in the basement. Day after day he played out the fantasy, until finally he found himself actually doing it. He stayed behind on a Friday night until everyone else had gone, said good-bye to Frank, and then walked around the block a few times until the light in the reception area had gone out, too. Then he let himself into the secret rooms and went down into the basement.

Snezhna was asleep. The breaking-in process was physically and psychologically shattering for most of the girls; they slept for a lot of the time when they weren't being abused or lectured or threatened. Rich climbed in beside her, he told me—on top of her, his memories insisted—and put his lips on hers.

She woke up in a panic, too cowed to fight but terrified of the whole agonizing process starting up again. She tensed to endure the new ordeal, and then she saw who it was on the mattress with her.

Instantly her whole manner changed. She went straight from rigid passivity to spitting, cursing frenzy, screaming obscenities as she clawed at him. She went for his eyes and came within a half inch or so of having them, but he was able to grab her arms and use his weight to keep her pinned. Still she yelled and spat into his face: Bastard! Judas! Monster! Liar! Devil!

Rich got angry in return. All he wanted was sex; it couldn't be any big deal after what Snezhna had already gone through. He pressed the point, and she fought with everything she had to keep him out. The details became hazy, both in what he was telling me and in what he was remembering. There was pain. His hand was rising and falling, the keys clutched in his fist like a flail, and his wrist jarred with agony every time his arm came down. There was sex, too, and a thrusting, shuddering climax like an epileptic fit, but it was all mixed together in his mind, and there was no clear sense of sequence. He didn't know—didn't want to know; wouldn't let himself know—whether the woman was alive or dead when he finally succeeded in raping her. But if she was still alive then, she died soon after.

When he realized what he'd done, Rich felt a choking panic that was almost as strong in memory as it must have been at the time. He sat in the room next to Snezhna's corpse for a long time, unable to form a single coherent idea. He remembered talking to himself and to her. He remembered laughing like a maniac and whimpering like a beaten dog. He kept thinking of what Damjohn would do when he found out. He wondered what sort of death—besides painful—he'd end up being allocated. Then he'd tell himself that it was just a whore—he could make the next run to Eastern Europe for free, find a replacement, and the balance would be right again. Damjohn wouldn't care; Damjohn would let him off the hook. But after a moment or two, sick terror would set in again, and he'd be back where he started.

Finally, maybe an hour or two hours later, Rich began to pull himself together and think beyond the miasmic terror of the present moment. He had to tell Damjohn. It couldn't be hidden, and there was nowhere he could run where he wouldn't be found. Trying not to look at the ruined thing on the bed, he cleaned himself up as best he could with the blanket and then limped up the stairs, so oppressed by fear still that he thought he might faint and go tumbling all the way down again.

He called Damjohn at the strip club—the ICOE number. Well, if anything qualified as an emergency, this did. He made a halting, stumbling confession, which was met neither by fury nor by indulgence but by a cold, clinical pragmatism. Damjohn wanted the details. Where was the body now? What state was it in? How had the girl actually died? Had Rich remembered to lock the door behind him when he left? Had he ejaculated inside her? Had he used a condom? Had he brought his keys out of the room or left them with the body?

The catechism had a sobering effect. Rich was able to get a handle on what he'd done by describing it in such objective terms. By the time he'd finished talking, he was calm. Damjohn told him to go home and clean himself up—seriously clean himself up, with special attention to fingernails and what was under them. He should also soak his keys in bleach overnight, then boil them in a saucepan. His clothes had to be burned, but not in the backyard with the neighbors watching. The best option, Damjohn said, was to take them out to some waste ground in the middle of the night, soak them in kerosene, drop a match on them, and stay long enough to make sure that they were entirely reduced to ash.

Rich did as he was told. Having a program to work to helped, and so did the feeling that someone else was making the decisions now. When he'd raped and murdered Snezhna, it had felt as though he'd jumped the tracks of his life and was hurtling through empty space. Now he felt like he'd landed on the far side of a ravine, and things might be starting to make sense again.

All the same, the weekend was nastily surreal. He wandered around his flat, afraid to go out, afraid to be seen by anybody, afraid even to use the phone. His hand, which he'd gashed with one of the keys when he was hitting Snezhna, throbbed hypnotically and swelled up to agonizing tautness. He soaked it in antiseptic and popped cocodamol like Smarties.

There's a T. S. Eliot poem about a guy who murders a girl, keeps her in his bathroom in a bathful of Lysol, and ends up getting confused about whether it's him or the girl who's actually dead. That was sort of the way it was for Rich, or so he said—and the anguish that squirmed in his mind as he said it gave some weight to the words.

Scrub dropped in on the Saturday afternoon to deliver a message from Damjohn: it was all sorted. Rich was by no means to go to the secret rooms. They were out of bounds for him now. But the body was taken care of, so nobody would ever connect it to him. And now he owed Mr. Damjohn a big, big favor, which he could bet his bottom dollar would someday be called in. In the meantime, he should go to work on Monday as if nothing had happened. Mr. Damjohn would take a grim view of it if Rich drew attention to himself by pulling a sickie, bursting into tears in public, failing in his professional duties, or whatever.

It was ironic, Rich said with a sobbing laugh. He was suddenly like one of the girls in the flats: told what to do and what to say and how to behave; having to choke down his own emotions and put on a performance that he thought might actually tear him apart.

But he forced himself to do it—to shower, shave, get dressed, go to work. He felt as though he was walking through some kind of fucked-up hallucination based on his own previous life, but nobody looked at him twice or seemed to sense anything odd about him. He went down to the reading room at lunchtime and went through the papers from cover to cover—nothing about a female body with a ruined face being found in Somers Town or anywhere else in London.

As always, normality began to work its healing spell on Rich. He got through the day with no slipups, no sign that he was anything other than himself. He even managed to enact a fake "accident" with a drawer that would explain his injured hand and allow him to keep it bandaged until it healed. He was keeping it together: riding out the waves of insane discontinuity that the murder had set off in his life.

At five-thirty (half an hour's overtime—safely within the usual parameters), he went home, ate, watched TV, and drank a beer. Okay, he flaked out at about ten, exhausted by the emotional intensity of the eventless day, but still, he'd made it. If he could do it once, he could do it as many times as he had to.

Then, on the Tuesday, his world fell apart again. One of the part-timers came up screaming from one of the basement strong rooms. She'd seen a ghost: a woman without a face. When Rich heard those words, he fled to the gents' toilet and threw his guts up. It was half an hour before he dared to venture out again, and he spent the rest of that day staying at the edges of all the eager discussions about the ghost, all the lurid speculation. He knew he wouldn't be able to keep the mask up if he had to talk about it. He had to pretend to keep an austere distance from such a childish subject.

On the Wednesday, he did call in sick. He just couldn't face the thought of meeting Snezhna in the stacks: coming face to face, or rather face to not-a-face-anymore, with her in some dark, narrow space where no one could hear him scream. He told Alice that he had gastric flu. Then he drew the curtains and hid.

Somehow, Damjohn found out. Rich got another visit from Scrub, and it was a lot more painful than the first one. Scrub wanted Rich to understand that Mr. Damjohn expected high standards of professionalism from his employees, particularly in the area of doing what they were fucking told. He made the point imaginatively, using everyday objects from Rich's kitchen to illustrate what would happen if Rich let Mr. Damjohn down in this respect. He also reminded Rich that if he didn't pull himself together, he'd end up facing a murder charge. He had—in Scrub's vivid phraseology—a big bastard sod of a lot to lose.

Rich did his best, with mixed results. He was able to go back into the Bonnington the next day and get back to work—where everyone was very solicitous about him, because it was obvious that he was still a bit shaky after his illness. And he was able to put a brave face on it through the days that followed, even though he felt like a condemned man whose execution was going to be sprung on him as an impromptu party rather than being set for a fixed time and place.

When the worst happened and he finally met the ghost, not in a strong room but in the middle of a corridor, he pissed himself—literally, physically, with a great access of terror so pure that it made him forget who and where he was. When he could think again, he was sprawled on the floor behind a desk in an empty storeroom, his drenched trousers cold and clinging, his hands shaking so hard he couldn't even pull himself upright.

As soon as he could walk, he got up and headed straight out of the building. He knew that if he met anyone and had to talk to them, he'd break into pieces.

In the evening, Rich went to see Damjohn at Kissing the Pink. To his horror, Damjohn found the whole situation vastly amusing. Oh, it had its serious side, of course: a woman in whom he'd already invested a certain amount of money and time was now dead, and he'd had to go to some degree of inconvenience in the resulting cleanup. But he was, he told Rich, a man who'd always believed that the punishment should fit the crime—and in this case, the fit was exquisite.

In short, he told Rich to live with it, and in passing he renewed the threats that Scrub had already made. If Rich found that he *couldn't* live with it, there was another option that would serve just as well from Damjohn's point of view.

"The man's a sadist," Rich moaned. "A fucking sadist. He liked it that I was scared. He was getting off on it."

I didn't comment. The sense of the ghost's presence was palpable now, so intense that it was like a thickening of the air. Snezhna was here; she was listening. She was hanging around Rich like a shroud, and although she still hadn't shown herself in visible form, I was amazed that he couldn't sense her. The room was full of her.

"Where did Gabe McClennan come in?" I asked, and Rich bared his teeth in a panting snarl.

"McClennan! That bastard! That was just part of the joke, wasn't it? I went back, and I kept my nose clean. I did everything Damjohn had fucking well told me to do. And I made it all the way through September. But can you imagine what it was like, Castor? I mean, Jesus Christ! Every time I turned around, she was there. I kept on seeing her. Everyone kept on seeing her. And whenever she showed up, she was saying the same thing: asking where Rosa was. *Gdyeh Rosa? Ya potrevozhnao Rosa.* Again and again and again, never fucking letting up.

"I told Damjohn he couldn't let it carry on. She might name me.

She might name him. He'd sorted out the body, but now he had to sort out—the rest. What was still left of her.

"And he agreed. And he brought McClennan in." Rich twisted his head around to look up at me, his haggard face contorted into a look of half-insane appeal. "But McClennan didn't exorcise her—he only put that ward on her, so she couldn't talk. Damjohn was just protecting his own arse. He still wanted me to go on suffering!"

Rich lapsed into silence, twitching slightly from time to time, his head once more clasped in his hands. I thought through everything I already knew in the light of what he'd just told me. It seemed to fit. And the emotional commentary track that I'd accessed by gripping the back of Rich's neck had agreed with the words on every major point. He was telling the truth, as far as he knew it and believed it.

"What about the documents?" I asked. "The Russian collection? Where did it really come from?"

He rubbed snot and tears away from his face with a hand that still shook.

"One of the girls—not Snezhna, one of the earlier ones—had that stuff in her flat. Family heirloom sort of thing. I saw it, and I thought—yeah, that lot's worth something. I could sell it to the archive. So I said I'd bring it over for her and get it valued. I used one of Damjohn's flats—a vacant one—as a postal address, and I set the whole thing up. I said I was liaising with this old man, but it was just me."

That was something else I should have worked out sooner. Scrub and McClennan hadn't turned up in Bishopsgate by accident. Rich had probably phoned Damjohn as soon as he'd hung up from talking to me.

"And Rosa?" I asked him. "Did you ever see her again?"

Rich shook his head miserably without looking up. "Damjohn wouldn't let me. He told me not to go back into the club or any of his other places. And he's only used me on the talent run once since then. He says I'm on probation. He says I've got to wait, and he'll call me when he needs me."

Bizarrely, after all I'd heard, it was then that my stomach chose to turn over. It's not likely that I'd have felt much pity for Rich in any case, given what he'd done. But the fact that he'd been able to go back to his old routine of picking up girls put him outside the human race, as far as my categories went—into some other conceptual space that he shared with the likes of Asmodeus.

But I still needed him for one thing more.

"Listen to me, Rich," I told him. "Rosa's gone missing. Damjohn's got her hidden somewhere, in case she talks to me and helps me to put two and two together. She knows that her sister's dead. Maybe he told her, or maybe she found out in some other way—but she must know, because she attacked me with a knife, thinking that I'd exorcised Snezhna's ghost. So she's in the same boat as you—she knows enough to bring the police down on Damjohn. He'll probably kill both of you once the dust has settled on all of this—and the only reason you're running around free right now is because you disappearing would be too damn suspicious.

"So your only chance of coming out of this alive is to cooperate with me. Do you understand?"

He looked up slowly and nodded. "And you'll keep it quiet?" he asked, his tone approaching a whine. "You won't tell anybody about—"

I exploded with all the pent-up emotion of the past half hour. "Jesus, of course I won't keep it quiet!" I shouted. "What, are you sick in the fucking head or something?" He flinched at the caustic contempt in my voice, shrank back against the wall. I brandished his keys in his face. "The only choice I'm giving you is between serving time for murder and hitting the wall right now. And make it fast, Rich. I've got other places to be."

But Rich was shaking his head. I'd pushed him too far, and he was finally pushing back. "No," he said. "No. I can't do it. I can't go to prison."

"I think you'll like it better than the other option," I assured him grimly.

"I can't!" he moaned, groveling on his hands and knees with his head bent under him, "I can't!"

I stood back, realizing that I wouldn't get any more sense out of him until he'd got over this whelming flood of panic. I was itching to get moving, only too aware of how much might hinge on me getting to Rosa before Damjohn's nerve failed. But I had to contain myself. There was no way of applying any more pressure to Rich without him breaking altogether.

No way for me, anyway. At that moment, the darkness in the corners of the room began to stretch and flow. Rich hadn't noticed, because he was incapable of noticing anything, but whatever was happening, he was the focus of it. The shadows ran toward him, circled him like water circles a drain, darkening and deepening. It didn't look like her, but I'd been waiting for her to make her move for ten minutes or more, so I knew it when it came.

I suppose it shouldn't have surprised me. Okay, she'd been fighting against the pull of this room ever since she'd died, but Rich's churning emotion was a beacon burning through the darkness and confusion of death. She had to come.

Only she didn't come as herself. No woman stood over Rich as he rocked and moaned. It was just the darkness, curdling and thickening.

When he did finally realize that something was wrong, he looked up at me, startled, as if it was some trick that I was trying to pull on him. Then he raised his hands and tried to swat the shadows away. That was as futile as it sounds. He gave a little shriek and rolled away toward the wall. The darkness followed him, zeroed on his face, sank into and through him.

"Castor!" Rich screamed. "Get it—get it off—don't—"

I didn't make a move. There probably wouldn't have been much I could have done in any case. Not now. The shadows sank into and through Rich's skin, drawn in by some psychic osmosis. His scream became muffled, liquid, inhuman. His hands flailed, groping blindly at his own face.

Except that he didn't actually have a face—not much of one, anyway. From forehead to upper lip was just a red, rippling curtain of flesh. Chestnut-brown hair hung in lank ringlets over it, and the mouth that gaped formlessly underneath was rimmed by blood-red lips.

The illusion—if that's what it was—held for the space of a long-drawn-out breath. Then it was gone, as if someone had thrown a switch, and it was just Rich there again, screaming and babbling, his fingers gripping his face as if he was trying to tear it off his skull. I waded in and stopped him from blinding himself in his panic.

"I'll help," he promised, raising his hand as if to ward off a blow. "Please! I'll help, Castor. I'll cooperate! You can tell her I cooperated. Don't let her touch me! Please!"

"That's great, Rich," I said. "But I'm going to need you to get your breath back first."

That took a while. When his breathing was close enough to normal that I thought he might be able to talk, I took out my mobile phone and threw it into his lap.

"Make a call," I told him. "There's another emergency."

Twenty-one

RICH TURNED THE PHONE ON, WAITED FOR IT TO LIGHT up and find a network. Nothing happened. He stared at it nonplussed, robbed of all initiative by the psychic gut-punch he'd just taken. He looked at me with a mute appeal.

"Oh, for fuck's sake," I snapped. "Hand it over."

It was the usual problem: no charge. With an inward curse, I flicked through some unworkable alternatives and then had a sudden inspiration. In my inside breast pocket, I found the mobile phone I'd taken from Arnold after I'd coldcocked him in the toilet at the Runagate in Chelsea. I gave that to Rich instead.

He dialed clumsily, taking three goes before he managed to get the number right. Then we both waited, eavesdropping on some etheric limbo while the call wound its way through cyberspace. I was listening in, my head right up close to his. I didn't trust Rich to fly straight on this unless he had a copilot. In my mind's eye I saw the phone ringing in the foyer of Kissing the Pink, Weasel-Face Arnold picking up.

"Yeah?"

"It's Rich Clitheroe," Rich said. "I've got to speak to Mr. Damjohn." There was a pregnant pause, and then he added, "It's about Castor."

"Hold on," the voice muttered.

They kept him hanging. Damjohn wouldn't make himself imme-diately available to anyone, let alone to someone as lowly as Rich. As the pause lengthened, though, I wondered if they were having trouble reaching Damjohn. Maybe he was somewhere else altogether.

After about a minute, Arnold came back on. "He's on the boat," he said, sounding slightly disgruntled—as if, maybe, he'd been torn off a strip for disturbing his boss's repose. "He said you should call him there." He rattled off the number, and Rich made a pretence of writing it down while we both did our best to commit it to memory. Rich made the follow-on call, his shaking hands causing a number of false starts. We got the ring tone, and it went on for what seemed like forever. Then, finally, someone picked up.

"Hello?" Damjohn's voice. "Clitheroe?"

"Mr. Damjohn, I've got to talk to you. I don't know what to do. I don't know what to do here." I had to admit, Rich sounded suitably scared and agitated, but I guess that was mostly because he was. You couldn't fake that degree of abject terror.

"Calm down, Clitheroe," Damjohn said, his tone clipped. "You shouldn't even be trying to contact me, but since you have, tell me what the problem is. And please—no hysteria."

Rich flicked a frightened glance at me, looked away again quickly.

"It's Castor," he said. "He just came to my house."

There was silence on the other end of the line. Then Damjohn's voice said, "Why? What does he know?"

I shook my head silently at Rich. We'd already rehearsed this whole conversation, but I wanted to make sure he didn't ad-lib. I didn't want Damjohn panicked enough to do anything to Rosa.

"Nothing," Rich said. "He doesn't know anything. But he's—he's asking a lot of questions."

"And who is he talking to? Just you, or everybody?"

"I don't know." Rich put a convincing edge of anguish in his voice. "Look, I don't think I can take any more of this. I'm facing a murder charge already—a fucking murder charge. Mr. Damjohn, where's Rosa? She knows about me, doesn't she? Where is she now? If she goes to the police, I'm fucked. Unless I go there first and get my story in. I can tell them it was an accident, because it was."

I heard Damjohn's breath hissing between his teeth.

"Killing someone while you're trying to rape them doesn't count as an accident, Clitheroe," he said with icy calm. "Even on a manslaughter plea, you'd draw down twenty years and end up serving at least ten of them. That's what you're facing if you can't keep your nerve. Rosa isn't talking to anyone, and neither are you."

I made a winding-up motion with my index finger—get to the point—and Rich nodded, showing me he understood.

"Where is she?" he repeated.

"What?" Damjohn's tone was pained.

"Where's Rosa? I want to talk to her."

"I've already told you that that's impossible."

Rich's voice rose an octave or so. "That was before Peele called in his own fucking exorcist, man. I'm sweating this. I'm sweating it. Okay, maybe I don't need to talk to her. But I want to make fucking sure nobody else can. You've got her out of the way, right? I mean, she's not still turning tricks? Castor could just walk right in there and—"

"She's here with me," Damjohn snapped. "At the boat. I'm looking at her right now. And she'll stay here until Castor is dealt with. How long ago did he leave you?"

"I don't know. Maybe ten minutes. Maybe a bit longer."

"Did he say where he was going?"

"Yeah."

"Good. Where?"

Rich blinked twice, on the spot, realizing that he'd painted himself into a corner. I made the "it's a book" sign from charades. "To the—back to the archive," Rich stammered. "I think. I think that's what he said."

Another pause. "It's Sunday," Damjohn pointed out, his tone gentle but precise. "Isn't the archive closed now?"

"No, there's a function on there today. A wedding."

"At midnight?"

"He—he's got my keys."

A longer pause. "You let him take your keys?"

"It's all right," Rich blurted. "I already took the keys to the safe room off the ring. He's only got the archive keys."

"Well, then that isn't a problem for us. I'll arrange for someone to meet him there. Clitheroe, listen to me. Stay where you are. Scrub will come and collect you and bring you out here to the boat. Until we've sorted the Castor situation out, which will be soon, this is the safest place for you."

Rich looked both wistful and tragic. "I can't do that right now," he mumbled, his eyes filling with tears.

"You can, and you will. Stay there, and Scrub will come."

We played charades again. I pointed to him and then waved the matchbook from Kissing the Pink, which had been in my pocket all this while. Rich nodded to show that he understood. "I'll meet you at the club," he said.

"What?" Damjohn didn't sound happy at all at this show of defiance.

"I'll meet you at the club. It's more central. I'm—I want to be where there are lots of people, okay?"

"You don't trust me, Clitheroe?" You could have used the edge in Damjohn's voice to shave, if you were into cutthroat razors.

"I just want it to be somewhere public. I told you, I'm scared. I don't want to go all that way out there, in the dark, and—"

"The club, then. You're closer, so you'll get there first. Wait for me." And Damjohn hung up. Rich turned to me for further instructions.

"What's the boat?" I demanded.

"It's a yacht. He's got a yacht."

"Where does he keep it?"

Rich gave me a look in which a pathetic spark of defiance flared and died. "You think he ever invited me?"

No, that would have been too easy, wouldn't it? But one idea came to me, even as I was cursing. I turned to Rich again, fizzing and crackling with impatience.

"When he was wining and dining you," I snapped, "where did he take you?"

"What?"

"The snazzy hotel. Where was it?"

"Oh." He frowned for a second, then fished it up from somewhere in his memory. "The Conrad, out in Chelsea."

Bingo.

But it was still only a best guess. And since I was working against the clock, I had to get moving. I pointed to the phone, and Rich held it out to me, which meant that when I swung with the handcuff, he couldn't get his arm down to block in time. I caught him full in the stomach, putting all my weight into it. He hit the wall and slithered down it, his eyes wide and his mouth gaping. While he was still dazed, I got his hands behind his back and tied a double reef knot around them with the rope that was lying so conveniently to hand.

"Wh—what was that for?" he gurgled when he could swallow enough breath to speak. "Castor, what are you doing? I said everything you told me to!"

"I know," I agreed, passing another loop of rope over his head and starting on another knot. He kicked a little, but I had the leverage, and he was still weak from the sucker punch. "But I've got some errands to run now, and the last thing I want is for you and Damjohn to get together and patch up your differences." I passed the free end of the rope through the steel ring in its concrete mooring and made it fast. Rich was on his stomach and didn't see me, but he guessed a second or two too late what I was going to do and rolled over frantically, struggling to get to his feet. No use. There was only about eighteen inches of play on the rope. He could get into a kneeling position, but that was all.

"Castor, no!" he screamed, the expression in his eyes coming close to madness now. "Don't leave me here! Don't leave me here with her!"

Retrieving the phone from the floor, I stood up. I stared down at him without pity, without any feeling at all except premature relief that I was going to be able to get out of his company soon.

"You'll be fine, Rich," I assured him insincerely. "She doesn't even like this room. She remembers what you did to her here. She's spent every night since she died fighting against the pull of this place, trying not to be brought back here, but not able to get away from it. You see, she's got unfinished business. And tonight, I'm going to be doing my bit to finish it. In the meantime, the best advice I can give you is to try to stay calm. Heightened emotion is what's most likely to bring her."

Rich was still screaming at me as I went up the stairs, locked the door at the top, and crossed the upper room. I paused at the door and listened. I could just about make out his voice, but only because I knew it was there. The soundproofing really was excellent.

The outer door slammed behind me with the finality of a coffin lid.

Considering it used to be a coal wharf for London's various railway lines, Chelsea Harbour has done pretty well for itself. Location, location, location, as they say; it didn't hurt that it was a coal wharf stuck in the middle of some of the most upwardly mobile real estate in the whole of London. In the late 1980s, some smart developers moved in and built a marina, and then the Conrad Hotel went up a couple of years after that. It's not Henley, but you could think of it as a sort of miniature, portable Henley that's more convenient for Harrods and Harvey Nicks.

I approached it cautiously, because I'm not the sort of element that the Conrad and the Design Centre and the Belle Époque are strenuously trying to bring in. The taxi dumped me at the top of Lots Road, at the entrance to a maze of gated communities from where it was easier and quicker to walk.

Five past midnight. It had taken me just over an hour to get here from the Bonnington, with one stop along the way to pick up some bolt cutters and a crowbar from Pen's garage. I was only going to get one crack at this, and time was going to be tight, so I needed to make sure I was ready for anything. As it was, sixty minutes gone meant that Damjohn was probably already looking at his watch and wondering where Rich had been held up. I probably didn't have much of a window before he realized that Rich wasn't coming and started to wonder where he'd gone instead. That might lead to a general desire to tie up loose ends before they unraveled for good and all. I quickened my pace as I walked past the antiques shops, furniture importers, and bijoux residences.

Circling the great, elegant spike of the Conrad itself, I came to the marina's entrance. There was a security hut, but the florid, uniformed guard inside was talking on the phone and didn't particularly register me as I walked on in. I was guessing that this was where Damjohn's yacht was berthed, because it was barely ten minutes' walk from the pub where Scrub, Arnold, and McClennan had met up the day before. And then when Rich had confirmed that Damjohn had brought him here to eat, it gave me just enough confidence to bet Rosa's life on it. In any case, looking at the whole thing another way, if the boat wasn't here, then it wasn't anywhere where I could find it, and I was stuffed before I started.

Most of the berths fronted onto the main marina, which was where I soon found myself. It's a broad basin shaped like three-quarters of a circle, with a gap of about ten yards between the outreaching arms, beyond which lay the Thames. I looked around for somewhere to start, hoping vaguely that there might be a list of vessels that I could read through, looking for inspiration. But there was nothing like that.

I walked on along the planking—which was probably sun-bleached in Ostia before being shipped here in individual packages and reassembled—looking at the name of each boat in turn. All I had to go on was what Scrub had said to Rosa in Jasmine's hazy recollection: "It's the nice lady for you." None of the ships had a female name except for the *Boadicea*. That would be a bit of a stretch, I thought.

On the far side of the marina, past the harbor entrance, the berths continued around the outer face of the harbor wall. I took that direction now, still glancing at each boat as I went by. There were a few empty berths here. Presumably, the farther you got from Lots Road and its swinging night life, the less desirable the space was. Another woman's name: the *Baroness Thatcher*. No. Surely an even less likely candidate for the title of "nice lady" than *Boadicea*.

Finally I was left with only one boat to check on this side of the marina, and it was a long way out from the others. If I got no joy here, I'd have to retrace my steps and try the other arm. But from twenty feet away, when I was able to read the name painted on its side, I knew this was the one. It was called the *Mercedes*. Not only was that the Spanish word for "kindhearted," it was also the name of the woman I'd seen in Damjohn's mind when I'd shaken hands with him the first time we'd met—the woman of whom he had such bloody and such happy memories.

I approached more stealthily now, although there were no windows lit on the yacht, and it seemed deserted. From ten feet away, I got all the corroborative evidence I needed when I saw Scrub standing up on the top deck. He was leaning on the rail at the stern end, staring out across the river toward Battersea. He was facing away from me, but there was no way of mistaking Scrub for anybody else, particularly since he was lit up romantically by the yellow radiance of a Victorian streetlamp, complete with scrollwork and nonfunctional gas mantle. I already knew Scrub was strong and mean. I wouldn't have expected running water to deter him, although it ought to make him itchy and irritable. But there was no sign of that in his absolute immobility, his air of dense, unfathomable calm.

I looked ahead down the walkway past the *Mercedes*: nothing to see there. The planking just ended about twenty feet farther on, where presumably there was a last, unoccupied berth. As setups went, it wasn't perfect, because it was remote, and that dead end might turn out to be a problem for me if things went wrong. But you do your best with what you've got.

I retreated off the walkway into the shadow of the last boat I'd passed—the *Baroness Thatcher*. I wondered inconsequentially which Tory grandee owned it and what perverse fantasy had made him name his toy boat after the Iron Lady. On the other hand, maybe it was a former wet who got a nostalgic kick every time he leaned hard on the tiller and proved that she was for turning after all.

I took off my shoes and dumped most of my tools—the lock picks and the bolt cutters; the crowbar I kept hold of. My best chance of surviving this encounter was if Scrub didn't see me coming. Someone once bullshitted me that there's a Welsh martial art called Llap-Goch, where the key to victory is to take out your opponent before he even knows you exist. I can get my head around that.

I rummaged in my pockets, checked that I still had the handcuff where I could get to it, and then took out my secret weapon. No point setting it up here—too far away. I started to pad stealthily down the walkway toward the *Mercedes*, unwinding the tangled length of cable as I went. It was weighted at its ends, like a bolas, but it was something else entirely. Scrub still hadn't turned, which with luck meant that he was lost in whatever passed with him for thought.

About twenty feet away from the boat, I stopped and knelt down. I put the disk-shaped payload down at the very edge of the planking, where it was less conspicuous. I paid out the cable to its full length and pressed the button. I'd given myself two minutes of lead-in. Two minutes ought to get me to where I needed to be, and after that, we'd see. With good timing, I might even come out of this with my head still attached to my shoulders.

Three more steps brought me to the *Mercedes*'s gangplank. She was a big ship—Mercedes had been a big woman, God rest her soul. There were three decks, and on the lowest one—the one I could see from where I stood—there was a door that obviously led down into the cabins. I toyed with the idea of getting out my lock picks and taking a crack at that door; it looked ridiculously easy. But no. Scrub was a dangerous man to have at your back. There was no point in getting in there if he was still extant and blocking the way out—and in the meantime, my two minutes were ticking away.

So I climbed the companionway steps to the middle deck and kept on going to the top. The crowbar was reassuringly heavy in my hands, but I wasn't pinning much of my faith to it. I was counting off the seconds in my mind, and forty had gone by already. I could see Scrub up ahead of me, still contemplating the iconic chimneys of the Battersea Power Station.

I took a few quiet steps toward him, the crowbar raised in my hand. Then, when I was about ten feet away, I let my foot fall heavily on the deck. The big man turned and saw me.

"You don't look any prettier by moonlight, Tinkerbell," I said.

Scrub bared his teeth and growled. I think that meant that he was happy to see me. He lifted his elbows off the rail and came up to his full height, which was every bit as scary as I remembered it being.

"Castor," he said, spitting out the word.

I didn't answer. I just backed away, the look of terror on my face not at all difficult to assume. Scrub made a lunge, and that was nearly it for me. He was a hell of a lot faster than I would have expected, and if I'd gone backward, he would have had me. I jumped to the side instead and vaulted over the rail onto the middle deck.

It was too dark for acrobatics. I landed in a sprawl and scrambled up again as Scrub came charging down the companionway steps. He'd cut me off from the gangway now, so I stepped up onto one of the scuppers and made another death-defying leap down onto the wooden walkway below. The crowbar was still in my hand, and as an added bonus, I managed to avoid breaking my leg with it.

Scrub came down the gangway at his leisure. He had me trapped in the little dead-end section aft of the *Mercedes*, where there was nowhere to go but down.

"You little fucker," he burred deep in his throat. Ninety seconds gone.

I took a few experimental swipes with the crowbar, making the air whistle in a way that I hoped was intimidating. But Scrub just laughed and started to lumber down the walkway toward me. "I wish you'd stuck with the whistle," he said, smirking horribly. "I was looking forward to jamming it down your fucking throat."

I backed away, dipping my free hand into my pocket. "Scrub," I warned him, "I've got a secret weapon. Coincidentally, it's behind you."

He ignored that and just kept coming toward me. I was hoping that the crowbar might give him a moment's pause, but he must have been threatened by bigger men than me and had probably eaten them for breakfast. (I really wish some other metaphor had occurred to me.) I brought my hand out of my pocket; the metal arc across my knuckles flashed bright in the light of the streetlamp. Scrub's eyes went to it—not scared or even wary, but mildly curious.

"It's silver," I said. "You know what silver does to your kind. Keep your distance."

Scrub shrugged massively. One of his huge hands reached out toward me, fingers spread wide. Out of options, I blocked and jabbed at him with the cuff. The metal grazed the skin of his wrist, and he flinched, feeling the pain. He hesitated, then took a step back. I did, too, taking advantage of that moment's respite to shift my balance. That was when he charged me.

It was like a bull's charge—no finesse, but lots and lots of momentum. His forearm hit me first, and it was rising, with all his weight behind it. That offhand, almost negligent swipe lifted me off the walkway and threw me ten feet through the air. I came down on my back at the very end of the planking, my head over the water and all the breath slammed out of me in one jarring gasp.

I tensed myself to roll aside, but Scrub was on me before I could move. His foot came down on my chest, pinning me to the ground and sending a jolt of electric pain through my stressed ribs. He glared down at me; one hand fumbled in his jacket pocket and came out with a knife. It would almost have counted as a sword in anybody else's hands: a thick-bladed dirk with a recurved tip. He bent from the waist, caught a handful of my lapels in his other hand, and hauled me half upright. The edge of the blade touched my cheek.

"I am fucking gonna love this," Scrub rasped.

One hundred and twenty.

The first blast of music split the night. Actually, "music" is far too generous a word for it; it was a mauling shriek like the sound a dying cat might make. It was a whistle playing three octaves above middle C. Scrub stiffened, a look of wonder and dismay crossing his face. Still with his foot planted on me, he swiveled to look for the source of the sound. But we were alone on the walkway; no piper, pied or otherwise, hove into sight.

The whistle modulated through three slurred discords, dropping from screeching treble to skirling bass. There was no tune, just burst after burst of raw noise hacked into a barely perceptible pattern. It made strange shifts from major to minor, from key to ham-fisted key. It polluted the night with its imperfection.

And it made Scrub let out a startled grunt of protest, like a stuck pig. He cast his head about, triangulating on the sound. Obviously it was coming from behind us—from the empty planking thirty feet or so away, back in the shadows between the *Mercedes* and her nearest neighbor.

The sound rose in pitch again, and Scrub screamed in pain and rage. He took his foot off my chest, probably just in time to stop my whole rib cage from caving in, and ran back toward the harbor entrance. That meant he was running toward the weird music, which seemed to be as hard for him to do as swimming against a riptide. His headlong pace slowed; he staggered and seemed for a second to be about to fall sideways into the water. Then he saw something on the ground ahead of him and forced himself to take a few steps more, toward it.

I sat up, sucking in an agonizing breath around ribs that seemed to have been reduced to needle-sharp splinters. I watched Scrub try to bend and pick up the thing he'd seen on the floor and fall down instead. I saw him scrabble at the boards and come up holding the Walkman in his huge hand. He stared at it as if he was having trouble making his eyes focus. Then he bellowed like an ox and threw the thing from him. It shattered against the side of the *Baroness Thatcher* before falling into the waters of the marina, its harsh voice silenced midnote.

Loup-garous are different from regular ghosts—harder or easier, depending on what it is you're trying to do. On the one hand, the invading spirit has burrowed its way deep into flesh and then resculpted the flesh around itself like a cocoon; so doing a full exorcism can be a bastard. But (and it's a *big* but) the flip side of that is that the flesh remembers its original shape. The line of least resistance is to make host and parasite fall out with one another—to set up an interference, so that the borrowed flesh reverts to what it was before the ghost came in and redecorated.

I'd been half convinced that the afternoon I'd spent in Pen's kitchen, teasing out that tune and getting it down on the Walkman, would be so much wasted time. But I knew I could never take Scrub one-on-one, no matter how many low blows I threw. So if I ever did come up against him, I'd need to have an even more unfair advantage.

The big man lurched to his feet again, but it took him a Herculean effort. His head snapped around, and he looked at me across ten meters of planking with a glare of insane, incendiary hatred.

"Castor," he growled. "I'll kill you for this. That's a promise. When I—"

He stiffened, and a tremor ran through his body like a wave through water. He stared at his arms and groaned. They were writhing, not like limbs but like snakes, like puppy dogs in a sack. He tried to take a step toward me, managed, started work on another. That was as far as he got.

"When I come—back—" Scrub was having to force the words out, his voice bubbling and fluting. He began to melt from the legs up, and he shrank in on himself spectacularly. But he wasn't melting; that was just the way it looked from where I was sitting on the walkway. What was actually happening was a whole lot more disgusting.

He turned into rats. The whole of that big, solid frame dissolved and separated, tore itself asunder, and a wave of brown, furry bodies struggled out of the folds of his greasy suit to sweep off along the walkway in a filthy tide, heading away from the water. If Scrub's consciousness had still been animating them and welding them together, they could have eaten me alive, but Scrub—the mind and personality that used that name—was a ghost. When the music punched him out of the flesh that he'd wrapped around himself, the individual little rat minds all kicked back in and took up their own agendas again.

I thought back to the time when I'd unlocked the door of my room and found Scrub sitting on the bed. Now I knew how he'd managed to get in through that barely open window. I gave a reflexive shudder at the thought. When he'd threatened to kill me, it wasn't just farting in the wind. I hadn't exorcised him, just broken his concentration and stolen his body out from under him. He could find another body, given time—could and probably would. *Loup-garous* are like weeds in that way; you think you've got rid of them, but they pop up again when you least expect it, kill off your prize geraniums, eat your dog, and crush your skull like an eggshell.

But that was a thought to linger on during some warm summer evening yet to come. Right now I had other things to think about. Picking myself up off the planking, I retraced my steps along the walkway and retrieved the rest of my stuff: the lock picks, the bolt cutters, the cone-bore flute, the whole dodgy tool kit. Then I put my shoes back on, boarded the *Mercedes* again, and made a beeline for the cabin door.

I gave it the once-over as I hauled out my lock picks. Bog-standard Yale, slightly sexy Chubb. Not the piece of cake that I was hoping for, but far from impossible. I got to work, occasionally looking over my shoulder back toward the harbor entrance to see if anyone was coming down the walkway in my direction. Nothing. I worked undisturbed, got the Yale inside of ten minutes, but then lost time on the Chubb. It was a real fucking boojum, with an impossibly narrow barrel and a double detainer. Bouncing the pick didn't help at all, so I was reduced to working out the set pins laboriously, one by one, the skin on the back of my neck prickling the whole time. Then it was one pass for each pin, with the minutes ticking by.

When the lock finally clicked and the door gave inward a fraction of an inch, I was taken by surprise and almost fell in with it. Recovering my balance, I stood up and stepped into the dark space inside the cabin.

I stood still for a few moments, listening. Nothing. I didn't really want to turn a light on, because if Damjohn came home suddenly, I wanted to be the surpriser rather than the surprisee. I ought to be able to hear footsteps and maybe voices as he came along the walkway toward the boat, but if he saw a light, he'd send the heavy mob in first, on tiptoe, and before I knew where I was, I'd be replaying Custer's last stand with only a couple of vowels out of place.

The faint movement of air on my face told me that the cabin or galley that I was in was fairly large, but it was impossible to see a thing. My nerves more or less screaming now, I forced myself to wait for my eyes to adjust to the darkness. The room built itself up around me, piecemeal, as the darkness separated out into discrete volumes.

There was a table right in front of me—long, low, and really convenient to trip over. There were two couches built into the sides of the room and something in the middle distance that looked like a tall cabinet of some kind against the farther bulkhead wall, with a squat, blocky object standing off to one side of it. In between me and the cabinet there was a chair, and the more I squinted at the chair, the more convinced I was that someone was sitting in it.

I stepped soundlessly to one side so that I wouldn't be silhouetted against the open door behind me. It made no difference, of course—if anyone was sitting there, they'd already seen me and had plenty of chance to respond to my entrance. But the stillness and the silence persisted, and I reminded myself that taking things slowly wasn't a luxury I could afford right then.

So I skirted the table and advanced into the room. That brought me broadside on to the chair and confirmed my first impressions; it was definitely occupied by someone who was sitting stock-still in the dark, rigidly upright, facing front even though I'd moved a quarter-circle around to the left.

I thought again about turning on the light, came to the same conclusions. My flesh creeping a little, I closed in on the chair and its motionless occupant. I put out a hand and brought it down gently on the silent figure's shoulder.

Instantly it convulsed, its head snapping round in my direction, its back arching. It tried to twist away from me, but didn't manage to get very far. The combination of squirming effort and more or less total failure to go anywhere left me mystified for about half a second. I realized that the figure was tied to the chair around about the same time that something hard and cold slammed into the back of my neck, dropping me to my knees. I didn't stay there for long, though. The foot planted in my stomach sent me rolling and gasping, full length, on the floor.

The lights clicked on, blinding my dark-adjusted eyes. It wasn't as much of a handicap as you'd think; winded, dazed, and curled up in a fetal ball, I wouldn't have been able to see a whole hell of a lot in any case.

Damjohn's unctuous tones intruded on my pain. "I have caller display, Mr. Castor," he said with dripping scorn. "When Richard called me on Arnold's phone—a phone that he'd previously lost to you in a brawl in a public house—what was I supposed to think?" He said a few other things as well—or at least he was still talking when I faded out.

Twenty-two

I WAS PROBABLY ONLY UNCONSCIOUS FOR A MINUTE OR so. As I bobbed my way painfully back up from the black well that Chandler used to get so lyrical about, I could still hear Damjohn's voice. He was speaking in a clipped, commanding voice—giving orders, from the sound of it. Heavy footsteps moved across the cabin in response. Good. If he was talking to someone else, I could go back to sleep.

But the someone else hauled me roughly upright and gave me a hard shake to dislodge the cobwebs—almost taking my head along with them. I blinked my eyes open, took in a scene that was skewed at a nauseating angle and had a very depressing effect on my spirits.

Damjohn was sitting on one of the couches, at his ease, lighting a black cigarette. Behind him stood Gabe McClennan and Weasel-Face Arnold. Arnold's battered face gave me a moment's low satisfaction, but under the circumstances, it didn't do a whole hell of a lot to warm the cockles. Two more bravoes to whom I hadn't been introduced stood on either side of me, holding me up in the absence of any meaningful efforts from my rubbery legs.

The woman tied to the chair had a gray Parcelforce bag tied around her head.

"Mr. Castor," said Damjohn with just a hint of paternal sternness.

"At one point in this sad, complicated business, I paid you the compliment of trying to bribe you. I honestly wish you'd accepted."

"Go fuck yourself," I suggested. "What you tried to do was seduce me, because that's what you like to do best. Now you're about ten minutes away from a lobster quadrille with the Vice Squad, so let's cut a deal. You drop the Blofeld act, and I won't ask for a martini." I was chagrined at how quavery my voice sounded. That whack to the top of the spine had knocked a lot of the fight out of me. I was going to need to play for time; a couple of weeks would do nicely, so long as I got bed rest.

Despite appearances, though, Damjohn hadn't settled down for a nice long chat. He turned to glance over his shoulder at McClennan. "What are you waiting for?" he asked mildly. "A pay rise?"

McClennan jerked to attention as sharply as a West Point graduate. He came around the couch and crossed to stand in front of me.

"You wouldn't take a fucking hint, would you?" he asked, glowering at me. He pulled my coat open, snapping off a couple of the buttons in the process, then did the same thing with my shirt. He seemed to enjoy it. I wondered for a brief, unsettling moment if I'd misunderstood the situation—if I was going to be raped before I was murdered. But then Weasel-Face handed Gabe a tray full of implements I vaguely recognized, and Gabe got busy.

There was a pot of henna, another half full of water, and a couple of brushes—one fat, one thin. Gabe dipped the bigger of the two brushes in the water, then in the henna, and painted a broad, messy circle on my chest. I gave an involuntary gasp; the water was cold. I began to get an inkling of what was about to happen, but if I let myself think about that and froze up with fear, I'd be dead for sure. In the absence of any better ideas, I continued to play the few paltry cards I had left.

I looked across at Rosa—assuming that it *was* Rosa trussed up like a parcel over there. The ragged rise and fall of her chest was a hopeful sign, anyway.

"You should quit while you're ahead," I told Damjohn, slurring my words only slightly. "If you let her go, all you're going to get is accessory to murder and wrongful imprisonment. Kill her, and you'll do life. But not here. They'll deport you back to Zagreb. You fancy twenty years in a Croatian prison? I reckon the time off for good behavior would arrive at the sharp end of an ice pick."

Damjohn just smiled, as if I'd made an unfunny joke that he was going to be magnanimously polite about.

"I'm not going to kill Rosa," he reassured me. "Not while she's still a saleable asset. Eventually, if drugs and disease and distempered clients don't get her first, it will be necessary to draw a line under her. For the time being, though, she's fine. She's young, she's healthy, and she's earning her keep. I'm actually quite fond of her. Don't worry about Rosa, Castor."

"Then why have you got her tied to a chair?" I asked. It seemed like a reasonable question, but Damjohn waved it away.

"I needed to make sure she didn't speak to you. In the short term, I arranged that by keeping her here. But it was only ever an interim measure. You really should have just exorcised the ghost at the archive and taken your pay. Or, conversely, accepted my foolishly generous offer. You've got no one to blame for this but yourself."

"Let me see that she's all right," I said, sounding for all the world like someone who still had a bargaining position to maintain.

Damjohn put his head on one side, frowned at me either in puzzlement at the request or in annoyance that I'd presumed to give him an order. Whatever went through his mind, he finally made a gesture to Weasel-Face, who walked over to Rosa and pulled the mail sack off her head. Underneath it she was gagged with a plug of cloth and a few loops of rope, and her right eye was swollen closed. Her other eye was open, though, and her expression as she stared at me, though terrified, was alert. It seemed as though she might get out of this with her life after all. On the other hand, from what Damjohn was saying, that would just be a suspended sentence.

"There," said Damjohn, smiling at me almost mischievously. "I'm a man of my word, when I care to be." I wondered whether that was really why he'd shown her to me—whether it was because after a lifetime of lying and betraying and raping and murdering, he felt on some level as though he was left with something to prove.

Gabe had switched to the thinner of the brushes and was painstakingly dabbing at my midriff. An unpleasant tingle was building in my stomach. The two men on either side of me were holding my arms so tightly that they were in danger of cutting off the circulation. Even if I wasn't still weak and sick from the skull massage I'd got earlier, I could never have fought my way free.

"This is a pretty roundabout way of killing me," I observed.

"But it has the right *look* to it," Damjohn countered. "You're an exorcist. You bit off a little more than you could comfortably chew. That must happen all the time."

I wondered briefly about what had happened to my flute. Then I saw it on the floor at Damjohn's feet, incredibly still intact. He followed my gaze and saw it, too. He snapped his fingers and pointed, and Weasel-Face played fetch.

"This isn't what you used at the club," Damjohn mused, turning the instrument over in his hands. "What is it? It's not a flute."

"It's a cone-bore flute," I said. "Earlier version of the same instrument. When Boehm invented the modern valve system, this went in the dustbin."

Damjohn looked at me and nodded. "Which is where you're going," he acknowledged. "Arnold, I'll need those bolt cutters, too."

He pointed to the cutters, which had fallen half under the farther couch. Arnold harkened to his master's voice again, picked them up, and handed them over. Very deliberately, Damjohn got to his feet and crossed over to me. In the narrow cabin, it only took him three steps. He held the flute up in front of my face, put the blades of the cutters around its midpoint, and squeezed. The wood of the flute splintered and then gave, shattering into fragments, enamel flaking off like red-brown dandruff. Damjohn wiped the flakes off on his sleeve and let both the bolt cutters and the remains of the flute fall to the floor again with a heavy clatter.

"In case you were hoping to pull off a last-minute miracle," he said.

"Actually, I had it in mind to" I began, but I wasn't destined to finish that sentence, and I can't even remember what merry quip was on my lips. Pain flowered in my throat, cut off my breath, left me gasping soundlessly as my knees once again buckled under me.

Gabe backed away from me, rubbing his henna-covered fingertips together.

"Your trouble is that you talk too much, Castor," he said with a nasty grin. "Or at least you did. But I just took care of that."

It took a few seconds for the agony to subside. When it had, I spat out a few choice swear words at him, but my jaws were working in stealth mode; not the slightest sound came out of my mouth. I knew then, as I guess I'd known all along, what sigil Gabe had painted on my chest. SILENCE. He'd taken my voice again.

"Now take care of the rest of it," Damjohn said, standing up. "I have other places to be."

Gabe pulled himself up to his full height and became almost comically solemn. He began to declaim in barnstorming style—Latin, of course, but the medieval stuff where the word order is all to fuck and you can't follow a damn word of it. Trying to pick sounds out of the flow, I caught the word *pretium*, which means "price;" *imploramus*, which means "buddy, can you spare me a dime;" and *damnatio*, which is self-explanatory.

It was a summoning, the first I'd ever seen, because I tend to steer clear of black magic on the perfectly reasonable grounds that it's a pile of arse. Well, 99 percent of it is. Unfortunately, it looked as though Gabe had latched onto at least one spell that did what it said on the box.

His words rolled around the small cabin, raising an echo that seemed somehow displaced, as if it belonged to a vast, cavernous space a long way from chic and cheerful Chelsea. Gabe was looking strained and uncomfortable, sweat running down his pale face as he forced the words out like some kind of human die-stamp machine punching measured indentations into the air we breathed. Looking at the twinges of pain crossing his face, I realized why he'd looked so wrecked when I called on him in his office—and why he'd swallowed those black bombers like they were Smarties. That was a few scant hours after my first close encounter with the demon. He must still have been in the deep pits of a psychic hangover.

Arnold and the two other heavies took the whole procedure in their stride at first, staring at Gabe with a kind of amused contempt. But they got very tense as the temperature climbed a few perceptible degrees. Then, when the pungent smell hit them, they started to sweat. I'd been there, too, and I knew it had sod all to do with the heat. Rosa moaned around her gag, her one visible eye rolling in her head, and even Damjohn lost something of his sangfroid.

I missed Ajulutsikael's entrance. Demons are like that; you think they're all about big, showstopping numbers, but they come up on you as softly as the dawn. Maybe the darkness behind Damjohn deepened for a moment, and then again maybe it didn't. My gaze passed over the place, jerked back, and she was there.

Damjohn moved hastily aside as she stepped forward, and every man in the room drew in his breath with an audible, almost painful catch. Every man except me, that is. I couldn't make a sound if my life depended on it. Sorry, that should have read "even though."

What caused that communal swallowing of tonsils was the fact that Juliet was naked—and if that conjures up an image in your mind, forget it. She wasn't naked like that. Oh, I suppose it was no more sensational a body than Helen of Troy's, say. On a ship-launching scale, maybe a straight thousand, give or take. But with the raw stench of her pheromones supersaturating the air, she looked like every woman you ever loved or dreamed about loving, miraculously combined, miraculously open and willing, like a solid sign of God's mercy.

Damjohn's muscle boys were staring at her slack-jawed. Weasel-Face had a spreading puddle on the floor at his feet. The man to the left of me groaned in despair or spontaneous orgasm, and Rosa made a muffled, balking sound. But they had one advantage over me—Juliet wasn't looking at them.

Her stare held me like a vice—the kind of vice you give way to in the dark behind a locked door, your hot blood ashamed and quickening. She advanced on me with the unhurried grace of a panther. Just for a minute, that predator's stalk let me see through the veil of her scent and recognize her for what she was—the top carnivore in an ecosystem that offered no challenge to her, her long legs shaped for the chase, her exquisite curves only adaptive camouflage. There was a very faint music that I'd heard before, like wind chimes.

"Do him slowly," said McClennan's voice, strained but clear. "He's fucking earned it."

The men on either side of me stepped back in a hurry, and without their support, I crashed down instantly, agonizingly, to my knees. My head swiveled as I fell to keep my eyes locked on hers. I couldn't look away. I couldn't even blink. Her terrible perfection flooded my mind, shattered any thoughts except fear and desire into random shards.

"Mortal man," she growled deep in her throat. "You made me run. Made me bleed. I'll make this good for you—make you so happy in your agony that your soul will never be free of me."

Not like wind chimes. Like church bells, incongruously and ridiculously, like church bells ringing at the limit of hearing in an octave so high they must be rimed with permafrost. And now I thought I recognized it.

I closed my eyes. Both of them. It was the hardest thing I'd ever done, like shoving two trucks backward up a ramp. My mind screamed in protest, the animal hindbrain wanting only to feast on the sight of Juliet until she'd done sucking out my marrow. With my eyes closed, a fraction of that mesmeric power was shut off. I listened to the sound, and I turned my head fractionally downward, toward it.

Juliet's hand closed on my shoulder, her nails puncturing the skin. She squeezed, and I howled in pain—without, of course, making the slightest sound. My eyes snapped open again. I was staring at her left ankle, which was still encircled by the silver chain.

She was trying to haul me to my feet, her claws hooked into my shoulder right next to my throat. I fought back not against her strength—I couldn't have resisted that for a second—but against the weakest link, which happened to be me. The flesh of my shoulder strained and then tore, and I screamed again—with the volume turned down to zero, but I'm sure it was music to Damjohn's ears all the same. My right hand, which isn't my strongest, groped and scrabbled on the floor for a moment or two, finding nothing except the sad remains of my flute. Then something cold and hard touched the heel of my hand, and my fingers closed around it. The handle of the bolt cutters.

Juliet bent from the waist and took hold again, her hands this time closing on either side of my head. Pinpricks of pain at temple, cheek, chin told me where her claws were embedded. I shut it out, shut her out, although ghost images of her still danced obscene tangos in my brain.

It was almost impossible to aim, to focus. My hand was a balloon sculpture, nerveless and fragile; it wouldn't do what it was told. It wavered and wobbled, the lower jaw of the cutters finally catching on something at least, but I didn't know what, and now she was pulling me upright again. If I struggled against her this time, my whole face would come off. In my head I uttered a prayer that didn't even have words, and I squeezed the cutters closed. There was a slight but audible *clack* as the blades met.

Then I was lifted, Juliet raising me without effort to her own shoulder height, her hands cupping my head like a goalie about to punt the ball past the centerline. My feet flailed but found no purchase as she drew me close, her mouth open, her hypnotic pupils so wide she had no irises.

But her lips didn't close over mine. She just held me there, dangling uselessly, an inch from my death and damnation and so much in her thrall now that I even felt slightly aggrieved that it had been postponed.

She was looking down, staring fixedly at the ground. No, at her own left foot. She was holding my head completely immobile, and my eyes couldn't traverse that far, but I could see Damjohn and Gabe. They were also looking down, and a kind of sick horror spread in slow motion across their faces. Gabe's first, because he had the summoning spell down word-perfect, and he knew exactly what he was looking at.

Juliet let me go, and by some supreme effort of will, I got my balance as I fell so that I only staggered back and slammed against the wall instead of taking yet another pratfall.

For a moment, the cabin was a frozen tableau. Damjohn, Gabe, Weasel-Face, the two anonymous heavies, even Rosa with her one good eye all were looking at Juliet, hushed, expectant, as if she was about to propose a toast. Her shoulders slightly bowed, Juliet flexed her ankle experimentally. The broken chain slid off and tinkled to the floor.

"H-hagios ischirus Paraclitus," Gabe quavered without much conviction. "Alpha et omega, initium et finis . . ." Juliet swiveled from the hip, without undue haste but still moving almost too quickly to see, and kicked him in the stomach. He folded in on himself with a sound like water going down a partially blocked drain. From the floor, in a defensive crouch, I could hear him trying again to frame a word, without any breath left to force it out. Juliet stamped down on his neck, and it snapped audibly. It had all happened inside three seconds.

Both feet back on the ground, Juliet drew in a deep, lingering breath. For a moment, she closed those exquisite eyes; her face wore the sensual calm of someone who was about to enjoy themselves on a very deep, very visceral level. Then her eyes opened wide again; she flexed her long, elegant fingers once, twice, and turned to face Damjohn.

"Do as you're told," Damjohn snapped, pointing across at me. "Finish him off." He knew damn well that this was a kite that wouldn't fly, of course, but his whole life had consisted of outraging the natural order in various indefensible ways. You lose nothing by spinning the wheel. Except that this time he did. There was a sound like silk tearing, and he lost his look of contemptuous superiority, a surprising amount of blood, and what looked like a loop of his entrails. Again, Juliet didn't even seem to have moved. She licked a trickle of blood from the heel of her hand and laughed a throaty, appreciative laugh as Damjohn fell heavily back onto the couch with a grunt of unhappy surprise.

There was a clattering of booted feet on planking as Weasel-Face Arnold tried to run. The other two guys drew a knife and a gun respectively, but Juliet walked through them with her arms flicking to left and right, and blood blossomed as they fell. Arnold was lucky enough to be looking the other way when she got to him. He was trying so hard to get the door open that he didn't see her come, and his death as she smashed his face forward—into and through the bulkhead wall—must have been mercifully quick.

Then she turned back to stare at Damjohn. The expression on her face told me everything I needed to know. She hadn't left him alive by carelessness or accident or whimsy, she was going to take her time with him. She even smiled in unholy anticipation.

With what little volition was left to me, I staggered over to Rosa, stumbled across her, and shielded her with my own body. I kept my own eyes firmly shut. It was one thing to be caught up in Juliet's feeding and mating ritual, quite another to have to watch it. Damjohn's whimpers and sobs went on for a very long time, until eventually they faded, Juliet's sighs of satisfaction drowning them out.

When everything was silent again, I straightened up. Rosa's one eye was staring up into mine, imploring, terrified. Slowly, without turning to look at Juliet, I started to untie Rosa's gag. It wasn't easy. Someone had gone to town on the knots, and I couldn't get my fingertips between them. It didn't help that I was so rigid with tension that I could barely make my hands move at all—or that the wound in my shoulder was sending irregular pulses of agony down my left arm, making my fingers spasm every few seconds.

The skin on my back was crawling, anticipating Juliet's touch. I was expecting every second for her to take hold of me and turn me around, and since her tastes were catholic with a small "c" and polymorphously perverse, I was hoping to leave Rosa in a position to run while I was being devoured.

No such luck.

"Face me," Juliet murmured.

With huge reluctance, I turned. She was standing exactly where Damjohn had been sprawled. The bodies of Gabe, Arnold, and the other two bully boys still lay where they'd fallen, but of Damjohn himself there was no sign.

"You set me free," she said, her tone glacially cold.

I gestured toward the sigil on my chest, shrugged in mimed apology. My heart was tripping and stammering like a telegraph machine. She stared at the daubed pentagram as if she'd forgotten it until that moment. Then she drew her hand across in front of me—a single horizontal slash in the air—and McClennan's chains of compulsion fell from me as if they'd never existed. I knew that at once, because suddenly I could hear my own harsh breathing.

"To bind and to loose," Juliet said, and her face twisted now in almost physical disgust, "these are games that men play. And you *dare* to play them with me."

I couldn't think of anything to say to that. All I could do was shrug again. Her power over me was undiminished, and it was still hard to think around the searing fact of her nakedness. She turned her attention to Rosa, who was staring at her in hypnotized terror. The gag was still in her mouth; I was only about halfway through untying it. She made an urgent sound around it, pleading with me or with Juliet or with God.

"What's your purpose with this woman?" Juliet asked after a heavy silence.

I forced myself to speak. My voice came out as an unlovely croak. "I was going to untie her and then take her to visit her sister."

Juliet considered this, her face a hard mask.

"The other bound one? Under the ground?"

"Yeah, her," I agreed. "I wanted them to see each other again. Maybe say good-bye to each other. I was thinking that that would probably—"

Juliet's snarl cut across my words. "I said that binding and loosing are men's games. I didn't say I was ignorant as to the rules of them. Do you think I'm a child, mortal man? Flesh puppet, would you *patronize* me?"

She was walking toward me as she spoke, one slow step at a time. Now she was right in front of me, and I was a rabbit in the headlight stare of her eyes. I bowed my head; just like before, I had to force myself. On one level, all I wanted to do was to look at her until I died of thirst or exhaustion or an overlabored heart.

Juliet leaned forward, brought her face up close to mine. "My mark is on you," she growled in her throat. "I can whistle for your body or for your soul, and you'll bring them to me and beg me to take them. You wear *my* chain, which can't be broken."

Without looking up, without meeting her gaze, I nodded. I stayed like that for a long time: three or four minutes, at least. The silence was unbroken, and her perfume was dissipating. When I couldn't smell it anymore, when the last hint of it had faded from my lungs,

I allowed myself a quick glance from under lowered lids. She was gone.

I exhaled shakily, only then realizing how long it had been since I'd drawn a proper breath. Finding that I could move again despite the extensive damage reports coming in from my neck, my back, my shoulder, my face, I turned to Rosa and made a second attempt at removing her gag.

It took another five minutes. When it was off at last and she was able to spit out the saliva-drenched wad of cloth that had been in her mouth, she let loose with what I'd guess was every swear word she knew. Fortunately for my modesty, I don't speak a word of Russian. She might just as well have been saying her prayers.

I released her hands, which had been tied behind her back with blue nylon washing-line string, and her legs, which were attached to the front legs of the chair by about a hundred turns of duct tape. Her body was so racked with cramps that she could only stand with my help. Slowly, patiently, I walked her back and forth across the cabin as her circulation returned. Every few seconds, she let out a moan or a sob or another curse, and after a while, she had to sit down and rest her protesting muscles. I watched her in silence. I didn't have a clue what to say to her. But after a while, she looked up at me with a frown that was frankly suspicious.

"Why she didn't kill you?" Rosa demanded in a sullen murmur.

Fair question, but not one I felt in any mood to answer. "I don't know," I admitted. "I think—if this makes any sense—it was because she felt something for you. You and Snezhna." She started at the sound of her sister's name, and her one good eye flared wide open, but she said nothing. "Maybe it was because she was in the same position you were in. You know how you were tied to that chair with rope and tape? And Snezhna was trapped in that room after she died by fear and unhappiness and worry about you? Well, the chain Juliet wore around her ankle was the same kind of deal. I think she might actually have killed me for setting *her* free—that was an insult almost as great as binding her in the first place. But she saw me trying to untie you. And she saw that I wanted to untie Snezhna, too. So she thought what the fuck—she could always come back and kill me another time."

I was saying this for my own benefit as much as Rosa's, thinking it through as I spoke. It made as much sense as anything would. You can't try to explain demons by reference to human emotions or human motives.

Rosa picked herself up, and since she was walking more or less normally, apart from a residual limp, we went out onto the deck. The cool night air hit us like a kiss on the cheek from God. I made her wait there while I went back inside and, picking my way around the corpses, collected everything from the cabin that I'd brought with me or that might have my fingerprints on it.

She seemed relieved when I rejoined her, although I'd only been inside for a minute at most. We both had to take the companionway stairs slowly, like two old codgers coming down from the top deck of a swaying bus.

When we were back on the terra-comparatively-firma of the wooden walkway, I turned to her.

"She wants to see you," I said as gently as I could manage with my still-hoarse voice. "She wants to know that you're okay. That's why she's still there. In that room. That's what she's waiting for."

It took a second or two for Rosa to get her head around what I was saying. Then she nodded. "Yes," she said.

"Are you ready?"

No hesitation this time. "Yes."

I led the way.

Twenty-three

It was way after two A.M. by this time, and Eversholt Street was as silent as a necropolis. Even the night buses, rolling empty out of Euston with all their lights on, looked like catafalques bound for some funeral of princes.

Rosa flinched visibly when she saw that door, but she stood her ground. I took care of the locks using Rich's keys, and we stepped into the upper room of the archive's secret annex. Rosa looked around her, shook her head, and laughed without any trace of humor. I stopped still to listen, gestured to Rosa to do likewise. There was no sound from the room below.

"You'd better wait here," I said, aware that her nerves probably couldn't take too many more surprises tonight, and Rich would probably be a surprise of the nastiest kind.

I unlocked the door to the stairs, turned on the light, and went down. Rich was still there, but the atmosphere down in the basement didn't seem to have agreed with him all that much. He was slumped on the floor, staring slackly at his drawn-up knees. He didn't respond when I called his name, and his eyes didn't move by any visible fraction when I waved my hand in front of them. The lights were on, but it was clear that, for the moment at least, nobody was home. I surmised that Snezhna had visited him again while I was gone and that she hadn't been restful company. Well, if a guy gets what he's been begging for, you don't waste tears.

I went back upstairs and beckoned Rosa over to me. I explained briefly about Rich and what he was doing there. Her eyes narrowed, and her lower lip jutted out.

"I'll kill him," she hissed.

"To be honest," I said, aware that I was echoing what Cheryl had said to me a week before about the ghost herself, "I think you'd be doing him a favor. But there's been enough killing done tonight, and it's a fucking rotten spectator sport at the best of times, so here's the deal. You promise not to kill him, and we'll go and see Snezhna, all merry and bright. Okay?"

But I realized as I said it that it had just become moot in any case. A familiar feeling was stealing over me, coming in on whatever extra sense I have that's perpetually tuned in to Death FM.

I led the way down the stairs, and Rosa followed. She bared her teeth in a snarl of hatred when she saw Rich. He stared back at her, slack and invertebrate and without any sign of recognition.

I turned to look down at the stained, spavined mattress. Nothing to be seen there, but that was where she was—that was where it was coming from.

I pointed, and Rosa followed with her eyes.

"There," I said. "Don't be afraid."

To do her justice, she wasn't. Snezhna's faceless ghost emerged from the floor like Venus from the waves, the red fringes of her ruined face waving like a silk scarf in a wind we couldn't feel. But Rosa stood her ground, her eyes filling with tears.

When Snezhna got to ground level—or a few inches above it—she stopped, and the two women faced each other across a gap of about ten feet. The tears were rolling freely down Rosa's face now. She said something in Russian. Snezhna nodded, then answered. Rosa shook her head in wonder.

Discretion is another virtue I've never really got the hang of, but I decided at that point that a breath of fresh air would do Rich and me a world of good. I untied him, hooked a hand under his arm, and pulled him, unprotesting, to his feet. I led him up the stairs, and he went as docile as a lamb. Just once his eyes half focused, and he looked at me, his gaze intensely troubled. He seemed to be about to speak, but evidently he couldn't find the words or forgot what it was he had to say.

I stood the sofa upright again and sat Rich down on it. Then I picked up one of the remaining water bottles, unbuttoned my shirt, and slopped it over my chest, trying without much success to clean off some of the henna. It wouldn't budge—that would take a lot of soap and water and a lot of time. In the meantime, I'd have to hope that my husky voice sounded sexy rather than just ridiculous.

I gave the sisters plenty of time, because what Rosa was doing had to be done right. I knew that better than anybody, because what she was doing was my job. It's the other way to make a ghost move on from this place to wherever. You just give them what they want—tie up the loose ends for them, let them see that everything's going to be okay after all.

My mind went back to Damjohn's offer. *I have knowledge that comes with a price many would consider too high.* Yeah, way too high for me, sport. I'd find out in my own way. In my own time.

After half an hour or so, I went back down. I found Rosa sitting alone on the mattress, looking almost as spent and catatonic as Rich. I held out my hand, but she didn't take it. She stood under her own steam.

"She's gone," she said, but with an inflection that might have made it into a question.

"Yeah," I confirmed. "She's gone. She just needed to know that you were out of that shit-hole. Now she's happy."

Rosa didn't seem convinced. She stared at me, a solemn frown on her face. "*Where* has she gone?" she asked with very careful emphasis.

"I'll get back to you on that one," I promised. "Sometime."

Twenty-four

ONE OF THE REASONS WHY I NEVER GET UP-TO-DATE with my paperwork is that I can't seem to find the kind of job where you can sign off and say it's all done. Maybe it's just me. Everything in my life has a more ragged shape than that, tapering off at the end into bathos, bullshit, and bittersweet absurdity.

The headlines were all variations on a theme, the *Sun*'s CHELSEA HARBOUR BLOODBATH being my personal favorite—although the *Star* came a close second with CHELSEA'S ORGY OF DEATH. The stories all leaned very heavily on Lucasz Damjohn's dodgy reputation and suspected involvement in various kinds of organized vice for which, notwithstanding, he had escaped the indignity of even a single conviction. Now there had been some sort of gang war on board a yacht that was registered to him, a number of men were dead, and Damjohn himself had apparently gone to ground. They identified one of the corpses as a known associate of Damjohn's—a man glorying (posthumously now) in the name of Arnold Poultney. That was Weasel-Face Arnold, presumably. The three remaining bodies belonged to John Grass, Martin Rumbelow, and a certain Mr. Gabriel Alexander McClennan, who was survived by a grieving widow and daughter.

That was a disturbing thought. I'd had no idea up until then that McClennan had ever married, let alone bred. There ought to be licensing laws that stop that sort of thing happening, but since there weren't, I'd just torpedoed—along with the unregenerate bastard himself—an entire family unit. I considered blagging an address from Dodson, or more likely from Nicky, and going round to see them, but what the hell would I have said? I killed your husband, your dad, but it's okay, because he deserved it? I chickened out. That was one last reckoning I wasn't ready for just yet.

But leaving all the imponderables off to one side, there was a certain pleasure to be had in dumping the whole day's papers down on Alice's desk and telling her she could add them to the Bonnington collection. It was Alice's desk, because Peele was already on secondment to the Guggenheim, who were so keen to get their hands on him that they were paying the Bonnington to let him work out his notice in their employ. And Alice was where she'd wanted to be all along—a happy ending that, by Cheryl's account, had left hardly a dry eye in the place.

"This changes nothing," Alice told me coldly. "The fact that nobody has seen the ghost since last Sunday doesn't prove that she's gone, or if she's gone, that you exorcised her. By my reckoning, you still owe us three hundred pounds—and you can be grateful that I didn't involve the police over the theft of my keys."

I didn't let any of this spoil my sunny disposition. "You're right," I said. "When you're right, you're right. I can't prove I did the job. No witnesses. No physical evidence. That's the nature of the beast, I suppose. Most of what I do doesn't leave a trail."

She was waiting for me to leave, with barely concealed impatience.

"No," I went on, musing aloud. "For a good, solid trail, you need a good, solid crime. Now I know you caught up with Tiler because I made it my business to find out. You turned up on his doorstep with two solicitors and a gent from the cop shop, and you took possession of twenty-seven boxes full of miscellaneous documents, with no fuss and no charges brought. Then the next day, he gave his notice in."

Alice was still looking like someone with a lot of better places to be. "And what's your point?" she demanded.

I shrugged disarmingly. "Far be it from me to have a point. It's best to do these things discreetly. Nothing gained by making a big noise about it. Okay, the screwy little fucker tried to kill me, but I know as well as anyone that there's a greater good. Tell me, Alice, did you do what I asked you to? Did you go next door and have a look in that basement?"

She just stared at me for a moment or two.

"Yes," she said at last—and I could hear the strain under the neutral tone she held so well. "I did."

"Come to any conclusions about it?"

She nodded slowly. Very slowly. Again she took her time answering, making sure every word did what it was supposed to. "I took legal advice. Those premises never came into the possession of the archive in the first place. They remained with the Department of Social Security when the rest of the building was made over to us in the 1980s. So I let the police know that the rooms had been broken into and left it at that."

"Of course you did. Was that you as in Acting-Chief-Administrator-of-the-Bonnington-Archive you, or private-citizen-cooperating-with-the-police-out-of-disinterested-sense-of-civic-duty you? I mean, did you leave a name or just ring them anonymously from a call box?"

She opened her mouth for an angry reply, but I hurried on. "Whichever," I said, "I'm sure you made the point that you, Jeffrey, and Rich were in possession of keys to that door, and that therefore, any inquiries about possible unlawful imprisonment, rape, and/or murder ought to start with the three of you."

There was a very long, very painful silence.

"I've checked my own and Jeffrey's keys very thoroughly," said Alice. "There are no keys to that door on either ring."

"That's interesting," I said. "I mean, I saw Rich letting himself into those rooms with his Bonnington key ring only a few short nights ago. It stands out in my mind because of the very vivid events it's associated with. Now obviously, Rich is in a secure ward in the West Middlesex right now, sedated up to his eyeballs and consequently unable to speak up for himself. But I could maybe point the police in his direction in case he ever gets better."

Alice's conscience might have been bothering her, but she wasn't in the mood to be pushed around. "Then maybe you should," she said. "What you do is your own affair, Castor. Good-bye and good luck."

"How about the Gug? Do you think we should put them in the loop, too?"

No answer at all. Alice had the slapped-in-the-face look of a little kid who's just been told that there isn't any Father Christmas. I laid my cards on the table. This wasn't sadism, it was just business.

"Apart from you," I said, "Peele made three appointments during his time here. Cheryl's solid gold, but out of the other two, one was stealing from the archive on an industrial scale, and the other has only managed to escape a murder investigation by going conveniently insane at the eleventh hour. That's a great record, isn't it? Something you might definitely expect to come up at the recruitment interview when the Guggenheim board formalize this temporary appointment of his."

Alice still hadn't found anything to say, so I just kept on going.

"Now I figure it this way. There was no reason not to throw the book at Tiler except a desire to let sleeping dogs lie. And you've tried to keep at least an arm's length, if not a barge pole's distance, between the Bonnington and the Snezhna Alanovich murder investigation, although you must be very well aware that it's going on right next door to you. I believe the police even dropped in to ask you a few questions, but obviously I wasn't privy to that conversation, so I can't possibly tell what they asked you and what came up in the general chitchat.

"Probably you've come to the conclusion that whatever happened in that basement is none of your business. Possibly you've decided that

Rich has already been punished for whatever he did and would never stand trial anyway, in the state he's in. Maybe you've also reflected on the potential embarrassment to Jeffrey if he was dragged into not one but two criminal trials at a time when he's anxious to build on his capital in the art history world and make a big forward move in an already impressive career.

"It would be a shame to have to drag him back, really. It's impossible to tell when another opportunity like this one would come up again. For either of you. And on the other hand, I kept Rich's set of keys—which ought to make an interesting contrast with yours and Jeffrey's. Just a thought, Alice. Perjury being a crime, and all that."

I gave her all the time she needed to think that speech over. I'd worked on it for a long time and practiced the delivery on Pen, and we both thought it had a lot of dramatic highlights. Alice got up and crossed to the door, which was just a little open. She closed it firmly. We looked at each other across the length of the room.

"You're a real bastard, aren't you?" Alice said, but with less rancor than I would have expected.

"I did the job," I reminded her. "All coy bullshit aside, I did the job, and I almost got killed doing it. You owe me. I'm sorry I had to remind you about that."

We haggled some, but it was pretty much plain sailing from then on. Alice agreed to give me the seven hundred that was owing on the original exorcism and another grand and a half as a finder's fee for the stuff that Tiler had stolen. Under the circumstances, I didn't think it was exorbitant. It was more or less exactly what Pen needed to pay off the debts on the house, so all I was doing was keeping a roof over my head. Business is business.

As I got to the door, though, I felt her stare on my back. I turned around, and we looked a question at each other across the room. Well, I looked a question, she looked an accusation, but it was the same thing going both ways.

"You saw her," I said.

Alice started to speak and then didn't. After a long moment's silence, she nodded.

"I was playing her in instead of out." I groped for words. "The tune was the tune that described her for me. The one I'd normally wrap around her if I was doing an exorcism, until she couldn't get away again and had to fade when the music died. I think—I guess—the tune described her for you, too, so that you could see her this time. You won't see her again, though. I can promise you she won't be back."

For whatever reason, that didn't seem to help very much, but I couldn't think of anything else to say. I consoled myself that Alice was a lady who would always get by.

On my way out, I stopped by the workroom, where Cheryl was toiling alone. She looked up from her keyboard, gave me a nod and a half smile.

"Thanks for everything," I said.

"You're welcome."

"I'm really sorry about your mum's wedding."

"Yeah. You said."

A pause. I walked over to her, but she held out her hand quickly, emphatically, palm out, before I could touch her. I did as I was told and kept my distance.

It took her a long time to find the words. "I'm glad you did what you did," she said. "I think it was cool. There's got to be someone who'll stand up for people like Sylvie—Snezhna, I mean—and make sure they get their justice. After all, there's a million people out there protecting the living against the dead. Someone's got to protect the dead against the living. There's gotta be that balance, right? And I don't think you even knew yourself, up until now, that that was what you were for."

Cheryl blinked a few times, quickly, as if she might be about to cry. I could have been imagining that, though; it didn't show in her voice, and she had no trouble looking me in the eye. "The thing is, Fix," she said mournfully, "you lie too easily. You lied to yourself, all that time, about how ghosts were just things, not people. So you didn't have to feel guilty about screwing them over. And then you lied to me when you didn't even have to. When I would've helped you anyway, if you'd told me the truth. That's a shitty basis for a relationship."

"Relationship?" I said. "Hey, it was a good bang, and I like you and everything . . ."

She recognized her own words and laughed. But she got serious again.

"We can still be friends," she said. "I'd like that. But I can't—you know. I can't open up to a man I don't trust. It just doesn't work for me."

She let me kiss her once, very lightly, on the lips.

"Well, now you've tried it," I said. "So you've got every right to say that you don't like it."

Just like with Alice. It was all I had, and I knew it wasn't enough. The sound of Cheryl's typing accompanied me down the corridor, but was lost in the vast coldness of the place as I descended the stairs.

Twenty-five

YOU MOVE ON. YOU MOVE BACK. ON BECAUSE YOU'RE always getting older, back because there's always a set of habits and routines to catch you and suck you back in when your guard is down.

Before that happened, or before it finished happening, I borrowed Pen's car and drove over to the Charles Stanger Care Facility in the early hours of a Sunday morning. I parked up, skirted the front door, and walked on around into the formal gardens. The place was as quiet as it ever gets, at least from this perspective. No screams or weeping to be heard; no rushes, charges, or scuffles. Just the flowers waving in the moonlight, the furious barking of a distant dog, and an occasional moth trying unsuccessfully to immolate itself on a twenty-five-watt solar-powered garden light.

I chose a bench and sat down. Then, for a while, I just waited, letting the mood sink into me, and finding the closest approximation to it in the key of D. When I thought I knew what I was doing, I took out my whistle and started to play.

It was another Clarke that I held in my hands, but not an Original. For whimsical reasons connected with turning over a new leaf, I'd gone for a green Sweetone. I hadn't trained my mouth to it yet, though, and I was also still stiff from the wound I'd taken to the shoulder when Juliet sank her claws into me on the *Mercedes*, so the rendition of "Henry Martin" I launched into probably sounded a little wobbly and wild, rough enough, in fact, so that I was afraid it might not work at all. I played it through all the way, careful not to raise my head until I'd reached "*. . . and all of her merry men drowned.*"

When I did finally look up, they were there—the three little ghosts with their pale, solemn faces, the oldest about thirteen, the youngest not more than ten. Two of them were neat and clean in 1940s school uniforms, berets and all. The third wore a torn blouse and rumpled skirt with stains like leaf moss across the front.

Now that I had their attention, I played a different tune, a quicker one with a jauntier and more complex rhythm. It wasn't a tune that had a name, particularly, or one that I'd ever heard before. It was a musical incision into reality, at a slightly different angle to the tunes I usually played. They listened silently and attentively.

When it was done, they exchanged a glance that cut me out entirely, as it cut out all the living. Then, all at the same time, as if at some signal I couldn't hear, they ran. Across the gardens, through the boles of trees, through the distant wire mesh of the fence, over the eight lanes of the North Circular, and on out of sight.

I couldn't do for them what Rosa had done for Snezhna because I didn't know what it was, besides the fear and indignity of their deaths, that kept them tied to the Earth. But I could set them free to this extent, so that now they could at least choose what place they haunted.

Fuck knows, it was little enough.

———

And later still, I was back in Harlesden, sorting through the mail again—which, since it was a solstice thing, meant that about half a year had passed. Quiet outside, because it was after midnight. The breath of cherry blossom coming in through the open window, like news from another world. I was sitting with my feet up on the dwarf filing cabinet, a glass of whisky at my elbow, and a sense in my heart of what passes with me for peace.

The immediate trigger for that feeling wasn't the whisky. It was a letter from Rosa Alanovich, now back in Oktyabrskiy and apparently doing very well for herself as the proprietor of a small grocery store. The payout she'd got from the Criminal Injuries Compensation Board had been insultingly small, but only by British standards. In the wilds of Primorsk, it was serious stake money—and Rosa had hit the ground running.

So I was miles away, and my guard was so far down it was nonexistent. Then in an instant, the freshness of the cherry was cut wide open by a hot, miasmic stink of fox, which in another instant was refracted into a thousand shades of unbearable sweetness. My head came up, and my feet crashed down as though a celestial puppet master leaning forward out of the sky had tugged hard and sharp on my strings.

She stood beside the open window, her hair lifted slightly by a cool spring breeze. She was naked and, as before, her terrible beauty stirred me and cowed me in equal measure. For a long time we regarded each other in silence. The smell faded instead of building, which gave me hope she wasn't hunting that night; but just in case, I didn't move. Succubi react to a running man as cats do to a running mouse.

"I was summoned for a specific task," Juliet said at last, her incredible shot-silk voice caressing me like the flat of a razor blade.

I nodded. I knew damn well what that task was.

"And I can't go back home until I finish it."

There was no way I'd get to the door before she got to me, and the only thing at hand that would be any use as a weapon was the whisky bottle. I let my hand fall on it, as casually as I could.

The moment stretched.

"It never occurred to me before," Juliet said, "that failure would bring such extensive benefits. But then—while I wore the chain, failure wasn't an option. I really ought to thank you for that."

I shook my head. It was meant to indicate that unbinding demons was all part of the Castor service, and that no thanks were needed or expected. Of course, I realized numbly, home for Juliet was Hell—or at any rate, a place for which Hell was the only word we had. It probably wasn't a place that anyone ever got nostalgic about.

"So I need something else to occupy my time," Juliet finished. "And I believe the job that you do would suit me well. But clearly there are rules, and some of them will be alien to me. So I've come here looking for instruction—you being the only human I've met who's still alive."

It took me a while to get a coherent answer out, because first I had to run what I'd just heard through my internal logic circuits, many of which had shorted out at the first sight of her.

"Work experience," was what I managed to say after a pause that stretched out almost to breaking point. "You want a work-experience placement."

"If that's what it's called, yes. To work with you. To watch you. To learn how it's done."

I sat down again, slowly and carefully, so that I wouldn't fall over and so that there wouldn't be any sudden movements that might make her change her mind and eviscerate me.

"Okay," I said. "Yeah. Yes. I'm prepared to—take you on. It's a hell of a lot better than the alternative. But—if you don't mind me asking this—could you please put some clothes on? Because I need some blood to be in my brain. Otherwise I'm probably going to lose consciousness."

Juliet quirked an eyebrow, glancing down at my agonizing erection where it tented the cloth of my trousers as if she was noticing it for the first time.

"Sorry," she said, and without there being any interval of time or any sense of movement, she was dressed in the outfit that she'd worn when I'd first met her—the black shirt, the black leather trousers, the ice-pick heels.

It was an impressive ensemble, and it did the job. But did it—just maybe—lack the proper sense of professional gravitas?

I sat back in my chair, frowning judiciously as I rubbed the line of my chin with forefinger and thumb. After a moment or so, inspiration came.

"I've got this trench coat," I told her. "One careful owner."